HOW TO BE DEAD

HOW TO BE DEAD
PAPER CUTS
OLD HAUNTS

DAVE TURNER

Aim For The Head Books

Aim For The Head Books
149 Long Meadow
Aylesbury, Buckinghamshire, HP21 7EB

www.daveturner.co.uk

Cover design by Paul Turner

How To Be Dead / Dave Turner. -- 1st ed.
ISBN 978-1-5272-0251-1

For Zoë and the Infinite Monkeys
Max, Grace and Joseph

HOW TO BE DEAD

ONE

Death watched the city sleep.

He gazed down at humanity's glow from the top floor of the office block. A sleek and thrusting tower made from glass, chrome and undisguised wealth.

He was waiting. He was good at that.

He checked his pocket watch. A gift from three old friends. Crafted for him by Patek Philippe & Company in 1933 with a movement as complicated and precise as the dance of the stars that he had counted for millennia.

Sometimes, as he gazed up at the night sky, he wondered if the universe was some kind of in-joke that had got out of hand and was working up to an awkward punchline. He had explained his theory when he and Einstein had briefly met. Nice guy. Good hair. That was back in 1955 and Death had not seen anything since to change his mind.

He did not know how long he had existed. He thought he remembered the dinosaurs. An asteroid killed them, hadn't it? Was he there? Or had he merely read it in a book? All he was sure of? It's the sort of thing that happens when you live in a world without Bruce Willis.

Then humanity arrived. They loved. They fought. They died.

He had seen the worst that they could do, but he had also witnessed them at their finest and he loved them for it. Their compassion. Their bravery. Their wisdom. The Billy Joel album 'An Innocent Man'. Cake.

Especially the cake.

He took his mobile phone from the folds of his cloak and dialled the only number in his contacts.

'Did I wake you, Anne?' The groan at the other end of the phone answered his question. 'Who would win in a fight between Bruce Willis and Billy Joel? I mean, Billy Joel used to be a professional boxer. I think he'd be a bit tasty.'

'No, I don't know who would win, but the fact that we're even discussing this at half past two in the morning means I'm pretty sure I know who the losers are here. What do you want?'

'Today is the day. Are we sure he is the one?'

'You should know that Death isn't allowed to doubt.'

'Are we sure?'

'Yes.' Anne sighed.

'There are portentous skies. I haven't seen them like this since Beezelbub was defeated.'

'I'm sorry. Who?' Anne stifled a giggle.

'Satan. Lucifer. Beezelbub.'

'You mean Beelzebub?'

'Yes. Beezelbub.'

'Repeat after me,' she said. 'Bee.'

'Bee.'

'Ell.'

'Ell.'

'Zee.'

'Zee.'

'Bub.'

'Bub.'

'Beelzebub.'

'That's what I said. Beez-el-bub.'

'You're an idiot,' she said. 'Shouldn't you be working?'

'I will be. Stockbroker. Heart attack. Another one who'll tell me how much he regretted spending so much time here. They never bloody learn.'

'How are you going to play it?'

Death drummed his fingers against the window, considered his options. 'Old school, I think.'

He heard a thump from the office next door. 'I have to go. You should get some sleep.'

'Do you think?'

'Sarcasm is the lowest form of wit.'

'Oh, is it now?' asked Anne, sarcastically.

'Touché.'

Death switched the phone off and looked again at the infinite blackness. This was all created from stardust, born in the furnace of a long dead sun. Humanity. Earth. The city below. The stapler on the mahogany desk. One day, the sun would expand beyond the realms of the inner planets and consume it all in its burning belly. Which was a shame. It really was a very nice mahogany desk.

He glided through the wall into the equally splendid office next door. A well dressed, yet confused, middle-aged man looked down at his own limp body.

The dark figure stood in front of him and whispered three little words.

'I. Am. Death.'

TWO

Some days you are Godzilla. Other days you are Tokyo.

Beneath the office lighting scientifically engineered to both increase productivity and crush the spirit, Dave Marwood stared out of the window. At twenty-five, he had learned that there were three key stages to employment:

A) 'Oh. This is new!'

B) 'I don't know what I'm doing.'

C) 'Could someone please stab me with this pen?'

Dave was toying listlessly with a chewed biro when he noticed Fiona marching over to his desk like some corporate Stormtrooper. A rictus grin carved into her face, she brandished her phone like a weapon.

'No fancy dress, Dave? Did you not get my email?'

Dave looked over at a nervous zombie using the photocopier for personal business, then down to the calendar on his desk. 31st October. Halloween.

'I think I've made my feelings on enforced wackiness in the workplace clear,' he said.

'Remember, last week, I asked you to compile the weekly ACR figures into a report?' Dave had perfected the art of the non-committal shrug. 'You appear to have provided me with this.' Fiona held up a drawing of a pony. Dave winced. It wasn't his best work.

'Is that not what you wanted?' he asked. Fiona's smile intensified. Dave was sure the temperature in the room rose with the corners of her mouth.

'I've noticed that your KPIs are in the horizontal rather than the vertical. I think we both know what that means.'

Confident that her point was made, Fiona sat on the desk and knocked over the action figures that Dave had spent most of the morning arranging. Something shifted inside of him, rising up from the pit of his stomach and spilling out of his mouth.

'Have you ever wondered if there might be more to life than this?' he asked.

'I'm sorry. I don't know what you mean?'

'My life feels like a Bruce Springsteen song.'

'Well, who doesn't like the Boss?' Fiona smiled.

Dave turned from his keyboard and looked Fiona squarely in the eye. 'It's not that I don't like my job. It's more that I have absolutely no opinion about it.'

Fiona considered this. One of her flock had questioned the faith. A corporate heretic. She licked her lips and leaned forward.

'Can I pass onto you what I have learned over the years?'

'Please.' Dave sighed.

'Take all this doubt, fear and anger, screw it up into a tight ball of rage and bury it deep down.'

'But...'

'Deep, deep down.'

'I never thought I'd say this, but I think I'd like to get back to work,' said Dave. Fiona visibly relaxed. Her smile stretched even further. Dave thought he could hear tearing.

'My door is always open,' Fiona said, beaming. 'Except for when it's closed. But when it's closed, I'm usually shouting at someone so you wouldn't want to come in anyway.'

'Thank you. That's very... reassuring.'

Fiona's phone beeped. The call to prayer. Targets and milestones. Paradigms and synergies. Forever and ever. Amen.

'Good talk,' she said, and marched off towards one of the meeting rooms.

Dave spent some more time arranging his action figures so that they were returned to rows of military precision. He then took a moment to try to figure out exactly how many fucks he did not give, but the calculator's display ran out of digits, so he just watched his fellow drones. They danced around the open plan office to the rhythm of tapping keyboards and ringing telephones. The administrative ballet was soon halted by a stack of paper dropping onto his desk.

'These need to be done by the end of the week,' said James. Or was his name John? Did it really matter? Dave needed a break. He picked up a spreadsheet printout from the top of the pile and walked away.

Melanie Watkins stood by the vending machine as it spat out its acrid brew. She was no moon. She was a space station. Even dressed in a cheap witch's costume, the very air around her seemed to glow. Dave had never been in love before but, if love felt like a fat man - on a space hopper made of pure misery - bouncing on your heart until all that was left was soul-crushing pain, he was pretty sure that this was the real thing.

'Nice hat,' Dave said as casually as his crippling self-doubt would allow. His heart was beating like John Bonham and Keith Moon locked in a devastating heavenly drum war.

'Thanks.' A tight smile. No teeth.

'How's the coffee today?'

Melanie took a sip and grimaced. 'It's like there's a party in my mouth and everyone is drinking creosote. Can I get you one?'

'Sounds awesome. Please.'

'What are you having?' she asked.

'I like my vending machine coffee like my women. Cold and of mysterious origin.' Dave considered the series of poor life decisions that had led up to him uttering that terrible line.

Melanie pressed a button and the machine spluttered and whirred into life.

Dave tried again. 'How's your day going?'

'There's rumours of cake in the office, so it's all gone very Lord of the Flies. The IT department have barricaded themselves in the kitchen and the accounts and marketing teams have formed an alliance and have laid siege.' She pointed to the piece of paper in Dave's hand. 'Anything important?'

'I have no idea,' said Dave, 'but if I carry it, I can walk around the office for hours without anybody questioning what I'm up to.'

'Impressive.' Dave relished the compliment. 'Are you going to the Halloween party tonight?' she asked.

'UberSystems International-endorsed employee-focused entertainment set between pre-defined boundaries?' Dave quoted from the employee handbook. 'Don't you think it's a bit lame?'

'No,' said Melanie, 'but, then, I did organise it.'

Dave could feel his face redden, hot needles of embarrassment pricking his cheeks. He hoped, briefly, that the ground would open up and swallow him, but then he remembered that he would just wind up landing in the Human Resources office on the floor below. That would probably make things more awkward than they already were.

'Thanks for the drink,' he said with a smile as weak as the coffee. He spun on his heels and headed back to his desk, forgetting to take the cup from the machine.

That afternoon, Dave watched an axe-wielding maniac attempt to unjam a printer. He had been temping at UberSystems International for two years now. In his opinion, there were three types of people who did this kind of work: those that were trying to find a job, those that had just lost a previous job and those that couldn't think of anything better to do. Dave was concerned that he had become the latter. Some mornings he laid trapped in his bed, crushed under the weight of his own apathy. He was stuck on amber. What if he just stood up, walked out and never came back? Would anyone notice? Would anyone care? Would Melanie?

He played their last conversation over again in his mind. An infinite loop of humiliation. Squeezing his eyes closed did nothing to shut out the image and when he opened them again, he saw Melanie striding purposefully across the office. Another drone tried to engage her in conversation and she deflected him by holding a spreadsheet up in his face. Dave allowed himself a smile. Of course he would come in tomorrow. What else was he going to do?

At precisely five thirty, Dave stepped from the glare of the office into the soft phosphorous glow of the streets. He sidestepped a family staring at a mobile phone as they slowly spun around trying to align themselves with Google Maps.

'Bloody tourists,' Dave muttered under his breath.

Some people are born in London, some move to London and some have London thrust upon them. The city had lost its charm for Dave. Like the seaside pebbles he had collected as a child, what once sparkled with pretty promise had quickly faded to dull stone. The cynicism hung in the air like the commuters' breath. It stuck to them like the grime pumped from the idle engines of the gridlocked cars. The unknown soldiers in the city's war of attrition against the soul.

He followed the path of least resistance and was swallowed by the anonymity of the crowd flowing into the underground station; a waterfall that splashed down the escalator and pooled on the platform. He jumped on the first train and, as it pulled away, he put his wrap-around headphones over his ears. Normally the warm cocoon of sound would be his one chance to unwind, but not this evening. Something was distracting him in the corner of his eye; almost imperceptible, like a smudge on a photograph.

It was the young man stood across from him. At first, Dave put his spectacular moustache, fedora hat and tweed suit down to a hipster affectation, but he seemed out of place. More than that, he seemed *out of time*. They made eye contact. A schoolboy error. The man said something to Dave, but was muted by the music. Gripped by the traditional English fear of awkward social situations, he reluctantly removed his headphones.

'I'm sorry?' said Dave.

'You can see me?' repeated Fedora Man, who seemed genuinely relieved.

'Of course.'

'You're looking at me. Not through me. At me.'

'You're not trying to sell me something, are you?'

Dave felt the woman next to him take a step away. Looking around, he could sense that all the other people on the carriage were deliberately avoiding looking his way. He turned back to the man but he was no longer there. Dave knew that he hadn't been in the first place. He had been talking to the dust motes dancing in the air.

This was not the first time that this had happened. As a child, he soon learned not to mention to others what he saw for fear of ridicule or worse. It started with his imaginary friend, Emily. His parents had been concerned with the amount of time he spent in his room playing on his own – playing with Emily – but she had disappeared from his life as he grew older and the matter was eventually dropped. Dave sometimes wondered where in his unconscious she had gone to play hide-and-seek.

The visions had increased since he had moved to the city. Dave often saw and heard things in the dark shadows of the architecture. Things that nobody else noticed. Odd things. Odd even for London. He originally put it down to working too hard, but conceded to himself that that theory was probably unlikely. As with everything in life, Dave took a pragmatic approach to his hallucinations and decided that, as long as they weren't telling him he was the Messiah or that he should hurt himself or others, he would treat them as a mere inconvenience, like a delayed train or a poor mobile phone signal.

Once he was back on the surface, Dave joined the hordes of vampires and zombies roaming the East End streets where he lived. Rows of Victorian houses that had somehow survived the blitz and slum clearance, but not the property developers. Their interiors ripped out, shifted, squeezed and reshaped into barely affordable flats. After his conversation with the man who wasn't there, Dave wondered whether he should relax a little. As he reached his front door a plan began to formulate.

A two birds, one stone interface as Fiona would probably have called it.

He let himself into the flat and walked into a living room that would have tested the euphemisms of the most devious estate agent. His housemate Gary was sprawled on the sofa, staring blankly at the television. A grunt and a fart was his acknowledgement that Dave was home and welcomed.

'Remember,' said the show's presenter. 'You can get in touch by phone. Or text. Or email. Or Twitter. Or Facebook.'

'Television has turned into my mum,' Gary shouted. 'That's how they track you. It seems innocent enough, but that's how they know what you're thinking. Where you are. What you're up to. Where's the remote control? I swear there's a wormhole in time in this house through which all my stuff disappears. A prehistoric tribe probably worshipped three remote controls and nineteen odd socks as Gods.'

Dave believed that Gary was a man who would start an argument with himself if left alone in a room for long enough. As far as Gary was concerned, the glass was not only half empty; it also contained a mind control drug placed there by the military-industrial complex. He had recently split up with his girlfriend by telling her: 'It's not you. It's them.'

Dave rolled his eyes, took a deep breath and asked the question that would change everything. 'Do you want to go for a drink?'

THREE

Number Fourteen, Meadow Close was a deceptively large and well-appointed three bedroom semi-detached house situated in a sought after location. Close to well-regarded schools and within walking distance of the local amenities and railway station, the property benefited from a south facing rear garden, a newly refurbished kitchen and an unspeakable horror lurking within.

Sarah Davidson tripped over the collection of sour milk bottles left on the doorstep. She attempted to hide them behind a dying pot plant. It disappointed her that, in this market, some vendors still did not make an effort. She was the fourth agent to take the property onto her books. Stories had begun to spread through the local industry that it was unsellable, but nobody could say exactly why. It happened from time to time. A house doesn't sell for a while, the price is dropped and buyers become suspicious. This did not deter Sarah. She was not one to back away from a challenge.

She let herself in, shoving the door against the pile of mail that had gathered on the hall floor, and turned the lights on. They flickered, hummed and crackled. Sarah did not like evening viewings. Lamps and downlights were less forgiving than the natural glow of the day, no matter what the property shows on the television might tell the public. She swept the envelopes and flyers up into her arms and dumped them on the hall table.

Sarah gave the house a quick inspection. Half drunk coffee cups on the kitchen sideboard, books scattered on the living room floor. She began to suspect why this was a difficult property to sell. It was structurally and aesthetically fine, but the vendors took no pride in it. Why should others imagine they could? She put away what she was able to, sighed and saw her breath on the air. She looked for the thermostat and turned it up until she heard the dull, distant thud of the boiler starting up.

The house was filled with a welcoming warmth by the time the viewers arrived. A young couple, Peter and Victoria. Sarah was happy to see that Victoria was pregnant. The nesting instinct always helped a sale along.

'Shall we start in the lounge?' Sarah asked. The couple nodded and followed her into the room. Sarah looked down on the floor in horror.

'How embarrassing. I'm sure I put those books back on the shelf.'

'Not a sign of subsidence, I hope,' said Victoria. Sarah laughed too hard.

'As you can see the room is generously proportioned...' The television burst into life. The three of them jumped as if they had been physically slapped by the noise. Sarah picked up the remote control from the coffee table and began punching buttons at random. Nothing seemed to work, so she ran over and yanked at the plug socket until it came loose and the television winked into a dark silence.

'Are the electrics safe?' Peter's face was a picture of concern.

'Fine,' said Sarah, trying to sound reassuring. 'I'm sure it was just on a timer. To deter burglars. Not that there's any problem with crime around here,' she said, breathlessly. 'The vendors must have gone away without informing the office. Shall we move through to the kitchen?'

Sarah scanned the plug sockets. She was relieved to see that they were all switched off.

'This has all been refurbished. Built-in dishwasher and dual sinks...'

'It's freezing in here. I thought there was central heating.' Victoria shivered. Sarah would later find it hard to describe, but it wasn't just cold. There was a palpable absence of warmth, as if it had been locked out of the room.

'Can you hear that?' asked Victoria. Whispers. Indecipherable and innumerable voices brushing past each other. The memories of every conversation ever held in this house being played back at once. Sarah looked around, but they were coming from everywhere and nowhere. The fear sat heavily in her chest, like a shard of ice had been plunged through her ribcage. She focused on what she knew. The sale.

'Shall we try upstairs?' she asked, enthusiastically. They hurried out of the kitchen and back into the hallway. Sarah went first, up the stairs and onto the landing. She listened carefully and was rewarded with silence. She sighed with relief.

'It's Halloween, isn't it? It's probably just some kids playing pranks,' she reasoned. Peter and Victoria replied with nervous smiles. 'Let's start with the master bedroom. It's en suite.'

Sarah placed her hand on the brass handle of a bedroom door, her body heat warping the shine of the cold metal. Her unease returning, she tentatively opened the door. It creaked open slightly, but then closed again as if someone on the other side had pushed back.

Sarah pushed again with her full weight. The door slammed back, throwing Sarah across the landing. Then the scratching started. An insistent scraping like nails chipping away at Sarah's soul. Victoria, Peter and Sarah looked at each other with wide eyes and scanned around for the source of the noise. Victoria saw it first and let out a scream that sang along with the rasping in a harmony of fear.

An invisible hand was slowly carving thick lines into the wall at the top of the stairs. As the dust and plaster fell to the floor, Sarah realised with growing horror that the marks were forming words.

GO AWAY.

This was not a childish prank. The estate agent and her clients ran down the stairs, their feet thumping as fast as their heartbeats. They fell out of the front door and began fumbling for car keys.

'We've thought about it,' said Peter, gasping, 'and we've decided not to make an offer.'

'Is there any way the vendor could improve the property?' asked Sarah, always keen to hear feedback.

'Fire. Lots of fire,' Peter replied as he lunged into his car and started the engine. The couple sped off, neither of them looking back.

FOUR

'Do I want to go for a drink?' Gary asked himself. He ran the unfamiliar sequence of words around his mouth to see if they were a good fit. 'But "My Big Fat Geek Wedding" is on. Your favourite. Footage of brides crying because they can't find a vicar who speaks fluent Klingon.'

'But we never go out. We never meet new people.'

'You know my motto,' said Gary. 'A stranger is just an arsehole I haven't yet met. And, anyway, we went out for your birthday.'

'That was a terrible night.'

'It was a brilliant night! We gave you the bumps!'

'You pushed me down the stairs!'

Gary sighed. It had been two years since Dave had moved in, a new arrival to London. He had seemed the safest choice from the parade of artists, graduates and hipsters that came to look at the small room. Gary had only been looking for help with the rent, but - as it is with men who care for each other - their conversation soon dissolved to nothing but personal abuse. He would grudgingly admit that he had also found a friend. He had learned from bitter experience that, if he refused

Dave, the inevitable outcome from this conversation would be his friend sulking for the rest of the evening.

'If you want to go out, I know somewhere holding a pub quiz,' Gary suggested.

Dave could feel the evening slipping from his control.

'I'd be useless. I don't know anything about pubs, but my work is holding a Halloween party.'

A knowing smile broke out over Gary's face.

'I presume that girl from your office going to be there? Melissa?'

Dave was prepared for this, but still tripped over his words.

'Melanie? I think so. Maybe. Perhaps.'

'I knew it. I don't know why you just don't admit you like her.'

'I do not. That's ridiculous. What makes you say that?'

'Every time you tell a lie an angel punches a unicorn in the face with a kitten.'

'I am not lying!'

'Whenever I bring this up, you react in the same way as when I ask if you've eaten the last biscuit. I'm not judging you or anything. All I know is that it's been a long while since I had a custard cream.' Gary sighed. 'We'll go. What are we going to do about costumes?'

'We'll get something on the way.'

Dave always ate the last biscuit.

And so Dave found himself back on the streets, surrounded by people so desperate to have a good time that he feared they may burst a blood vessel. He and Gary stopped at the corner shop on the way to the tube station and discovered their costume options were limited. Gary suggested that he could go as a zombie victim who had been bitten but had not yet turned, going so far as to try and bite a chunk from his own hand. Dave felt that this would not be in the spirit of a Halloween party, so he picked out some flashing devil horns. Gary settled on a pair of fluffy pink bunny ears because, according to him, both of them wearing the same thing would make them look 'fucking stupid'.

'Dave!' someone called above the noise of the crowds. He turned around to see Melanie and an unimpressed friend forcing their way through the tide of bodies. Her face painted like a cat's, Melanie teetered on high heeled shoes. Dave gazed at Melanie like Professor Brian Cox eyeing up a particularly thought-provoking mountain range. Suddenly the night was bursting with promise and opportunity.

'Is that her?' Gary had an impressed tone to his voice.

'Yes.' Dave's voice revealed his nervousness.

'Just be yourself. Actually, don't. You're a dick. Try and be someone cool and interesting.'

'No, you're right. I should just be honest with her.'

'What? Be honest? With a woman? And start a dangerous precedent?' Gary decided to ignore Dave's implicit admission that he was attracted to Melanie. There would be plenty of time for ridicule later.

Dave adjusted his devil horns to what he believed to be a jaunty angle. *Can devil horns ever be jaunty?* he thought. *Yes. This is the area to focus on right now.*

'Nice devil horns. Very jaunty,' said Melanie. 'What are you up to?'

'Oh. We're just on our way to the party.' Dave shrugged.

'UberSystems International-endorsed employee-focused entertainment set between pre-defined boundaries?'

He smiled sheepishly. 'I can't get enough of it.'

Gary cleared his throat. Dave supposed he was asking a lot to hope to avoid introductions.

'Melanie, this is my housemate Gary. Gary, this is Melanie.'

'Hi,' said Melanie. 'This is Emma.'

'Pleased to meet you,' said Emma, the iciness of her voice indicating that she was nothing of the sort. The four of them began to walk in silence. Dave decided to blunder blindly into the world of small talk.

'So how do you two know each other?'

'We went to university together,' said Melanie.

'Mel's crashing with me since she and her loser boyfriend split up.'

'Oh, I'm sorry to hear that.' He wasn't.

'Don't be. We'd been drifting apart for a while. He was... Well... He made things complicated, shall we say? He tried to make an effort at the end but it was all too little, too late. As opposed to his bedroom proficiency, which was too little too early. Clitoral stimulation? Give it? He couldn't even spell it. I'm not entirely sure why I told you that. I may have had a drink.'

Dave opened and closed his mouth a few times, but no words came. He was slightly relieved when Melanie stumbled over on her ridiculous heels. But she continued to stagger and slipped off the kerb into the road. Dave saw the oncoming headlights, like the bright eyes of a predator bearing down on its prey. He heard the brakes squeal. He stepped into the glare, as if an unseen force had propelled him towards the inevitable. He instinctively shoved Melanie out of the path of the oncoming car.

Everything was a blur. Sound. Space. Time.

Then.

Stillness.

Dave barely felt the wet tarmac beneath his broken body; a rag doll thrown by the petulant child that is chance. He was surprised by how uneventful his last moments were. There was no tunnel of light. Nothing flashed before his eyes.

With as little fuss as he had lived, Dave Marwood died.

FIVE

Dave opened his eyes. He could not feel any pain. He could not feel the ground beneath him, nor the cold night air against his skin. The only sensation was panic. He remembered a TV show in which a paramedic asked a road accident victim to wiggle their toes. This little piggy went to market. He went through all the piggies and their activities. Somehow, it was the world that was numb, not his body.

He pushed himself up onto his elbows. A fog had descended, reducing everything to a ghostly presence. The streets were empty. No traffic. No people. No life. After the noise of the crash, the silence screamed in his ears. How long had he been lying there? He couldn't understand it. Surely his friends wouldn't have abandoned him?

The mists parted and a figure that haunts all of humanity's nightmares glided ethereally towards him. Its black cloak absorbed the street light. The scythe in its hand glimmered with the memory of a thousand dying suns. This guy had really made an effort with his Halloween costume. The image was ruined, though, when he crashed to the ground like he had been shot. His feet waving in the air, Dave could see the roller skates.

'A little help, please?' the figure cried out.

Dave pulled himself up and helped the struggling and swaying man to his feet.

'Sorry about that. I was just trying something new.'

'Good night? Had a few drinks?' Dave asked slowly and loudly. He searched for a face under the cowl, but all he found was an all-consuming darkness that tugged at the loose threads of his being.

'Oh dear, Dave,' replied the grim stranger. 'This is going to be awkward. I am Death.'

Dave looked confused. Death pressed on regardless.

'The whisper on the lips of the damned? The dark companion who walks in the shadows of humanity's souls? But that's terribly depressing. I'm thinking of calling myself something else. Steve, perhaps.'

Dave knew somehow that the words the stranger said were true. The shock hit him harder than the car, a punch to the gut that caused him to double over.

The Living World crashed down around him. Dave saw that a worried crowd had gathered around his own shattered body lying in front of the car. Gary frantically paced back and forth, shouting into his mobile phone. Melanie, smeared with Dave's blood, pumped his chest with her fists. She locked her lips over Dave's in a kiss that he would never taste.

'What? I'm dead? But there were so many things that I wanted to do.'

'Really?' asked Death.

Dave wondered if it was worthwhile taking offence to things when you were dead.

'Well, I hadn't finished watching all my DVD box sets.'

'You're not going to cry are you? Oh, I don't like it when you lot cry.'

Dave decided that it was worthwhile to take offence to things when you were dead.

'No!'

'I shouldn't worry,' said Death, in what Dave assumed was an attempt at a reassuring tone. 'This is what you Meat Puppets call a Near Death Experience. You'll be up and about in no time. If it makes you feel more comfortable, I'm thinking of this as a Near Dave Experience.'

Relief flowed through Dave's body in exactly the way that his blood currently did not.

'Oh. Right. Lovely. Sorry about the shouting. So, what happens next? Do we just...?'

'Pretty much.'

Dave was standing before Death. He could ask him anything right now. Questions on the fabric of space and time. The past. The present. The future.

'You know you're a lot shorter in person?'

Death shrugged and nodded as if this observation had been regularly made to him since the dawn of creation. He then took a very expensive pocket watch from his cloak and examined it.

'Do you fancy a quick pint?'

Dave was having an out-of-body experience. More accurately, Dave was having an out-of-body-down-the-road-and-in-the-nearest-pub-with-two-pints-of-bitter-and-some-bar-snacks experience. This was not how he had imagined his evening would turn out; having a drink with Death. Actually, Death was the only one doing the drinking. Being a ghost, whenever Dave went to pick up his pint glass, his hand passed straight through it with the sensation of running his fingers through water. The pub was tatty and so dark Dave wasn't sure where the barmaid's nicotine stains ended and her fake tan began. Ignored by the customers, Death was just another drunk muttering to himself in the corner.

'This is the only night of the year when I can go out for a drink,' he said. 'Halloween has become so commercialised now. You lot have forgotten the true meaning of the undead walking the Earth.'

As Dave concentrated on picking up the beer in front of him, he remembered his last living thought. 'I'll be honest with you. I was expecting a tunnel of light or something. My life flashing before my eyes at least.'

Death choked on his pint. He wiped his hidden face with the sleeve of his robe. 'Tunnel of light? Load of rubbish. I got bored and held a toilet roll people's faces while shining a torch do want to see your life flashing before your

Did he? Perhaps Dave could learn something this. His past actions could give an insight into his destiny. His old life replayed and reset before his rebirth. Also, he might get to see Lisa Daniels naked again.

'Yeah. Alright.'

Death clicked his fingers and reality lurched aside.

Dave found himself watching the Long Dark PowerPoint Presentation of the Soul. His achievements had been reduced to a series of slides smashed together with every kind of heavy-handed dissolve, transition and clip art file.

And written in Comic Sans.

Dave saw himself aged seven years old, winning a cuddly toy from a seaside grabber machine. Then time jumped forward ten years and he was successfully parallel parking a beaten up car into an impossibly narrow space. Then a fruit machine hitting the jackpot, coins cascading everywhere. Star swipe to Dave sitting at his desk at UberSystems International. Late at night, he throws a screwed up ball of paper across the length of the office. It bounces off of the wall into the waste paper basket. Dave punches the air.

End of slide show. Click to exit.

'Is that it?'

'What are you talking about? That was a really good piece of parking.'

'And nobody saw it. That's the sum total of my existence?'

Dave wasn't expecting much, but that was pitiful. He resolved to become a better person, to look at this second chance as a gift. He turned to Death to tell him this, but he was concentrating on his mobile phone.

'What are you doing?' Dave asked. 'I'm having an existential crisis here.'

'I'm just updating my Twitter.' Death showed Dave the phone screen. 'I am currently talking to the world's most miserable man.' He pressed the send button.

'I am not the world's most miserable man!'

'I'm sorry, but you must be. It says so on the Internet.'

Dave never imagined that death would be like this. Tragic? Yes. Devastating? Inevitably. Annoying? Not so much.

'I am Death. I am merely a ferryman between your world and the next. I am not here to judge. I will mock, though.' Death looked at Dave's untouched drink. 'You not drinking that?'

Dave shook his head. Death picked up the glass and quaffed the contents with noisy gulps. He slammed the glass back onto the table and let out a supernaturally long burp.

'I'm going to let you into a secret. Magic exists in your world, Dave. The way shopping trolleys stop at supermarket car parks should be evidence enough. Though the bags for life are a source of constant disappointment to an immortal being.'

Dave had no idea what to do with this information so just let Death continue. 'If there's one thing I've learned in this job, you always cut the blue wire, never the red one. Another thing is that life is hard. People are cruel. But remember that... Nope. I don't know where I'm going with this. That's it. Life is hard and people are cruel. But you have an untapped gift, Dave. You're a good man. You could be the best.'

Death slid a business card across the table. Dave picked it up and turned it over. Expensive, weighty and black. It was embossed with simple white text that said: '1 CROW ROAD'.

Dave was aware that something important had happened here. The moment was heavy with expectation and meaning. Then Death's mobile phone began to ring. Dave had never considered what Death's ring tone would be, but if he had, 'Uptown Girl' would have been pretty far down the list.

'Do you mind if I get that?'

Dave shook his head and Death answered the phone.

'Steve speaking... Well, I didn't agree that it was a silly name... Really...? I'll be there in a minute.'

Death threw the phone back down on the table.

'Busy?' Dave asked.

Death let out a long weary sigh.

'I'm always busy.'

'How do you find the time to do it all?'

'Time is relative. In fact, he's my cousin. Who owes me money.'

'Time travel?'

'It's not time travel as such. It's more that I exist simultaneously at all points in time. Or something. I wasn't really paying attention. Quantum physics was put together on a Friday afternoon. That's why humanity will never figure it out. Some of the bits are the wrong way round.'

An ambulance siren cut through the awkward silence.

'Sounds like your taxi's here.' Death nodded towards the door.

Dave could feel himself being pulled from his seat. The voices in the room grew dim and the walls faded away. Before he went, Dave realised that he should probably ask at least one metaphysical question.

'Answer me this. What's the one true religion?'

Death seemed disappointed.

'It's not a bloody competition.'

Dave's heart kick-started and he slipped back into the warm embrace of life.

SIX

The pain reminded Dave that he was alive. He did not know exactly how long he had been in the hospital bed, but the antiseptic smell had become familiar and the electronic pulse of the machines reassuring. He opened his eyes and saw a dark blur standing over him. Since he had arrived on the ward, Dave's dreams had been haunted by an anonymous black figure always looking over his shoulder. For a moment, Dave worried that this unknown creature had stepped into reality to take care of whatever business he had with him. The world swam and snapped into focus. Melanie smiled down at him.

'Welcome back,' she said. 'How do you feel?'

'I am never drinking again.' Dave licked his cracked lips.

'Don't say that. I owe you a pint. What was it like?'

'What was what like?'

'You know. They said you were clinically dead. How was the afterlife?'

Dave tried to remember that night, back to a time when he was apparently between worlds. It was like his tongue probing where a lost tooth had been in his mouth. He could feel the shape of what was missing, but couldn't see it.

'I don't know,' he said. 'I think there were pork scratchings.'

Then he decided to slip into something more comfortable, like unconsciousness, and the world was dark.

The next time Dave opened his eyes he was alone. His memory staggered like a drunk bouncing from one recollection to the next.

His name was Dave Marwood. He had been dead. Now he was not. His mind stumbled further back. He was born twenty-five years ago, the only child of Bob and Susan Marwood. He had a happy childhood, but there had been bad dreams and strange occurrences. His mum and dad would come to his bedroom and comfort him and he knew that they would always protect him from the monsters in the world. They knew, as all parents do, that they could not. His father had died when Dave was seventeen; a heart attack brought on by a job that did not deserve that kind of a reaction. Six years later, cancer ate away at his mother.

Once he had smiled bravely at her funeral and taken off the only black suit that he owned, he had taken his father's ashes from the cupboard, mixed them with his mother's and scattered them. Somewhere that had been special to them. He remembered green, but no more than that. Maybe it had been a forest. Perhaps they had seeped into the earth, or had been gathered up by the roots of a tree. Maybe it stood there now, tall and proud amongst the leaves. Maybe some small part of them remained in this world, entwined together. This gave him comfort. He would visit their resting place, wherever it was, once he was out of the hospital.

His mind moved forward, sure-footed now. Like a homeless Dickensian orphan, he decided to seek his fortune. With a media studies degree and the small amount of money his parents had left him, he had taken a train to London. He'd thought it a romantic adventure. It'd turned out to be a series of tiny disappointments. He'd found himself at Gary's door. Soon after that, he'd started at UberSystems International. Later, Melanie had joined the company and he had fallen in love. Then he was hit by a car, which hurt slightly less. That brought him back to the present.

He was tired now; so tired that even his eyelashes hurt. He closed his eyes, drowning in the darkness, and felt the black figure once again at his shoulder.

'No matter how you look at it, Emperor Palpatine was the democratically elected leader of the Senate. Then the Rebel Alliance comes along without any mandate and starts blowing up anything within a twelve parsec radius,' Dave said. He was sitting up in bed now in his own hospital room. Melanie was perched on an uncomfortable plastic chair.

'You've obviously been thinking about this a great deal,' she said.

'I've had a lot of time on my hands. The way Luke, Yoda and Obi Wan kept banging on about their religion, it's obvious they saw it as a holy war.'

'Yeah, but those space teddy bears were cute.'

'Ewoks? Ewoks cook their prisoners and use the helmets of dead Stormtroopers as drums. You call them space teddy bears, I call them war criminals. And another thing. Even though he can backflip and lightsaber duel, Yoda claims he needs to use a walking stick. What's that all about? Apart from claiming disability allowance?'

Melanie laughed. 'Are you saying that the Rebel Alliance were religious terrorists and Yoda was a benefit cheat?'

'I'm just saying that when it comes to intergalactic civil war, nobody is squeaky clean.' After a brief silence, Dave decided to say something that had been on his mind. 'You don't have to keep coming here.'

'I enjoy our theological debates,' Melanie said, smiling warmly. 'Do you want me to stop?'

'No! I mean, I don't get many visitors. Probably why I chew your ear off. Sorry.'

'Does Gary not drop by?'

'No. He thinks that the MRSA bug is exactly that. A bug. A genetic tag released by the government to mark and monitor the weaker members of society.'

'Right.'

A bell rang in the corridor to indicate that visiting hours were over. Dave had a sinking feeling in his stomach. She would be gone in a moment. He should say something.

Melanie got up from her chair, causing it to squeak against the polished floor.

'Is there anything you want me to bring next time?' she asked.

You're all I need, Dave thought. 'No, I'm good, thanks.'

She squeezed his hand and he squeezed back, feeling her warmth against his cold skin. Then she was gone.

He should have said something.

Dave recovered quickly and the doctors were baffled by the fact he'd not sustained any permanent injuries. His interior had been ripped out, shifted, squeezed and reshaped. There had been operations and procedures. Metal had been grafted onto bone. Dave didn't mind this too much as it technically made him a cyborg and therefore fulfilled a childhood ambition. The police came and questioned him about the accident. It was a formality so that they could put a tick in a box. The car had been stolen earlier that night and the driver had fled the scene. No accurate descriptions and no evidence.

One morning, Dave was woken up by a rhythmic clicking. He pulled himself up in bed, tangling himself in the wires that were stuck into his skin. The door to his room was closed against the bustle of the corridor. An old lady in a dressing gown sat knitting in a small armchair by the window. Her knotted leathery hands moved the needles nimbly, yet the garment she was making did not seem to grow in size at all.

'Hello,' said Dave. As an opening gambit, it was a tried and tested method. The old lady looked up over the frame of her glasses, smiled and returned her attention to her work.

'You're awake, then? Your friend has been worried about you. Nothing good ever came from worrying. I tried to tell her that; but I were wasting my breath, so to speak. She comes here when you're asleep, that Melanie. She says she owes you.' Dave knew he owed her more. He had stopped her leaving this life, but she had brought him back. They were forever bound while they were in this world.

'Are you a patient here?' he asked.

'I was, but that's by the by. I heard about what you did to help that pretty young thing. What you did to end up in here. It was either very brave, or very stupid.'

Dave shifted his weight and felt a sharp pain shoot up through his legs.

'A little from column A and a little from column B,' he replied through gritted teeth.

There was a sharp, efficient knock on the door and a nurse briskly stepped into the room.

'How are you this morning, Dave?' she asked.

'Good, thanks.'

'Talking to yourself again?' She consulted his notes at the foot of the bed. Dave looked over at the empty armchair by the window. The nurse tapped the clip-board. 'Looks like we'll have to sort out that medication if we're going to send you home.'

The medication. That was it. Seeing ghosts at his bedside? It was understandable considering what he had been through. Pills and potions telling him what he wanted to hear.

Doctors and nurses came and went throughout the rest of the day. Forms were updated, waivers approved and prescriptions signed. Dave's thoughts soon drifted away from the old lady to plans of watching box sets of 'My Big Fat Geek Wedding' on the sofa.

SEVEN

Death stood at the back of the small church. A plaque over his shoulder informed visitors that it had been built in the mid-fourteenth century, funded by the wealthy town elders as an appeasement to their Lord in the hope that they would avoid the Black Death. Those same town elders had all been buried in the graveyard outside before the construction had even been completed. *You pay your money and you make your choice,* he thought.

The congregation shifted awkwardly in their seats and stared at the cold stone floor while the priest spoke from the pulpit. Some furtively glanced at the coffin in front of them, imagining their own lifeless body within, and shuddered. When the priest had finished, a piper wrestled a set of bagpipes like he was dealing with a drunk and surly octopus. Death was glad that he had stood at the furthest point that the room would allow. He was deeply suspicious of any instrument whose sound was improved the greater the distance between the performer and the listener.

'Play Free Bird!' Death chuckled to himself, disappointed that nobody could appreciate his wit. Every joke was a private joke these days.

Famine and War. Beelzebub had learnt the harshest of lessons. One does not anger Death. For the one and only time, he took satisfaction in the snuffing out of a life.

After they had buried their dead, Conquest and Death shook hands and parted ways. They had decided that they had no right to bring about Armageddon upon those that had fought alongside them. Death had had a few problems adjusting as a solo artist. Mistakes had been made and he knew that these needed to be put right. He did not know what had happened to Conquest, but sometimes thought of him. He hoped he would see him again some day.

Death looked at his watch; a gift from three old friends. Perhaps it was time to make new ones.

EIGHT

November turned into December. London was ablaze with lights as if a city-sized mother ship, crewed by drunken office workers, had crash-landed on the banks of the Thames. When Dave's money and patience with daytime television had run out he'd drifted back to work. He was happy to be busy. He had spent the last two Christmas days on his own. He'd walked the quiet, deserted streets and it had felt like the aftermath of the Zombie Apocalypse. It made sense; at that time of year people hoarded food, barricaded themselves in their homes and wanted to hit family members over the head with a shovel.

Offices thrive on private drama so it stands to reason that Dave's first day back at work was filled with handshakes and pats on the back. He smiled and modestly downplayed his involvement on that evening over a month ago. He just wanted to get back to his desk and be near Melanie. With no reason to call around to his flat, Dave hadn't seen her since he'd been discharged from hospital. He had missed her and over the next few days, they slipped into the conversational rhythm of old friends.

Melanie looked over from her seat opposite Dave. 'How's it going with the Meyer project?'

'It's been better.'

'Is all not well in the Shire, Frodo?'

'I think we may have a very big problem with the systems upgrade.'

'Remember what Fiona says,' said Melanie. 'There are no such things as problems, only opportunities to shine.'

'Okay,' said Dave, ' I think we may have a very big opportunity with the systems upgrade.'

Dave clicked a button on his mouse and the printer behind him chugged, whirred and spat out paper. He pushed himself away from the desk and glided along on his chair. When he reached for the printout, his left foot brushed the floor.

'Gotcha!' Melanie punched the air with her fist.

'What?'

'Your foot touched the ground.' Melanie looked at her watch. 'You've got no lives left and there's three minutes to go.'

'This game is so rubbish.' Dave sighed and shoved himself back towards his desk.

Melanie pouted. 'It was your idea!'

Dave shook his head as his phone began to ring. He picked up the receiver.

'UberSystems International... I don't know about that, Mr Meyer. I'll just need to grab the file. Please hold.' He pressed a button on the phone.

'Who's got the Meyer file?' he shouted across the room.

Over the other side of the office, on another bank of desks, John (or was it James?) held the file above his head, an evil smile on his face. Dave looked from James (or was it John?) to a smirking Melanie and, finally, to the clock on the wall.

He carefully pulled his feet up onto his chair and, wobbling, stepped onto his desk. He leapt onto a vacant chair. The momentum wheeled him across the floor until he reached the other island of workers. He scrambled up and trod carefully between computer keyboards, telephones and notepads. He snatched the file from his stunned work colleague and spun on his heel. Another leap back onto the chair and he sailed back across the ocean of stain-resistant carpet like a victorious pirate captain grasping plundered booty.

His battered joints aching, Dave clambered up onto Melanie's desk and stepped back over to his own. People began to applaud. Dave allowed himself a smile in his moment of triumph. Pride comes before a fall and physics is a harsh mistress. He stepped too heavily on the chair and it rolled away from under him. Dave hit the ground hard, paper exploding everywhere.

Worried, Melanie jumped up from her desk. She ran around and pulled Dave to his feet. Crouched down, the two of them gathered up the filing. She flashed him a smile.

'Very impressive.'

'Thank you.'

'I think you'll find I've won, though.'

Their eyes met over a spreadsheet. A memory emerged from the fog of Halloween night; jumbled fragments of a promise he had made to himself. The words tumbled out of his mouth.

'Do you want to go for that drink? You and me?'

'What? Like a date?'

'Not like a date. An actual date.'

The words hung in the air like subtitles on the paused DVD of Life.

'I think I'd like that.' Melanie tucked her hair behind her ear and Dave's heart came close to exploding. An office drone leaned over the desk.

'Dave?'

'Yes?' Dave looked up.

'Fiona's office. Now.'

Dave looked back at Melanie.

'You go. I'll take care of Meyer,' said Melanie.

Dave stood outside Fiona's door. As he knocked, he thought back to their last conversation before the accident and what a closed door meant.

'Come in!' A deep breath and Dave stepped into the room, attempting to exude a confidence he did not truly feel. Initially, the view from the window commanded his attention; the stark lines of glass and steel brutally etched against the crisp blue sky. Below, the Thames snaked like a predator ready to wrap itself around the city and consume it in its dark belly.

Then Dave realised that Fiona was not alone. A middle-aged man sat across from her. He was tailored to within an inch of his life and seemed to have been chiselled from some kind of tanned stone.

'Thanks for coming, Dave. I'm sure you know Mr West,' said Fiona. Conrad West. CEO of UberSystems International.

'Please. Call me Conrad,' West said. Though he smiled, his handshake felt like a threat.

'Good to meet you,' Dave said nervously.

'Take a seat. Fiona and I are just finishing some business.'

Fiona grinned. 'As I was saying, I took the initiative to crunch the numbers and, by my calculations, changing the vending machine suppliers and charging the staff for refreshments could save the company almost five hundred pounds a year.'

'Jesus, you're so tight that you'd probably skin your own farts for the grease.'

'I'm sorry, Mr West?'

'Let them have their free tea and coffee. It tastes like shit, anyway.' West rolled his eyes at Dave. *Get a load of her.* 'What do you think of the coffee, Dave? Do you drink it?'

'Yes, and now I know what regret tastes like.' West barked a big, harsh laugh and slapped the desk, causing pens and notepads to jump across the surface as if terrorized.

'I love this guy!' he boomed. 'Dave, I suppose you want to know why you're here?'

'A bit.'

'Firstly, I wanted to come down here to thank you for what you did to save Melanie.'

'Not a problem.'

'Not a problem?' West looked over to Fiona. 'He throws himself in front of a car to save a fellow team member and it's not a problem? I love this guy! But, anyway, I'll get to the point. Fiona's being reassigned.'

'There's a problem in Tokyo,' Fiona explained.

'Godzilla?' asked Dave hopefully.

'No.'

Dave sighed. 'It's never Godzilla.'

'Ha!' West clapped his hands together. 'Where have you been hiding this guy? That's why we want to know if you'd be interested in moving into Fiona's role? We need someone like you. Someone who can lead from the front. Someone who thinks outside of the box.'

'I think that if you always have to think outside of the box, then you probably need to get a different box,' Dave found himself saying.

'See? This is exactly the kind of blue sky thinking that we need. I love this guy!' West slapped Dave on his bruised shoulder. Dave winced. It was tough love.

'When do you want me to start?' he asked.

'Five minutes ago. Fiona's really got to get moving on her project. You wanna try her chair out for size?' Fiona slipped from behind the desk, relinquishing her authority to Dave.

He crossed from one side of the desk to the other and sunk into the expensive, ergonomically-designed chair. Within the space of ten minutes, he had arranged a date and secured a promotion. Though he did not miss the irony that he had to die to begin to live, none of it had seemed that complicated after all.

But you don't have to make life complicated. Sometimes it can get that way all by itself.

NINE

She wandered through the house. She drifted past the landslide of letters up against the front door and around the islands of books stacked haphazardly on the floor. She knew she didn't belong here, but she had nowhere else to go. She was cold and alone. People used to come and live here in her home. She didn't like the people. They ignored her. This made her angry and she broke things. They noticed her then. People did not come here any more.

A boy used to live here. She missed the boy. She liked him. He didn't ignore her. They talked and played games together. Hide-and-seek was her favourite. She always won. Then he left. That was a long time ago. Now, she waited at the top of the stairs. She had turned it into a game. She told herself she was hiding and, one day, he would find her again.

The boy would come back.

The boy would find her.

TEN

Sunlight tumbled down through a canopy of leaves above Dave's head. He had been here, in Green Park, once before during his first summer in London. It had been a good day with old university friends. He hadn't seen them since. They had been swallowed up by their new lives.

He was reminded of that day now. Young families picnicked on tartan rugs. Hipsters threw frisbees at each other. At the end of the path that cut through the trees he could see Buckingham Palace. Tourists scampered excitedly around it like ants around a greying lump of sugar. Behind him he could hear the hum of traffic on Piccadilly. He was sitting on the shady grass across from Death; a chessboard between the two of them. Death contemplated his next move.

'This is a dream, isn't it?' Dave asked.

'You don't have to worry if you dream of Death. No, you only have to worry if Death dreams of you.' Death moved a rook.

'We've met before, haven't we?'

'You recall that night?'

'A bit,' said Dave. 'I recall being annoyed. Is this going to take long? I've got work in the morning.'

'Oh, yes. Your new job. I've heard about that.'

Dave shrugged. 'You've got to pay the rent somehow.'

'Have you thought about getting a job you enjoy?'

'A job I enjoy? I'm sorry, I don't get you. I mean, I understand the individual words. Just not in that order and not in that sentence.' Dave picked up a bishop from the board. 'How does this move again?'

'Diagonally. I think. It's been a while. Mostly people want to play Hungry Hippos.'

Dave leaned back, his hands clutching at the green grass beneath him. Green. He thought of his parents again. Had they met this creature? Did they try to bargain or reason with him? Did they accept their fate or did they fight for a few more moments in this world?

'Do you remember my parents?' he asked.

'I'm sorry, but I don't. I have met so many of you. My time with each soul is brief. I'm basically just admin. Your myths and legends bestow upon me responsibilities that I do not possess.'

'Oh, that's a shame.' Dave sighed with disappointment.

'Let me explain something to you. Bodies are just meat puppets for the soul.'

'Meat puppets?'

'If Star Trek has taught humanity one thing, it's how to bang hot alien chicks. If Star Trek has taught humanity two things, it's also that you will transcend your corporeal forms and become entities of pure energy. I don't know where you'd put your bloody car keys, though.'

'Why are you telling me this?'

'I could show you so much. But you never write. You never call.' Death sighed as he pushed a pawn along the board.

'I don't know how to.' Dave moved a knight to capture Death's pawn.

'I think you do,' said Death.

'Checkmate,' said Dave triumphantly. A confused Death looked down at the board.

'What the fu--'

Throwing off his sweat-soaked bed sheets, Dave gasped awake as though he had surfaced from deep, cold, dark water.

Unable to get back to sleep, Dave showered and put on his best suit. He was checking his reflection in the chrome kettle when Gary stumbled into the kitchen, bare feet padding on the laminate floor.

'You vain bastard,' he said.

'It's not vanity, it's damage limitation.'

Gary peered blearily inside the fridge.

'Shouldn't you be at work?' he asked.

'I'm going in a bit.' Dave's head ached. It felt as if somebody had pushed their fingers into his brain; probing and stretching, pressing it up against his skull. He had thought about phoning in sick, but it was the first day in his new role and he was pretty sure the personification of death invading your psyche wasn't on the list of acceptable reasons for absence. He told himself that it was just a dream. Nothing more than a subconscious manifestation of his anxiety about work, but it had felt so real. Death had seemed so close.

Gary removed a pizza box from the fridge and sniffed the contents. His nose wrinkled.

'That's disgusting!' He shoved the box back in the fridge.

'Why did you put it back, then?' Dave asked.

'Because there's no room left in the bin.' Gary pulled out a cheesecake.

Dave grimaced. 'Cheesecake for breakfast?'

'What's the problem? It's dairy and cereal. It's practically a bowl of cornflakes.'

'Can I ask you something?'

Gary's eyes widened. 'I'm not explaining where babies come from again.'

'What do you think happens when you die?'

'That accident's opened a whole can of philosophical whoop ass, hasn't it? Honestly? I don't know.'

'That's unusual for you,' said Dave.

Gary thought for a moment, then said, 'Life is like a box of chocolates. It doesn't last very long if you're morbidly obese.'

'That's not very helpful.'

'All I know,' said Gary, arms outstretched, 'is that God is dead and I am an insignificant speck in an uncaring universe. But there's cheesecake. So, y'know, swings and roundabouts. Cheese and cake. You have to admit, as a concept it's faultless.'

By ten o'clock that morning, Dave had settled himself into his new office. He had failed to set up his laptop and smartphone and had been unable to programme his extension into the desk telephone. He rearranged his action figures for the ninth time that day. He looked proudly at the business cards printed with his name and a job title he didn't quite understand. He stared out of the window that stretched from the ceiling to the floor. His fingers gripped the soft leather armrests of the chair. He imagined he was Captain Kirk ordering the Enterprise to swoop over a previously undiscovered civilisation; one whose society was based on the service industry.

'Permission to come aboard?' asked Conrad West, his knuckles rapping sharply on the door. Dave pushed himself back to his desk and grabbed a spreadsheet.

'Oh, Mr West. I was... just... '

'Please, call me Conrad. How are you settling in?'

'Good.'

'Everything working?'

'No. They're all just very expensive paperweights.'

'Have you told IT?'

'I spoke to a guy on the floor below us who put me through to someone in Newcastle who phoned a support engineer in Mumbai who emailed another bloke who sits next to the guy I originally spoke to on the floor below us.'

'At least the process is becoming more streamlined, but I'm not here to discuss our poor business decisions. How are you feeling? Nervous?'

'A little.'

'That's good. It's just another type of fuel for the engine. I have high hopes for you, Dave. You're a good man. You could be the best.'

A memory stirred. The pressure behind his left eyeball grew until he thought it would pop out of his head and roll around the desk. He put a hand out to steady himself.

'I'm sorry? What did you say?'

'I don't enjoy repeating compliments. I said you could be the best. Are you alright?'

'Just a headache.'

'Take some aspirin. You good to come to the boardroom in ten minutes?'

'Of course,' said Dave.

'Great. Is there anything else you need?'

'I don't think so.' West was halfway out the door when Dave thought of a question.

'Just one more thing, Conrad, if that's OK?'

'Sure. Shoot.'

'What do I actually do?'

The UberSystems International boardroom had been designed with understated good taste and an overstated budget. If Dave had known how much the leather chair he sat in cost, he would probably have stopped picking at the stitching. He was surrounded by middle management; cheap suits and expensive ties. The room hummed with fear and buzz words.

This was where he spent the rest of the day, in meeting after meeting. At one point he was pretty sure he was having a meeting about a meeting he was going to have later in the day. Dave reckoned that he could recreate his work day by slamming his head in a door while someone poured cold coffee over him and repeatedly shouted, 'Synergies!'.

At five thirty, Dave escaped back to his office. The mythical computer engineer was staring at Dave's computer with a look of disappointment.

'Dude, you don't need an engineer. You need a priest. What did you do?' he said.

'Tried to change my password. I'm not very good with technology.' Dave pressed buttons on his phone in a futile attempt to retrieve his messages. Melanie looked around the open doorway.

'Well, don t you look the very model of a young professional,' she said playfully.

'I like to make an effort every now and again.' Dave continued to punch the phone's screen.

'What is that?' Melanie asked.

'It's a smart phone.'

'What do you need one of those for?'

'It means I can be contacted any time, day or night,' he said with an air of self-importance.

'That doesn't sound very smart to me. We're going to the pub. You coming?'

Dave sighed. 'I can't. I've spent so long in meetings about the work I have to do that I haven't had time to actually do the work.'

'Fair enough. You still got time in your diary to fit me in tomorrow?'

'Of course.'

'Don't work too hard.'

'I won't.'

A large green plastic bag labelled 'PATIENT PROPERTY' was waiting for Dave when he returned home late in the evening. He had the flat to himself. Every

Thursday night, Gary attended his conspiracy theorist support group, though he insisted on calling it a Truther Symposium. He had taken Dave along to a meeting once. Fourteen passive-aggressive men drinking real ale and all insisting they sat with their backs against the wall opposite the window.

He tipped the contents of the bag onto the living room floor. The clothes he had died in; smashed devil horns, torn tee shirt and jeans. Then a moment of clarity. He remembered everything. That night. The accident. The pub.

Dave picked up the crumpled trousers and turned them over. Nervously, he put a hand in the back pocket. He pulled out a creased business card. Ran his fingers over the raised text. 1 Crow Road.

He would definitely be phoning in sick tomorrow.

Dave slept fitfully that night. Whether awake or dreaming, the same thought occupied him like the last chorus of a song he had caught on the radio. He told himself that he didn't believe in any of this. His near-death experience had been his body's biochemical reaction. It was caused by a combination of oxygen deprivation and hormones overloading his system. Then he saw the business card perched against his bedside lamp. He felt like he had as a child when he'd worry about the monsters hiding in his wardrobe. The world now seemed even bigger and even more frightening.

Dave had been staring at the ceiling for thirty-four minutes when his alarm went off. He had been counting down the minutes; a tally drawn on the wall of his mind. Mechanically, he climbed out of bed, showered and made a phone call to the office. He explained about the physiotherapy session he had forgotten about. He was very sorry and would be contactable on the phone. Human Resources understood, wished him good luck for it, hoped he had a good weekend and would see him on Monday.

Dave had been surprised to discover there was only one Crow Road in the whole of London. It had taken several strolls up and down the length of the main street until he found the entrance where he was sure there had once been a coffee shop.

Crow Road, NW1, was a cobblestoned cul-de-sac lined with office buildings whose brickwork had been smoothed and softened by decades of wind and rain. This unassuming passageway didn't look like a location where worlds collided. Dave pulled his winter coat close, wrapping himself against a chill that was not meteorological.

Dave walked down the alleyway until he reached the last door. He went to press the buzzer, but hesitated as he considered the ridiculousness of the situation. He had been brought here by a supernatural business card.

It must be a practical joke. Gary had heard him talking in his sleep the other night, had printed a card out and had hidden it for Dave to find. But such an operation would require a sense of purpose and effort that Gary did not normally possess.

The intercom crackled to life.

'Dave Marwood?' asked the woman on the other end. Flustered, Dave pressed the button.

'Erm... Yes.'

'We've been expecting you.'

The door unlocked with an electronic buzz.

Maybe they have cheesecake, Dave thought hopefully. He pushed the door open and stepped through to the other side.

ELEVEN

The office was cramped and uncomfortable. Desks and filing cabinets were jammed next to each other like a giant game of analogue Tetris. Sometimes, Anne would look longingly across the rooftops towards the gleaming air-conditioned towers of the City, but only sometimes. This was a vocation. A calling. Like a teacher, surgeon or those people that sell cupcakes on the Internet. She moved with a crisp efficiency. A quick check that the coffee was warm, a hand combed through her hair. She was ready. It was time.

The stairs creaked beneath Dave's feet like old men's bones. The air smelled of accountancy and failed start-ups. He arrived at a door and knocked three times.

'Come in!' Anne called.

Dave stepped into the small office. The watery winter sunlight splashed over the furniture, bathing Anne in its glow. Dave guessed that she was in her early thirties and overly attached to her cat.

'I'm Anne. Can I get you a drink?'

'Hello, I'm Dave. But you already know that. I'll have a coffee, please. Black.'

Anne poured him a cup from the pot and passed it over. Dave sipped the finest coffee he had ever tasted.

He drifted away with thoughts of home and comfort. This was coffee beyond the skills of mortals.

'You found us, then?' Anne smiled.

'Yes. What have I found, exactly?'

'Perhaps we should go and see the boss?'

'Perhaps we should.'

Anne walked over to another door and rapped her knuckles on the frosted glass. She let herself in and Dave followed.

Death sat in a forest of Post-it notes and files. His feet were up on the keyboard of an untouched computer. A sign that read 'You don't have to be dead to work here but it helps' was stuck to the side of the monitor. Death was shouting into a telephone.

'I just want to know my bank balance... My mother's maiden name? I was born of chaos and pandemonium... What do you mean that's not what you've got on the computer? Right, mate. You're on my list.' Death slammed the phone down and took a long swig from a takeaway coffee cup. It was then that he noticed Anne and Dave.

'Oh, hello. You made it in the end.'

'I had a dream about you...'

'Let me stop you right there, Dave. The only way you could make this conversation any less interesting is if you were dreaming about showing me your holiday photographs.'

Anne stepped forward. 'I think somebody is having a bad day.'

Death sighed and picked up a newspaper from the desk. He threw it towards Dave.

'Humanity. I love you all, but you've really got to stop being wankers to each other. When will you learn? Whatever your gender, race, religion or sexual orientation, you're all as insignificant as each other. Lots of you are going to be very embarrassed when you find out there's no supreme being, no divine plan and we're all just making it up as we go along.'

Dave felt he should make an effort to defend his species.

'But people need something to cling to. Some order. Some reason.'

'Yes, everything happens for a reason,' Death said, 'but sometimes the reason is that life is cold, random and awful. Like telephone banking. I need a biscuit.'

'I'll warn you now,' said Anne, 'we're out of chocolate HobNobs.'

Death was enraged. 'What? The chocolate HobNob is humanity's crowning achievement.'

'I can go and get some if you want?' said Anne.

'No. Screw this. I can manipulate time and space. If anyone needs me, I'll be at Friday. Dave, Anne will give you the tour. I don't know what I'd do without her.'

Death disappeared, slipping through a gap in the fabric of reality.

'I'm sorry about that,' said Anne, 'He can get a bit grumpy.'

'What is this? I'm still in a coma in hospital, right?'

'You know those moments when you've seen someone nobody else can?'

'Hallucinations?'

'Death's mistakes,' she said.

Anne took the opportunity to get on with some filing while she waited for Dave to arrive at a conclusion. It was as though he was trying to work out the sixth character of an Internet password without using his fingers.

'Ghosts?' Dave finally asked. Anne nodded her head. His eyes widened as he looked her up and down. He reached out and prodded her with his finger. Anne looked cross.

'Please don't do that. A while back, it all got a bit too much for him. Some slipped through the net. He was all, 'Keith Richards is still alive? Bloody hell. Who did I collect in 1971, then?'. I was brought in to help with the paperwork.'

'Are you telling me ghosts are administrative errors?'

'In a manner of speaking.'

'And I'm here because...?'

'We're hiring.'

The conversation seemed to clog up Dave's brain. The words jammed themselves between the neurons and coated the synapses.

'I've already got a job. Thanks for the coffee, but I'm going to have to go now.'

Dave opened another door, but a wave of chattering and shrieking knocked him back. The noise and smell almost overwhelmed him. He staggered back and slammed the door shut.

Dave gasped. 'What was that?'

'That's the room of infinite monkeys working at infinite typewriters. They were left here by the last tenant.'

'What do they do?'

Anne picked up a bound stack of paper. 'Just a screenplay for an Adam Sandler movie so far. It's not much, but it's a start.'

Death. Monkeys. Drinkable coffee in an office. Dave realised that these were all figments of a deranged imagination. The only rational explanation for all of this was that he was heading for a spectacular breakdown. He had to get out. He looked around for another door and made his way towards it.

'But you've not even seen the Deathmobile,' said Anne in an attempt to make him stay. Dave stopped. He turned around.

'The Deathmobile?'

TWELVE

Anne opened the garage door. It rattled up into the roof to reveal a black Morris Minor. She gave the car's bonnet a quick polish.

'That's it, is it?' Dave asked, unable to disguise the disappointment in his voice.

'Get in,' she said, 'There's something I want to show you.'

They travelled in silence away from the choking streets at the heart of the city. Soon, the buildings began to shorten and spread out as if the world had relaxed and opened its belt a few notches.

After half an hour, they pulled into a car park and Anne killed the engine. Dave could see a forest steadily darken as the late afternoon light grew fainter.

'Come on,' said Anne as she stepped out of the car. Every nerve in Dave's body sang out a warning, yet still he followed. They headed deeper into the woods, the branches above their heads growing ever thicker. Anne moved with a practised grace, while Dave tripped over exposed roots and snapped twigs underfoot.

'In 1828, a young man and woman fell in love,' Anne whispered. 'He told to her to wait for him for a year, while he went off to find his fortune so that they could marry. She retreated to a cabin in these woods. A year came and went. When he didn't return, she threw herself into the lake just over there.'

'Wow,' said Dave, rather loudly.

'Ssh!'

They stepped into a clearing, the forest circling them like an attentive audience. A beautiful young woman in a white dress floated serenely between the trees. An other-worldly light illuminated her path. Dave swore it came from within her. She entered the clearing and he could see clearly that she was, in fact, hovering. There was only mist where her feet should have been. Even with his limited knowledge of anatomy, Dave realised that wasn't quite right. He started to back away, but Anne gently placed a hand on his arm.

'It's alright to be freaked out the first time.' She stepped towards the spirit.

'Rebecca?' she asked gently. The creature that was once Rebecca turned its head towards them. Dave held his breath for fear that it might shatter the moment into a thousand pieces. Then his mobile phone began to ring. He took it out of his pocket and looked at the number. It was Melanie. Anne and the ghost of Rebecca looked over at him.

'Sorry. I need to get this,' he said sheepishly. He answered the call. 'Hello? Fine. You...? Oh. No. I just had a hospital appointment... That's tonight? Of course it is...

No. Tonight's fine. Look, I'm in the middle of something. Sorry. See you later. Bye.' Dave hung up. 'Got a date tonight.'

Anne and the ghost of Rebecca looked less impressed than Dave had hoped and turned their attention back to each other.

'Are you friends of Jerome?' Rebecca asked.

'Yes. We'd like you to come with us,' Anne replied softly.

'I cannot. I must wait here for my love. He will return for me. He promised.'

'I know. He did return. The day after you took your life. You see, 1828 was a leap year. You forgot.'

This information hung in the air for a moment before Dave burst into laughter.

'What? That is the stupidest thing I've ever heard!' he said between snorts. Anne looked angry. Rebecca reacted to Dave's outburst by retreating into the forest.

'Don't go,' Anne said. 'We can take you to Jerome. You just need to take my hand.' She took a careful step towards Rebecca, her hand outstretched. Rebecca floated towards Anne, her fingers reaching for the warm touch of the living. An intense blinding light flashed when their fingertips met and Rebecca was gone.

From the passenger seat of the car, Dave stared at the darkness stretching out before him. He munched thoughtfully on a chocolate HobNob.

If Dave had learned anything from listening to Gary's convoluted analysis of everything from 9/11 to the moon landings, it was that the simplest explanation was usually the correct one. If he wasn't schizophrenic, and the CAT scans in hospital had shown nothing to suggest this, and he wasn't a vegetable in an intensive care unit, then this was the only remaining answer. Terrorists crashed the planes. People walked on the moon. He could see ghosts.

'This is what we do,' said Anne. 'We find the lost. We rescue those who were left behind. We bring comfort to those who are afraid.'

'You've been practising that, haven't you?' Dave asked between biscuit bites.

'A bit. Yes. Since you crossed over, you too are a link between this world and the next. You could only see them before. Now you can help them cross over. They were read-only, but now it's all rewritable. Sort of.'

'Why doesn't he sort it out?'

'I don't know. Pride?'

'So how did you cross over?' Dave made speech marks with his fingers and immediately regretted it. Partly because he thought it made him look foolish, but mainly because he dropped crumbs over the car's pristine interior.

'I don't know you well enough to talk about it.'

'Oh. Embarrassing, was it?'

It started to rain on the drive home. Dave watched the water on the passenger window. The streaks split, merged and ran down in paths that shimmered in the light of the approaching city. A thought had been playing hide-and-seek with Dave since they had left the forest.

'When I was a kid, there was this girl. Emily. We played together. Then we moved house. The last time I saw her, she was staring down from my old bedroom window as we drove off. I'd never seen anyone look so sad. Do you think she's still there?'

Anne just continued to stare at the road ahead.

Anne and Dave arrived back at Crow Road and parked the car in the garage. They ran to the shelter of the building, splashing in puddles pooled in the pockmarked road. As they climbed the stairs, they could hear music playing loudly. They entered the office and it was coming from behind Death's door. Dave realised that it was Blue Oyster Cult's '(Don't) Fear The Reaper'.

Anne knocked on the frosted glass and then marched in uninvited. Death was dancing to the music, his scythe a replacement for a guitar. Anne turned the music off and it was replaced with an awkward silence.

'Before you say anything, I've had a very hard day. Have you got a song named after you? No, I didn't bloody think so,' Death said indignantly. Anne placed the half-eaten packet of biscuits on the desk. 'Oh, bloody hell,' he shouted. 'Who's been eating these?'

'Yeah. That'll be me,' said Dave. 'Can I ask you something? Jesus rising from the dead. Was that one of your mistakes? I ask because I'm concerned that wars have been fought and millions of lives lost over what was essentially a cock up.'

'You take one day off for the Easter bank holiday and you never hear the end of it. And how do you guys commemorate the resurrection? By spending Bank Holiday Monday walking around DIY stores wishing you were dead too. Anyway, what are you still doing here? Haven't you got a date?'

'How did you...?'

'Do you really need to finish that question?' said Death.

Dave looked at his watch. 'Oh no. I'm going to be late.'

'Go. I'll see you soon.'

'You do know that saying stuff like that doesn't get any less creepy?' said Anne.

'Thanks for the biscuits,' Dave shouted as he sprinted out through the door.

THIRTEEN

It looked like rain, but it fell like stones. It stung Dave's skin as he made his way across the city as fast as he could. He found Melanie sat in a corner of the bar. Illuminated by the candlelight in her white dress, Dave was reminded of souls glowing in a dark forest. As he shivered and dripped water onto the stone floor, Dave truly felt that he was punching above his weight. He was soon warmed, though, by the wine, the fire and the company. So what if she was out of his league? Weirder things had happened to him that day.

'How did it go at the hospital?' Melanie asked as she poured the last drops from their third bottle of wine into her glass.

'What?' said Dave, confused. 'Oh. Yes. I don't think there's any permanent damage.'

Melanie pointed to her hairline. 'You wanna feel something permanent? Just put your hand there.' Dave leant across the table and, gently brushing away her hair, felt Melanie's forehead. 'You feel that little lump? St Paddy's Day. Dublin.'

Dave slumped back into his seat and thought for a moment.

'I got that beat,' he said as he rolled up the sleeve of his shirt, grabbed Melanie's hand and placed it on his arm. She rubbed his skin. 'Moron let his dog loose at a beach party,' he said. 'Bit right through my jacket. The dog. Not the moron.' Under the table, Melanie threw her leg over Dave's. She hitched her dress up slightly to reveal a dark scar against her smooth, pale thigh.

'Thresher,' she said proudly.

'Thresher?'

'It was an off-licence. New Year's Eve in Glasgow. A guy fell through the window. Shard of glass caught me.' Dave put his leg over Melanie's and rolled his trouser leg up. He rubbed a patch of rough skin on his calf.

'Glastonbury last year.'

'You were there?'

'No, I fell off the ladder trying to adjust the satellite dish so I could watch it on the telly.'

'You wanna drink?' asked Melanie. 'Drink to your leg?'

'I'll drink to your leg.' He looked at the empty wine glass in front of him. 'Shall we get another bottle?'

Dave swung his arm to attract the attention of a passing waiter, but knocked Melanie's full glass over. Time seemed to slow as he watched the dark liquid splash all over the table and onto Melanie's pale dress. She leapt up as if an electric charge had been put through her chair. Panicked, Dave attempted to dab the growing dark stain with a napkin.

'What are you doing?' she yelled. 'Oh God. I'm going to have to get this in to soak. It'll be ruined.' Melanie grabbed her coat and wrapped it around herself.

'I'm so sorry!'

'It's okay. Accidents happen. Thanks for the drink. I'll see you at work on Monday,' Melanie said, already heading for the door. She walked out of the bar without looking back.

Dave decided to have that bottle of wine. Time flew by as he sat there alone and before he knew it, the bar was closing. He just wanted the night to end. Everybody thinks that they are the star of the story of life, but Dave knew that he was just a bit part; a minor character, a blink-and-you'll-miss-it cameo in the drama that was humanity. He had realised that throughout the day. Life wasn't a romantic comedy. Nobody learns a lesson. Life wasn't an adventure. Few have the chance to get the girl and kill the baddie.

He knew tomorrow morning would hurt, and not just from the hangover. He had to win Melanie over. He pulled his phone from his pocket. With his head and fingers like marshmallows, he punched at the keyboard. Drunken logic told him he should tell Melanie everything. No secrets. She would respect him. He wrote about ghosts and Death and biscuits.

Send.

He stumbled through the streets, battling the tide of Christmas party goers; wave after wave of drunk executives crashing against him. His stomach rumbled and he realised that he had not eaten since those stolen biscuits. He wanted to get some takeaway and a taxi back to his bed. The alcohol would keep the dreams at bay. A quick inspection of the contents of his wallet soon stopped those thoughts, until he walked past a pizza parlour. He had a brainwave. Actually, in his current state, he considered it a brain tsunami. The greatest idea ever. He double backed, entered the shop and slapped his money down on the counter.

'I'd like to order a pizza for delivery, please,' he slurred to the bored-looking shop assistant.

Dave woke slowly. His head throbbed painfully in time with his heartbeat. His skin was cold and clammy, his mouth dry. Maybe this wasn't a hangover. Maybe he was patient zero in the Zombie Apocalypse. That would be the only way he could explain how bad he felt. He was glad that he had made it to his bed, even if he had only been able to remove one shoe. He turned over and found a half-eaten pizza spread across the duvet, greasy meat leaving a dark smear across the fabric. He didn't remember buying that. Some memories, though, bubbled to the surface like farts in a bath.

He felt under his bed until his fingers wrapped around his mobile phone. One new message.

LEAVE ME ALONE.

Dave dropped the phone back onto the carpet. The wine and pizza in his belly had been replaced with a mixture of lead and crushing embarrassment. The realisation of what he had done made him close his eyes and offer the traditional prayer of the drunk and remorseful: 'I am never drinking again.'

Then, after a moment of sombre reflection, he groaned, 'You idiot.'

'Don't be so hard on yourself.'

Dave jumped when he saw Death sitting at the end of the bed, a cup of coffee in his hand.

'Oh no. Am I dead again? I feel like it.'

'No. Social call. Is that cold pizza?' Death asked, helping himself to a slice before Dave could answer him. 'You like that girl, Melanie, don't you? Personally, I believe that love is merely a chemical imbalance that makes you forget your credit card limit.'

Death offered the cup to Dave. 'Strong coffee is the answer.'

'Is it strong enough to punch a hole through time to before I started drinking?'

'Funny you should say that. Would you like another go at last night? Best out of two? I can arrange that. I once had a chat with Einstein. Apparently the theory of relativity is nothing to do with time running slower the closer you get to your relatives.'

'And you'd do that for me?' Dave asked with suspicion.

'Of course. You'd just have to come to work for me in return. I like your style. Getting a lift with the pizza delivery guy? Inspired.'

Dave had no idea what Death was talking about. 'My mother warned me never to make deals with anthropomorphic personifications.'

'Sounds like she was a smart woman.'

Maybe it was the hangover or the desperation, but Dave told himself that everybody deserved a second chance. He just never thought that it could be so literal.

'Okay,' Dave said. 'This isn't going to screw up the space-time continuum or anything?'

'Nobody will realise I've done anything. I just need you to sign this.'

Death produced a thick contract and a silver pen from the folds of his dark cloak. Dave skimmed through the pages.

'Death accepts no responsibility or liability for any loss, injury, embarrassing family encounters or changes to documented historical fact. This liability includes, but is not limited to, becoming your own father and/or mother, the rise of Hitler or the inexplicable success of Coldplay.'

'It's pretty standard temporal law,' Death explained as he inspected his fingernails. Dave shrugged and signed his name at the bottom of the last page. If at first you don't succeed, torch the place and claim on the insurance.

'So, what happens now?' he asked as he passed the pen and contract back to Death.

'I think the question should be "what happens then?"' said Death.

'You wanna drink?' asked Melanie. 'Drink to your leg?'

'I'll drink to your leg.' He looked at the empty wine glass in front of him. 'Shall we get another bottle?'

Dave swung his arm to attract the attention of a passing waiter, but knocked Melanie's full glass over. Before it could complete its trajectory, time juddered to a halt. Panic was frozen on Dave's face as the room was caught in a moment of existence.

Death strolled over to the table and picked up the wine glass that was balanced at an impossible angle. He drank the contents and placed it back into its halted free fall. He then moved Dave's arm, like he was playing with an oversized action figure, so that his hand was beneath the glass. Death stepped back like a sculptor admiring a newly completed work of art, and vanished.

Time lurched back into motion. In an instant, Dave caught the now empty wine glass before it bounced off of the table.

'Wasn't that full? Where did it go?' He put the glass down and scanned the floor.

'That's two times you've saved the day now,' said Melanie.

'I suppose.'

'Why did you do that?'

'Well, wine stains are a nightmare to remove.'

'I'm not talking about tonight.'

Dave knew that this was his chance. His heart seemed to fill his whole chest and his tongue became as dry and heavy as desert stone. 'Because it's a better world with you in it.'

They looked at each other and it was as if time had halted once again.

Dave and Melanie decided to have that bottle of wine. The time flew by as they sat there together and, before they knew it, the bar was closing. Neither of them wanted the night to end, so they decided that it didn't have to.

As they walked along the bank of the Thames, they were the stars of their own romantic comedy. The heroes of their own private adventure. The rain made London sparkle in the flat orange glare of the street lights and the city belonged only to them. Melanie slid her arm through Dave's. Her fingers searched for his and entwined with them. Dave realised what those skinny boys with acoustic guitars had been singing about on soundtracks all these years.

They found a twenty-four hour café and talked about their lives before that night, as if everything had merely been a prologue to that moment. Melanie played with a silver cross; a christening present, while she talked about her family. It caught the light and sparkled just like her eyes. Her parents were still together. She was the eldest of three girls who had spent their lives playfully bullying the only man in the house. As an orphaned only child, Dave didn't feel jealous of this, instead he was happy that her family brought her such joy.

They talked about their ambitions and dreams and neither one laughed at the other. Even the silences were comfortable when the conversation ran dry. Dave revealed secrets he had never told anyone, such as how he felt it was him against the world, and she returned his trust by telling him hers. He had briefly considered telling her the biggest secret of all, but decided that admitting you could talk to ghosts was probably a third or fourth date confession.

Soon tiredness took hold and, hiding yawns from each other, they headed to the nearest underground station to catch the first train of the morning. Unsure of what to say, or how to say it, Melanie leaned forward and kissed Dave. She tasted of coffee, mints and hope. Pressing her body next to his, she felt real and warm and alive.

'Call me,' she whispered before heading into the station. Dave watched her until she turned around, smiled, and went past the ticket barriers.

He decided to walk the quiet streets for a while. That's what the leading man would do in the movies. He splashed in the puddles and wondered if he would ever stop smiling. He didn't have to wonder for much longer.

FOURTEEN

'Nice weather for ducks,' said a voice behind Dave. He turned around to see Death standing before him on the pavement. 'I could never figure out what you meat puppets meant by that. For a time I assumed that ducks were very romantic creatures and enjoyed walking in the rain thinking about other ducks they had loved.'

'What are you doing here?'

'I'm guessing it all went well with Melanie? There's no need to thank me.'

'Thank you for what?'

Death pulled the contract from his cloak. He looked at the last page, but Dave's signature was no longer there.

'Oh bloody hell. Stupid linear time. Can't causality take one for the team just once? Change of plan. Can I show you something?'

'If it's quick.'

Death grabbed Dave by the wrist. It felt as if he was a cocktail being poured from one place to another. Suddenly, they were standing in a dark bedroom. An old man was perched at the end of the bed while his body lay beneath the covers. Dave had never seen a dead body, other than his own, and he was surprised by how little it disturbed him.

'Hello, Michael,' said Death.

'I wondered when you'd get here,' said the old man with a sigh.

'Sorry I'm a bit late. Traffic's a nightmare.' The old man smiled, then pointed a finger at Dave.

'Who's he?'

'Work experience,' said Death.

Michael turned his attention back to the dark figure. 'You know you're a lot shorter in person?' he said.

'So I've been told.' Death glanced at Dave.

'What's it like, then? Eternity?'

Death thought for a moment before answering.

'Long,' he said, 'I've been watching a lot of Scooby Doo recently. Have you got any biscuits?'

'In the kitchen,' said Michael. 'The cupboard by the window.'

Death turned to Dave. 'Make yourself useful.'

Dave went downstairs. The walls of the hallway were lined with framed photos that told the story of a long life lived. Michael as a small boy, carried in his father's arms. Michael as a young man, surrounded by friends. A woman joined him in the pictures. They grew older together. Children and grandchildren appeared alongside them. Then, the woman was gone. Michael as an old man; an image of the person Dave had just left in the bedroom.

As he rummaged through the kitchen cupboards, Dave looked at the meals for one and the soups and realised that Michael had lived and died alone. At that very moment, he couldn't think of anything sadder.

When Dave returned to the bedroom with the packet of biscuits, Death had settled into a chair with his feet up on the bed.

'I just can't see where they got the money from,' Death said as he helped himself from the packet. 'Ooh. Garibaldi. Lovely.'

'Example?' said Michael.

'In one episode, Scooby and the gang were investigating a haunted hotel. It turned out that the janitor, it's always the janitor--'

'Or the theme park owner,' said Michael.

'--or, indeed, the theme park owner. Anyway, the janitor was pretending that the hotel was haunted to drive down its value so he could buy the place cheap. But the holographic and laser equipment he used must have cost thousands; hundreds of thousands, even. He would've got the place at a rock bottom price. But he would've owed a huge whack on the military hardware. It was a completely false economy.'

'If it wasn't for those meddling kids,' said Dave.

'And they always find a rational explanation for the supposedly supernatural events, but nobody ever mentions the talking dog. "Hmmm. Egyptian exhibition possibly haunted by a mummy? Let's investigate!" You're having a conversation about this with a Great Dane and he is actively disagreeing with you! Deal with the issue at hand!'

'Do you think we could get on with this?' Michael asked. Dave felt that he was intruding on a very private moment and quietly slipped out of the room.

'Yes. Of course. Sorry. Take my hand.'

Dave returned to find Death turning the pages of a half-read murder mystery novel that had been left on the bedside table. He flicked to the last page.

'I should've told him how it ended. There's nothing worse than not knowing.' Dave pulled the duvet up to Michael's chin, as though he were simply in the deepest of sleeps.

'I phoned for an ambulance,' Dave said, 'I didn't know how long he'd be here otherwise.'

'Thank you. I guess there's nothing more for us to do,' said Death, as he put the book down. He grabbed Dave's wrist. Once again, he was sucked up and spat across the country.

When Dave dared open his eyes, he saw that they were standing outside his flat. The rain had finally stopped and fingers of sunlight crawled over the dark glossy roofs.

'I'm not bad, or evil, Dave. I'm here because you all need me. Are you defined by your job? No.' Death sighed. He seemed tired. 'But there are probably things you need to do. I'll see you around.'

'Maybe.'

'Oh, you will. Eventually,' Death said as he disappeared into the ether.

Eventually. Dave understood. The soul was just too strong, too full of life, to be stopped. It had a momentum of its own and all Death could do was deflect its path of travel. Sometimes you needed a companion for a journey. Nobody should be alone.

His exhaustion forgotten, Dave knew what he had to do. He quickly showered, changed his clothes and quietly closed the flat's door behind him so as to not wake Gary, who had fallen asleep on the couch again. Dave made his way through the waking city until he arrived at Marylebone station.

'Where are you going?' asked the bored woman in the ticket office.

'Stratford. Warwickshire. I'm going home.'

'You can't go home.'

'Well, that's your point of view.'

'No, I mean there's a signal failure just outside the station. You'll need to take the Bakerloo to Oxford Circus, then take the Victoria to Euston. Take a train from there to Birmingham New Street, walk over to Birmingham Moor Street and then get a service to Stratford.'

'Oh, right. Thanks. I'll do that then.'

FIFTEEN

Dave made his way to Euston station, where he found buying a train ticket was an altogether less philosophical experience. He bought a cappuccino with so much chocolate topping it was technically a coffee Revel and boarded his train. He finally succumbed to his tiredness and fell asleep before the train had even left London. He dreamt that he had died but nobody had noticed. Everybody he knew continued with their lives, oblivious to his absence. Terrified and alone, he called and screamed at them as if behind a glass wall, but nobody responded. When he woke with a cry, he had arrived at his destination.

Dave left the station and, as Meadow Close was only a few minutes' walk away, he thought the crisp winter air would clear his head of the cotton-wool helmet that sleep had bestowed upon him. He was struck by the odd juxtaposition of the familiar and the new. There was the newsagent he had bought sweets from. A block of flats that had once been a pub.

The pub. The Green Dragon. Where his parents had first met. He remembered now. He had come here, the urn tucked away in a bag, and got heroically drunk. Then, he had wandered into the garden and had spread their ashes in the bushes and the flowerbed. The beginning and end of their life together.

Dave crossed the road and tried to look over the garden wall, but it had been rebuilt and raised since the last time that he'd been drinking here. He peered through a gap in the woodwork. Though it was now a private garden, the borders looked the same. Dave smiled to himself.

'See you later, mum. Goodbye, dad.'

Soon, he was walking past the bright Christmas decorations and tidy lawns of Meadow Close. The suburban perfection made the shock of seeing his childhood home even more intense. A bleakness infected the abandoned Number Fourteen. The overgrown front garden and boarded windows made it look like a decayed tooth in an otherwise shining and healthy mouth. Dave wondered what could have happened in the two decades since his family had left the street. He knew where he could potentially find answers. He walked to the house next door and rang the bell. An old lady answered. Stooped over a walking stick, she warily looked Dave up and down.

'Mrs Van Dresch?' Dave asked.

'I'm not buying anything,' said Mrs Van Dresch in an indeterminate accent, and began to close the door.

'I'm Dave Marwood. Bob and Susan Marwood's boy? Do you remember?'

Mrs Van Dresch peered over her glasses and smiled. 'No! Little Dabbie Marwood?' A nickname he had not heard spoken in almost twenty years. 'Come in! The kettle has just boiled. How long has it been?' Dave stepped into the hallway and was shepherded into the kitchen.

'About eighteen years, I think.'

'Look at you. So big now! Why do you come here?'

'I'm just visiting an old friend.'

'And parents? Bob and Susan? How are they?'

'They're both dead. I'm sorry.'

'Oh, Dave, I'm so--'

'Don't be. I think they're in a good place now. I'm not sure if it's better than here, but I think they're alright.' The kitchen was silent as Mrs Van Dresch performed the solemn ritual of the making of the tea until Dave asked, 'What happened next door?'

Mrs Van Dresch put a cup of tea in front of Dave and let out a sigh.

'Very bad things. Strange things. Everybody frightened. Nobody want to live there. Very sad. It has good parking and south-facing garden.'

Dave finished his stewed tea and ate a slice of inappropriately named sponge cake. He and Mrs Van Dresch made small talk, but he couldn't make her elaborate on what had happened next door. He said goodbye, promised to stay in touch, and when she had shut the door behind him, walked into the front garden of Number Fourteen.

Dave tried to look into the house but the boards over the windows were too tightly rammed together to offer any view. Hoping he would have more luck at the rear, he climbed over shopping trolleys and broken pieces of furniture in the side alley.

The back garden was in a worse state than the front, but the kitchen door had been exposed by somebody in the past. One of the small panes of glass had been smashed and the door opened easily when Dave tugged at the handle.

Daylight splashed over the grey, stale sideboards and cupboards. The house seemed to shift, as if it knew it had been invaded. Dave could have sworn the cup on the table in front of him moved an inch or two. Nerves made the tea and cake bubble in his belly, but he forced himself to take a step forward.

The cup flew from the table. Dave ducked and it sailed over his shoulder and shattered against the wall behind him. He choked on the dust and waited for both the grime and his heart rate to settle.

'Haunted house. No meddling kids. A janitor could make a healthy profit with a place like this,' Dave muttered to himself. He trod carefully through the hallway to the foot of the stairs. Dave had just mounted the first step when he heard a low rumble. It grew in intensity until his whole body shook as if caught in an earthquake. He gripped the bannister to steady himself and could hear items in other rooms crash to the floor. Soon, the groans of the house died down until the only movement was the dust motes dancing in the thin shafts of light.

Dave relaxed again, and that was when an invisible energy sucker-punched him off his feet. He crashed to the floor, gasping as the wind was knocked out of him. Something in his head screamed for him to run out the front door and never look back, but he couldn't tell if the voice belonged to him. He stood up, dusted himself down and renegotiated the stairs. Dave climbed and turned the tight corner when he reached the top.

'GO AWAY' had been scratched thickly and deeply into the wall. He ran his fingers across the rough relief of the letters. Layers of paint and wallpaper peeked through at the edges like rock strata. He walked across the landing to his old bedroom door. The paint was peeling and it hung off its hinges. With some effort, Dave pushed it open, the bottom scraping and catching on the bare floorboards.

There stood a little girl, no older than eight years old. She wore the same summer dress and sad expression Dave had last seen all those years ago.

'Hello Emily,' he said.

Her eyes narrowed. 'Go away!'

'It's me. Dave. We used to play hide-and-seek together. You always won. Remember?'

'You can't be. You're a grown up.'

Dave smiled sadly. 'That's what happens.'

'Not to me. You left. That made me cross.' Emily's lower lip jutted out.

'Is this what this has all been about? You've been sulking?'

Emily shrugged and stared at the floor. Dave could feel a smile beginning to curl at the edges of his mouth. All the terror and fear these walls had witnessed had been caused by a hissy fit.

'I'm sorry. I didn't want to leave.' It was all he could think of to say and he didn't know what to do next. He remembered what Anne had done in the forest, and took a step forward. Emily turned away from him. He decided a different approach would be needed.

'Do you want to play a game?' he asked. Emily spun round.

'Like what?'

'Whatever you want.'

They spent the day playing hide-and-seek (Emily's suggestion), Princes and Princesses (Emily's suggestion) and Killer Zombie Kung Fu Cyborgs (Dave's suggestion). They laughed and teased each other. As the evening drew in, they sat on the bedroom floor.

'I spy with my little eye something beginning with "D",' said Dave.

'Door?' asked Emily. Dave looked over his shoulder.

'Yeah, that'll do.' He winked at her.

'This has been the best day.'

'It has been, hasn't it?'

'Dave?'

'Yes, Emily?'

'I'm cold.'

'I know.' Dave held his hand out towards her. Emily smiled, though her eyes were heavy and wet with tears. She placed her hand in his and it was as if he was holding a breeze. They were surrounded by light and then, for a fraction of a moment, they *were* the light, until the darkness enveloped them and Emily was gone.

Dave stepped out into the chill of the evening air and quietly closed the door behind him. From the pavement, he looked back at Number Fourteen, Meadow Close. It was now just another neglected house; a spooky story, an urban myth. Dave made a promise to himself that he would never again forget Emily.

Once back in London, Dave transferred to the underground. It was the Saturday night lull, a time during which people were neither going out nor staggering back home, so he had the train carriage to himself.

The exhaustion seeped into him and spread through his bones. He wondered what touching a ghost's soul did to the living. His head fell forward and his heavy eyelids closed. Blissful silence. All of a sudden, he felt as if he was falling and jerked back upright, the back of his head banging against the carriage window. A man in a tweed suit and fedora now sat opposite him. He doffed his hat to Dave. 'It's you!'

'How nice to see you. Even better to be seen,' the man said. 'Fred Drayton.'

'Dave Marwood. I'd shake your hand, but it would get all pan-dimensional and stuff.'

'I see,' said Fred, who obviously didn't. 'You look tired.'

'It's been a busy day.' Dave sighed.

'Have you always been able to do this?'

'Apparently so.'

'It must be very unnerving.'

'I'm starting to get the hang of it. How long have you been down here?'

'Since August 12th 1957. They call it the Glorious Twelfth. Not so glorious for me, it turns out.'

'How did you... well... y'know?'

'It is not considered polite to ask a gentleman the cause of his demise,' Fred replied haughtily.

'I'm sorry.' Dave hadn't realised that there was a whole new etiquette he would have to learn. He felt that it would be good manners to offer his services. 'It must be very lonely down here. I can help you... well... cross over to the other side, if you'd like.'

'I get by. There are a few of us down here. Our paths cross from time to time. It's very kind of you to offer, but I'm just not ready to leave all this behind. I know this sounds foolish. I watch everyone making their journeys each day and it almost feels like I'm still alive. Almost.'

It did not sound at all foolish to Dave. The train began to slow down and he wobbled to his feet.

'This is my stop,' he said apologetically.

'Of course. I'm sorry to have gone on.'

'Not at all. I'll see you around? I'm always up for a chat and if you ever get bored of this...'

'Thank you, Mr Marwood. That would be lovely.'

Dave stepped out onto the platform and the doors closed with a hiss. The train pulled off and he waved it on its way. Fred Drayton disappeared into the darkness of the tunnel, continuing his journey with no destination.

Dave walked back home and went straight to bed. Almost as soon as he sank under the covers, he fell asleep. This time, though, he slept like he had never been afraid.

SIXTEEN

Conrad West burst through the door of the UberSystems International boardroom like a small, yet well-dressed, explosion. He slipped off his jacket and slid into the chair at the head of the table in one silky movement.

'I'm here to kick ass and chew bubble gum. And I'm all outta bubble gum. Wait. There's some in my back pocket. Sorry.' Nervous laughter rippled through the executives in the room. 'Where was I? Oh yeah. Monday morning. Let's grab the week by the throat,' he said as he clapped and rubbed his hands together.

'Or smother it with a pillow,' Dave said with a yawn. He tried to stop himself sliding down the smooth leather chair.

'What was that, Marwood?' West asked.

'Nothing, sir. Just very excited.'

Dave returned to his thoughts, tuning out the white noise of corporate-speak. He had not spoken to Melanie since Saturday. After he'd returned home that night, he had fallen asleep, missed Sunday entirely and hadn't surfaced until this morning. He'd hoped to speak to her when he got into work, but he'd been dragged into this meeting and had only managed to wave to her across the office. Was this playing it cool? Too cool? Not cool enough? Should he wait longer? Being a grown up was rubbish, Dave decided.

'I've looked at the figures. Right now, the market's colder than a witch's tit,' West told the room. 'We've been looking at new investment models. People already regard us as monsters that feed on faded dreams and broken promises made to small children. Let's not piss about. The Heart of Darkness Fund. Tobacco companies, arms manufacturers, petrochemical giants.'

Brochures were passed around. Though the figures and formulas contained within them were incomprehensible to Dave, others gave low whistles and murmurs of approval.

'As society crumbles, markets crash and governments fall, the returns could be phenomenal,' said West. The enthusiasm in the room made Dave feel uncomfortable. He raised his hand to speak.

'Yes, Dave?'

'I'm sorry, Mr West, but is this ethical?' There was a moment's pause before the room erupted in laughter. The suit next to him tapped him on the shoulder.

'You're new here, aren't you?'

'I love this guy! Listen, Dave, UberSystems International takes its employees' concerns very seriously and I'm sure we can allay them. Now if there are no more questions, then we'll move on. Bowen will talk to us about the company's new vision statement.'

Bowen had entered the room unnoticed, like a ninja accountant. He took his place in the seat at West's right hand side. Meticulous in his movements, he removed a single piece of paper from a folder and placed it on the table.

'The board have been working with one of the country's top consultants for several months in order to re-write our corporate narrative. Here's what they have agreed upon.' Bowen cleared his throat and read from the paper.

'UberSystem International's vision is to always be true to our vision.'

'Punchy, don't ya think?' West grinned.

Dave looked around at the people applauding with fervour in their eyes; wanting to be led, no matter where. He raised his hand again to disapproving glares.

'And how much did that cost?' Dave asked.

'I don't have the exact figure to hand,' said Bowen, 'but around two hundred thousand pounds.'

This time Dave saw his whole future flash before his eyes. A near-life experience.

'Life's too short for this,' he said, shaking his head. Silence. Dave made up his mind. He stood up, smoothed out his suit, and walked right out.

Dave returned to his office and began filling his pockets with his Star Wars action figures. West didn't knock on the door; he strode in as if he owned the place. Which he did. That was fair enough, Dave thought.

'Dave!' West smiled benignly. 'UberSystems International is like a big family. We laugh with each other, we fight with each other. Sometimes we hit one member over the head with a shovel and bury them under the patio for the insurance. But we don't stay mad at each other.'

Dave let out a long sigh; one that had been growing since he had first walked through the doors of the building.

'I'm sorry.'

'Hey, it's alright. Nobody died.'

'We're all dead, Conrad. Everybody in this office is dead and we're all just killing time until somebody comes along and puts us in the ground.'

The office was bursting with the kind of silence that follows a detonation. Dave could tell by the look on West's face that nobody had dared talk to him like that for a long time, if ever. A crowd had gathered outside what Dave now assumed was no longer his office. Melanie fought her way to the front with a concerned look on her face.

'Is everything alright, Dave?' she asked.

West snarled. 'You walk out of that door, Marwood, and it will be the biggest mistake of your life. I guarantee it.'

Accepting the challenge, Dave walked up to Melanie. He looked into her eyes and it felt, once again, as if she was the one and only thing keeping his heart going.

'Did you know, the only reason I came into this place every day was to see you?'

The kiss that followed was the most real and true thing Dave had ever experienced.

'Is that a Stormtrooper in your pocket or are you just pleased to see me?' Melanie asked slyly when their lips finally parted. She smiled.

'Han Solo, actually,' Dave croaked.

On this occasion, it only took Dave two attempts to find Crow Road. The weathered and faded brick buildings were a welcome contrast to the sharp edges and hard lines of the office he had just left for the last time. He was about to ring the bell of Number One, Crow Road when the electronic buzz of the lock revealed that he was already expected.

Anne was waiting at the top of the stairs. She didn't say anything and simply led him inside. Death was leaning against the door to his office.

'Glad to have you on board, Dave. The pay's terrible and the hours are awful, but I'll offer you this one bit of career advice. There's no 'I' in team. But there is 'tea'. So put the kettle on,' he said before disappearing into his office.

'Just so you know, that was your orientation,' said Anne.

'Thanks. Is Emily...?'

Anne nodded. 'Yes. You did well. Little girl ghosts are the scariest.'

Dave smiled. The weight of two worlds, the living and the dead, lifted from his shoulders.

'I can't hear anything boiling!' Death shouted from the other side of his door. Anne dropped a heavy stack of folders into Dave's arms.

'These need to be done by the end of the week.'

PAPER CUTS

ONE

2 September 1666

London was burning.

A raging firestorm roared and shrieked through the narrow streets, consuming the tinder-dry wooden buildings. Thick, choking clouds of smoke rose into the sky, blocking the sun and plunging the city into a false night. Attempts at extinguishing the fire had been abandoned and people were fleeing the destruction with whatever possessions they could carry. Carts and panicking horses filled the roads making it impossible for the fire fighters to get through. The turbulence of the boiling air made the wind veer erratically and the flames spread insidiously in all directions. Soon they would creep to the paper warehouses and gunpowder stores on the riverfront and all hope of saving the city would be lost.

Four horsemen watched the inferno from its very heart. Embers and burning flakes drifted and danced around them like a blizzard in hell. Their cloaks were not singed by the flames, nor their armour tarnished by the smoke. Their steeds remained calm as tongues of fire licked at their hooves. They'd seen this sort of thing before.

Shiny of hair and proud of bearing, Conquest sat sure and true atop his white stallion. On top of the red horse sat he who was known as War. Barrel chested, he looked as if he was made almost entirely of auburn hair and anger. Next to him, Famine shifted in the saddle of his black horse. Horseback riding was uncomfortable for one with a frame as slender as his.

The rider of the pale horse needs no introduction.

'Is this it, then? The end of days?' asked Famine in a thin voice.

'I don't know,' Conquest replied. It certainly had an end of the world vibe. He turned to the Pale Rider. 'Death, is this happening elsewhere?'

Death shook his head solemnly.

A fireball flew over their heads with a high-pitched whine and crashed into the thatched roof of a house. It collapsed in on itself and the explosion threw sparks onto the neighbouring properties. These, in turn, caught alight with a hungry crackle and rained down fire.

'I'm bored,' bellowed War.

Conquest thought for a moment, came to a decision and tugged on the reins. His horse obediently turned away from the blaze. 'Come on,' he said to the others.

'I'm going to find an alehouse. If this is the apocalypse, I'll be damned if I'm doing it sober.'

The Four Horsemen made their way through the narrow and winding cobbled alleys until they reached London Bridge. The bridge was a haphazard jumble of shops and businesses that precariously balanced over the murky waters of the Thames. The crowds instinctively parted to allow the riders through. As they trotted over, Conquest noticed that the buildings that spanned either side of the road were beginning to smoulder at the edges.

After much delay and many assurances that they did not require any of the goods or services offered by the tradesmen, they finally passed through the Stone Gateway on the opposite bank and crossed into Southwark. They rode along the riverbank for a short while until they found a tavern that would suit them.

They hitched up the horses and ordered the stable boy to bring grain and water. Once the horses' needs had been met, the Four went in search of their own refreshments. The south bank of the river was congested with onlookers, the fire obviously the entertainment of the day. Despite the inn's popularity their armour, weapons and general demeanour meant that the Four found an outside table overlooking the conflagration with little difficulty. The first drink did little to quench their thirst, so Conquest was sent to the bar to see if a second would do any better.

Death looked out over the Thames. It was smeared orange and seemed to burn like the River Styx that he supposedly guarded, if you listened to the more popular poets of the time. On the north side, families wrapped in blankets stood in pathetic huddles as they waited for the usually reasonably priced river taxis which, in a textbook example of supply and demand, had become a lot less reasonably priced overnight. A ragged flotilla of lighters, barges and rowing boats was making its way upriver from the East. Never underestimate a Londoner's ability to make a quick shilling from someone else's misfortune.

Conquest returned with four pints of cloudy brown liquid and bags of pork scratchings. Famine grabbed the snacks from the tray before he could even sit down. Conquest placed a glass each in front of his three companions and took a large gulp from his own. War eyed his glass's contents with suspicion.

'What's this?' he growled.

Conquest was now having trouble breathing. He wheezed, 'The innkeeper informed me that this was favoured by his most discerning clientele.'

'You mean the drunkards?'

'Yes.' Conquest wiped his eyes on the back of his riding gloves.

War beamed. 'Excellent!'

Conquest regained his composure. 'I was talking to a fellow named Samuel at the bar. Apparently, it all started in a bakery on Pudding Lane.'

'Don't talk about pudding,' Famine moaned, wiping crumbs from his tunic. 'I could really go for some pudding.'

The Four settled in and sampled several more of the ales that the tavern had to offer. They all agreed that the beer was excellent and there was little chance that the world would end today, but tomorrow's hangovers would make them wish that it had.

The afternoon had turned into early evening when a tall, elegant man glided over. He was dressed in a long red coat stitched from the most exquisite material and balanced a wig the size and shape of a substantial bush on his head. He drank from a glass containing the finest claret while his eyes darted around like he was looking for something to steal. Probably souls. He tapped the silver tip of his cane on the table in a demand for attention.

'Good afternoon, gentlemen.'

War jumped clumsily to his feet. His hand grasped for, and missed, the sword at his side. 'Beezelbub!'

Beelzebub looked hurt. 'Do none of you have the courtesy to pronounce my name correctly?'

Conquest looked him up and down, his head wobbling. 'What are you wearing?'

Beelzebub pirouetted so that everybody had a good view of his marvellous garments. 'Oh, these rags?' he said with false modesty. 'Just a little something I threw together.'

'You look ridic-- ridic--. You look like a tit,' War said, falling back into his seat.

'You were all wearing those same clothes the last time I saw you,' Beelzebub said with disdain. 'After the Battle of Bosworth.'

'Ah, yeah.' Conquest turned to Famine. 'How did we do in that one?'

'I don't know. I stopped counting after Agincourt,' Famine slurred.

'Look at you. It's like the Restoration never happened,' Beelzebub said. 'Everyone at court is wearing this style. In fact, I've just come directly from Whitehall. His Majesty has ordered the destruction of all the buildings in the fire's path. Travelling south of the river usually gives me a nosebleed, but this has the best view.' He gave a smile that War wanted to punch into the Thames.

'You did this, didn't you?' Conquest tried a dramatic sweep of his arm, but only managed to slap Famine in the face.

'Just passing the time. I really thought we were getting somewhere with that plague, but it seemed to just peter out. Most disappointing.' Beelzebub looked down the table. 'You're being very quiet, Death. I thought this would be your kind of thing.'

'He's sulking. It's been twenty years,' Conquest answered.

'Twenty-three years, to be exact, and it's starting to get on my bloody nerves,' said War.

'Famine ate the last of his biscuits,' Conquest continued.

Famine stared at the ground. 'I bought him some new ones.'

'He's never been the same since he made that vow to never kill,' said War.

'How's that going?' asked Beelzebub. Death rocked his flattened hand. So-so.

Beelzebub looked at the empty pint pots that covered the tabletop. 'What's the cause for celebration?'

'The world made it through another day. That's reason enough.' Conquest raised his glass and the other three clinked theirs against it.

'But the end of everything is your raison d'être.'

'Don't mention bloody raisins. You'll set Famine off again. You know what he thinks about health food.' War laughed loudly at his own joke.

'Is it, though?' Famine asked quietly. 'Is it our responsibility? The end of the world, I mean.'

'It is our destiny,' War replied.

'Because they say so? Just because they believe it's going to happen doesn't mean it should. We don't bow to them on any other topic. We don't know why we're here. We've heard nothing.'

Beelzebub's face turned as red as his coat. 'He said so!'

'Did He?' replied Famine.

'There were burning bushes and prophets and all sorts.'

'Have you spoken to Him personally?'

'No. But...'

'I've been thinking about this for a while. We've been abandoned,' Famine said. 'If He put us here at all. Perhaps we only exist because they want us to. "Don't blame us," they'll say. "We didn't break the world. It was those Horsemen".'

Conquest thought this over. He had been leading them for millennia, but where was he leading them to? His memories of the early days were hazy now. He remembered the excitement, though. A whole world, new and green, that was theirs to explore at leisure. They had crossed continents and navigated oceans. They had been privileged to witness the rise of humanity, though they had stumbled many times on the way. They had watched the construction of the pyramids of Giza and the destruction of Babylon. They were instrumental in the rise of the Roman Empire and, after they had switched sides, had brought it to its knees. There would be more great achievements and, no doubt, great failures in the future. This wasn't the first city they had seen burn to the ground and he was certain it wouldn't be the last.

A scuffle broke out between two drunkards further along the towpath. 'They seem to do a pretty good job of breaking things on their own,' Conquest said. 'I don't see why they need any help from us.'

'What about that volcano in Sumatra? The ash cloud that killed off almost every living thing?' Beelzebub said. 'We didn't think they'd make it. They're a resilient bunch. They'll need a push.'

'I've kind of got used to having them around the place, Famine replied. 'Think of everything we'd lose. Art. Music. Ale.'

There was a general murmur of approval at the mention of the ale. Conquest winked at a buxom serving wench. 'And the women. I'd certainly miss them.'

War rattled his scabbard. 'So this flaming sword is just for show, is it?'

Conquest patted him on the arm. 'I'm sure there'll still be plenty for you to do. Their wars will grow bigger and they'll think of more imaginative ways to be unpleasant to each other.'

War relaxed a little. If previous behaviour was an indicator of future action, then Conquest was right. Humanity had evolved from simply hitting each other over the head with blunt objects to intricate instruments of warfare with breathtaking speed. They really had a knack for it. Now that he'd had a few beers, the end of the world seemed like an awful lot of hard work.

Two thin wisps of smoke snaked their way out of Beelzebub's nostrils. 'I want my thousand years of glorious rule! I was promised!'

People were beginning to look over to see what the commotion was all about. Witnessing a bar brawl would be an excellent way to round off the day's excitement.

'Be a poppet and keep your voice down,' Conquest said.

'That's it, then?' Beelzebub asked in a more measured tone. 'Death. Talk some sense into them.'

Death merely shrugged and waved his empty glass. It was time for another round.

'What do you think you're doing?' Beelzebub hissed.

Conquest looked back towards the city. Against the bruised sky, London Bridge was an arrow of fire pointing to a future that was no longer clear. He gave one of his smiles that, in a few hours, would persuade the barmaid to accompany him to his chambers.

'I think we're retiring.'

TWO

It was the last night of James McCann's life.

Unaware of this disappointing end to the working week, he was sat at his desk on the empty twenty-second floor of UberSystems International Tower and shouting into a phone clutched in his meaty, sweaty hand.

'You are an idiot wrapped in a moron inside another idiot. If I was there, I would punch you and I abhor violence, so you actually make me hate myself. You're going to hang the phone up, go and fix the problem and call me back tomorrow morning.' He slammed the receiver down several times, imagining it was the caller's head. A row of clocks across the wall told the time in each of the UberSystems International offices around the world, boasting the company's reach. James looked for the one showing London time. Midnight.

He thumbed through the MI reports and ERQ alert readouts until the RSI in his wrists screamed. He laughed bitterly as he considered how his life had been reduced to a series of meaningless measurements and indecipherable three letter acronyms.

His had not been an existence worthy of note. He'd spent twenty years working in the Risk department of

UberSystems International. He'd come to realise there had been something rotten at the heart of the company for some time and he was going to find it. Whenever he felt he was getting close to the unpleasant truth, though, it slipped away from him. All he had to show for his efforts was a divorce, a handful of grey hairs and an irritable bowel.

He opened an encrypted spreadsheet on his laptop and began to work on some formulas, but received only error messages in return. He was so tired it was like trying to change a duvet cover while wearing mittens. And there was a cat inside the cover. And the cat was pointing out all of his mistakes. He closed the file without saving the changes and rubbed his sore eyes with his aching hands. He thought about getting another coffee, but he'd drunk so much already he was pretty sure he could hear the building breathing. One more cup and he would be able to see time.

He thought he felt something move behind him. He looked over his shoulder, but saw only shadows. Definitely no more caffeine. No matter how often he worked late, an empty office was always eerie. The darkness and silence where there was normally light and industry made him uneasy.

He stared blankly at the computer screen's wallpaper. It displayed the UberSystems International logo, which focus groups had assured the Public Relations department made them think of both 'family values' and 'the brutal decimation of enemies'.

He opened his desk drawer and took out his emergency packet of cigarettes and lighter. Perhaps five minutes away from the computer would clear his head. He took his crumpled suit jacket from the back of the chair and walked past the empty banks of desks towards the lifts.

Before he was halfway there, he stopped. Had he heard laughing?

'Hello?' he called out. Silence. Satisfied that he was alone, he continued to the lifts and pressed the down button. He impatiently tapped the lighter against the cigarette packet as he waited for the doors to open. Shadows shifted behind him. Double doors swung back and forth in the half-light. He was being watched. He was sure of it. His finger jabbed repeatedly at the lift button.

The doors slid open with a *ping* and James jumped at the sound. Inside the lift stood Conrad West, CEO of UberSystems International. West was a financial rock star and his story was told in hushed tones in boardrooms across the land. He had exploded onto the scene from nowhere during the boom years of the 1980s and had built an empire of glass and steel that stretched from New York to Tokyo. He had an uncanny ability to spot trends and patterns in the swirling chaos of the markets. His competitors respected and feared him and his management team were unwaveringly loyal to his cause. James hesitated despite his unease with staying on the floor. It would be like getting into a lift with an immaculately tailored nuclear device. It never felt safe being in an enclosed space with so much energy.

James stepped into the lift, pressed the button for the lower ground floor and felt the smooth descent begin

'Still here, James?' West asked with an expensive smile.

James tried to avoid eye contact. 'Yes, Mr West. It's the Meyer project.'

West groaned. 'Is that still dragging on?'

'I think we're nearly at the end.'

West looked at the cigarette packet. James could sense the disapproval. 'Those things will kill you, you know.'

'I've been meaning to quit, but work's been rather stressful recently.'

'I know. Don't think it's gone unnoticed. We run a healthcare programme for smokers. Maybe you should sign up for it?'

'I will, Mr West.'

The lift stopped its gentle fall, bobbed slightly and the doors slid open. West turned and rested a reassuring hand on James's shoulder. 'What's our most valuable asset, James?'

'That really big diamond you bought at that auction last year?'

'People, James. People are our most valuable asset. I don't like to see those assets eroded.'

'Yes Mr West. Thank you. Good night.'

'Good night James. Don't work too late.' West stepped out of the lift. The doors started to close behind him, but he turned and held them open. 'It really was a very big diamond, wasn't it?'

'Yes, sir,' replied James.

'Excellent.' West let go of the door and the lift continued its journey. James slumped against the wall. He could feel the warm stinging pricks of sweat on his brow. He stumbled out of the lift into the car park beneath the building and collided with a body on the other side of the doors.

'Steady on there, Mr McCann.' James looked up and stared into the face of Keith, the ancient night shift security guard. His skin was like thin white paper, dried and stretched across a stick frame. An origami version of a man, delicate paper folds and creases where limbs should've been. James thought he would snap and tear in half if someone grabbed him too roughly. He didn't understand why they just didn't let Keith go. Not that there was much for him to do. Danger didn't walk up to the front desk of major corporations. It was usually already inside the building. James knew this from experience.

'Off home?' asked Keith. 'I didn't see your car here?'

James held up the cigarette packet. 'Just getting some fresh air.'

'Right you are. Just you, the document management guys and Mr West left.'

'He's just gone.'

'Really? That's a pity. I wanted to talk to him about the security cameras.'

James smiled. Wherever he'd worked, there was always one security guard who thought that he owned the building.

'See you later, Keith.'

'Good night, Mr McCann.'

A fluorescent light blinked and buzzed, making the shadows jump and dance around James. He walked quickly across the empty bays and pushed open the fire door. He was grateful for the cool spring air on his hot face. He rubbed a hand on his wet forehead, matting his thinning hair. He lit a cigarette and hungrily drew the harsh smoke into his lungs, listening to the crackle of the burning tobacco above the soft murmur of the traffic above him. He exhaled as the nicotine flooded his body. A thought dropped into his pleasantly spinning head. He knew what was needed on the spreadsheet. It was obvious. He stubbed the cigarette out on the ground, crunching it under his foot. He had to get back to his desk before the answer fell out and disappeared forever.

The shadows reached out, grabbed him by the collar of his jacket and threw him back through the fire door. He crashed onto the tarmac with such force he felt the dull snap of the bone in his left arm. Pain and panic gripped his palpitating heart so tightly he thought it would squeeze the life out of him then and there. He heard somebody crying and realised it was him.

James pushed himself up onto his knees with his good arm, the other hanging limp and useless. He began to crawl towards the lift, agony running through his body with every heavy sob.

Whoever, or whatever, had attacked him lurked close by in the shadows. James could feel the heat of its excitement; hear its breathing and smell the stench from its exertion. It was stalking him, toying with him. He felt a boot under his chest and he was flipped over onto his back. He kicked and floundered like a newborn turtle unable to right itself.

James stared up with wide eyes. The tears had reduced his vision to nothing but dark smudges and smears.

'Please...' James gasped. Then teeth were at his throat, ripping at the flesh, puncturing and tearing into his windpipe. Thick warmth filled his mouth. He couldn't breathe. James was choking on his own blood. It spilled out and pooled around his head like a dark halo. He could feel himself draining away, his body leaking life with every misfiring beat of his heart. The world grew darker. As James had always suspected, there were no Pearly Gates. No choirs of angels or family members waited to receive him into the afterlife. There wasn't even a guy carrying a scythe.

There was nothing.

THREE

The sun shone down from a piercing blue spring sky, illuminating the sheer majesty and beauty of the world in all its form and splendour. It was Monday morning and the universe was basically taking the piss.

Dave woke slowly. A sunbeam punctured a gap in the bedroom curtains and hit him square in the eyes like creation's flashlight. As he shifted under the duvet, he remembered that somebody was in bed with him. Somebody who turned over and slid an arm across him. Somebody who murmured nonsense and nuzzled his neck.

Since he'd started going out with Melanie at Christmas, he knew that this was how he wanted every morning to start. This simple moment; this fraction of a lifetime that he'd fantasised about on a hundred conference calls and craved through innumerable sleepless nights was now his. His breath fell into rhythm with hers, his chest rising and falling beneath her embrace. She stirred and pulled herself closer.

The four months he'd worked for Death had taught him about the vast, frightening randomness of life, but love was a conspiracy of two. They were atoms clinging together, tumbling and spinning through the infinitesimally small gap between birth and the grave. Love was a binding force.

'Good morning,' Melanie said, her voice thick with sleep.

Dave smiled. 'Morning.'

'Sleep well?' Dave nodded. 'Excellent. Care to finish what we started last night before you fell asleep?'

'I'd had a really hard day at wor--' Dave began before Melanie's hand slid down Dave's chest and beneath the covers, causing him to forget the entire English language.

In the warm, sleepy glow afterwards, Dave knew that he would have to drag his heavy body from Melanie's embrace and mentally prepared himself for what waited for him in the bathroom. Since starting his new job, he had learned a great deal about quantum physics. Theories stated that reality was a delicate balancing act and all the universal forces tiptoed along a knife edge. There was a central pivot around which all possibilities teetered precariously, ready to plunge into the chaotic abyss at any given moment. Dave was pretty sure this point was on the hot and cold taps of his bath.

Melanie's hand instinctively slid up to her naked neck and then felt the surface of the bedside table.

'Have you seen my necklace?' she asked, a sliver of panic in her voice.

'No,' Dave blearily replied.

Melanie sat up sharply. 'It's got to be around here. Oh, it was a christening present.' She leaned over the side of the bed and looked underneath. 'It's filthy under here.'

Dave struggled to a sitting position and ran his hands along the carpet beneath the bed. A finger caught the thin chain and he pulled it up with a flick of the wrist. She gratefully took it from him and placed it around her neck. She played with the silver cross, stroking it with her fingers, then let it fall against her soft skin. 'I couldn't lose this. The Watkins are big on Catholicism.'

'Are you?'

'Me? Not so much but once a Catholic, always a Catholic. I'm guessing you put Jedi as your religion.'

'Lapsed. I had a crisis of faith after Episode I.'

Melanie hugged her legs beneath the duvet. 'I think we should all just worship cake.'

'That's a religion I could get on board with.'

'I bet we'd still find a way to ruin it, though. We'd soon break into factions. Victoria Sponge worshippers fighting the Battenberg heretics.'

'The streets running thick with ganache.'

'Cake, hope and charity. But the greatest of these is cake.'

'Amen.'

Melanie leaned forward and wrapped her arms around Dave's neck, pulling him down onto the bed. They kissed long and slow. Eventually, Dave's head reached emotional escape velocity from his heart's gravitational pull and he unwrapped his limbs from hers.

Dave negotiated the Quantum Shower of Doom with the minimum of shocked screams. He dressed in black jeans, black hoodie and black Doc Martens and checked himself in the mirror. It was a look he was trying out. He'd experimented with dark suits and smart shoes, but they lacked the practicality and comfort of a heavy pair of boots and hard-wearing trousers.

He carried out a handful of household chores, made two fresh cups of coffee and went into the living room. He handed one to Melanie and perched on the arm of the chair in which she sat. Gary, Dave's flatmate, was laid out on the sofa watching children's television; his natural state of being. Dave had seen many strange things, but was still in awe of Gary's almost supernatural ability to do absolutely nothing.

'I've put the rubbish out,' Dave said to him. 'That's your one area of domestic responsibility.' Gary had been playing Bin Jenga again, trying to balance the rubbish as high as he could before it collapsed on the floor.

Gary's eyes didn't move from the creepy toy mice singing a high-pitched song on the screen. 'And you've snatched it away from me. I feel I'm no longer the master of my own destiny.'

'I'm just saying--'

Gary put a finger to his lips. 'Shhh. Can you hear that? It's Monday morning. If we keep still and stop talking, maybe it will pass us by.'

Melanie patted Dave on the knee. 'Yes, we're trying to watch telly.'

'Are you two ganging up on me? Why don't you form a little club?' asked Dave. 'Oh God. You're going to form a little club, aren't you?'

'We'll need a cool secret handshake,' said Melanie.

'Oh, definitely,' agreed Gary.

What are you watching?' Dave asked.

'Bagpuss. You know it?'

Dave sipped his coffee. 'It's a bit before my time.'

'It's very interesting. It was made at the height of the Cold War and is basically a metaphor for Communist Russia.'

'You what?'

'You see those mice? They're the workers, the proletariat. They happily sing "We will fix it! We will fix it!" to show that they are content with what they have with no need for obtaining new material goods. Make do and mend.'

Dave watched a bookend in the shape of a woodpecker walk stiffly across the screen. 'Who's that then?'

'That's Professor Yaffle. He represents the bourgeois intelligentsia.'

From a wicker chair, a rag doll looking down serenely at the mice and woodpecker. 'That's Madeleine. She's the aristocracy,' Gary said before Dave could ask. 'It's all very simple.'

'And Bagpuss?'

'He's just an old, saggy cloth cat. Baggy and a bit loose at the seams, but Emily loved him.'

Melanie glanced at her watch. She jumped out of the chair. 'Oh, shit. Look at the time. I've got to get to work.'

'Yeah,' said Gary. 'That office window isn't going to stare out of itself.'

'Actually, it's hectic at the moment. We're ridiculously understaffed. Every department is haemorrhaging workers,' she replied. She turned to Dave. 'You remember James McCann?'

Dave did, vaguely. 'Yeah.'

'They say he was working late a few days ago, then just got up and left. Nobody's seen him since. Stress got to him, they say.'

'They always know these things, whoever *they* are.'

'They do, don't they? We're having to get a load of temps in. Nobody knows what they're doing. It's chaos. I've got to go in early just to clear some of the backlog. Anyway, see you later.'

She ruffled Gary's hair, who scowled up at her, and went into the hallway. Dave followed her.

'So, I'll see you tonight?' she asked as she pulled on her dark overcoat. 'Mum and dad are looking forward to meeting you.'

'I can't wait.'

'Eight o'clock. Let's not have another incident like Valentine's. Those computer networks are going to have to learn to look after themselves.'

Struggling for a suitable cover story, he'd told her he now did "something with computers", which he'd correctly assumed would be dull enough to avoid having to go into any specifics. As well as love, Death claimed that St. Valentine was also the patron saint of crushing disappointment, humiliation and Chinese set meals for one. That night, Melanie ticked all those boxes. Even though his heart fractured a little every time he lied to her, Dave couldn't tell Melanie what he was really up to. Like the fire brigade on Bonfire Night, Valentine's Day was one of his busiest times of the year. The afterlife was filled with yearning as spirits tried to contact their loved ones.

The dead had given up on the idea of keeping to office hours and Melanie had become used to the cancelled dates, forgotten rendezvous and nights dozing in front of the television. Dave stifled a yawn and stretched his tired, knotted muscles. He felt as clumsy and rigid as one of the stop-motion models on the television.

'Aw, babe.' Melanie stroked his cheek softly. 'I don't like what this job is doing to you.'

'I'm alright.'

'I still can't believe that you accepted a job from a man you met in the pub. For all I know, you're a henchman to a criminal.'

'He's a good guy. He's taught me a lot.'

'You could always come back to UberSystems. Christ knows we need the help. Nobody would think any less of you.'

'Wouldn't you?'

She just smiled and kissed him. 'Eight o'clock. Don't be late.'

FOUR

Death's office was located in an affluent area of the city where the local economy was supported by boutiques and artisan bakeries. Rows of Victorian buildings were chaotically squeezed together, rising up over a shallow hill. God's finger could've pushed the last one over and they'd tumble into each other like dominoes. Behind them, cranes scratched the grey sky as steel and money travelled upwards.

With his hoodie pulled up against the early morning chill, Dave walked past rows of BMW's and Chelsea Tractors and turned into Crow Road. He buzzed himself into the last unit at the end of the alley and climbed the stairs to the first floor.

The office was a small room full of filing cabinets and Scandinavian self-assembly furniture. Three doors led off it. One was the door Dave had just stepped through and one led to Death's inner office. The Infinite Monkeys with Infinite Typewriters were behind the third. They'd just signed with the William Morris Agency and had secured a three picture deal with Universal.

Anne, Dave's manager, was stood at one of the cabinets. With her shock of short blonde hair, long skirt, bracelets and bangles, she had a certain New Age quality about her, but he'd learned that she had a steely resolve and an edge that could only have been formed by something dark in her past.

'Good morning,' he said as he helped himself to a cup of coffee. 'What's today's plan?'

Anne looked up from her filing. 'Morning. First, I need you to finish the paperwork on yesterday's exorcism.'

Dave sipped his drink and shuddered at the memory. 'That was a messy one. Do you know how difficult it is to get ectoplasm out of clothes?'

'Then we're going on another field trip.' Anne passed him a newspaper and tapped an article with her finger. Dave skimmed it. Letitia Bowen, a thirteen-year-old girl who had recently moved into a house in East London, was at the centre of a series of inexplicable phenomena. Items moved in her presence without anybody touching them. She had been seen levitating above her bed and the walls of her flat ran with blood. This sort of thing unnerved the landlord as it hadn't shown up on the original property survey and wasn't covered in the rental agreement. He was threatening to evict Letitia and her mother unless all supernatural activity ceased immediately.

'Weird,' Dave said.

'Weird is what we do.'

'It's not going to take too long, is it? I've got plans this evening--'

'Anne! Could I get some coffee, please?' Death shouted from behind his door. Dave and Anne rolled their eyes at each other. Dave fetched a fresh cup and they went into the inner office. Death sat with his feet up on the desk as he read something on an old cathode ray computer monitor.

'Good morning, Death,' Anne said.

'Steve.'

'I'm not calling you Steve.'

'Try it. You'll get used to it.'

'I doubt it.'

Dave put the coffee mug on the desk. He was suddenly aware he still had his black hood pulled over his head and pushed it back down.

'Thanks, Dave. No, keep it up. It's a good look,' said Death.

'Anything to report from last night?' asked Anne.

'The world's oldest man died. Again.'

Anne tutted. 'He keeps doing that.'

'I'm surprised the newspapers haven't started calling it the curse of the world's oldest man.' Death and Anne smiled at their joke. At least, Dave assumed Death smiled. He had never seen what was beneath the hood. 'Then there was a food poisoning at an Elvis convention. Twelve Elvis. Elves. Elviseses. What's the plural of Elvis?'

Dave frowned as he pondered the question. 'Elvii?'

'Twelve Elvii. That'll do. Doomed to forever impersonate The King. They were all very impressed that I'd met him, though.'

'He's actually dead, then?' Dave made a mental note to challenge that particular conspiracy theory the next time Gary brought it up.

'Yes. What are you two up to today?'

'Looks like we've got something over in Stratford,' Anne replied. 'It shouldn't take too long and then Dave can make his evening plans.'

'What are you up to?' Death asked.

'Dinner with Melanie's parents,' replied Dave.

'Well, we'd better make sure you make that,' Death said. 'We don't want another Valentine's Day cock up.'

'Is that never speaking of it again?'

Anne tried to see what was on Death's computer screen. 'What are you actually doing?' she asked. She always felt uneasy when Death was on the computer.

'Just checking my emails. Now that I've managed to log in. Soon, passwords will need to contain at least eight characters, a story arc, a major theme, subtext and pass the Bechdel Test. And why do people use that handwritten font on their email signature? Do they expect people to go "oh, how sweet. He signed it himself?"' He sat bolt upright. 'Hey! I've won the Spanish lottery! I just need to give them some bank details.' He began typing on the keyboard then stopped. He looked up at Anne. 'Did I enter the Spanish lottery?'

Anne leant over and hit the 'delete' key on the keyboard. 'No, you didn't. I'm constantly surprised by how stupid a centuries-old being can be.'

'I'll have you know that the other three Horsemen and I were the Wise Men in Bethlehem.'

'No you weren't,' replied Anne.

'Four Horsemen?' asked Dave.

'Yes,' said Death.

'As in Four Horsemen of the Apocalypse? You see, you say "Horsemen", I hear "Apocalypse".'

'Yes.'

'Death, War, Famine...' Dave tried to remember the last name. '... And Ringo?'

The air between Death and Dave crackled. 'His name is Conquest,' Death muttered darkly, 'and I would ask you to say his name with the respect it deserves.'

Dave looked at the ground. 'Sorry,' he mumbled sheepishly. 'Wasn't there a Pestilence?'

'A human construct from the beginning of the twentieth century. An attempt to personify the guilt you felt for the disease and plague you carried with you in your attempts to civilise the world.'

'Right.'

'Conquest, Famine, War and I heard on the grapevine there was something going on, so we went to have a look. Those three only get mentioned because they brought presents. I couldn't find anything, but that's what happens when you leave your Christmas shopping until the last minute. To be honest, if we'd known what a big deal you lot would make about it, we would've made more of an effort. I said to War afterwards, who buys a baby myrrh?' He sighed sadly. 'Good times.'

When Death talked like this, Dave was never sure whether he was telling the truth, misremembering or just plain making it up. He once told him that there was a curve in the space-time continuum on Friday afternoons, which explained why they went on for so long and nothing got done. Dave didn't mind. He enjoyed hearing his stories.

'I thought you said you'd never met God?' Dave said.

'Nope, never met the fellah. But, wherever he is, I'm sure he's looking down on you lot and shouting "Bloody hell! That's not what I meant at all!". The Ten Commandments? They're such a downer. Don't get me wrong. They're a very good starting point, but they're so negative. Thou shalt not do this and thou shalt not do that. What about things you shalt? Thou shalt have a nice cup of tea and a biscuit, for example.'

It wasn't even nine o'clock and Dave was dealing with the fundamental nature of humanity and the universe. He wouldn't be doing that if he'd stayed at UberSystems International. 'But he exists?'

'No idea, but I knew the other guy and I speak from personal experience when I say you lot are better off when their type doesn't get involved.'

FIVE

Anne and Dave headed east from the office in the Deathmobile. Clouds gathered above them and soon the patter of rain rattled off the car's thin metal roof. Anne was hunched forward, trying to see out of the windscreen.

'So, what happened to the other Horsemen of the Apocalypse? They decide they weren't needed, or something? That we're more than capable of throwing ourselves in the abyss?' Dave asked.

Anne simultaneously hit the car's brakes and its horn as a lorry pulled out from a junction in front of them. Dave gripped the door handle tighter. Anne was a terrible driver and he didn't want to deal with Death as a customer instead of an employee. 'I don't know the whole story,' she said, 'There was some unpleasantness. With Satan.'

'Wow. I'm sorry I asked.' Dave stared out at the crowded streets. He thought of the billions unaware of the bigger world on their doorstep. He was almost envious of them as he weighed up the burden of his ever-growing knowledge. 'Anne?'

'Yes, Dave?'

'Are we henchmen?' he almost whispered.

'What makes you say that?'

'We work for a demon. One who was sent here to destroy the human race.'

'He's over that now. It was just a phase he was going through.' She made a rude gesture to a pedestrian running out into the road. 'I wouldn't call us henchmen.'

'Then what's my job title?'

Anne thought this over for a moment. 'Trainee With Afterlife Transition Senses.'

'That spells T.W.A.T.S.'

'Does it?' Anne asked innocently.

The car pulled up outside a mid-terrace house Dave estimated had been built some time before the Luftwaffe bombed large chunks of the surrounding area.

Anne got out and ran to the back of the car where she opened the small boot. She returned with a rucksack over one shoulder and leaned into the car.

'Come on. Just follow my lead. Keep your eyes open for anything unusual.'

They jogged down the front path, their jackets pulled up against the rain. Anne rang the doorbell as they both tried to squeeze beneath the small porch.

'It's the glamour that attracted me to this job,' Dave muttered as the rainwater ran down his neck. Through the frosted glass, he could see a blurred figure approaching. The door opened and the blur solidified into a short, stocky woman with a kind face. She didn't just look tired, Dave thought. She looked like she had been drained of all her energy.

'Christine Bowen?' Anne said, thrusting her hand out. 'Anne Mitchell from Ghost Watchers Productions. We spoke on the phone yesterday about appearing on the show?'

Christine Bowen, caught off guard, limply grabbed at Anne's hand. 'Oh hello. Yes.'

'This is Dave Marwood,' Anne pointed a thumb over her shoulder. 'He's one of our junior researchers. May we come in?'

'Junior?' Dave repeated.

Before Christine could answer, Dave was carried into the hallway by the force of Anne's words.

'Let me get you a towel,' Christine said. She went into a cloakroom by the stairs and came out with two fluffy white towels. Dave enjoyed the warm fuzz of the cotton against his face and neck. When he was finished, he looked at the blank magnolia walls and sanded floorboards. He could detect the faint odour of fresh paint and remembered that the newspaper article said Christine was a relatively recent tenant.

'How are you holding up?' Anne asked with genuine concern.

'Not too well, actually,' replied Christine and she gasped back a sob. Anne smiled sympathetically, giving her a second to compose herself. 'Look, I'm not sure about this. After the newspaper article...' She trailed off.

'I promise you we'll handle this with the utmost discretion. Isn't that right, Dave?'

Dave gave what he hoped was his most understanding smile. 'The utmost.'

'Is it possible to have a chat with Letitia?' Anne asked.

'Yes. She's in her bedroom. She doesn't come out of there much now.'

'Shoes off, Dave,' Anne ordered.

'Yes, mum,' Dave replied. He kicked off his scuffed boots. Christine, Anne and Dave climbed the stairs, Christine leading the way and Dave bringing up the rear. He smiled to himself. Forget about impersonating a police officer or a government scientist. These days, if you want to impress someone just tell them that you could get them on television.

Christine knocked on a door across from the top of the stairs. 'Letitia, love. The people from the telly are here. The ones who say they can help. Do you want to talk to them?'

Dave heard a muffled response and Christine turned back to them. 'Come in.'

Letitia's bedroom generally resembled that of most thirteen-year-old girls. Posters of well-scrubbed boy bands were stuck to the wall. Cuddly toys that she was too old for, but couldn't bring herself to get rid of, sat on shelves. A surly teenager sat cross-legged on a pink duvet covering a metal-framed bed.

Where it differed was the collection of objects floating in the air. Hairbrushes, books and make-up boxes lazily orbited Letitia's head like tiny pastel-coloured planets.

'I think this counts as unusual,' Dave said.

'You see our problem?' said Christine. 'Nobody believes us, so nobody will come here to help.'

Acclimatised to the strange over the last few months, Dave was curious more than anything. 'Have you thought about filming it? Putting it online?'

'Whatever it is, it burns out whatever we try and use to film it. I went through three phones before I worked that one out,' Christine replied.

Dave took a step forward. 'How are you, Letitia?' he asked, trying to ignore the pencil case hovering into view.

'How do you think?' Letitia pouted.

'Letitia!' barked her mother. 'It started just after we moved in. It seems to centre around her.'

Anne took a computer tablet out of the rucksack. 'There are lots of poltergeist cases that focus on adolescent girls. We think they're attracted to the life force as they approach womanhood. Like moths to a bright light.'

Dave walked back over to Anne. When he saw what she was reading on the tablet he said, 'Can I have a quick word with you outside?'

They stepped out of the room and Dave pulled the door closed. 'Are you using Wikipedia?' he hissed angrily.

'It's worked perfectly well in the past,' Anne said defensively.

'We're not going to screw her up or anything, are we?' Dave asked.

'No. Poltergeists are rare and tricky to deal with. It's all a bit hit and miss. The problem is they have no form, so our usual methods don't work. They're angry energy. Trust me on this.'

Dave was in unfamiliar territory and Anne was the closest thing to an expert. 'Alright, but the moment that it looks like we're frying her brain you stop.'

'Of course.'

They plastered grins on their faces and walked back into the room. Dave's mobile started to ring. He took it out of his pocket and looked at the number. It was Melanie.

'Sorry. I need to get this,' he said sheepishly. He answered the call. 'Hiya. Fine. You? That sounds great.' He glanced up. 'Hold on a second.' He put his hand over the phone's mouthpiece and nodded to Letitia. 'Should her head be doing that?'

Letitia's eyes had rolled back up into her head, which was slowly revolving on her shoulders. Christine began to scream, but smothered it with a hand over her mouth. They watched in horror as Letitia's head reached a point where her neck should've snapped, but it just kept on going until it had rotated a full three hundred and sixty degrees.

'I get the feeling that, whatever this thing is, it doesn't like mobile phones,' Anne said.

Dave remembered the phone in his hand and spoke into it. 'Look, I'm in the middle of something. What time tonight? No, I won't be late. I'll see you there.' Dave hung up.

'If we've all finished taking personal phone calls in work hours, let's get started, shall we?' Anne said.

Several hours later, it wasn't just the restless spirit that was cross. They'd tried everything from Pagan rituals to Christian prayers, but still the poltergeist refused to leave Letitia alone. Dave's frustration was coiled tight around an iron core of impatience. A teddy bear floated through the air and gently bumped into the side of his head. 'Oh, come on! I've got a date this evening!' he roared. He took a step forward and an unseen power swatted him to one side like he was an annoying bug. He crashed into the wall and slid down onto the floor. Dave groaned in agony. Sometimes, his job seemed like a fairground ghost train; scary and exciting but safe. Moments like this reminded him he was confronting the dead and he didn't know what they were capable of.

Anne was studying the tablet's screen and barely noticed the fuss around her. 'Here's something we haven't tried. Apparently, burning fresh sage will cleanse the spirit.'

'We've got some mixed spices in the kitchen,' said Christine.

'I don't think that's going to work. Is there anywhere we can get some?'

'There's a Tesco Express at the end of the street.'

'Perfect. Dave, can you pop out?'

Dave rolled onto his back. 'I really need to go. I'm going to be late for meeting Melanie's parents.'

'Nothing less than the fate of a young girl's soul hangs in the balance this night,' Anne said.

Dave picked himself up off of the floor. If the stars and, more importantly, the trains aligned he might still be able to complete his task and make it to the restaurant in time. 'Alright. I know it's serious when you start sounding like a bad fantasy novel. Can I claim it back on expenses?' The look Anne gave him made him realise that this wasn't the best time to discuss this.

'You're not actually television researchers, are you?' Christine asked, passing a set of door keys to Dave. 'It doesn't matter anymore. Let yourself in. I don't want to leave Letitia.'

Dave went to the shop and bought some sage. He also picked up a chocolate bar because he'd learned you really shouldn't try to communicate with the dead on an empty stomach. When he returned to the house, the interior had darkened as the evening light grew fainter. He stood at the foot of the stairs. The staccato sound of the rain against the window filled the silence of the house.

He mounted the first step and heard a low rumble. It grew in intensity until his whole body shook as if caught in an earthquake. He gripped the bannister to steady himself and could hear items in other rooms crash to the floor. Soon, the groans of the house died down until the only movement was the dust motes dancing in the thin shafts of light.

Dave relaxed again, and that was when the invisible energy punched him off his feet for a second time. He crashed to the floor, gasping as the wind was knocked out of him. Something in his head screamed for him to run out the front door and never look back, but he wasn't sure if the voice was his own. He stood up, dusted himself down and renegotiated the stairs. Dave climbed and turned the tight corner when he reached the top.

Uneasy, he opened the bedroom door. The room beyond was black and as silent as the grave.

'Hello?' His hand grasped for the light switch on the other side of the wall, but nothing happened when he flicked it. He stepped into the gloom and the door behind him slammed closed, plunging the room into total darkness. Dave fumbled in his pocket for his phone, which had a built-in flashlight. When he turned it on, he found himself staring into the blank eyes of Letitia floating an inch away from his face. Dave stumbled back and fell to the floor, screaming in shock and terror. In the beam of the flashlight, he could see the unconscious bodies of Anne and Christine.

Her feet six inches off of the floor, Letitia drifted towards him. Dave shouted out the first thing that came to mind, 'The power of Christ compels you!'

Letitia stopped in mid-air, her face twisted in agony. 'Not that bloody film,' she said in a voice that wasn't her own. 'I saw that when it first came out in 1973. What a load of rubbish.'

'Wh-- What?' Dave stammered.

'Load of rubbish. I don't normally go in for that sort of malarky, but everyone else was goin' so I thought I should see what all the fuss was about.'

'What?' Dave asked again, because he couldn't think of anything else.

'That picture house 'as gone now, of course. Used to take my Dorothy there when we was courtin'. Everything's changed now. You can't stop progress, she'd tell me, but it'd be a bit bloody nicer if it didn't go so bloody fast. Like those phones you all carry around with you these days. Don't get a minute's peace, but I'm stuck 'ere.'

It was becoming apparent Letitia was possessed by a grumpy old man. 'It's not really fair on the girl, is it?' Dave said.

'I suppose you're right. She seems a nice enough lass. She just felt so warm and it's so, so cold when you don't have a body. Especially since the dark appeared.'

'What dark?'

'Can't you see it? Can't you feel it? It's bloody everywhere.'

'What does it look like?'

'It's drifting down the streets like a wind is blowing it around. It gets everywhere. It clings to everything. It chokes you. We used to get some right pea soupers back when I were a kid. Couldn't see your hand in front of your face.'

Dave took a step towards Letitia, trying to avert a trip down memory lane. 'That's incredibly fascinating, but I'm working in a time frame here. If you could possess me, please, I think I can help you now.'

'Really?'

'We can give it a go.'

'You're not as warm as she is.'

'It'll only take a second. If you don't like it, you can go always go back to her. Please.'

'If you say so.' Letitia's eyes closed and she slumped lifelessly to the carpet. Dave tasted rolling tobacco and his head felt uncomfortably full, as if there was something sharing the space. The pressure pushed against his skull and he worried that it might explode. Then there was a flash of magnesium white behind his eyes and he was alone in his mind. Exhausted, he dropped to his knees. The bedroom light flickered back into life. Christine, Letitia and Anne woke slowly and groggily.

'It's gone,' whispered Letitia and hugged her mother.

Anne rubbed her temples. 'How did you do it?'

Dave shrugged his shoulders. 'I asked politely.'

'You asked politely?' Anne repeated and then she laughed.

'See?' Christine said to Letitia. 'That's where good manners gets you.'

Christine saw them to the front door. She insisted that they take some cake with them. It was the least she could do to say thank you.

'Our boss will appreciate this,' Anne said.

Dave checked his phone. There was a collection of missed calls and text messages from Melanie growing exponentially in anger as he scrolled through them. He tried calling her, thinking of an excuse as he waited for the call to connect, but it went straight through to her voicemail.

When they were back in the car, Dave told Anne what the poltergeist had said.

'What's the dark?' he asked when he'd finished.

Anne shook her head. 'No idea. Never heard of it.' She looked at her watch. 'It's getting late. Where do you want dropping off?'

Anne drove Dave across town. The whole while, Dave fidgeted in the passenger seat like a man being transported to his own execution. Every nerve ending fizzed with dread and terror, even more than when he was contacting the dead. He rehearsed what he would say to Melanie, but his mouth was full of teeth and tongue.

Sooner than he'd hoped, he was stood at Melanie's front door and he couldn't put off the inevitable.

'Good luck,' Anne called out of the car's window as she drove off. He pushed the buzzer for Melanie's flat.

'Yes?' a voice crackled through the speaker. Emma. Melanie's flatmate.

'Is Melanie there?'

'She doesn't want to talk to you, Dave,' Emma replied with undisguised glee. Since he'd met her, she had made it very obvious that she didn't like Dave. She'd probably said more words to him in that one sentence than she had in the entire time he'd known her. The shrug was her primary form of communication.

'I just need a couple of minutes. Can you let me in?'

There was a pause before Emma replied, probably while she consulted with Melanie. 'No.'

Dave sighed and pressed the button. 'Just tell her there was this work thing. Lives were in danger. It's all a bit complicated.'

'She says you're a terrible liar, Dave,' Emma said. 'Personally, I'm sure your employers wouldn't trust someone like you with that kind of responsibility. Just go home.'

The intercom went dead, leaving Dave standing miserably in the rain.

SIX

21 October 1872

The ritual was about to begin.

The sigil of the Four Horsemen of the Apocalypse had been drawn with salt on the cold stone floor of the cellar; a diamond within a circle. Black candles stood at the four points of the diamond, their flickering light painting shadows across the blood red fabrics hanging from the brick walls.

Seven robed figures stood before the crude altar. Archibald Christou, occultist and self-appointed High Priest of the Righteous Order of Armageddon, clutched an ancient and heavy leather bound book to his chest. It had taken many years and a large chunk of his family's fortune to obtain the last remaining copy of The Dark and Unusual Works of Cedric the Perpetually Baffled. He savoured the moment. This would be an event to be remembered until the end of time which, if he'd interpreted the prophesies correctly, was about five minutes away.

The group waited patiently until Christou felt the energies in the room align themselves. Satisfied, he opened the grimoire and, with great reverence, began to read the evocation from its dry pages.

'War, with your sword of flame, I summon you. Famine, with your scales of judgement, I summon you. Conq--'

'I really want a wee,' whispered one of the other cult members.

'I asked if anybody needed the bathroom before we started,' Christou replied testily.

'I didn't need to go then.'

'Maybe some of us shouldn't have drunk so much ceremonial wine,' suggested another worshipper.

'You're just going to have to hold on to it. I'm not stopping now.' Christou turned his attention back to the sacred text. 'Great. Now I've lost my place.' He ran his finger along the page. 'War... Flaming sword... blah blah... Famine... Right, here we are. Conquest, with your crown so that you may rule over the dominions, I summon you. And Death, with your scythe so that you may reap the souls of all men, I summon you.'

The ritual was complete. Cedric the Perpetually Baffled had been unclear about what should happen next, but Christou reckoned it'd be pretty bloody spectacular. The Righteous Order of Armageddon waited. Nothing. They waited a bit longer. The awestruck hush became an awkward silence. Somebody cleared their throat. 'I don't think it's--'

The candles erupted into fountains of fire, the flames licking at the low ceiling. The air above the sigil ripped apart with a sound like all of humanity sighing. The room was filled with a light so intense the bones could be seen in the hands the onlookers used to shield their eyes.

When the flames, smoke and light had faded, four dark figures stood in the circle. The worshippers fell to their knees, their eyes cast down in supplication to their masters.

'What the bloody hell was all that about?' asked War.

Christou raised his head. The Four Horsemen were not as he had imagined them, especially War who was naked, wet, covered in bubbles and holding a rubber duck. The room was silent but for the soft hiss of a candle being snuffed out by the bath water dripping from his body. Slowly, all eyes in the room turned to him.

'What are you lot staring at? This is just how I like to unwind.'

Christou cleared his throat. This wasn't going how he had expected, but he pressed on regardless. 'In the name of my Lord and Master Beelzebub--'

'That idiot?' muttered War.

'--Beelzebub, I have summoned you so that you may carry out the sole task for which you were created.' He bowed his head with what he thought was the right amount of respect.

'We'd rather not,' replied Conquest.

'Pardon?'

'No, thanks. If it's all the same to you.'

Christou was confused. Had the ritual gone wrong somehow? 'Are you not the Four Horsemen of the Apocalypse?'

'Yes.'

'And are you not charged with the destruction of the world, bringing about the glorious rise of Beelzebub?'

Death coughed loudly. It sounded, to Christou, like a rude word.

'We're not into that any more.'

'What?'

'That whole wrathful, end of days, fire and brimstone thing? Not our bag.'

'Oh, I don't know. I still like a bit of wrath every now and again,' said War.

'Is this going to take long?' Famine asked. 'I've got tickets to the theatre tonight.'

'Famine makes a good point,' Conquest said to the room. 'This all a bit rude, isn't it? There we all were, enjoying our evenings and then, without so much as a by-your-leave, you babble some incantations and inconvenience us.'

'Well, pardon me for trying to end the world,' said Christou defensively.

'And why would you want to do that?'

'The prophesies said so,' Christou replied, a note of doubt creeping into his voice.

Conquest gave him an understanding smile. 'They always do.'

'But we have been preparing for this day for years.'

Conquest placed a comforting arm around Christou's shoulder. 'It must be very disappointing. How about we go and have a pint and see if we can't sort this whole thing out?'

'That'd be nice.'

'Beer? Excellent,' said War. 'Could somebody get me a towel?'

Everybody shuffled out of the room and up the stairs.

'This is the worst end of the world cult I've been in so far,' somebody at the back muttered.

War, in a borrowed robe, dragged everybody into the first hostelry he found. The saloon bar was hot and cramped, the working classes trying some of the new-fangled binge drinking that had been created by the recently introduced licensing laws. Thick grey clouds of tobacco smoke circled above the drinkers' heads, threatening to create their own weather pattern and rain down sweat and spilled beer.

The Righteous Order of Armageddon sat nervously at a large table at the back of the pub nursing their pints of ale. They were a small group of middle-aged men and Archibald Christou was the most middle-aged of them all, grey and bland. Most of the order saw it as an eccentric gentlemen's club, and an excuse to get out of the house once a week. Not only was Christou a prophet, he was a prophet with an excellent wine cellar. They were more than happy to put up with a bit of chanting and incense as long as he opened a few bottles of claret afterwards, but they were totally unprepared for any of the rituals actually working.

They listened politely as Famine complained about missing his play and War told them stories of his victories in battle. Death sat there in silence. He was just happy to be drinking with his friends. Since fashions had changed, it had become more difficult for him to be seen in public without looking conspicuous.

Conquest sipped his pint and looked Christou in the eye. 'So what's all this nonsense about ending the world?'

'Have you seen the state of the place?' replied Christou. 'Wars in the colonies. Disease rife at home. Our cities are awash with the destitute, who we're choking with the coal we burn in the factories where they earn a pittance. We're killing each other and ourselves. We're too sick to survive. It seemed the kindest thing to do. Wipe the face of the Earth clean and start again.'

'So how long have you been trying to do this?'

'Twenty years or so. Since my fiancée died.'

'So you decided to end it all? That's a bit unfair on everyone else isn't it?'

Christou's nervousness turned to anger. 'She was the only good and pure thing in this filthy world and she'd been taken from me. Is that fair? Without her here, there didn't seem to be much point to anything else. I looked for signs and I found them.'

'There are always signs if you look hard enough.' Conquest turned to the other end of the table. 'Famine, do you remember that fellow in Hungary?'

Famine stopped his conversation about nineteenth century theatre. 'The one who thought that potatoes were the work of the devil?'

'They had eyes, you see,' Conquest said to Christou. 'If you ate them, he said, the devil could watch your soul.'

'That's just mad,' said Christou.

Conquest shrugged. 'One man's madness is another's philosophy.'

'So what do I do now?'

'Have you thought about getting a hobby? Some charity work, perhaps? Philanthropy is very popular right now.'

'I don't know...'

'You can't change the world with grand gestures. You have to do it in tiny increments. Now, who wants another drink?'

The drinking continued and once they let their hoods and their hair down, the Righteous Order of Armageddon were a decent bunch of lads. If you forgot that they'd tried to destroy the world earlier on in the evening.

When the singing started, Conquest excused himself and stepped out into the crisp autumn night. Once again, a human had surprised him. Compared to the centuries that Conquest had walked the Earth, Christou's sad and lonely existence was but a blink of an eye. Yet he had experienced something that the Horsemen never had. Love. All the millions who'd lived and died in his time had too. They gave their mortal hearts to each other knowing that every romance was doomed.

And when the inevitable happened, this man would prefer that the world did not exist, rather than live in it without his lost love.

It was about a girl.

When it came down to it, it was always about a girl.

SEVEN

Death stepped out of his office. 'Why did the chicken cross the road?' he asked.

Dave looked up from his computer. He'd spent the day researching hauntings, grabbing snippets of information from newspaper articles, blogs and urban myth websites, but was finding it hard to concentrate. All he could think of was Melanie. She hadn't replied to any of his text messages or phone calls since the night before. 'Pardon?'

'Why did the chicken cross the road?' repeated Death.

Anne sipped her cup of tea. 'I visited a farm when I was a girl. Have you ever looked into the cold, unfeeling eyes of a chicken? Some things are best left unknown.'

'Seriously,' said Death. 'Do it properly. Why did the chicken cross the road?'

Dave exhaled heavily. 'I don't know. Why did the chicken cross the road?'

'To get to the other side.'

'Excellent,' Anne said. 'Is there a reason why you're telling us a joke older than you are?'

'Don't you see?' replied Death. 'To get to the other side.'

'It doesn't get any funnier if you repeat it.'

'It means that the chicken is dead. It never occurred to me before. It's blown my mind.'

Dave looked at his watch. 'I could spend the rest of the day talking about the spiritual life of poultry, but that's me done.' He turned the computer off and pulled an extravagantly large bunch of flowers from under the desk.

'Going to see Melanie?' Anne asked.

Dave brushed the heads of the roses. 'Yeah, I'm going to surprise her after work and take her to her favourite restaurant.'

'I'll never understand human displays of affection,' Death said. 'I want to see you naked. Here, have some dead foliage.'

'Don't listen to him,' Anne said to Dave. 'I think it's romantic.'

Dave picked up his bag and threw it over his shoulder. 'Thanks. I just hope she does too. Wish me luck.'

'There's no such thing as luck,' Death said. 'Just a series of probable outcomes perceived from a certain point of a certain reality.'

'You smooth talker,' Dave replied as he shut the office door behind him.

Dave stared up at the thirty floors of UberSystems International Tower pointing up to the blue evening sky. The glass geometry seemed smaller than the last time he'd seen it. Over-caffeinated office workers spun in and out through the revolving doors. He followed a smartly dressed group into the foyer, his footsteps instinctively falling in time with theirs.

His boots squeaked on the polished marble floor as he passed Doric pillars stretching up to the glimmering lights on the high ceiling. The large space had been constructed to convince visitors that an intimidating slab of Roman architecture had been squeezed into the ground floor of a modern office complex. He asked for Melanie at the reception desk that seamlessly rose up from the floor as if the whole lobby had been carved from one solid piece of stone. He stood to one side and waited, self-consciously playing with the bunch of flowers. He watched the banks of lifts behind the reception as they whisked passengers up to the gladiatorial arenas of middle management. Soon, his attention was grabbed by the sound of a metallic tapping on glass. Death was stood outside, banging the tip of his scythe against the window. Dave looked around and, when he was satisfied that nobody else could see him waving from the street, he walked back outside.

'What are you doing here?' Dave whispered.

Death produced Dave's mobile phone from beneath his cloak. 'You left this in the office.'

Dave casually glanced over his shoulder and then took the phone. He held it up to his ear, pretending to talk into it; a technique he'd developed as a way to hold conversations with Death in public.

'Thanks very much. I'll see you tomorrow.'

Death looked up and carefully examined the steel and glass structure stretching up into the sky. Dave could tell something was on his mind. 'What's bothering you?'

'You used to work here, right?'

'Yes.'

'Did you notice anything unusual?'

'Apart from everyone who worked in I.T.?'

'Unusual in a supernatural sense.'

'Not that I can remember. Why?'

Death started to push his hands against the window as if he was feeling for something and then looked back at Dave. 'I'm sure it's nothing.'

'What are you doing here? You dragged me out of a meeting,' a voice from behind Dave said. He span round to see Melanie, her arms folded across her chest and an unimpressed look on her face.

'I'll call you back,' Dave said into his phone.

Death patted him on the shoulder. 'I'll leave you to it.'

Dave felt a faint breeze behind him as the air rushed in to fill the gap where Death had stood.

He smiled and thrust the flowers towards Melanie. 'I got these for you.'

He felt foolish when she ignored them, but he continued with the speech he'd rehearsed on the way over. 'Look, Melanie, I know I haven't been the best--'

'Maybe you should let me speak first?' Melanie said. She sighed and played nervously with her necklace. 'I know this probably isn't the best time to do this, out in the street, but when is a good time?'

The mental scaffolding supporting Dave's fragile smile fell away and his face crumbled into a frown.

'At the start, it was all very romantic, with your declarations in the office and stuff,' Melanie said, 'but you've got to have something to back it up, y'know?'

'I'll make it up to you,' Dave replied, 'If you'll let me.'

'You've let me down too many times. My birthday...'

'I can explain that.'

'That weekend away...'

'I had a good excuse.'

'Valentine's Day, last night. Do you know how humiliating it is?'

Dave looked at the ground, ashamed. 'I'm sorry.'

'I can't begin to put into words how angry I am with you.'

'You could always try it through the medium of interpretive dance?'

Dave wanted to hear the sound of laughter; a sign that there was hope.

'You're not going to joke your way out of this one,' Melanie snapped. 'When you do show up in my life, all you want to do is sit around in your pants eating crisps.'

Dave looked up. 'That's not fair!'

'Isn't it?'

Dave looked back down at his shoes. 'It's not always crisps.'

'I want to go out with someone I can spend quality time with. I want to go out with someone because I like them and we have fun, not out of a sense of morbid curiosity wondering how they'll let me down next.'

Dave was reminded of his car accident a few months ago. Time slowed as he braced himself for the grim inevitability of impact.

Melanie took a deep breath. 'I think, perhaps, we need a break.'

The sound of pedestrians and snarled-up traffic reduced to a distant hum in Dave's ears. His stomach dropped as if he was plummeting from the top floor of the building he stood in front of.

A man appeared at Melanie's shoulder. 'Is this guy bothering you?' he asked in a cut glass accent. With his muscular frame, expensive suit and golden mane of hair, he looked like a lion that had been privately educated and given a gift card for Savile Row.

Melanie wiped a finger under her eye. 'No, this is Dave. Dave, this is Jeremy.'

'The mythical Mr Marwood!' Jeremy said, snatching Dave's free hand and shaking it firmly.

'Hi,' Dave managed to mumble.

'I was beginning to think that you were an excuse that Melanie uses when I ask her out.' Jeremy laughed; a braying guffaw that Dave wanted to stop by removing his larynx. 'So, tell me, what brings you back to these parts?'

'If you don't mind, Jeremy, Melanie and I were in the middle of something,' Dave replied coldly.

'Of course. Very sorry to bother.' Jeremy touched Melanie lightly on the shoulder, looked into her wet eyes. 'I'll see you inside?' he asked, a note of concern in his voice. Melanie nodded and Jeremy took this as the signal to leave them alone.

When Jeremy was out of earshot, Dave said, 'I'll try harder. I'll be better.'

Melanie's voice caught on the edge of a sob. 'What you need to do is sort out what's important to you.' She looked at her watch. 'I need to get back.'

'Whatever,' Dave replied sulkily.

Melanie looked as if she was about to say something, but then turned and went back into the building.

Through the glass, Dave could see that Jeremy had waited for her. He offered her his handkerchief, touched her elbow to guide her towards the lifts. Each moment of contact sent a jolt of jealousy through Dave. He'd seen Jeremy's type many times before. Dave was already imagining him offering his well-tailored shoulder for Melanie to cry on, suggesting drinks after work if she wanted to talk about things. He'd tell her how she could do so much better, undermining her already shaken confidence in Dave.

Dave took a calming breath. Now was not the time for petty envy and rivalries. This situation required a mature, measured approach. He knew what needed to be done.

He would get very, very drunk.

EIGHT

Needing the emotional anaesthetic that only alcohol could provide, Dave found a pub, went in and bought himself a pint. Then a second one to keep the first one company. A third followed. Then another because three's a crowd, while four is a gathering. He bought a fifth along with some pork scratchings, because he decided he might as well make a party of it.

A band were playing by the time Gary arrived. Tucked away in the corner, as if they were an embarrassment, they weren't so much murdering the songs as bludgeoning them to death and then violating the corpses afterwards. Sat across the grubby table from Dave, Gary listened to him drunkenly describe the events of the evening.

'Why didn't you call me sooner?' he asked as he slurped his frothy bitter.

'I needed some time to think.'

'Come to any conclusions?'

'Yes. The pork scratchings here are terrible. And I've written a haiku about relationships.'

He pushed a scrap of paper across the table. Gary picked it up and scanned the words. 'You've just written the word "AAARGH!" seventeen times?'

'I admit that it needs some work.'

'It's good to see you're taking it so well. As my mother always told me, if you love someone set them free. There's a possibility that they won't press charges.'

They sat in silence for a moment, listening to the band. 'Is this how you thought that life would turn out? Sat here listening to the wankers up there?' Dave nodded towards the musicians, tiredness creeping into his voice.

'I know they're not very good, but there's no need to be like that.'

'No, that's what they call themselves.' Dave picked up a beer-soaked flyer from the table and passed it to Gary. 'The Wankers. I was talking to the drummer. It's meant to be post-ironic or something.'

Gary put the flyer to one side. 'So, what are you going to do?'

'Well, I was planning on getting drunk.'

'I meant about Melanie.'

Dave winced. Just the sound of her name was like a stab to the heart. 'I don't know. Being a grown up is not the rich sophist-- sophist--' Dave took a long linguistic run up. '--Sophisticated experience I had been led to believe it would be.'

'I think the definition of a grown up is somebody who orders a hot drink with their McDonald's meal.'

'Very deep. You should put that on a tee shirt.'

Gary folded his arms. 'You know what you need, don't you?'

Dave shook his head. 'No. What do I need?'

'Drunken monkey sex.'

'Drunken monkey what?'

'We'll have a couple more here, a few shots, find a club and get you some action. Get back on the horse, so to speak.'

'No, besides I have work in the morning.'

Gary picked up the crumpled piece of paper with Dave's haiku written on it. 'If this is what I'm going to have to put up with - poetry - we need to get you laid as soon as possible, for my sake as well as yours.'

Dave put his pint down and looked Gary squarely in the eye. 'I am not going clubbing.'

Dave and Gary staggered up to the club. The owners had obviously taken the decision that it was too cool a venue to publicly advertise its location. The only clue that anything laid beyond the doors was the thick-set bouncer who stepped from the shadows. An unfortunate combination of stubble, interesting scars and green neon light made his round head look like an angry tennis ball. He gave the two friends the kind of intimidating smile that was usually followed by a request for the recipient's wallet and valuables.

'Evenin'' he growled as he opened the door for them.

The club was self-consciously hip and filled with second hand furniture, no one piece matching another. Behind a turntable and a laptop, a DJ was playing music at such volume it was as if he was waging an ideological war on the concept of conversation itself.

Dave was not a natural party animal. He was an inefficient mingler and often discovered that he had gone out with an insufficient number of conversational topics. As a child, on the rare occasions he was invited by classmates, he'd go to fancy dress parties dressed as a ninja. He would find somewhere quiet to hide and only emerge when it was time for the prize giving. As he had gone completely unnoticed by the adults, he had proved himself to be an excellent ninja and invariably walked away with the first prize.

The place was heaving with bodies; quick drinks after work that had spiralled out of control, and it was way past everybody's bedtime. Sweaty accountants filled the dance floor. Illicit couples hid away in the dark corners in unsuccessful attempts to avoid being tomorrow morning's water cooler gossip. While Gary was at the bar, Dave had found himself dragged into a conversation with a twenty-one-year-old UberSystems International sales assistant he vaguely knew named Sophie. What had started as a quick 'How are you?' had grown into a full-blown analysis of her relationship with her ex-boyfriend. At least that's what Dave assumed it was as she talked almost entirely in textspeak, shouting over a bass line so deep and powerful it threatened to rearrange their internal organs.

'I WOZ ALL, LIKE, OMG, UR MAKIN ME H8 U. HASHTAG FACEPALM. U C WOT IM SAYIN?' She laughed. Dave didn't see what she was saying, but laughed anyway.

'STILL,' she continued. 'U NO. YOLO.'

'What-lo?'

'YOLO. You only live once.'

'You'd be surprised.'

'WOT?'

'Never mind.'

They fell into an awkward silence, but Dave could see that Sophie was preparing for another indecipherable rant. He smiled. 'Well, I'd better leave you to it. Good to talk to you. Hope it all works out with your boyfriend.'

'C U L8R,' she called back after him.

'NOT IF I C U 1ST,' Dave muttered under his breath.

He headed up to the bar's roof terrace. From there, London's lights shone like a thousand fallen stars climbing invisible towers, trying to return to their home in the empty black sky. Alcohol's warm hug protected him from the chill of the night. The low rumble of the city ebbed and flowed as it was whipped around them by the swirling winds. The sound of a sleeping monster breathing.

Dave remembered that he'd been here once before, in the early days of his relationship with Melanie. Her friend had organised a seventies disco night. They'd slipped between the other dancers until they'd found a small piece of dance floor to call their own. Melanie moved with a grace and poise that suggested she could feel the music around her and shape herself around it. Dave, on the other hand, hopped and jerked as if the floor was made of hot coals burning through his shoes. Like so many activities with Melanie though, what he lacked in natural ability he'd more than made up for in enthusiasm.

The density of dancing bodies had forced Melanie and Dave closer together, until they brushed against each other. Dave had felt electricity between the two of them. Or it could've just been the static from the manmade fibres that surrounded them. His memories were hazy.

Right then, he didn't want to see ghosts. He didn't want to commune with the dead. He wanted to snog Melanie Watkins. He wanted to go for drinks with her, dance to terrible pop songs and look disinterested at gigs listening to challenging bands. He wanted to go on holidays and business trips. He wanted to make executive decisions, own a decent suit and impress people with his knowledge of current affairs. He wanted to do all the things that you're supposed to do when you're young and living in a big city. He wanted a normal life. He wanted Melanie.

NINE

Death looked up to the night skies from the flat roof of One Crow Road. He would come up here to gaze up at the silent majesty of the universe when he needed to think. He was saddened that the stars had dimmed and disappeared from the London skyline over the centuries, obscured by a veil of smog and light, but the city was his home now. Death liked the English. He enjoyed the real ale, biscuits and cricket. Any nation that could invent a game that went on for five days and invariably ended in a draw truly grasped the futility of existence.

Sometimes, though, he liked to travel to a desert far away from civilisation and lay staring up at the Milky Way's thick, glowing ribbon looping around the Earth. A galaxy that contained more stars than there were grains of sand beneath him and every atom of each of those grains was born out in the cosmos. Death didn't understand why humanity didn't spend more time and energy on space travel. It wouldn't be exploration. It would be going home.

Anne climbed up the fire escape, breathing heavily as she clambered over the rusting metal onto the rough felt roofing. 'I thought I'd find you up here. UFO spotting again?'

'Don't mock. Aliens are real, Anne. They show up every few years in their mothership, look down on humanity, go "Nah, they're still dicks" and bugger off again. Did I tell you I've got the deeds to the universe somewhere in the filing?'

It was true that Death held what appeared to be the deeds to the universe. He'd come across them while having a clear out, but had no idea where they came from. Perhaps Conquest had won them in a card game. One night after humanity had once again done something to disappoint him and he'd drunk too much cheap red wine, he decided that it all had to go and placed the following advert on an internet auction site:

"Due to an increase in running costs in these times of financial hardship, the decision has been taken to put the entire universe up for auction.

Started not with a Big Bang, but with a Big Sigh of Resignation 13.7 billion years ago, it's in need of some modernisation. There are some black holes, but these can be sorted with a lick of magnolia paint. Though it's quite roomy, we'd suggest knocking through an extension into a parallel universe.

Included in the sale:

30 billion trillion observable stars. We think there may some more in the attic. If we find them, we'll throw them in.

A number of planets – Some rocky. Some gas. One – interestingly – made entirely of nougat.

Dominion over all living beings. If you can get them to do a bloody word you say. Good luck with that.

An indeterminate amount of dark matter. It's possibly Marmite.

Full deeds and meaning of life written on the back of a cigarette packet.

Instructions.

Would suit Pan-Dimensional Overlords of unspeakable horror.

Please note that the photo is not to scale. Buyer collects."

Some Pan-Dimensional Overlords of only moderate horror were the highest bidders, but the cheque bounced. Death left them negative feedback and filed the deeds away.

'So, what's bothering you?' Anne asked. She knew Death well enough to know this was where he came when something was on his mind.

'I went to Dave's old office today,' he said, not taking his eyes from the heavens. 'He'd left his phone behind here, so I thought I'd drop it off. He was in the reception and I was going to surprise him. Y'know, appear right behind him and there'd be screaming and stuff--'

'That's never been funny, by the way,' Anne interrupted.

'--But I couldn't do it. It's like the building spat me out onto the street.'

'Spat you out?'

He looked down and back at Anne. 'Like a piece of chewing gum. It didn't want me to be there. That's the only way I can describe how it felt. I've not come across anything like that before. There's something going on in that building. Something sinister. Something dark.'

Anne stiffened at Death's words. 'Yesterday, Dave said that Letitia told him the dark was coming. I didn't know what she meant. Do you think it has anything to do with that?'

'I don't know, but I think we need to get in that office and find out.'

'How are we going to do that?'

'I've got an idea.'

'I thought you might.'

Anne and Death fell silent, the city humming in tune with the whistling wind the only sound between them.

'It's getting worse out there,' said Anne finally.

'How do you mean?'

Anne thought for a moment, looking for the right words. 'Usually, they're benign.'

'You know I don't like talking about them,' Death said.

'Lost and aimless,' Anne continued, ignoring Death's embarrassment at his past mistakes. 'Bored, even. But they're getting restless. Angry. They're starting to bleed into the everyday. They're getting noticed.'

Death's shoulders slumped. The ghosts were a constant reminder of his failures and of what he had lost. Anne placed a comforting arm around him. It made him shiver in a way he didn't understand.

'You should get inside,' she said. 'You'll catch your death out here. Well, you know what I mean. Die Hard is starting on the telly. You like that, don't you?'

Death perked up. 'As far as I'm concerned, Die Hard is humanity's greatest artistic achievement. Hamlet and the Mona Lisa are fine in their own way, but do they have explosions in a lift shaft? No.'

TEN

Dave woke up alone. His brain thudded painfully against his skull in time with the kick drum of his heartbeat. Soon, his stomach joined in with a bass solo and the ringing in his ears added some treble. He rolled over to the other side of the bed, his limbs twisted up in the covers.

He looked at the alarm clock. This was the beginning of one of seven billion daily rolls of the dice. Seven billion games of chance where the odds eventually decreased to zero. The teenager in a car crash. The middle-aged man felled by a heart attack. His mother eaten away by cancer until it was burned away along with what remained of her. All of it played out in an apathetic universe.

He pulled himself up and looked around the bedroom. He had changed so much since the start of the year, it had taken on a strange yet familiar quality as if he had gatecrashed somebody else's life. The film posters and photographs of drunken nights out pinned to the wall seemed juvenile now. The action figures and comic books sat on the shelves belonged to another, younger Dave Marwood. He threw the Star Wars duvet cover off his legs. As he stumbled towards the wardrobe to pick out the day's clothes, he decided that he'd buy some more suitable bed linen as soon as he could.

Dave was surprised to find he was the first to arrive in the office. He immediately headed to the kettle, filled it with fresh water and set it to boil. He carefully measured out two heaped spoonfuls of instant coffee granules and dropped them into a mug. When the kettle clicked off, he looked at the contents of the mug and decided that it wouldn't suffice. He poured the steaming water into the half-full coffee jar instead, stirred and drank.

Death and Anne arrived within a few minutes of each other. When Dave had made drinks for them both, he blurted out, 'Can I be frank?'

Death and Anne looked at each other. 'Only if I can be Steve,' Death replied.

'Stop that,' Anne admonished.

'I mean, can I speak frankly?'

'Sure.' Death sat back in a chair, waving a hand to indicate Dave should continue.

Dave suddenly felt nervous. He screwed his confidence up into a fist and he cleared his throat. 'First, I just want to say thank you for everything you've taught me. If nothing, this whole experience has been educational.' He turned to Anne. 'Thank you for all your help and guidance, but I think the time has come for me to move on.'

'Oh,' replied Death. 'We'd be very sorry to see you go. Do you have anything lined up?'

'I was thinking about seeing if I could go back to work for UberSystems International, actually. I really don't think I'm cut out for this.'

'Don't worry. I thought the same when I started,' Anne said. 'In fact, I'm still learning. So far, I've been responsible for fourteen insurance claims, accidentally caused the deaths of all the squirrels in a Royal Park and I'm pretty sure the burning down of a stately home was my fault.'

'Well, I think it's a splendid idea,' Death said.

This wasn't the reaction that Dave had expected, but he realised that he shouldn't have been surprised by this. That was part of the problem. Lack of consistency. 'You think I should do it?'

'Yes. In fact, I've taken the liberty of updating your C.V. and sent it over to them this morning. Tamsin in Human Resources would like to see you today.' Death took a typewritten piece of paper from a drawer and passed it to Dave, who scanned it with a quizzical expression.

'Under other skills, you've written "good gaydar",' Dave said.

Death sipped his coffee. 'Yeah, well, I had to pad it out somewhat.'

Dave scrunched the paper in a ball. He was angry and hurt that Death would go behind his back like this, that he would be so quick to dismiss both him and all that they had been through together. Those feelings, though, were quickly replaced by suspicion as he remembered who he was dealing with. He looked from Death to Anne.

'What's going on here?'

'There's something happening at UberSystems International,' Anne said.

'What?' asked Dave.

'Haven't the foggiest,' said Death. 'But it's supernatural and powerful.'

'So you want me to snoop around? See what I can find out?'

'See, that's what I like about you, Dave. You're on the ball.'

'Do I get any say in this? What if it's dangerous?'

'If it's dangerous, then everybody who works in that building could be in trouble,' said Anne.

'Melanie?'

Anne nodded. Dave sighed. He knew then that leaving this job wouldn't be as simple as handing in a resignation. Perhaps it was something he could never truly leave behind. 'You better tell me all you know about this. And then I want to talk about those squirrels.'

Dressed in a hastily selected suit and tie, Dave waited in UberSystems International's HR department as young women with names like Jemima and Poppy bustled around him. He reckoned he could work in Human Resources. As far as he could tell, it mostly involved letting people go and eating cake. That wasn't too far off what he did already.

Taking in the clean lines and monotone colour scheme, he wondered what strangeness could've entered such a bland, vanilla world. The oddest thing that had happened in his time working here was a spate of stapler thefts about eighteen months ago. He didn't know what to look for and wouldn't know what to do if he found it. He guessed he'd cross that bridge when he came to it.

More important matters weighed on his mind. Like what was he going to tell Melanie? Would she be happy that he'd apparently come back to work, or would she be disappointed that he'd seemingly given in? His train of thought was derailed by Tamsin, the Head of Human Resources. 'David Marwood?' she asked.

'Yes.'

'Mr West will see you now.'

The colour drained from Dave's face. 'Mr West? Conrad West?'

'Yes. He's taken a keen interest in your application. Follow me, please.'

Dave let Tamsin lead the way to the interview room. He hadn't seen his old boss since he'd walked out of his previous position to go and work for Death. He assumed West now wanted to humiliate him in some way before kicking him out of the building. He decided to get it over and done with, so thanked Tamsin and let himself into the room.

Conrad West was sat at a small table. He indicated the empty chair opposite him, inviting Dave to sit down.

'The prodigal son returns,' he said with a warm smile. 'I can't begin to tell you how surprised I was when we received your curriculum vitae. What have you been doing with yourself, Mr Marwood?'

Dave sat down. 'You know. This and that.'

West folded his hands on the table and the atmosphere grew colder. Dave was grateful for the table separating them. 'I'm afraid I don't know,' West said. 'Please enlighten me.'

Dave could feel itchy pricks of sweat on his forehead. 'I've just been doing some administration for a small start up.'

'Financial services?'

Dave thought for a second. 'No, a different industry. It's got a few fingers in different pies.'

'That sounds very intriguing. Why would you want to return to us?'

Dave had been practising his answer. 'It's like you said to me before. UberSystems International is a family. I miss my brothers and sisters. Together we can be the best. One team striving towards a common goal. Synergy, Conrad. It's all about synergy.'

'That's a very commendable attitude. It's tough here at the moment, I'll be the first to admit it. How do you think you would handle the stress this time?'

'Once you realise life is a futile struggle against the inevitable, it's a breeze,' replied Dave with a smile.

'That's an unusual approach.' West sat back in his chair. 'I like you, Dave. Always have. Always will. You've got potential. One day you could be sat where I am, but I can't just let you stroll back into your old position. You need to prove your commitment to the organisation. You need to prove yourself to me. I want you to learn about every facet of this company. You'll start in the Document Management Centre, on the midnight to eight in the morning shift. If you perform well there, then we'll look to move you up. Do we have a deal?'

Dave considered the offer. West had offered him the perfect solution. Working the night shift meant that he'd have access to a virtually deserted building and the hours would allow him to avoid Melanie, at least until he'd figured out what to tell her.

'I'll take you up on it, Mr West.' Dave held his hand out and West shook it firmly. 'I won't let you down.'

'Excellent. Be here at midnight and ask for Kirsten.'

ELEVEN

17 June 1933

Death's head pounded behind his closed eyes. He was hot and sweaty underneath his robe. His stomach performed somersaults at such speed it was as if he'd swallowed a Russian gymnast during the night. He was hungover. Unsure of how much of a good idea it was, he opened his eyes. He was laying on top of a giant bed, its pillows and covers piled up thick and soft like marshmallow. He rolled onto his back. An expensive chandelier hung from the Rococo ceiling, the crystals sparkling and winking with a strange, otherworldly light. He realised he was in a very expensive hotel room. He tried to remember the events of the previous evening, but there was a supermassive black hole in the centre of his mind dragging all thoughts down into a drunken singularity.

War shifted next to him and began to snore; loud, skull splitting snorts and wheezes. Death prodded him, but War was in his full armour and it made no difference. Death shoved with all the strength he could summon and War tumbled off of the bed and onto the deep cream-coloured carpet. He was immediately on his feet, sword in hand, but then he wobbled and staggered back until he collapsed into a mahogany Louis XVI armchair. The chair's legs creaked under the weight of man and steel, but held firm.

'Are we able to die?' War croaked as he rubbed his forehead. 'Because I think that would be the sensible option right now.'

Famine crawled out from under the bed. He looked even more pale and gaunt than usual. He hugged the carpet. 'The floor is my friend. The floor is not moving.'

Death sat up very slowly as if he was balancing a delicate glass bowl on his shoulders. 'Where's Conquest?' he finally managed to ask.

There was a thud from inside a white wardrobe across from the foot of the bed. Death noted it was in the French country style as the door opened and Conquest, a crown balanced on his head, flopped out onto the floor.

'Is he dead?' asked War. 'Lucky git.'

Conquest gave a groan muffled by the deep carpet fibres. 'I wish. This better be the only time I get married.'

It had been Conquest's stag night. He who had taught Casanova everything he knew was settling down and getting hitched. War had decided that this was worthy of note and celebration. They had worn the uniforms of their former office and gone for a couple of quiet drinks around their old London haunts.

'Where are we?' Famine asked. War pulled himself from out of the chair and stumbled over to the window. He pulled the curtain aside and the room was flooded with a shimmering silver light. The other three cried out in agony and shielded their eyes with sleeves and pillows.

'Big. Shiny.' War dropped the curtain back and the cool darkness returned. He collapsed back into the chair.

'What?' asked Death. He gingerly crossed the room being careful not to step on Famine or Conquest, nor bump into War who was already snoring. He peered through a gap in the curtain. The sun hung in a powder blue sky. Boats lazily drifted along the flat mirror surface of a lake, framed by rolling green hills dotted with small towns and villages. On any other occasion, this would've moved Death to tears as he took in the sheer beauty sketched out on the world's living, shifting canvas. Instead, he just muttered 'Lake Geneva. It's Lake bloody Geneva.'

'What?' said Conquest. 'Are you sure?'

'I've been here a few times,' Death replied curtly.

Famine flopped onto his back like a dying fish. 'But we were in the Hen and Chickens yesterday afternoon. Why are we here?'

Before anyone could reply, the black Bakelite telephone on the bedside table began to ring. War, who had no truck with new technology, was back on his feet. 'Whatever is making that infernal racket, kill it. Kill it with fire.'

'It's just the bloody telephone,' mumbled Conquest. 'Somebody please answer it.' War threw himself across the room and grabbed the receiver.

'What?' he bellowed into the mouthpiece.

'Bonjour, monsieur. Je suis vraiment desolé pour l'intrusion,' said the caller.

War offered the telephone to Death. 'It's some mad French bastard.'

Death took the phone from War. One of the perks of being the Grim Reaper was that he could converse in all of humanity's dialects. 'Bonjour?' said Death.

'I'm very sorry to disturb you, sir. There is a gentleman here at reception to see Mr Quint.' Quint was the name that Conquest was using at that time. 'He says that he has Mr Quint's order.'

'Merci,' said Death and he hung up the telephone. 'There's someone waiting in reception, Conquest. He says he's got something for you.'

Conquest climbed to his feet. 'I'd better see what he wants.'

'Good idea,' replied Death. 'I'd lose the crown, though. The Swiss might regard that as a tad ostentatious.'

Conquest was gone for around ten minutes, during which time War made a futile attempt to order some tea from room service. On his return, Conquest was carrying an envelope and a small wooden box. He placed the box on the bed and his three friends gathered around. He opened the lid. Four silver Patek Phillipe pocket watches of unequalled design and delicacy were nestled securely in the black suede lined interior. This must've been why they had travelled to Geneva, home of humanity's finest watchmakers.

'What's in the envelope?' Famine asked in a hushed tone as he stroked the face of one of the watches. Conquest tore open the envelope and took out a handwritten letter. His eyes scanned over the contents. 'It's addressed to us. From us. "Hi. If you're reading this, then you survived the night. You are blessed with infinite time and possibilities. These four watches are a gift and a reminder to each of you from the others. All the best, the Four Horsemen of the Apocalypse (Retired). P.S. War owes the landlord of the Hen and Chickens a new billiards table. They weren't built for what he did to it yesterday".'

They each took a watch from the box. They were all inscribed on the back. One with a picture of a scythe, one with a crown, one a pair of scales and the other with a sword.

'Thank you, gentlemen,' Death whispered.

'I'm sorry to ruin the moment, but are these watches accurate?' asked Famine.

'The most accurate in the world,' Conquest replied.

'That's a pity. Because that means you're getting married in Scotland in just under two hours.'

The castle sat squat and dark against the grey Highland mountainside. In the bridal suite at the top of one of the towers, Conquest's bride Julia looked at her reflection in the mirror. Amongst the bustle of pageboys and bridesmaids, she was calm and cool. She was twenty-five and her groom a few years older, which had raised some eyebrows. It had been a whirlwind romance, but that was long enough for her to know that she wanted to spend the rest of her life with him. She examined every inch of herself. Her dark hair intricately sculpted upwards, the full red lips, the dress and down to the dainty shoes. She smoothed the ivory silk that clung around her hips and smiled. The dress. The dress was as perfect as the setting. She was a princess waiting in the tower for her prince. She had always dreamed of marrying in the church in the Cotswolds where her parents had, but Quint had insisted that the ceremony shouldn't be religious. She loved him and granted him this compromise. She was glad she had. This would be their moment and theirs alone.

Howard MacDonald, Julia's father, came into the room. He seemed as squat and wide as the building he stood in and the seams of his morning suit strained against the load placed in them. He stopped dead when he saw his daughter. 'Oh Julia. If only your mother could see you now,' he said with a lump in his throat. She ran to him and took his hands in hers.

'Is he here?' She bit her lower lip nervously.

Howard smiled, raising two of his three chins. 'Yes. He turned up a little while ago with those two friends of his. They looked the worse for wear.'

'Well, boys will be boys.' She squeezed his hands.

'Are you sure...'

'Yes, father,' she said, cutting him off. 'He's a good man.'

'There's something about him. How does he pay for all of this?' Howard indicated the sumptuous fabrics and heavy antique furniture that dominated the room. 'Does he really have no family at all?'

'Should you be saying things like this to your daughter on her wedding day? And having no family just means that I don't have the burden of any in-laws. Unlike him, who's stuck with you.'

Howard laughed. 'True, true. I'll say this, though. He certainly knows how to throw a party.'

In a room in the other tower, Conquest was putting on a grey morning suit. He looked effortlessly handsome and smart, as if he had been poured into his clothes. War and Famine were dressed identically, with varying degrees of success. War looked as if he had been forcefully shoved into his top hat and tails, while Famine resembled a consumptive romantic poet.

Death sat against the stone wall drinking a fine champagne. As usual he was in, but not of, the moment. War tugged at his collar with thick fingers. 'I'm a warrior. I should be in steel and chain mail, not dressed like a mincing dandy.'

'You look fabulous,' encouraged Death, topping up everyone's glasses. 'A toast, I think. To Conquest and Julia. I always feared that one of us would leave one day, but it couldn't happen under happier circumstances.'

'To Conquest and Julia,' echoed Famine and War. They all clinked their glasses and downed the contents.

Conquest checked himself in the mirror one last time and adjusted his shirt cuffs. He checked the new pocket watch hanging from his waistcoat by a thin silver chain. 'You two had better get downstairs. As my best men, you need to make sure that everything is in order. I'm sure they'll be serving nibbles and drinks by now.'

'Excellent,' said Famine. 'Aren't you coming?'

'I just want to have a word with Death. Do you have the rings?'

War patted his waistcoat pocket. 'Yes. We'll see you down there, then.' Famine and War headed out, pulling the heavy oak door shut behind them. Conquest and Death were left alone in an awkward silence.

'Do you remember the last time we were here?' Conquest asked.

'1374, I think. This castle would be yours if you'd accepted the Laird's daughter's hand in marriage.'

'I was not ready to take a wife.'

'And you are now?'

Conquest laughed. 'No, but she's who I've been looking for in all my years of walking this world. I just didn't realise it until I met her. When I looked into her eyes that first night, I was excited, amazed, scared and unsure of myself. I knew what it was like to be human.'

'She's a fine woman. Not that we've been formally introduced.'

Conquest placed his hands on Death's shoulders. 'I'm sorry you couldn't have taken a more active role in this.'

'I will meet her in the end, though, and I can't give favours. Even to my oldest friend.'

'I know.'

Conquest, Famine, War and - unseen by anybody else - Death entered the castle's library. Conquest had suggested the ceremony was conducted in there so that Julia could be surrounded by the three things she loved; her family, friends and literature. Leather bound volumes lined the walls and filled the air with their thick smell. Two suits of armour holding swords guarded either side of the doorway and War regarded them with disdain. 'Cheap tat. They wouldn't stand a chance against a mace or battle axe.'

The wedding guests sat in rows facing the far end of the room where the registrar sat at a large oak desk. She was a round, joyful woman who constantly peered over the rims of her half-moon glasses. Famine, War and Death made their way towards her, while Conquest shook hands, laughed and joked with the guests.

'You must be the best men,' the registrar said in a soft Edinburgh brogue that put everyone she spoke to at ease.

'Yes, just the three of us,' War replied.

'Just the two of us,' Famine corrected. 'Another one couldn't make it, but he's here in spirit.' Death shook his invisible head.

'And which of you is giving the reading?'

'I am,' bellowed War.

'Will it be something traditional?'

'I should bloody say so. Sun Tzu's "The Art of War".'

Famine turned to War. 'I thought we'd talked about this.'

Conquest slapped Famine and War on the shoulders and gave a sly wink in Death's direction. He shook the registrar's hand. 'Lovely to see you again. What are we talking about?'

'He's doing it again,' Famine complained. 'He's threatening to read Sun Tzu.'

Conquest put his arm around War. 'Well, Mr Warbuton and I had a discussion earlier and we agreed that he'd choose something more appropriate.'

'Alright. I'll read the bloody poem, but when you and your new wife are caught in a land war in Asia and don't know what to do, don't come running to me.'

A string quartet sat in front of the biography section began to play. Conquest had wanted a jazz band, but Julia had put her foot down over that.

'I think we're ready,' said the registrar. Famine and War took a pace back toward two empty chairs in the front row. Conquest rubbed his sweaty palms on his trousers. He could feel Julia and her father approaching, but he did not look behind him. He wanted them to be together, side by side, the first time he saw her.

Then Julia was next to him. She smiled and Conquest felt thousands of years fall away. He was new and reborn and the world was once again full of infinite possibilities. Howard MacDonald placed his daughter's hand in Conquest's and seemed reluctant to step away, as if he was surrendering the most precious thing in his life.

The registrar asked everybody to be seated. 'Thank you all for coming today,' she said. 'We are gathered here to join together Christopher and Julia in matrimony; which is an honourable and solemn estate and therefore is not to be entered into unadvisedly or lightly, but reverently and soberly. Into this estate these two persons present come now to be joined. If anyone can show just cause why they may not be lawfully joined together, let them speak now or forever hold their peace.'

Despite themselves, everybody looked around. Silence. The registrar chuckled. 'I always get a little nerv--'

'I've got just cause and it's a doozie,' someone said from the back of the room. Beelzebub was leaning against the doorframe. He'd dressed formally for the occasion.

War leaped from his seat, sending his top hat skittering across the carpet. 'Beezelbub!' he roared.

Beelzebub winced. 'Really?' He took a sword from out of one of the knight's gauntlets and made his way down the aisle until he stood in front of Conquest and Julia. He held the sword point down to the floor like a cane and looked as if he might break out into a soft-shoe shuffle. All eyes were focused on him.

'I'm very sorry. I know it's bad form to upstage a bride on her special day.'

Julia placed a hand on Conquest's arm. 'Who is this?'

Beelzebub looked hurt. 'You mean you've never mentioned me? I wonder what else you haven't told her?'

'I told you he was a fairy,' somebody muttered from behind.

'What do you want?' asked Conquest, taking a step forward to shield Julia.

'I just don't think it's fair on Julia for her to do this without all the facts. As the lady just said, it is not to be entered into unadvisedly or lightly. "Till Death us do part" is a rather hollow promise when he's your drinking buddy.'

'What's he talking about, Christopher?'

'Christopher? Is that what we're calling ourselves these days?'

Howard thought that he should step in and do something. 'What's going on? This is a wedding, you know.'

Beelzebub looked the father of the bride up and down. 'Is it really? How incredibly embarrassing, I don't appear to have brought a gift.'

Without warning, Beelzebub lifted the sword high above his head and plunged it through Conquest's chest. He buried it to the hilt and a good foot of the blade smashed into the desk behind, splintering the wood and pinning Conquest in place like an insect trapped in a display case.

Julia's high-pitched scream shredded the air and this was the cue for pandemonium to break out. Beelzebub pointed to the door and it slammed shut with a sound like a hand clapping with joy. He looked over to the suit of armour still holding the other sword and motioned with his hand. The sword broke free and flew over the heads of the guests. It landed in Beelzebub's grasp and, in one fluid motion, he pointed it at Julia's throat. Silence and stillness replaced the confusion and tumbling furniture.

Conquest writhed on the desk, trying to grab the handle of the sword. War ran over to help him. Famine took a step towards Beelzebub. 'What do you think you're doing?'

'Come on,' Beelzebub shouted out, ignoring Famine. 'Show yourself. It's not the same without you.' He pressed the point of the sword harder against Julia's neck. 'Come out, come out, wherever you are. Make it quick or the bride will be her own something blue.'

Death stepped out of thin air. A murmur of horror and shock ran through the room. Beelzebub smiled. 'There you go,' he said, his eyes twinkling. 'The gang's all here. It's just like old times. Julia, I'd like you to meet your husband-to-be's oldest friend. Death himself.'

'Nice to meet you,' Death said. 'I've heard a lot about you.'

One of Julia's aunts screamed and then the pounding on the library door started. Guests crowded up against it, pushing and hammering, but it wouldn't budge. During the bedlam, it took the combined efforts of Famine and War to pull the sword loose from Conquest. After that, it slipped easily from his chest, leaving a ragged tear in the front of his shirt.

'Why are you doing this?' Conquest asked.

'You took from me what I most wanted. I'm simply returning the favour.' Beelzebub looked at Julia. 'I can actually feel the love leaving you. It's leaking out from every pore. It's glorious. Well, my work here is done.' Beelzebub dropped the sword and Conquest made a grab for him. Before he could wrap his hands around his throat, Beelzebub fell out of reality. Conquest crashed to the floor, snatching at the air.

'Somebody call a doctor!' a voice yelled from the back of the room.

Conquest picked himself up and perched on the table. He rubbed his bloodless scar. 'There's no need for that.'

The colour had drained from Julia's face until she was the same pale shade as her wedding dress. Her eyes were fixed on the chest wound. 'That... That should... should've killed you,' she stammered. Conquest reached for her hand. She snatched it back. 'Don't touch me. What are you?'

'It's complicated.'

She turned and ran from the library, her dainty shoes falling from her feet.

All Death could do was watch.

TWELVE

Dave woke with the smell of tweed in his nostrils. There was a moment of heavy-eyed confusion as he wondered why the whole world around him was juddering until he remembered he was on a train rattling its way through tunnels deep underground. The carriage was empty save for him and the ghost in the seat opposite. It was Fred Drayton, formerly of Finsbury Park and now resident of the London Underground system since a particularly troublesome incident on the Bakerloo line in 1957. He greeted Dave with a doff of his hat.

'Mr Marwood.'

Dave wiped his bleary eyes and nodded back. 'Fred. How are you?'

'As well as can be expected in this post-mortem condition. And how are you? It's been a while since our last conversation.'

'I've been busy. Sorry.'

In the early days of his job, Dave often came down and travelled the sprawling Underground rail network where he found a small community of ghosts in the labyrinth tunnels and stations. Some were happy to accept the offer of Dave's services, whilst others like Fred were content with their half life amongst the bustle and commotion.

'How are things up on the surface? As baffling as ever?' Fred asked, smoothing his moustache with a thumb and forefinger.

'Even more so,' Dave replied.

'What brings you down at this time? It must be almost midnight. Business or pleasure?'

'Business, unfortunately.'

'That won't make the lovely Melanie happy, will it?'

Dave shifted uncomfortably. 'We're having some time apart.'

'Oh, I'm very sorry to hear that. I'm sure you can sort things out between you.'

Dave smiled. 'Thank you.'

Fred brushed a speck of non-existent dust from the lapel of his jacket. 'Of course, in my day we knew how to properly woo a lady. There'd be flowers, dancing and, if you were lucky, a quick feel in the back row of the picture house.'

'You little player, Fred. I had no idea.'

'What I'm saying is that perhaps today's youth should treat each other with a little more respect and dignity. A little romance never killed anybody. Maybe you'd all find it easier to find husbands and wives. You won't believe what I see down here on a Friday night.'

'Hang on,' Dave huffed, 'I'm not taking relationship advice from a ghost.'

The train slowed down as it entered the station. 'Just because I'm dead doesn't mean I don't have an opinion,' Fred replied. 'I believe this is your stop.'

Dave signed his name in the logbook sat on the UberSystems International reception desk and took a temporary pass card from Keith, the night watchman who seemed to have been with the company since forever. He took the lift to the fifteenth floor and found his way to the staffroom where six other new recruits sat huddled around two cheap plastic tables lit softly by the orange and red lights of the vending machines.

'You must be new here,' said Dave. 'There's still hope in your eyes. They'll soon trample all over that.' Six quizzical faces looked back at him. 'It's not my first time here,' Dave explained.

'Can I get you a coffee from the machine?' asked one of the recruits. In his suit and tie, he stood out amongst the jeans and tee shirts of the others.

'No, thank you,' replied Dave, taking a seat at the end. 'As I said, it's not my first time here.'

'Good evening everyone. I'm Kirsten,' said a voice from the doorway. Kirsten's skin was so pale Dave wasn't sure whether it was a lifestyle choice or a serious medical condition. The pitch black hair framing her face reminded him of Death's cowl and her red lips looked like a bloody gash against her white complexion. She glided into the room with a delicate grace. 'Before we begin, perhaps we should each say a little about ourselves? I'll go first. I'll be your manager in the Document Management Centre and I've been at UberSystems International longer than I care to admit.' Her lips parted into a smile revealing rows of perfectly white teeth. A smile that made Dave feel giddy. 'Who's next?'

'I will.' All eyes turned to the man in the suit and tie. 'I'm Christopher Love. I was a management consultant for ten years until they decided that there wasn't enough management for me to consult on. They let me go and I haven't been able to find anything since. So here I am. You need to be earning something, anything, if you've got a mortgage and children to pay for.'

'What do you have?' asked Kirsten.

'A three storey town house in Balham,' Christopher answered with pride.

'I meant your children.'

'Oh.' He hesitated for a moment. 'A boy and a girl. Eight and five.'

'That's lovely,' said Kirsten. 'Who's next?'

One by one, they introduced themselves. There was Jason Digby, a squat angry middle-aged man who had blundered through various jobs until he'd stumbled into this one. Dave could sense that Jason thought this company wouldn't be the last in the chain.

Sarah Barnes was twenty-six and had just moved to London to pursue a dream after working in provincial call centres. Quietly spoken, she told them that she hadn't really figured out what that dream was yet, but she was sure it would make itself know to her soon.

Young and ambitious Simon Austin and Jim Wilson were friends who were straight out of university. After hundreds of job applications for more senior roles had gone unanswered, their idealistic plan was to start at the bottom rung of the corporate ladder and work their way up to the very top through sheer force of will and character.

Emma Miller had travelled from Northern Ireland to study. A night job was the only way she could find to make money and keep up with her university work.

The last to speak, Dave told the others that he'd worked in a department several floors above where they sat now but had left to go travelling. He dropped vague hints of exotic experiences and tropical locations until Kirsten cut him off. She perched on a table, crossing her long legs, a high heel shoe dangling from her toes.

'The Document Management Centre is the beating heart of UberSystems International, pumping the lifeblood around the company. Would anyone like to tell me what the lifeblood of any organisation is?'

Christopher looked up from the notebook he'd been scribbling in. 'Information, Kirsten.'

He was rewarded with Kirsten's hypnotic smile. 'Exactly, Christopher.'

Dave drifted off. He knew what he was going to be doing. Even in the digital age, a company the size of UberSystems International generated a vast amount of paperwork. What came in needed to be collated, sorted and scanned onto the work systems ready for the administration teams when they came in the next morning. What went out needed to be packaged, franked and prepared for posting.

He found himself thinking of Melanie and what she'd be doing now. Would she be tucked up in her bed, or out with Emma? Or Jeremy? He pushed that thought out of his head with a shudder and gazed out of the window. He was surprised to see ghosts hovering serenely on the other side of the glass. After a second, he realised that they were just reflections of the room's occupants. He could see seven figures seemingly sat down on thin air, but the way the light was cast seemed to mean Kirsten had no doppelgänger. He stared back at himself floating free above the glow of the city and wondered what it would be like to swap places, to no longer be tied to gravity or responsibility.

'Are you joining us, Dave?' asked Kirsten. The others were heading out of the room.

'Yeah. Sorry,' he mumbled and got up to join them. As he headed deeper into the building, he looked back to see his ghostly double swoop away into the night.

The Document Management Centre was a large open-plan space filled with banks of workstations containing computers and scanning equipment. The only sources of light in the windowless room were headache inducing fluorescent strip lights that painted the sun-starved complexions of the twenty staff a sickly grey. They peered over their monitors like office-based meerkats as Kirsten led Dave and the other new recruits past them.

A big bear of a man waited by a row of empty desks. He smiled warmly as the group approached. 'Fresh meat.'

'This is Carl,' said Kirsten. 'He'll be your team leader. I'll leave you in his very capable hands. If you have any questions, he's the man to talk to. I'll come back later and see how you're getting on.' She spun on her heels and retraced her steps, stopping to talk to workers as she went.

Carl gathered his new team around one of the desks. He stroked a big slab of plastic and metal that looked like a printer with ideas above its station. 'I want to introduce you to a personal friend of mine. This is a ScanPro 3000 scanner and copier. Fifty sheet automatic document feeder with full file conversion capabilities. Respect this baby and it'll keep you out of trouble.'

Carl gave a brief overview of how the machines and the department worked and then gave each of the team a desk and a stack of documents to work through. He wandered between the desks fixing paper jams and answering questions with good-natured humour.

Dave took some comfort in the monotony of the mindless, repetitive work. Muscle memory soon took over as he scanned, processed and filed the work away. His brain switched off and shut out the thoughts of Melanie. Repression was the English way and who was he to fight hundreds of years of tradition?

He watched the others around him. Sarah and Emma worked silently through the pile of paperwork at their elbows. Jim and Simon talked animatedly about their plans for world domination. Christopher was already making suggestions to Carl on how the process could be made more efficient. Jason was regularly checking his phone and complaining about the lack of signal.

After a couple of hours of this, a long-haired teenager came around pushing a wire-framed trolley filled with more documents. As he replenished their piles of work, the music leaked out from the earphones he wore with an annoying rhythmic hiss of treble.

'What's your name, mate?' Jason asked him.

The youngster pulled one of the earphones out. 'What?'

'What's your name?' repeated Jason.

'Simon. Simon Dunnett. People call me Si'

'Good to meet you, Si. Like your music, do you?'

Si eyed Jason with suspicion, unsure where this was going. 'Yeah. It's alright.'

Jason leaned across the desk menacingly. 'That's great, but if you don't turn it down I am going to use those earphones as Japanese love beads and insert them into your person.'

Kirsten appeared at Jason's shoulder. She placed a hand on the barely touched stack of paperwork next to him. 'Jason, I'm sensing what I can only describe as an attitude problem.'

Jason sat back in his chair, his demeanour becoming less aggressive. 'Me? Nah. Me and Si were just having a bit of banter, weren't we?'

Si shrugged. 'I suppose.'

Kirsten drummed her fingers on the documents beneath her hand. 'Jason, could you join me in my office for a moment please?'

The murmur of conversation died away and everyone turned to look. Kirsten beckoned Jason with a finger and walked towards her office. He followed behind like an obedient puppy. When the door closed behind them, the hum of chat returned.

Dave turned back around and continued working. After a few minutes, Kirsten's office door opened and Jason walked back to his desk next to Dave. He sat down and silently began working with enthusiasm. Dave shared a look with Sarah, eyebrows raised.

'Everything all right?' he asked Jason.

'Great, thanks. Good talk.' Jason didn't slow down, nor look up from the documents he was jamming into the scanner's feed tray. As Dave watched him diligently carry out his task, he noticed two small red spots on Jason's skin just above his tee shirt's neckline.

'Nah,' Dave muttered to himself, shaking his head as if to throw out the idea that was forming there.

The shift continued without further incident until eight o'clock in the morning when Carl told them that it was time to clock out. Jason remained at his desk as the others packed their bags and pulled on their coats. 'You not coming?' Dave asked.

Jason looked up and smiled. 'No, I'm going to stay behind and do some extra work. Kirsten asked if I would.'

'What did she say to you in there?' Dave nodded towards Kirsten's office.

'Not much. She just put some things in perspective.'

Dave held his hands up. 'Whatever, dude. I'll see you tomorrow?'

'Certainly.'

Dave ran to catch up with the others as they were getting into the lift. As the doors closed, he turned to them. 'That was a bit weird with Jason, didn't you think? He was an dick one minute and then he became like a model employee.'

He was answered with noncommittal shrugs. 'Maybe that Kirsten's a good boss?' suggested Emma.

'Yeah. Maybe,' replied Dave as the doors slid open and the morning sun poured into the lift.

THIRTEEN

Dave was back at UberSystems International the next night. His body clock was broken. Between the daylight spilling through his curtains and thoughts of Melanie, he'd only managed to doze off for a couple of hours that afternoon. Then Anne had phoned to ask if he'd found anything out during last night's shift, to which he'd admitted he hadn't.

So, he found himself lurking in the foyer wondering what he should be looking for. Death said it felt like the building itself was rejecting him. Dave placed a hand on one of the pillars and was immediately struck by a wave of sadness. It was a palpable hurt and longing that hung thick in the air. Heartache and pain. But there was something else. As he let his mind wander, he could feel a quiet rage. Subtle, like a howl's echo, it drifted between the pillars and leather sofas. As he concentrated, he felt something relax in his mind. It ached and throbbed like a muscle that hadn't been used. He could sense a darkness creeping around the edges of the room. It flowed and danced, as intangible as smoke from a hellish fire but so cold Dave could feel the chill in his bones.

'Are you okay, Dave?' asked Conrad West.

Dave lost his tenuous grip on the feeling and the darkness retreated. 'Oh. Conrad. I'm fine, thanks.' He noticed the suitcase West wheeled behind him. 'Where are you off to?'

'I'm just flying over to Paris for a few days. How are you settling back in?'

Dave, muddled by exhaustion and what he'd just experienced, rubbed his eyes. 'Yeah. Great. They're a good bunch of people.'

Conrad looked at the clock that hung above Keith sat at the reception desk. 'Shouldn't you be on your way up?'

'Yes. I was just going.'

'Have a good night.'

'Thanks. Have a good trip.'

Conrad smiled. 'I always do, Mr Marwood. I always do.'

Jason was already working away when Dave got to his desk. 'Have you been home yet?' Dave asked, jokingly.

'Just wanted to get ahead,' Jason replied.

The others arrived one-by-one. Jim was the last to turn up, munching on a sandwich between yawns. 'When I'm CEO of this place, I'm going to allow people to call up and say "I'm not coming in today. I just feel too good".'

Emma smiled. 'Yeah, they'll be all like "Yeah, Jim. We don't want you spreading that around the office. Come back when the existential dread has returned".'

'Exactly.'

Kirsten approached the gang. 'I see you've all decided to come back for a second night. That's--' She froze. 'What's in that sandwich, Jim?'

'Garlic chicken. Do you want some?' Jim offered it to her. She flinched and backed away as if he'd threatened her with a weapon.

'I'm allergic to garlic.'

'Allergic?' Sarah asked. 'To garlic? Is that even a thing?'

'It's very rare, but it is a thing I'll have you know,' Kirsten replied. 'Now would be a good time to remind you all that no food is permitted at your workstations, so if you could kindly dispose of your sandwich I would be most grateful.'

As the shift ground on, Dave couldn't stop thinking about what happened in the reception. It was one of hundreds of new experiences he'd had, but this had a power that touched a hidden part of him. He needed to find out where that power was coming from.

'I'm just going to the stationery cupboard. Does anybody want anything?' he said to nobody in particular. When no reply came, he went out into the corridor. He walked slowly, running a hand against the wall. He tried to open himself up to any spectres that might be present, but soon felt foolish. He decided that the spirits, or disturbance in the force or whatever, weren't being receptive and so he went to the stationery cupboard.

He opened the door and switched the light on. Amongst the notepads and staples a couple were energetically necking, their limbs intertwined like the elastic bands on the shelf above them.

'I'm so sorry,' Dave said, trying to avert his gaze. One of the couple turned around and Dave saw that it was Jason. The woman beneath him had an enthusiastic love bite on her neck. Dave recognised Alice from one of the other DMC teams. They were both panting, their chests heaving with lust and arousal.

Dave smiled. 'Bloody hell Jason. You're a fast worker. I wouldn't let Kirsten see you like this.'

The way they stared at him made Dave feel like he'd interrupted dangerous wild animals. He reached up and grabbed a box of pencils. 'There we are,' he said, rattling the box. He smiled awkwardly. 'I'll leave you two to it.' He gently closed the door behind him.

When he returned to his desk, he said, 'You'll never guess what I've just seen.'

Before he could finish, Kirsten clapped her hands together and called for everyone's attention. 'I want all team leaders in the staffroom for a huddle in five minutes.'

'Ow!' Dave shouted.

'Something the matter, Dave?' Kirsten asked.

'Paper cut,' he hissed, waving a bloody, stinging finger in the air.

Kirsten was at his side in an instant. 'Let me take a look.' Her voice trembled with excitement. She held his finger tenderly and gently blew on it. Dave felt the pain subside. Then she placed her wet lips over the cut and gave a quiet low moan of pleasure. Horrified, Dave tried to pull away but her lips locked tighter and he felt her probing tongue run along the length of the wound, licking it clean.

'I... I... don't think that's very hygienic,' Dave stammered. Kirsten let a disappointed sigh escape and released her grip.

Dave wiped his finger with a tissue but the blood continued to flow. 'Is there anywhere I can get a plaster?'

Kirsten regained her self-control and said, 'In the kitchen. There's a first aid kit.'

Cradling his finger in his other hand, Dave jogged to the kitchen. He found the first aid kit in a cupboard next to the accident book. He rinsed the blood off under the tap and applied a waterproof plaster.

He absent-mindedly turned the pages of the dog-eared accident book as he tried to process what Kirsten had done. He was shaken by the way she'd looked at him. He'd seen the same look in Jason's eyes in the stationery cupboard; hunger and desire.

As he leafed through the book, he was struck by the sheer number of entries. Pages and pages of bloody injuries, flesh wounds and lacerations. It read more like a battle report than a health and safety requirement.

'Have you suffered an injury in the workplace?' he said to himself. 'Maybe it wasn't an accident. Maybe somebody's out to get you.'

He put the book and the first aid kit back where he found them and headed back to the DMC. As he walked past the staffroom, he heard Kirsten's voice trembling again. In anger this time.

'And what happened in the car park the other night? That was clumsy and foolish. We are here by invitation and you cannot go helping yourselves to members of staff.'

There was a tap on Dave's shoulder. He turned round to see Jason eyeing him hungrily. 'Your finger alright?'

Dave gulped. 'Yes, thank you.'

'Then perhaps it's time we got back to work.'

'Perhaps you're right,' Dave replied, his voice cracking.

Back at his desk, Dave stared at his monitor. The paranormal feeling of anger and fear in reception. Kirsten's lack of reflection and her aversion to garlic. Jason's neck wound. The accident book full of bloodshed.

He was finally sure of what he was dealing with.

FOURTEEN

'Vampires?' said Death. 'What a load of bollocks.'

Ignoring his tiredness, Dave had rushed across the city to Crow Road when his shift had ended. He'd arrived to find Anne out on an errand and Death struggling with the coffee machine. After cleaning the filter and making Death an espresso and a cappuccino for himself, Dave told of his theories and the discoveries behind them. Death didn't accept them.

'I've been around the block a few times and I've never come across anything like a vampire. They're just stories,' he said.

'I thought you were a story once and now I'm stood here talking to you. It makes sense. They've put some kind of magic or something over the building that keeps you from entering or seeing what goes on in there. Then they can get up to whatever they want, helping themselves to employees and blaming it on high staff turnover. '

'Yeah, alright Mulder. I think you're leaping to conclusions.'

'There are conclusions all over the place. Conclusions are right in front of me. I'm simply ambling up to conclusions in a casual manner. There's something evil going on.'

'That's a notion as old as thought itself,' Death said. 'You tell yourselves that if there's pure evil in the world, then there must be pure good. You put your faith in absolutes. Good and evil. Heaven or hell. Blur or Oasis. You're so sure of the universe and your place in it and who put you there. I speak from personal experience when I say it's a lot more complicated than that. Take wasps, for example. Wasps are made entirely from bastard. Whose grand design are they part of?'

'But--'

'When was the last time you got some decent sleep?'

A wave of exhaustion washed over Dave just hearing the word. 'A while ago.'

'It's your imagination running away with you. I can understand this. You've had a tough time with Melanie and everything.'

'Then why don't you go back to before she dumped me and make sure that I make the date?'

'We've talked about this in the past. I can't do that.'

'You did it before.'

'That was a one time, never to be repeated offer. You can't keep trying again and again until you get something right. It's like cheating at patience. A life without consequences is no life at all.'

Dave kicked the leg of the desk. 'I guess.'

'Tell me more about what happened in the reception. The answer lies there. What was it like?'

'Angry. Very angry. And frustrated. Odd as it sounds, it felt like a broken promise.'

'I'm used to odd.'

'But not vampires?'

Death shook his head. 'No. That's silly, not odd. I want you to go back there tonight.' He watched Dave rub his eyes. 'Concentrate on the reception area, but now I want you to go home and get some rest.'

Dave slammed the front door of the flat and stomped into the living room. Gary was sat playing video games. It looked like a bomb had come in, thought about going off, realised that Gary had got it covered and wandered back out again. DVDs were grouped into toppling plastic islands on the faded carpet between magazines, half-drunk cups of tea and unidentifiable food items.

'You back?' asked Gary. His eyes didn't leave the television screen.

'Yeah.'

'How's that new job working out?'

'I think my boss is a vampire.'

'Dude, they all are.'

Dave didn't have an answer for that so he skulked off to the shower to try and wash some of the weariness from his body. When he'd dried himself and dressed, he sat on the edge of the bed trying to work out his next move.

He picked up the phone on the bedside table and dialled Melanie's mobile phone number. He was unsurprised when it went straight through to her voicemail. He hung up and called her work number, which was answered almost immediately. He heard her laughter and the tail end of a conversation. Dave felt an irrational pang of jealousy knowing she was amused by somebody else.

'UberSystems International. Melanie Watkins speaking.'

He closed his eyes, at once enjoying the sound of her voice and hating that he wasn't there with her. 'Hi, Mel.'

There was a moment of silence before she spoke, 'Oh. Hello.'

Dave was trying to gauge the tone of her voice to sense whether this call was welcome. 'How are you?'

'Good. What do you want, Dave? I'm really busy here.'

That settled that. 'That's what I wanted to talk to you about. I think you need to get out of there. Like now. Just grab your stuff and leave.'

'What are you talking about?' I can't just leave. Some of us have to work for a living.'

He clenched his eyes shut, his brow furrowed. He knew it wouldn't work, but he had to try and persuade her. 'I know what this sounds like, but there's something bad going on here. Something dangerous.'

He heard Melanie let out a long breath. 'What are you talking about? Bad? Dangerous? Is this some kind of anti-capitalist thing?'

'No, it's not anything like that.'

Melanie put her hand over the phone's mouthpiece, muffling her voice, and said something indistinct to somebody. He heard a deep muted laugh.

'Who are you talking to?' he asked.

'Nobody.'

'Is it that Jeremy?'

'I haven't got time for this, Dave. Just leave me alone.'

Her voice was replaced by the dial tone. Dave smashed the phone back down on the table. He was infuriated. He felt nine years old again when nobody believed him about Emily. When he was ignored and patronised and told to forget about his imaginary friend.

He reached under his bed and pulled out his laptop from beneath a pile of clothes. After years working in a dull office job his Google Fu was strong. He jumped from page to page, learning the names of the UberSystems International employees who had been listed as missing over the years. The high staff turnover and the constant flow of people in and out of London meant that nobody had made the connection until now. He knew that every one of them had walked into the UberSystems International Tower and had never left.

He spent a few more hours trying to gather evidence to back up his theories, heading further down the rabbit hole with every click until he fell asleep.

The sun sat low in the sky and stained the clouds blood red when Dave woke up under a blanket of printouts. He'd never felt more in control. He had a plan. He'd never had a plan before. Sure, he'd had ideas, dreams and fantasies but never anything concrete. He knew what he had to do.

'You're in early,' Keith greeted Dave as he swiped his card and pushed his way through the turnstile.

'I just can't stay away,' Dave replied with a plastered-on grin.

'Have a good night.'

'You too.'

The lift arrived while Dave was still wondering whether the thumbs up he gave Keith was a tad over the top. He stepped inside and the doors closed. Gripped by a moment of doubt, his finger hovered over the button for the fifteenth floor. The lift waited patiently until he made a decision. He jabbed the button and the lift shook into motion.

The lift slowed its ascent and the doors dinged open onto an empty corridor. He crept quietly along the tiled carpet until he reached the kitchen. He snuck around the door and, taking a piece of paper from his pocket, tiptoed over to the spare water cooler bottles. Checking over his shoulder, he read the text on the unfolded A4 sheet and then retraced his steps. He checked his watch. There was still a few minutes until his shift started, so he decided to head down to the car park to see if there was anything he could find there.

He pressed the 'down' button and the lift doors beeped open. He found himself face to face with Melanie.

'What are you doing here?' they both asked each other at the same time.

'How did you get in? Are you stalking me?' Melanie asked. Dave felt a pang of longing. Once again, she was within reach, but untouchable.

'No, it's not like that. I work here now.'

Melanie checked the floor number. 'But there's just the DMC on this floor.'

'Yeah.'

'Oh. Right.'

'Conrad reckons I should learn about the company from the bottom up.'

'Why didn't you tell me? We only spoke a few hours ago?'

Dave noticed the packet of cigarettes and lighter in her hand. 'Have you started smoking?'

'I smoked before I went out with you. I've been under a lot of stress. It's just temporary. It's the end of the tax year, remember? That's why I'm here at almost midnight, but I don't think any of this is any of your concern,' she replied impatiently.

'You need to go. It's not safe.'

'Why? Why isn't it safe?'

Dave looked left and right down the corridor and then leant in closer to Melanie. 'James and the others. I think they were murdered.'

She gave a shocked laugh. 'Murdered? Who by?'

'I don't know. I've got an idea. I'm working on it.'

Melanie placed a hand on his shoulder. 'Dave, I'm worried about you. I don't know what's happened to you recently. I think you might need to see someone. You're sounding paranoid.'

Kirsten poked her head around the door to the DMC office. 'Dave, you're here early! Could you give me a hand with something please?'

Dave turned to Kirsten. In that moment, Melanie stepped back into the lift and let the doors close.

Melanie rode the lift down to the basement. When the doors sprang open on the utilitarian corridor that led to the car park, she looked at the packet in her hand

and pressed the button to return to the floor she had just journeyed from.

Why did it matter what he thought? She knew why. For all his faults, she still loved him and he was obviously trying to make amends by quitting that damned job that had taken so much of his time. His paranoid talk about the building unnerved her, but if she stopped worrying about Dave she wouldn't know what to do with herself. The lift doors opened. She stepped out and swiped her security card to pass through the double doors that led to her department. Her desk was an island of light in the half-light of the office. Jeremy was perched on it, turning his head when he heard her approach.

'You look like you've seen a ghost,' he said.

'Dave was downstairs.'

Jeremy crossed his arms, his lips pressed into a thin line. 'Oh, was he?'

Melanie assessed his reaction. 'Did you know he was here?'

'No.'

'I don't know why he didn't tell me.'

'Perhaps he was embarrassed.'

'Why would he be embarrassed?'

'I don't know, but it's not like they handed him back the keys to the executive office, is it?' He jumped off the desk and clutched her shoulders. 'You could do so much better than him. Tell you what, why don't we pack up here and go get a drink and talk about it. I think we've earned a night out.'

She shrugged his hands off and nodded towards her computer. 'I've still got to try and make those numbers work.'

'Maybe later, then?'

She smiled wanly and looked at Jeremy. Dependable, reliable Jeremy. 'Yeah. Maybe.'

FIFTEEN

Dave was starting to think that perhaps Melanie was right and he'd grown paranoid. Then two of his work colleagues exploded.

After he'd helped Kirsten carry some boxes of printer paper, he sat at his desk obediently carrying out his duties. His fellow workers arrived one by one, except for Emma and Jim who arrived together giggling and exchanging knowing looks. He kept one eye on the water cooler at the end of the room and, soon, the bottle was empty and a new one was fetched from the kitchen.

He watched Sarah fill a cup, take a long a swig and return to her desk opposite him. Curious, he ambled over to the dispenser as casually as he could, pulled a plastic cup from its holder and filled it up from the nozzle. He took a tiny sip, then a larger one and swished the cool water around his mouth. He let the liquid slide down his throat. It tasted perfectly normal.

He topped the cup up and carried it back to his desk. The plan wasn't working. He'd expected some kind of reaction by now. Maybe he'd been wrong. Then Carl and another team leader helped themselves to drinks, leaning against the water cooler and making small talk. As soon as they gulped the water down, Dave knew something was wrong. Their happy smiles were replaced by confused looks and then grimaces. They scratched at their throats as if trying to rip out whatever poison had infected their bodies.

Then, without warning, they were no longer there. A fraction of a second after Dave's brain had processed this impossible fact, thick ropes of putrid black blood and stinking flesh splattered against the walls and floor with a wet, sickening thud.

Everybody stood frozen in shocked silence. Kirsten's office door opened and she walked over to where Carl used to be, her high heels squelching in the entrails. She picked up a blood-smeared cup and sniffed the contents. Her nose wrinkled in distaste and she let out a disappointed sigh. She turned to the rows of stunned faces.

'Now I don't want to create a blame culture, but who blessed the water cooler?'

Dave drew rapid, shallow breaths as panic took hold. He hadn't thought this through.

Kirsten repeated herself, slower, 'Who blessed the water cooler?'

Next to Dave, Alice sniffed the air like an animal sensing prey. She turned to Dave, breathing deeply to drink in the fear. Dave watched her face shift, the bone and muscle beneath the skin reshaping into a demonic configuration. The smile turned to a snarl as the canine teeth lengthened impossibly, becoming weapons to puncture and tear.

Dave realised he was still clutching a pencil, his knuckles white with tension. With an instinct developed by years of horror movies, he plunged the pencil into Alice's heart. She stumbled back clutching at the thin shaft of wood protruding from her chest until she burst like an overinflated balloon. Dave turned, shielding his face from the worst of the gore with his arm.

Across the office, other workers were turning into something more evil and toothier. Dave could feel someone bearing down on him. Grabbing his cup of holy water, he spun around and threw it in the vampire's face. It screamed as if it had been attacked with acid, its hands flying up to its smouldering and melting face.

The slaughter had begun. Screams tore through the air as teeth tore through flesh and sinew. Half of Dave's co-workers were lost in a blood lust, ripping and biting at the other half.

'Behind you!' he yelled at Sarah, who stood wide-eyed with confusion and fear. Copying Dave, she emptied her drink into the face of a vampire running at her and it crashed to the floor with an inhuman wail.

Dave searched for a way out when his eyes fell on a heavy metal door in the wall nearest him. 'The fire escape!' he shouted to anyone who could hear him.

He sprinted towards the door. He could sense that there were others on his heels, but he didn't know if he was leading the charge or being chased. He smashed the door open with his shoulder and crashed into the wall opposite. Chris, Simon, Jim, Emma and Sarah quickly followed him. The fear in their eyes told him that they hadn't been turned.

Simon and Jim pushed the door closed, but it sprang open, slamming against the wall and throwing them to the floor. Jason leaped through the doorway and fell on Jim, blood and drool dripping from his gaping mouth.

Emma rugby tackled him from behind shouting, 'Leave him alone!' The two of them tumbled down the rough concrete steps onto the landing below. With a swift snap of her neck, Jason exposed the white skin of Emma's throat, sank his teeth into the soft flesh and feasted noisily.

Coming to his senses, Dave pushed the door shut and locked it before anyone or anything else came through. As it shook from the heavy blows from the other side, he knew that it wouldn't hold for long.

'What the fuck is going on?' asked Simon.

'I don't know but I don't think we should stay here to find out,' replied Chris.

Sarah turned her eyes from the frenzied feeding below. Her voice quivered. 'How are we going to get out?'

Dave realised everybody was looking at him. 'What are you looking at me for?'

'You're in charge,' said Simon.

'I think it's obvious that I'm not the sort of person you should give any kind of responsibility to.'

Still they continued to stare. Dave looked up at the loop of stairs stretching above them. 'We climb until we get enough distance between us and them and then call for help.'

Chris and Simon pulled a traumatised Jim to his feet. 'She saved me. She saved me,' he repeated to himself like a mantra.

Ignored by Jason, the five survivors ran up the stairs two at a time, pulling themselves up by the metal railings. A few storeys up, Dave suddenly came to a halt.

'What are you doing?' Simon said, his voice verging on hysteria.

'My girlfriend's down there. Well, my ex-girlfriend.' He felt their eyes burning into him. 'Look, it's complicated, alright? I've got to do this.' He started to head back down the stairs. 'Get to the thirtieth floor,' he shouted back up. 'You can get an express lift straight down to reception. If something goes wrong, regroup at the boardroom. It's got a solid, lockable door.'

Dave cursed himself as he flew down the steps, spinning around the stairwell. This need to prove himself right had put everyone in danger and now he was the only one in any kind of position to get them out of it.

His legs were burning when he reached Melanie's floor. He took a second to catch his breath and was glad that he could still hear Jason busy below. When he remembered what was keeping him occupied, a wave of guilt and shame washed over him. He grabbed the door handle and tugged at it. It was time to see Melanie.

Kirsten wasn't angry. She was just disappointed. In the two hundred and fifty-eight years she had been a creature of the night, she had never aroused any suspicion. Hiding in plain sight, she had been careful and considered in her existence. Now all that had been destroyed in two minutes of homicidal madness.

Blood had ruined dozens of documents and a lot of the office furniture would need to be replaced. She dreaded to think what the Full Time Equivalent impact would be to get the team back on track.

Bodies littered the floor. Some would rise again while others were gone forever. Such a terrible waste. She'd have to get onto the recruitment agencies again and their commission would come out of her budget.

'How many are missing?' she asked.

Andrew, one of the team leaders, counted the bodies. 'Seven. Six newbies and that Jason guy.'

The fire escape door opened with a click and Jason appeared, his face still smeared with Emma's blood.

'Where are they?' Kirsten asked him.

'They went up,' Jason replied.

'What floor?'

'I don't know. I was busy.'

Kirsten pointed to her bottom lip. 'You've got something on your face.'

Jason wiped his chin and licked the smears of blood from his fingers. Kirsten turned to the office. It was time to manage the situation, to bring things under control. That's what she was paid for. 'I want you to kill the lifts servicing the floors above the twentieth. Cut the phone lines. I want a floor-by-floor search until we find them. We've got less than three hours before we have to stamp our time sheets, if you know what I mean.'

'Yes, Kirsten,' her staff muttered.

She waved a hand at the carnage around her. 'And somebody clean this mess up.'

SIXTEEN

Simon reached the thirtieth floor first. He cracked the door at the top of the stairs open and stuck his head through the narrow gap.

'It's all clear,' he whispered to the others as they crowded around him, trying to put as much distance between themselves and the horror several floors beneath them. He opened the door wider and the four slinked through, clutching each other like the world's most depressed conga line.

Simon jogged over to the nearest desk and picked up the phone. He pressed some buttons and growled with frustration. 'It's dead.'

'Have you tried pressing nine for an outside line?' Chris asked as he clambered onto a desk, waving his mobile phone in the air in an attempt to get a signal.

Simon gave him a withering look. 'Of course I've sodding pressed sodding nine for a sodding outside line.'

'I was just trying to help,' Chris replied. 'Hang on. I've got a bar!' Being careful not to move the phone out of signal range, he dialled 999. Everyone held their breath as it rang. 'Hi. We're at UberSystems International Tower. We need the police. Some of our co-workers have gone crazy and attacked us. It was like they were zombies or vampires or something. They were eating each other... Yeah. They were running... What do you mean zombies don't run? What about "28 Days Later"...? Well, I suppose they weren't technically zombies... Look, I think we're getting off-topic. Can you just send someone? Sorry. You're breaking up.' He looked at the others. 'We got cut off.'

'Zombies?' asked Sarah. 'Really?'

'Come on. Let's get to the lifts,' said Simon.

They snuck past rows of desks sat like dark tombs in the dim light of the sleeping office. When they reached the lifts, Chris pushed the down button. No light came on. He pressed the up button. Nothing.

'Can they shut the lifts down?' Sarah asked.

'Apparently so.' Chris rubbed his eyes, trying to problem-solve his way out of the terror. 'I say we do what Dave suggested. Let's get as far away as we can from these things and just wait for the police.

Defeated, they turned around and headed back the way they had just come.

Dave quietly made his way around the office looking for Melanie. She'd moved desks since Dave had left the company - UberSystems International's continual struggle to find the optimal productivity model.

He decided that he'd complete a sweep of the floor and when he was satisfied that she'd left the office for the night, he'd get the fuck out of Dodge. Halfway through his search, he was disappointed to hear her voice.

'It's half two in the morning. I'm not going for a drink.'

'It's London. This place never closes. ' Jeremy's voice.

Dave's concern was replaced by anger. He quickened his pace and rounded the corner to see Jeremy perched on Melanie's desk while she was at the photocopier. Unused adrenaline coursed through Dave's veins as he ran over and grabbed Melanie by the wrist. 'Come on,' he barked at her. 'We've got to go.'

'What are you doing?' she screamed, pulling her wrist free from his sweat-slicked grip.

Jeremy hopped up from the desk. 'What are you playing at, Marwood?'

Dave pointed a finger. 'Don't. Just don't, alright?' He turned to Melanie. 'We have to get out of this office now.'

'What have you got on you?' Melanie asked, frightened.

Dave looked down at his blood stained clothes. 'Oh, it's not mine.'

Melanie took a slow step backwards. 'Dave, what have you done?'

'I've not done anything!' Dave said as he reached out to grab Melanie's hand again. She batted him away as Jeremy ran forwards and shoved him hard in the chest. Dave staggered backwards with a grunt.

'I wouldn't do that if I were you,' he told Jeremy. 'I'm a master in Feng Shui.'

Jeremy looked confused. 'The Chinese philosophical system of harmonising everyone with the surrounding environment?'

Dave realised that he'd got his Oriental references mixed, but decided to front it out. 'Yeah, well, I can kill a man with a well-placed vase of flowers.'

The lift across from them pinged a warning. Dave backed away, looking for a way out. 'Look, are you coming with me? There's some bad shit about to come through that door right now.'

The lift's doors slid open with a clunk and a round, middle-aged lady pushing a trolley laden with cleaning products stepped out. 'Am I interrupting something?' she asked with a friendly smile. Dave breathed a sigh of relief.

'Yeah, she looks absolutely terrifying,' Jeremy drawled sarcastically.

A second lift arrived. As soon as its doors parted, a blur leapt out with inhuman speed and knocked the cleaner to the floor. Blood splattered over Jeremy, Dave and Melanie, who screamed.

'See? That's what I've been trying to tell you!' Dave yelled.

Jeremy was already running towards the double doors at the end of the corridor when Dave grabbed Melanie by the hand and lurched after him. Jeremy crashed through and slammed the doors behind him, locking the other two in. Dave beat the glass with his fists.

'Let us in!' he screamed, but Jeremy was already through the next set of doors. 'Jeremy! You thundering cockwomble!' Dave shouted after him. He turned to Melanie. She was lost in fear. He wiped a drop of blood from her cheek. 'We'll get out of this, but I need you to focus, Melanie,' he said in as soothing a voice he could muster. 'Can you do that for me?' He searched her eyes for a sign that she understood. A tiny whimper escaped from her lips, but she nodded her head. 'Good.' Dave held her hand and they ran.

Gasping, Jeremy staggered into the darkened toilets. The motion-sensitive lights flickered on grudgingly as if unsure that they wanted to get involved.

He shrieked at his own reflection in the mirror that ran the full length of the wall above the sinks. Streaks of blood ran up his crisp white shirt and onto his face in a smooth, continuous pattern.

Running the taps, he could scrub the blood from his skin but not the shame. He shouldn't have left Melanie behind. He dropped his gaze from the mirror, but just met himself staring back up from the chrome.

'They'll be able to take care of themselves,' he told himself. He turned his attention to his shirt and cleaning the dark red stains smeared over the fine white cotton.

He didn't notice the door open. It closed with a quiet click, but the mirror showed Jeremy that he was alone in the room.

Then something was close behind him. He could smell the metallic tang of bloody breath, could hear the inhalation as it drew in his scent like a fine wine's bouquet.

Unable to turn, he stared straight ahead into his own tear-filled eyes. The mirror lied to him, telling him he was on his own, but the panting on the back of his neck told him the truth of the situation.

'You look like you'll taste expensive,' a voice whispered in his ear.

SEVENTEEN

9 November 1983

The early years of the nineteen-eighties were a terrifying and desperate time to be alive. The world was entering a recession and governments slashed welfare budgets so they could treat themselves to a nice war every now and again. The United States and Soviet Union stockpiled ever more powerful weapons in a game of Thermonuclear Chicken. Duran Duran walked the Earth unopposed like some New Romantic behemoth.

The world has faced annihilation on countless occasions, but it never came closer than 9th November 1983. The official versions are sketchy, but they say that forty thousand NATO troops were engaged in a Europe-wide exercise code named Operation Able Archer. The Soviet Politburo, made paranoid by decades of nuclear brinkmanship, became convinced that this was a smokescreen to disguise a first strike against the Warsaw Pact.

The United State's Pershing missiles, newly deployed in West Germany, could impact on Soviet soil within six minutes of launch. The Kremlin would have to pre-empt any aggression and unleash their arsenal first if they were to stand any chance of burying what was left of their enemies. Before the Soviet premier Andropov could press the button, cooler heads prevailed and the world stepped back from plunging headlong into World War III.

The true story, however, is buried deep in the underground vaults of the Pentagon and Kremlin, never to be released.

Beelzebub had been busy after Conquest's wedding day. The Second World War took up a large amount of his time. He hadn't been involved in the more heinous acts; humanity managed to be evil in ways beyond anything that even he could imagine.

In the last years of the conflict, he'd seen the awesome potential of the atom and had worked behind the scenes on the Manhattan Project. The bombs dropping on Hiroshima and Nagasaki signalled the end of the war and the birth of the Atomic Age. He regularly switched sides between East and West in the burgeoning arms race, his intention to make sure that neither superpower achieved superiority over the other. The odd blueprint would go missing and a piece of military intelligence would be whispered into the correct ear.

Intelligence. That made Beelzebub laugh. As far as he was concerned, humanity and intelligence were mutually exclusive.

Now, thirty-eight years after Enola Gay took off on its historic flight, Beelzebub stood in the control room of a nuclear bunker buried deep beneath a large chunk of the Latvian countryside. It was small and windowless with two banks of computers facing a backlit map of Europe and a digital clock on one wall. It came with all mod cons: Command and control facilities, hardwired comlinks direct to Moscow and thousands of megatons of fiery nuclear death.

Beelzebub liked the Soviets. Ever since the Greeks had come up with the concept of democracy after a few too many glasses of ouzo, he'd thought it was overrated. While the mood took him, he was a marshal of the Red Army and enjoyed the power, influence and really big hats. Say what you like about Communist ideology, but the Soviets didn't muck around when it came to using headwear to show who the most important person in the room was. Right now, Beelzebub was *Le Grand Chapeau.*

A young lieutenant, Grishenko, turned from the Cyrillic figures dancing across the green screen monitor and addressed Beelzebub. 'Approval for Dead Hand has been granted, sir.'

Beelzebub gave a smile that made Grishenko want to be anywhere but there, even the front line in Afghanistan.

'Excellent news, comrade,' Beelzebub replied in perfect Russian. Dead Hand was Beelzebub's masterpiece. He'd always fancied building a doomsday device and had taken full advantage of an unlimited research and development budget. Now the Kremlin had received his reports of unusual enemy troop movements on all borders, he took a step closer to revealing his work of art. This must've been how Leonardo Da Vinci felt when he had finished the last brushstrokes of the Mona Lisa.

A red light began to flash on the console in front of Grishenko. 'Sir, we have a perimeter breach in Sector Twelve.'

Beelzebub brushed a speck of dust from the long row of medals on his green tunic and smiled again. Grishenko considered requesting a transfer to a nice comfortable gulag somewhere in Siberia. 'That'll just be some old friends dropping in,' said his commanding officer. 'Be a good chap and pop the kettle on.'

The Four Horsemen of the Apocalypse (Retired) looked down from the crest of the hill. Their steeds' breath fogged in the frosty winter air and the snow crunched beneath their shifting hooves. Dark sullen clouds gathered around them. War looked up.

'Portentous skies,' he murmured.

The eighties were a particularly cruel decade fashion-wise. War had been watching far too much 'Magnum:

P.I.' and had shaved his fiery red beard down to a moustache. He had gone through his wardrobe and chosen his best Hawaiian shirt for today. Famine favoured an all-white ensemble of leather jacket and trousers. Conquest wore a wide-shouldered double-breasted suit from Savile Row, because the end of the world didn't mean you didn't have to look swish. Death was in his favourite hooded cloak because, as he always told the others, the classics never go out of style.

Chain-link fencing topped with barbed wire surrounded a square block of granite with blast shielded doors large enough for a couple of tanks to pass through side by side; the main entrance to the complex buried deep underground. War counted the conscripted soldiers sheltering from the cold in the guardhouse and patrolling the perimeter, cigarettes hanging from their chapped lips.

'Are we sure he's in there?' asked Famine.

'You saw the files that War's contacts brought back,' Conquest replied. Beelzebub had been hiding from them for the last fifty years and then, last week, he had appeared on the intelligence reports that War still received from MI6. He was now a high-ranking officer in the Red Army's Black Ops division and they'd all agreed that this was A Very Bad Thing. 'What do you think, Death?'

No answer. Conquest punched him on the arm. Death removed his Walkman headphones. 'Sorry. What were you saying?'

'You should probably take those off. You need to focus.'

'Yeah, I know. It's just that this new Billy Joel album is really good.'

Conquest shook his head. 'Are we all ready?'

They all agreed they were.

'Captain!' barked War.

A bush a couple of metres away stood up and became Captain Bill Hillier. He was in full camouflage, his face smeared with paint. He slung an assault rifle over his shoulder and quietly sprinted to War's side. 'Sir?' he asked, spitting bits of twig.

'I need your men to run interference. Engage at fifty metres. Do not attempt to detain the target. That's our job.'

Captain Hillier couldn't see how these fruity-looking Limeys were going to infiltrate a top secret Soviet military site and capture one of the Red Army's top officers. 'Yes, sir.'

War placed a hand on his shoulder. 'Make them think Judgment Day's come early.' His three friends looked at each other. They really hoped that it hadn't.

Hillier smiled grimly. 'With pleasure, sir.' He disappeared back into the undergrowth and fifteen identical bushes began to move silently down the hillside towards the main gate. The Four Horsemen were alone.

'So, what's the plan, then?' Death asked.

'Go in there and fuck shit up,' War replied.

Famine frowned. 'That's always the plan.'

'Hasn't failed so far.'

'How many times is this now? Saving the world, I mean?' Famine asked.

'This is different,' said Conquest. 'This is for what he did to Julia. If I stop everything being reduced to ash, well, that's a bonus.' It had been half a century since he'd last seen Julia. She'd be an old woman now, probably married with the children and grandchildren that he couldn't give her. Whoever said it gets easier with time never had an eternity alone stretching before them.

'It also makes my workload a lot more manageable,' said Death.

On an unseen signal, the Special Forces troops sprung up and opened fire on the guardhouse. The air sang with gunshots and screams. Intruder alarms howled in the winter wind. Spooked by the sudden noise, the horses reared up.

'Where did you get these bloody things?' asked War as he trotted around in a circle.

'Do you know how difficult it is to hire horses in this day and age?' replied Famine.

Conquest stroked his horse's mane and, leaning forward, whispered something in her ear. She whinnied and calmed down. As she did, so did the others.

'It's a pleasure and a privilege as always, gentlemen,' Conquest yelled above the gunfire. He snapped the reins in his hand and galloped down the hill. The others chased him into battle with the fury of the righteous. The ground beneath them rumbled like an approaching storm. Swords drawn, the Horsemen dashed past the ghosts of the fallen. Death would see to them later.

Hillier's men had already secured the guardhouse and were opening the gates when the Soviet reinforcements came up to the surface through the bunker's doors. The Four Horsemen were in the compound before the gates were fully open. When the guards saw Death charging towards them on horseback, most of them dropped their weapons and fled. Those that stayed fired bullets that passed straight through him. They were rewarded with a boot to the face.

War charged at a Russian firing indiscriminately from his Kalashnikov, but he couldn't reach him in time and bullets raked across his horse's neck. He was leaping through the air before she could hit the ground. He plunged his sword through the chest of the soldier, rolling when he landed. With the poise of a gymnast, War was back on his feet in an instant and pulled the sword from the dead man. He turned to the approaching guards. 'Come on then,' he roared, shaking his bloodied sword. 'One at a time or all together. Doesn't make any difference to me.'

None of them had signed up to fight what appeared to be a very angry and lost holidaymaker who had dressed completely inappropriately for the weather conditions. War returned to his dead horse and patted her flanks. 'Thanks, girl.' He strode towards the compound entrance unchallenged.

Conquest had finished dealing with an entire platoon that had been pinning Hillier's men down on the left flank. He cantered over to join War and jumped off his horse. He fed her some sugar lumps from his suit pocket and then straightened his tie. Death appeared from thin air. Famine was last to join them. His white leather jacket was splattered with dark red spots. He looked furious.

'Do you know how hard it is to get blood out of leather?' he grumbled.

Hillier jogged over. 'That was impressive.'

'Thank you, captain,' War replied. 'I need you and your men to fall back before the next wave arrives. My friends and I will take it from here.'

'Yes, sir.' Hillier saluted. 'Good luck.'

Hillier gestured to his troops and they all ran back through the gate and vanished into the countryside.

The Horsemen crept into the compound and down the entrance ramp until daylight had been reduced to a small white rectangle behind them. They found themselves in a deserted servicing bay. The alarm whooped and bounced off the concrete walls. Army trucks had been left with engines exposed and wheels missing. The engineers had no taste for battle and had disappeared into the bowels of the underground base.

In the shadows, a nervous young private fumbled with the safety catch on his pistol. When he looked up to fire it, the intruder wearing a long coat and hood had travelled across the length of the bay impossibly fast. He plucked the gun from the soldier's hand and shook his head. The private didn't hang around to find out what else he might do.

The Horsemen snuck through a small door at the end of the servicing bay and into a corridor that had been carved into the rock itself. It stretched off in both directions and caged lamps that hung from the ceiling cast shadows on the roughly hewn walls.

'Which way?' asked Conquest.

'I don't know,' said War.

'I thought you had a plan?'

'I do have a plan. I told you it on the hill.'

'I thought that was bravado.'

'They don't exactly hand out schematics to these places, you know. I thought we'd blag it.'

Conquest rubbed his forehead. He could feel a headache coming on, which was the usual result of a conversation with War. 'You thought we'd blag breaking into a top secret Soviet nuclear missile silo? Alright. Let's split up. Death and I will go one way and you and Famine can go the other.'

'Why do I have to go with him?' Famine moaned.

'I don't want to argue about it.' Conquest spoke with the tone of a weary father addressing a sulking child. The pairs headed off in opposite directions. Before Death and Conquest rounded the corner, Conquest turned back.

'War?' he called.

'What?'

'Try and keep the body count to an absolute minimum.'

War pouted. 'You're no fun anymore.'

War and Famine watched Conquest and Death disappear from view.

'Come on, you skinny streak of piss,' said War. 'Let's go and find this bastard.'

Keeping close to the wall, they made their way down the corridor. They turned left and right at various junctions, searching for clues to Beelzebub's location. Once or twice, they had to duck down tunnels and hide in doorways as troops ran in the opposite direction to join a battle that was already over.

Soon they arrived at a door covered in so many warning signs, it could only lead to the control room. Entrance was granted by swiping a security card through a keypad to the door's right.

'Do you think you can open it?' asked War.

Famine bit his lip and crouched down to inspect the keypad. 'I'm going to have to override the system. I'll need a pocket calculator, soldering iron, a twenty-five millimetre screwdriver, some chewing gum and a paper clip.'

The door slid open and a technician stepped out. The door hissed shut and he stared at Famine and War in stunned silence. War did the first thing that came to mind and punched him in the face. The technician slumped to the floor and War searched his clothes until he found a security badge with a magnetic strip. 'How about this?'

'Yeah, that'll do.'

War tossed the badge to Famine who grabbed it with one hand and swiped it through the keypad. The door locks opened with a thud.

Beelzebub was stood with his back to them. He was sipping tea from a delicate bone china cup and saucer and studying a computer monitor. Hearing the door open, he said something in Russian over his shoulder.

War answered, 'I'm sorry, but I don't speak commie.'

Beelzebub turned around. He placed the cup back on the saucer. 'Gentlemen! I'm so glad you could make it. Do you like what I've done with the place?'

'How did you slime your way into this gig?' asked Famine.

'You know how it is,' Beelzebub replied. 'Dark forces. I am legion. It's not about what you know, but who you know. How have you been?' Famine and War brandished their swords. Beelzebub smiled politely. 'Done with the small talk, are we?'

War sneered. 'What are you up to?'

'I'm glad you asked. What's the point of coming up with nefarious plans if you don't get to show off about them? Have you heard of The Dead Hand?' War shook his head. 'It's a little project I persuaded the powers that be to invest in.'

'Can I put this sword down?' Famine whispered to War. 'It's really rather heavy.'

'Alright,' War whispered back.

'Have you two finished?' Beelzebub asked impatiently. They nodded. 'If a nuclear strike is detected on Soviet soil by seismic, light and radiation sensors, it will automatically trigger the launch of all our ICBMs towards their primary targets. The Kremlin thinks that I designed it as a deterrent, but what's the point of building something if you're never going to use it?'

Famine was horrified. 'But if you launch all your nukes, then everybody else will launch theirs. Billions will die.'

'There'll be some collateral damage, I admit. You can't make an omelette without breaking some eggs. With governments left impotent, I shall take my place as ruler. True, it'll be Hell on Earth, but better to reign in Hell and all that.'

'But you need someone to launch a nuclear strike against you first,' War said.

'You're not as moronic as that ridiculous shirt suggests. If hostile forces attack a nuclear missile installation the highest-ranking officer is granted extraordinary powers up to and including the use of nuclear force, without requiring authorisation from Moscow. So, thank you for that.' Beelzebub looked over at the map on the wall. 'I was thinking London. Put those grumpy bastards out of their misery.'

Famine chuckled and raised his sword. 'Haven't you seen any movies? The bad guy should never reveal his plans for world domination until it's too late to stop him.'

Beelzebub tilted his head to the side sadly. 'Oh, but it is too late.'

The last sound War and Famine heard were the triggers of the guns pointed at the backs of their heads.

EIGHTEEN

Dave and Melanie were hiding behind a filing cabinet experiencing one of history's greatest awkward silences.

'Well,' Dave finally said. 'At least we're spending some quality time together.'

Melanie ignored his joke. 'Who was that?'

'John. No, wait. James. Or at least, that's who he used to be.' James Camp. That was his name. Dave had drunk coffee with him on their break less than twenty-four hours ago. He seemed like a nice guy. Now he was drinking blood from an office cleaner and Dave was trying to figure out a way to destroy him. You never really know your co-workers.

'What is he now?'

'A vampire.'

Melanie almost laughed at the suggestion. 'There's no such thing as vampires.'

'What bit is confusing you? The teeth? The pale skin? The blood sucking? That was a bit of a pointer. The way they get all explodey around holy water?'

'Holy water?'

'Oh yeah. You weren't there for that bit. I got ordained in an online church. One of the perks is that I can bless water.'

Melanie shook her head. 'I don't believe this is happening.'

'You get used to it after a while. Trust me.' Dave pulled himself up into a crouch, chanced a look over the top of the cabinet then ducked back down. 'I promise that I will tell you everything if we get out of here alive, but the coast is clear and we need to go right now.' Dave stood up. 'Are you ready?'

'No, but let's go.' She held her hand out and Dave took it, pulling her up.

'Head straight for the lifts. Whatever happens, don't stop,' Dave ordered. They left the safety of their hiding place and, half crouched, they dashed towards the centre of the office. As Dave passed a desk, he grabbed an aerosol can of compressed air and jammed it into his hoodie pocket.

'What are you doing?' Melanie hissed.

'I've got an idea,' he whispered back.

They reached the lifts and pressed the down button. Dave was relieved that it illuminated with a little ring of light. They waited, Dave impatiently tapping his foot on the stone floor.

The vampire James appeared at the end of the row of steel doors. Grinning, he slowly paced towards Melanie and Dave; a predator stalking its prey. Dave held his hand out to Melanie. 'Give me your lighter.'

'I know it's stressful, but now's not the time for a cigarette.'

Dave pulled the aerosol can from his pocket and showed it to Melanie. 'Give me your lighter.'

Melanie understood and passed him the disposal plastic lighter from her suit pocket. Dave gulped and beckoned James. 'Come on, then.'

James broke into a sprint. As Dave fiddled with the striker wheel, he regarded this as one of a long line of questionable decisions. The lighter sprang into life. As James pressed his hands on Dave, he sprayed the canister into the flame and a plume of fire caught James full in the face. He fell backwards, his hair and clothes catching alight. Dave pressed forward, keeping his finger held down on the improvised flamethrower and engulfing the vampire in a blaze.

James floundered and waved arms of flames. The lift arrived and, as the doors slid open, Dave aimed carefully and with his foot shoved the burning monstrosity into it. It fell to the floor, thrashing and screaming like a wild animal. Scorch marks blackened wherever its limbs struck the interior. Dave reached around into the lift and jabbed at the button to send it down to the ground floor. As the doors closed, Dave looked at the can in his fist and shrugged his shoulders. He tossed the can into the flames. The doors sealed, creating an oven plummeting to the ground.

Police Sergeant Graham Thomas was an old fashioned sort of copper who missed old fashioned policing of old fashioned crimes. He remembered a time before cyber fraud, tasers and - most recently - undead creatures engulfed in balls of flames.

The shift had started regularly. Graham and his partner P.C. Reynolds had been asked to attend an incident at UberSystems International Tower. A probable hoax call; someone claiming vampires and zombies were attacking office workers. Graham was betting on a bored kid.

Keith the security guard at the front desk, who was eighty if he was a day, was helpful. He'd let them have a look around and there'd been a bit of banter.

Then one of the lifts had exploded, sending burning shrapnel and glass over a wide area. The smoke cleared and a blazing figure ran out and collapsed on the floor. Graham tried to smother the flames by throwing his hi-vis jacket over the charred, writhing body. Soon, the only movement was a foot kicking pathetically against the stone floor.

Reynolds grabbed his radio as Keith impossibly leapt over the desk in a single bound. He clamped his jaws around Reynolds's throat and ripped his windpipe out, spitting it on the floor like an unwanted chunk of food. Reynolds gargled and clawed at the pulpy, bloody mess where most of his neck had been.

Graham barely had time to pull the pepper spray from his belt before Keith was biting down on him with incredible force. The initial sharp stab of pain and fear was replaced by a warm sensation flowing through his veins. He felt something important within him die at that moment, replaced by something stronger.

Hunger.

The blood pooling around Reynolds was fascinating. As the liquid shone darkly against the marble, Graham had never seen anything look more delicious and inviting.

Keith licked his own fingers clean. 'Take him. He's yours.'

Graham radioed back to the station. 'It's all fine here. False alarm. I'm just going to have a bite to eat.'

NINETEEN

Dave and Melanie scampered up the stairs, nervously glancing behind them every few floors.

'This reminds me of that Bruce Willis film,' Melanie said between laboured breaths.

'Die Hard?' Dave asked, wiping the sweat from his brow.

'No, "Look Who's Talking" because this is also a very bad idea.'

Dave took his phone from his pocket and redialled Death's number. He listened to it ring a few times before it went to his voicemail. 'You're through to Death. I can't take your soul right now, but please leave a message and I'll get back to you as soon as I can.'

'Hi. It's Dave. Nothing important. It's just that I was right and I'm being chased by vampires. No biggie. Give us a call when you get this.'

They ducked through the door to the thirtieth floor and skirted around the familiar layout quickly. This was where Dave's office had been.

He tried the handle of the boardroom's door and was relieved to find it was locked. Though the others hadn't managed to escape, some were still alive at least. He gently knocked on the door.

'It's Dave. Open up,' he whispered.

He heard the scraping of heavy furniture and the lock sprang open. Simon, about as pale as the creatures that were hunting him, opened the door. Melanie bundled Dave in from behind.

Chris, Sarah and Jim were slumped in the expensive leather chairs around the conference table. 'What kept you?' Sarah asked.

Simon and Dave pushed a sideboard back into place against the door. 'We ran into a friend.'

'Why didn't you get out?'

Melanie looked accusingly at Dave. 'Somebody's blown up the lifts.'

'I was improvising,' Dave said defensively.

Chris stood up and approached Melanie, his hand extended. 'You must be Melanie. Chris Love.' Melanie shook his hand. 'That's Sarah over there, Jim's the one having a nervous breakdown at the head of the table and Simon let you in.'

'Nice to meet you all.' Melanie gave a vague wave to the room. Manners were still important, even in survival situations. They were British, after all.

Chris turned to Dave. 'The police have been called.'

'I don't know how much faith we can put in the police,' Dave said, sliding into one of the empty seats.

'So, what is this? You seem to have a better idea than the rest of us.'

'Vampires.' Dave said.

Simon gave a mocking laugh. 'There's no such thing.'

'We can go round in circles debating what does or does not exist, or we can make an assumption that the things out there that want to suck our blood are vampires.'

'If it looks like a duck and quacks like a duck, it's a duck,' said Sarah.

'A duck that killed my new girlfriend,' Jim muttered.

'Alright,' said Simon. 'Let's say they're vampires. What do we do?'

'I've left a message with some friends who can help us, but until then we need to figure out a plan,' Dave said.

Chris realised that this was his moment to shine. 'Sarah,' he said. 'There's a coffee machine in the corner. Simon, I'm pretty sure there are some biscuits in one of the sideboard cupboards.' He leaned over and placed a hand on Dave's shoulder. 'There's not a problem I can't brainstorm myself out of.'

Chris set up a whiteboard while Simon and Sarah scurried around the table setting down cups and plates of biscuits around Jim, who simply stared off into the distance.

Dave looked down on the lights of the city. He sensed Melanie join him at his side.

'It's kind of beautiful, isn't it?' she said. Even now, he could almost believe it with her by his side. Her breath condensing on the window was illuminated by the city's glow. He felt her fingers tentatively brush his. 'Thank you.'

'For what?' he asked.

'Coming for me.'

Dave shrugged, faking nonchalance. 'No problem.'

'You said you'd tell me what was going on?'

'Do you trust me?'

Her fingers wrapped around his. 'I do now.'

Dave looked into her pale blue eyes, breathed deeply and spoke. 'London is full of lost souls. Not all of them belong to the living. I find them. I rescue those who were left behind. I bring comfort to those who are afraid.'

'You've been practising that, haven't you?'

Dave nodded. 'Yes.'

'Lost souls? Are you talking about ghosts?'

'That's one way to describe them. After the car accident, there were some - well - side effects. I've been able to see them my whole life, but since then I can help them if they haven't passed on in the usual way. That's what I do all day. That's why I've done so terribly at us.

I had to choose between you and them. I think I chose wrong.'

Melanie placed a hand on his cheek. 'Oh, Dave,' she sighed.

'You believe me?'

'I wouldn't have before tonight, but once you see your boyfriend fight off a vampire with an aerosol and a lighter you tend to be a bit more open minded about things. So what's the usual way? A tunnel of light? A choir of angels waiting for you at the Pearly Gates? A guy with a big scythe?' She laughed, but stopped when she saw Dave's face. 'The Grim Reaper? Really? Have you--' she paused, as she tried to form the words to a ridiculous question. 'Have you met him?'

Dave let out a long sigh. 'Melanie, I work for him.'

'Why isn't he here? People are dying.'

'I don't know. There's something stopping him entering the building. If you were to die in here, then he wouldn't be able to do anything. That's why I'm here. To try and find an answer.'

Chris cleared his throat. Dave was annoyed by the interruption, but this would have to wait. They all gathered at the table. Dave munched on a biscuit and considered how relationships seemed more complicated when the undead got involved.

'I thought we'd try brainstorming exercises,' Chris said, popping the lid off a marker pen. 'What do we know about vampires? What are their weaknesses? There are no wrong answers here. We just want to get some ideas flowing and see if we can solutionise this.'

Dave put his hand up. 'Yes, Dave?' said Chris.

'I'm pretty sure that's not a real word.'

'What isn't?' asked Chris.

'Solutionise.'

'Yes it is,' said Sarah. 'It means to heat a metal alloy to form a homogeneous solid solution.'

'Every day's a school day.' Dave turned back to Chris. 'Is that what you meant? To heat a metal alloy to form a homogeneous solid solution?'

'Obviously not,' said Chris.

'Then please don't use it again.'

'Can we get back to the topic?' asked Chris. 'What kills vampires? Just say the first thing that comes to mind.'

'Sunlight,' Simon shouted out.

'Good. When's sunrise?'

'Half past five,' said Dave.

Chris looked at his watch. 'That's just over two hours away. Let's park that one and we can come back to it offline. Does anyone have any suggestions that don't rely on the Earth's rotation?'

'Stake through the heart?' said Sarah.

'Stakes! Good!' Chris wrote the word on the board. 'Anything else?'

'Holy water,' Dave said.

'Excellent! We've got real world evidence of that one.'

'Crosses,' Melanie said, playing with her necklace.

'Crosses. Good.' Chris scribbled the suggestions down.

'Garlic?' said Jim.

'Do we have any garlic?' Chris asked.

'We could use Jim's breath?' Simon said.

'Fuck off,' Jim said with a hint of a smile.

'If you kill the head vampire, you kill them all,' Sarah said.

'And any that haven't fed yet have their condition reversed,' Melanie said.

Chris stood back and read the short list. 'How do we make stakes?'

'There's a caretaker's cupboard. Wooden mops and broom handles. We can use them,' Dave said.

'Brilliant. Crosses?'

'There might be something in the stationery cupboard? It's just a case of putting two long strips together,' said Melanie.

'And holy water?' asked Chris. 'Dave's our subject matter expert on that.'

'I don't know,' said Dave with a shrug. 'The water cooler?'

'That's not very portable,' said Simon.

'What about the fire extinguishers? You can aim it and everything,' said Sarah.

'And how do we kill the head vampire?' asked Simon.

'Let's cross that bridge when we come to it,' said Dave.

Chris clapped his hands together. 'Good work, everyone. Sarah and Simon, you're in charge of going to the stationery cupboard. Dave and Melanie, you're on stake duty. Jim and I will get the fire extinguishers. Let's all meet back here in five.'

As everybody stood up Dave said, 'Remember, they're no longer the people you work with. They're soulless monsters who will do anything to destroy you.'

'To be fair,' said Melanie, 'that pretty much sounds like the people I work with.'

TWENTY

Melanie and Dave sought out the mops and brooms amongst the chemicals and cleaning products in the caretaker's cupboard. They discarded those with metal and plastic handles and were left with three mops with wooden ones.

'What's he like?' Melanie asked suddenly.

Dave was looking in an old ice cream box for anything that could be of use. 'Who?'

'Death.'

Dave stopped and smiled as he thought about him. 'Funny. Annoying. Sad. Lonely.'

'Can I meet him?'

'I don't know. I think I really have to stress the annoying bit.'

'Where are the ghosts? If he's not here to do his thing, shouldn't they be hanging around?'

'I don't know where they are. I've got a theory, but it's incredibly depressing. Death by vampire is utter destruction. Death of the body and death of the soul. They're psychic locusts. They leave nothing behind.'

Melanie silently contemplated this. 'We'd better be extra careful, then.'

'Too bloody right.'

'What you do is important, isn't it?'

'I think so.'

'I think you made the right choice. I wouldn't want to be left alone for eternity. I'd be pretty happy if you showed up even if it was just to say goodbye.'

They looked at each other. Nothing else needed to be said.

'Come on,' said Dave. 'We've got some vampires to destroy.'

Dave and Melanie rushed back with the mops under their arms. Everybody arrived outside the boardroom at the same time. Sarah and Simon carried rulers and rubber bands. Chris and Jim had a fire extinguisher each and they'd found a fire axe as an added bonus.

'Fire extinguishers are heavy,' Chris said, dropping the red canister to the floor and wiping the sweat from his brow. 'I think we got the raw deal.'

The attack came from the shadows. Six vampires jumped from all sides in a blur of teeth and claws. Dave's first instinct was to lash out with a fist. It connected sharply with the jaw of one and it went sprawling over a desk.

Melanie and Sarah held rulers together to make rudimentary crosses. The vampires bearing down on them skidded to a halt and backed off, hissing like scalded animals. Simon and Dave impotently waved mop handles, failing to halt the attackers' advances.

A vampire leaped onto Chris's back, sending them both spiralling and bouncing off office furniture and onto a photocopier. Dave ran over to help, smashing the lid repeatedly onto the vampire's head, but its teeth were clamped tightly around Chris's throat. It lashed out an arm, sending Dave crashing to the floor.

Pulling himself back to his feet, Dave knew they had seconds to live unless he thought of something. A small object on the ceiling caught his attention. He clambered up onto a desk, kicking over framed photographs and ornaments, and pulled Melanie's lighter from his pocket. Stretching up, he held the flame to one of the fire sprinkler heads. The system kicked into life, spraying a fine rain down and soaking everything.

'Exorcizo te, creatura aquæ, in nomine Dei Patris omnipotentis, et in nomine Jesu Christi, Filii ejus Domini nostri, et in virtute Spiritus Sancti. Ut fias aqua exorcizata ad effugandam omnem potestatem inimici, et ipsum inimicum eradicare et explantare valeas cum angelis suis apostaticis, per virtutem ejusdem. Domini nostri Jesu Christ qui venturus est judicare vivos et mortuos et sæculum per ignem,' Dave shouted over the white noise of the water.

As soon as Dave finished speaking, the vampires howled and screamed as the blessed water stripped the skin from their muscles like boiling rain. Soon, the sprinklers ran dry and the vampires' bodies lay still in the silence.

'Great. My phone's water damaged. That's the insurance fucked,' Simon muttered to himself.

'Yeah, that's the thing to concentrate on right now,' said Sarah.

'Don't have a go at me!' shouted Simon. 'It wasn't me that got us into this mess! We'd all be still sat at our desks if it wasn't for him.' He pointed an accusing finger at Dave.

'If it wasn't for him, we'd all be gotten to eventually,' Sarah said. 'You saw what they did to Jason.'

Dave jumped down from the table and ran to Chris's side. He was slick with diluted blood. He tugged weakly at his sodden tie. 'They're burning,' he gasped. 'My clothes. My skin. On fire. I can feel it. I can feel it inside me. I don't want to become one of them. I'm a vegetarian, for Christ's sake.'

Chris was soaked in holy water. It would be a painful, lingering death as the change took place. Dave looked up at the others gathered around in silence like a sombre, mourning family. He knew he would have to be the one that did this. In the bad days after his mother's death, he'd resented his parents for not giving him a brother or sister with whom he could share the burden of grief. He felt the same loneliness now. He took a mop from Jim's hand and snapped the handle with the heel of his shoe. With a pen knife he whittled the sharp, splintered end to a vicious point. An executioner preparing his instrument of death.

He knelt beside Chris. He shifted the stake in his hand. Its weight was unbearable. He couldn't lift it up and do what was being asked of him.

'You're all going to die, you know?' Chris said through gritted teeth, his humanity slowly dying. 'You'll be sucked dry. There's no way out of it.' He gave a mocking laugh, blood bubbles popping from the gaps in his teeth.

Dave plunged the stake into Chris's heart and the laughter stopped.

The silence was worse.

'Shit. He had kids,' Dave said.

'Oh, Jesus,' Melanie muttered, placing a hand on Dave's shoulder. He shrugged it off.

He pulled the stake from Chris's chest, wiped the blood on his jeans and tucked it into his belt. He turned to the others. 'We need to get out of here. They'll know where we are now.'

TWENTY-ONE

9 November 1983

Conquest and Death had just discovered that they had been walking around in circles. They'd decided to start an argument with each other when the countdown began. The concrete, flashing red lights and ear-splitting klaxon reminded Death of a New York nightclub he'd been to for a fancy dress party once. He translated the garbled announcement from the Tannoy system for Conquest.

'They're locking down the base in preparation for launch. We've got a couple of minutes.'

'He's launching missiles? At what?'

'How should I know?' Death snapped, 'but if we don't do something about it, I'm really going to get it in the neck from a lot of very annoyed people.'

Conquest weighed up the options and came to a decision. 'You go and find War and Famine and get to the control room. I'm going to the missile silos and see if I can stop them from there.'

'Do you know where you're going?'

Conquest breathed in deeply. 'I can smell their power.'

'What are you going to do?'

'I'll blag it.'

'Good luck,' Death said.

'You too.'

Death ran back in the direction he'd last seen Famine and War heading, the hem of his cloak dancing up and wrapping around his legs, until he came across the unconscious body of a technician. It could only be War's handiwork. Without stopping for the laws of physics, he glided through the door to the control room.

Red lights flashed, casting demonic shadows that pulsed against the wall in time with the blaring sirens. Beelzebub was stood over the limp bodies of War and Famine, cast crimson in the dim light. A bullet fired into the back of the head from point blank range will make an enormous mess and kill both mortal and immortal beings alike. Where mortals and immortals differed, though, is that immortals didn't have souls. All that remained were two large holes punched through the universe.

Death could grasp the distance between the farthest stars, but the idea that his two friends were gone forever was too big. An unfamiliar feeling balled up and knotted inside him. Death screamed with rage. 'What have you done?'

Beelzebub sipped his tea. Irritated, he said, 'I'm not explaining it all again.'

Death picked up War's sword from where it had fallen. He shifted the weight in his grip. He hadn't held a weapon in centuries, but at this moment it felt right. Beelzebub backed away. The cup and saucer slipped from his fingers and smashed onto the floor.

'Now, come on. Remember your oath. You vowed never to take a life. You won't do anything.' There was uncertainty in his voice.

Death ran a finger along the blade. A thrill of pleasure ran up his arm and through his body. 'Yes, I remember. I vowed never to take a human life.' He took a step forward. Porcelain shards cracked and splintered under his feet.

Beelzebub had backed himself up against the computer terminal on the far wall. He was panicking now. He'd gone too far killing War and Famine, but his pride had blinded him to the consequences. 'Guards!' he yelled. 'Fall back. Protect me.'

The soldiers stood frozen in place. What was happening in front of them went beyond their understanding. Some of them were offering breathless prayers, silent beneath the sirens. Death gave the sword a couple of practice swings, cutting the air around him. It was all coming back to him. Back to a time when he spilled blood alongside his three brothers.

A warning light flashed on Lieutenant Grishenko's computer terminal. He cleared his throat. 'Sir, the missile silo doors are jammed. We're unable to launch at this time.'

Conquest had obviously thought of something. Beelzebub looked from Death to Grishenko. He was sweating, gasping for air and having difficulty multi-tasking. 'Get somebody down there and manually open them.' He turned his attention back to Death. 'I'm guessing that's Conquest interfering? Come on, Death. You were always my favourite of the group. You were definitely the smartest. You're different to the others. I always thought we had a lot in common.'

'One minute until launch,' Grishenko told the room.

Death held the sword up to Beelzebub's throat. 'Abort it.'

'I can't. I removed the override. Once the codes are entered, it can't be stopped. If those doors don't open, it'll blow up in the silo.'

Death headed for the door.

'I'm assuming that your normal mode of transport isn't available? I made sure there'd be too much electrical interference when they built this place. You'll never make it there in time. Maybe he's got out, maybe he hasn't. There's nothing you can do,' Beelzebub called out behind him.

Death turned back and pointed the sword back at the base of Beelzebub's neck. 'A very long time ago, when I was much younger, I assumed there must be something more than us. I mean, there you were; the embodiment of pure evil. I thought that, somewhere, there must be the embodiment of pure good. But the universe doesn't deal in such absolutes. There's just shades of grey.' He leant forward; close enough for Beelzebub to see the true face of Death. It was pale and awful and terrified even the Devil himself. 'You're not needed anymore.'

Death stepped back and swung War's sword. It cut cleanly through Beelzebub's neck, separating his head from his body. The body fell to its knees and then forward onto its chest; an empty vessel.

For a brief moment Death was victorious, but then he felt less than nothing. The sword fell from his grip and clattered to the floor, but Death did not hear it.

Grishenko was pressing buttons and turning keys, but it was futile. With seconds to go, he was swept by a wave of calm that pushed him back into his seat.

Three.

Two.

One.

Boom.

Compression waves pushed their way through the rock between the missile silo and the control room.

Files slipped from desks, half-drunk cups of coffee smashed and bodies were thrown around like rag dolls.

When the room stopped shaking, a fine shower of dust drifted down from the cracks splitting the ceiling. It coated everything in a layer of grey so it looked like a thousand years had passed in the brief moment of detonation. Grishenko climbed out from under his desk, bewildered. Death had disappeared. 'We're still here,' he said with astonishment.

'The payload wasn't armed. That was just the conventional explosives and rocket fuel going up,' one of the technicians replied through the haze. 'We'd better evacuate, though, in case there's been any kind of leak.'

Grishenko agreed and sounded the alarm. The control room door opened with a hiss of compressed air and the dust wafted out into the corridor. The survivors stumbled and staggered over the three bodies in their way, and out towards the surface.

Conquest did not return. Death followed the corridor back until it became a narrow service tunnel leading to the missile silos. He saw a flash of silver catch the dim light. Conquest's pocket watch dropped in the rush to get to the missiles. Death picked it up and put it in his cloak. He carried on until he arrived at the silo's access hatch. A young soldier stared dumbly at his own crumpled body. The silo's walls had done their job and contained the firestorm, but the blast had punched the life out of him.

The soldier looked up. 'Oh, it's you,' he said with a resigned tone.

'Have we met?'

The soldier's voice trembled with shock. 'I thought I saw you once at my babushka's bedside. Does this mean I'll see her again? I'd like that.'

'Possibly. I hope you do. Before that, though, did you see anybody go in there?' Death pointed at the sealed hatch.

'A guy in a good suit? Yeah. I thought I was seeing things. I mean, what's a guy dressed like that doing down here? I told him not to, but I don't think he understood me. He never came out.'

Death thanked the young soldier and did what needed to be done. He climbed through the access hatch and into a tall thin concrete tube. Flames crackled hungrily, consuming what little wreckage was left. The skeleton of the rocket, twisted and warped like some horrifying piece of art, pointed up towards the cracked hatch a hundred feet above his head. Conquest lay still in the corner, his clothes reduced to rags by the explosion. Death ran to his side. Conquest stirred and then rolled over slowly. He looked down at his body, checking that everything was still attached.

'Bloody hell. Do you know how much this suit cost?' he groaned. He looked up at Death. 'Where are the other two?'

Death found a tool shed, took a shovel and returned to the control room. He and Conquest carried the bodies of War and Famine to the surface. The storm clouds had passed and a thin plume of smoke split the clear, bright sky. They went to the top of the hill from where the Horsemen had last rode out together. Now that they were clear of the base Death could transport the bodies in an instant, but they carried them up the hillside. Their fallen comrades deserved the effort and the two remaining Horsemen honoured them with every slip and stumble.

Two deep graves were dug in the frozen ground and War and Famine's bodies were placed in them. They would decay and be washed from here by the meltwater. They would be carried in the rivers and swim out into the sea until their infinitesimal remains had spread and wrapped themselves around the whole world. They would approve of that.

'I'm done with this,' Conquest said after a while. 'Once again we've saved humanity from themselves, given them another chance, but they'll learn nothing from it.'

'Maybe they will this time,' Death said.

'They crave order, but fight amongst themselves like spoilt children,' Conquest replied. 'It's not our duty to save these mortals. We've done so time and time again and all I have to show for it is pain and loneliness.' He extended his hand to Death. 'It's time to part ways.'

Death knew that this is what Conquest had to do. The Four Horsemen were no more. He shook his hand. 'What will you do?'

'Head west. That's as far as I've got.'

'Goodbye, old friend,' said Death warmly.

'Goodbye.'

Conquest headed down the hillside. Death watched him until he disappeared over the horizon. For the first time in his existence, Death was alone. He stared at the two mounds of dirt and wondered whether he could go back and try to save them, but he knew from experience that it wouldn't work. He wasn't in control. The tragedy of life is that everything dies. The blessing of it is that nobody knows when. He wished the world would grasp that fact.

He didn't know how long he stood there. It might have been for a second, or maybe the whole of time had travelled full circle. He couldn't stay forever. He had work to do.

Death would always have work to do.

TWENTY-TWO

Kirsten searched the Document Management Centre. Her hunger was a dull ache nestled in the bottom of her stomach. In all the excitement, she hadn't had a chance to feed.

She'd been saving the Marwood boy for tonight. She was careful to farm the new recruits, but he'd tasted so sweet she thought she'd treat herself. Now he'd caused her incredible problems. She'd wanted to savour him, drink him down slowly, but now she just wanted to rip his head from his spine.

A group of vampires were torturing a cleaner who'd unfortunately blundered into the department. The torment made the victim taste better. The adrenaline and fear gave the blood a unique piquancy. But who had time to properly prepare a meal these days?

Jason approached her. She had high hopes for him. He was still learning the ropes, but she'd been impressed by the improvement in his attitude and work ethic. He led a stranger dressed in a police uniform. That couldn't be good, Kirsten thought. She sized him up. 'You're new.'

'Keith sent me,' he said. 'A fire alarm was triggered on the thirtieth floor. He's contacted the emergency services and told them it was a false alarm, but it might be a good place to start looking for the others.'

'Someone who uses their head as well as their teeth. You'll be handy to have around here. Take a group and see what you can find.' She signalled to those gathered around the cleaner. 'Stop playing with your food and go with...' She turned back to the ex-policeman. 'What's your name?'

'Graham, ma'am.'

'Go with Graham. We might know where the others are.'

'But, Kirsten, we were going to... y'know...' one of the group said, nodding to the cleaner begging for death.

Kirsten smiled. 'Leave it to me. I wouldn't let any of my staff do anything that I wouldn't be prepared to do myself.'

Dave searched around the twenty-eighth floor. It had been cleared of furniture for refurbishment and was an open expanse of carpet. All the doors were electronically locked so swipe cards wouldn't work. 'We can't stay here,' he said when he returned to the others. 'It's too exposed. Let's tool up and move on.'

They worked quickly and in silence. Mop handles were broken up and sharpened. Rulers were bound together with rubber bands to make crosses. Dave blessed the two fire extinguishers they'd hauled down with them. He didn't know why his blessing worked and didn't want to question it. Perhaps its power came from his need.

Everybody armed themselves with stakes and crosses. Simon had found a couple of rucksacks containing sweaty gym equipment and they placed a fire extinguisher in each one, tucking the fire axe in with one of them. He and Jim took a bag each and pulled them onto their shoulders.

'We can't go up,' said Dave. 'Let's go down to the next floor, find a bathroom and hide until sunrise. It's not the most dignified of plans, but it's all I've got.'

They headed back to the door leading to the stairwell. When they were sure they couldn't hear any footsteps coming from the other side Dave cracked the door open. He searched the landing and, seeing that it was clear, beckoned the others to follow him out. They inched down the stairs, their wet shoes squelching with each step.

As Dave reached the next landing, the stitching on the straps of Jim's rucksack gave out under the weight of its load. Melanie and Sarah reached out, but the material slipped through their fingers. The extinguisher tumbled and spun down the stairs, letting out a loud metallic chime with every step it struck.

Everybody froze as they imagined a dozen pairs of vampire ears pricking up.

'Leg it!' Dave ordered in a hoarse whisper. They could already hear the footsteps heading in their direction from above and below.

The five of them burst through the door to the twenty-seventh floor. They shimmied and danced between desks and reached the door leading to the next set of offices. They were fumbling for key cards to unlock the door when a snarling face appeared on the other side of the glass.

'How the fuck did they get in there?' Dave asked.

Reeling back from the shock, they fell over each other and headed back in the opposite direction as the vampire let himself in. Another vampire dressed in a police uniform flanked by three others blocked the exit back to the stairs.

'There's your police response,' Dave muttered.

Surrounded on all sides, Dave, Melanie, Jim, Simon and Sarah formed a tight huddle. They held their crosses out in front of them. The vampires backed off. They circled slowly, looking for a weakness to exploit and break the stalemate.

The fire door opened and, to everybody's amazement, Emma strolled in. Blood soaked and smiling lasciviously, she walked towards Jim with a seductive strut.

'Hello, babe,' she said. 'Did you miss me?'

Dave sensed Jim's mental defences drop. He grabbed him by the arm. 'That's not Emma,' he whispered.

His mind shattered, Jim broke free of Dave's grasp and walked to her in a trance-like state. The others bunched up to fill the gap he'd left.

'I thought you were dead,' Jim whispered as he stroked her cheek.

Emma smiled sympathetically. 'Oh, but I am.'

With lightning speed, she wrapped her mouth around his neck and drank deeply. The ruler and rubber band cross fell from his limp hand and bounced on the floor.

Graham, the policeman, took a step towards Dave. The cross in Dave's hand didn't waver and kept him at bay.

'We can do this the easy way or the hard way,' Graham said.

'What's the easy way?' asked Dave.

'You let us drink your blood.'

'And the hard way?'

'We still drink your blood, it just hurts a lot more.'

'Is there any way that doesn't involve anybody drinking anybody's blood?'

Graham shook his head.

Dave sighed and tightened his grip on the stake in his hand. 'I didn't think so.'

He leapt forward and drove the stake into Graham's chest with all his might. Stunned, they both looked down at it sticking out of the stab-proof vest he wore.

'You're an idiot,' Graham said. 'I'm going to enjoy hurting you.'

He picked Dave up by the throat and hurled him back into the group, knocking them over. Dave landed on the base of his spine. As he squirmed in agony, he wondered if he could go at least one week without being thrown across a room.

The fight that followed was short and brutal. Simon activated the fire extinguisher and took out two of the vampires in a frenzy of spray and smoke. Sarah sprang towards a third and stabbed him in his heart. As she shielded herself from his gory end, Graham was on top of her. As if opening a pickle jar, he snapped her neck with a twist of his wrist.

Dave pulled the fire axe from Simon's backpack and spun round to face a vampire wearing earphones. Even though his face was contorted and feral, Dave recognised him as Si Dunnett, the kid with the trolley. 'They didn't get you, too?' Dave asked, disappointed.

'What?' Si asked loudly, taking one of the buds out of his ear.

Dave rolled his eyes. 'I said... Never mind. What are you even listening to?'

'Coldplay.'

'Bloody hell. You *are* evil,' Dave said and buried the axe in Si's head.

The extinguisher's spray had reduced to a trickle, so Simon threw it at a vampire's head. It connected with a hollow thud. Simon took advantage of the confusion, quickly dispatching the vampire with a stake he pulled from his waistband.

Simon flashed a smile. 'I'm getting the hang of this,' he said, just before a stake spiralled through the air and buried itself in his chest.

'Two can play that game,' Graham said smugly.

'Cock it,' said Simon as he fell forward.

Dave looked around for Melanie, who was keeping Emma at bay with her cross. At the right moment, she dropped her guard and Emma jumped forward. With one smooth movement, Melanie thrust her stake between Emma's ribs.

Graham ran at Dave, teeth bared. Dave adjusted the weight of the axe in his hands and swung like a cricketer looking for a match-winning six. The blow severed Graham's head from his shoulders, the sharp blade cutting cleanly through bone and tissue. His body crashed to the ground at Dave's feet.

Dave dropped the axe and ran over to Melanie. He felt his legs give way but she held him up.

'Look out!' she shouted and shoved him away. She caught the full impact as a newly reanimated Jim crashed into her. They rolled on the floor as Melanie tried to avoid his gnashing teeth and clawing fingernails.

Dave repeatedly kicked out at Jim's chest, feeling the bones shatter against the tip of his boot, until he released his grip on Melanie. Fighting to control the kicking and screaming vampire, he grabbed his shirt and dragged him away. Dave scrabbled for the stake in his belt and blindly stabbed at Jim until he went limp.

Dave pulled himself out from under Jim's dead weight and noticed he was quietly chuckling to himself.

'What's so funny?' Dave asked.

'The sun's coming up,' Jim replied, his laboured breath rasping.

It was true. The bottom edge of the sky was starting to lighten with the first signs of the new day.

'I don't think that's going to be a problem for you,' said Dave.

'No, but it will be for her.' Jim nodded towards Melanie. She was clutching her neck, trying to stem the flow of blood. 'It's only a scratch, but I think it should be enough.'

Dave didn't hear anything else. He ran over to Melanie and pulled off his hoodie. He placed it around her throat and kept pressure on it.

'I'm sorry,' she said with tears in her eyes.

Dave's world collapsed. He was lost, unsure what to do next. He tried to think his way through the confusion of grief and guilt.

'It's going to be alright,' he told her, but he didn't know how. Then a thought rang clear and true. He stood with purpose. If he died trying to save her life, so be it. He'd done it before and he'd got himself out of it just fine that time.

'Don't leave me,' Melanie said, clutching at his hand.

'I've got to do something.'

'What?' Melanie was shaking. Shock was setting in.

'I'm going to do what everybody has thought about some time in their life. I'm going to kill my boss.'

TWENTY-THREE

It had been a good life, Julia thought in her last few moments. She had filled her one hundred and seven years with friendship, art and travel. If she had one regret, it was that she'd never had children. She'd never married. Of course, that wouldn't have made a difference in this day and age, but things were different back then.

She often thought of her wedding day and Christopher Quint. After the violence and chaos in the library, she'd locked herself in the bridal suite and refused all visitors. Christopher had waited outside like an obedient puppy. He'd tried to explain what had happened, but his words had faded over the years and didn't make much sense to Julia now.

When she had shed all the tears she could, she'd packed her bags and left. He didn't try to stop her. Over the next few months, she'd shut herself away from everyone and everything, with only her books for company. Christopher's phone calls were ignored and his gifts and letters returned unopened until they finally stopped. She never heard from him again.

Tired of sitting at home reading of others' adventures, she went out into the world and sought her own.

In turn, she wrote them down and achieved moderate success at the end of the thirties. The war interrupted her travels. The men of Britain were shipped out across the oceans from which she had returned while she did her duty trapped on the small island.

After the fighting had finished, she returned to her wanderings. The books didn't sell as well as before and she slipped into a comfortable obscurity. In her fifties, she was rediscovered and hailed as a pioneer of the feminist movement. She was invited to debates and talks and gave lectures to the young women of the sixties' generation.

Retirement saw her busier than ever. Environmental protests and campaigns demanding nuclear disarmament. During the eighties, she was a regular outside Greenham Common or Sellafield power station.

There had been dalliances and romances along the way, but no mortal could come close to the monster she'd loved. Sometimes she thought she saw his face in a crowd, or a glimpse of him on the television screen.

When her health had started to deteriorate a decade ago, she had refused to move from her home into care. She had no desire for communal living. She had watched her friends die one by one. Books and the characters in their pages were the only company she wished to keep. She decided that she would die in her own bed and there were no family members to dissuade her.

Now, here at the end, she wasn't afraid. She'd had more than her fair share of life. At least she'd tried and wasn't that the best one could hope for? Each breath came in a ragged gasp, every heartbeat in an irregular tempo. The orchestra of her body was out of time with itself and stuttering to a halt.

A dark, familiar figure stood over her, silhouetted against the winter sun. 'Hello, Julia.'

Julia squinted against the light. 'Long time, no see. Is that it, then? It's all over? I didn't feel anything.'

Death perched on the end of the bed. 'Not quite. I wanted to meet you in person. Properly, if you see what I mean, before we got on to the formalities.'

Julia held a frail hand out, which Death took gently in his. 'Julia MacDonald,' she whispered.

'Good to meet you.'

A cough rattled around Julia's chest. 'Don't expect me to get up and put the kettle on.'

'How's it all been for you? Life?'

'I can't complain.'

'That's good to hear.'

'How's Christopher?'

Death shifted uneasily, the bed squeaking beneath him. 'I haven't seen him for a while. We went our separate ways some years ago.'

'The Four Horsemen of the Apocalypse have split up?'

'War and Famine died.'

Julia was surprised by her capacity to still be shocked at this late stage of life. 'I thought you were all immortal?'

Death chuckled bitterly. 'Not as immortal as we originally thought.' Julia tried to sit up, but Death rested a hand on her shoulder. 'Try and rest.'

'I don't think it makes much difference now, does it?' she replied. 'How did it happen?'

'We were stopping a nuclear missile from launching. They died saving the world.'

'You don't do things by halves, do you?' Julia said wistfully. 'Puts my banner waving to shame. I'll have to thank them when I see them.'

'Unfortunately, it doesn't work that way for us. They're gone for good. They gave their lives saving humanity and nobody will ever know. They'll always be the Horsemen of the Apocalypse. They'll always be feared. That doesn't seem very fair.'

'So you're all alone?' Julia asked, patting him on the wrist.

'Yes, but I'm getting back out there. I'm meeting new people.'

'Good. It's important to make friends. To keep busy.'

She closed her eyes. Small movements now. She could feel life slipping away from her, like grains of sand running through her fingers.

'Julia?' said Death.

'Yes?'

'By the end of it all humanity, generally, disappointed Conquest. But not you. He always followed your exploits with great interest and pride. I don't think he was trying to save the world. I think he was saving you.'

Julia MacDonald died with a smile on her lips.

TWENTY-FOUR

Dave gently picked Melanie up from the floor and, with her arm over his shoulders, helped her to walk.

'Where are we going?' she asked weakly.

'The toilets.'

She managed to muster up some indignation. 'I'm not going to die in a toilet.'

'You're not going to die,' Dave said.

Melanie dragged her feet, scuffing the carpet until Dave ground to a halt. 'Where do you want to go, then?'

'I always fancied one of the corner offices, actually.'

Dave gave an annoyed sigh and changed to direction. He helped Melanie to one of the large empty offices.

'I want to see the sun rise,' she whispered.

He dropped her into the leather seat behind the desk and turned it so she could take in the panoramic view. The dark river lazily snaked between the sleeping monolithic buildings yet to be stirred by the new day. Blue flashing lights in the streets below bounced off the steel and glass. Anne or Death must have got his message. Even with only a handful of vampires left, it would be a blood bath when the unsuspecting police reached them. He'd have to act quickly.

'Can I get you anything?' he asked Melanie.

Her eyes half closed, she shook her head almost imperceptibly. With fumbling fingers, she unclasped her necklace and placed it in Dave's hand. 'Give this to my mum and dad.'

He gave her a reassuring smile. 'I'll get you out of this. I promise.'

'Are you going to keep this one?' The corners of her lips rose in a smile.

Dave didn't answer. He stuffed the necklace into his jeans pocket and readjusted the fabric around her neck.

'Keep the pressure on this. I'll be back soon.'

'What are you going to do?'

Dave stroked his chin. 'Don't ask me. I'm making this up as I go along.'

Melanie placed a limp hand on his. 'You can kiss me if you like?'

He leaned forward and placed a gentle kiss on her cold lips, then pulled back suddenly. 'No biting!' he ordered.

'Spoilsport.'

Dave hobbled down the stairs for what seemed the hundredth time that night. His entire body complained. Every muscle ached and screamed at him to stop and rest. He told himself that, if he got out of this alive, he'd take a holiday. And ask for a pay rise. And maybe look into health insurance.

He reached the fifteenth floor, where it all began and where it would all end one way or another. He ran through the plan in his mind. It was terrible, but it was all he could come up with. He gripped the DIY cross tightly. His hands wouldn't stop shaking. Walking through the door in front of him was walking towards complete death. Death of the soul. Head straight to oblivion. Do not pass 'Go'. Do not collect two hundred pounds.

The office was as quiet as a tomb. The night's carnage had been cleared up as if nothing had happened. Dave slowly approached Kirsten's office. The door opened and she stepped out as if sensing his presence.

'You're full of surprises, Mr Marwood. I don't think your monthly performance review is going to go very well, though. Not exactly a team player, are you?'

Dave continued to walk past the empty banks of desks keeping the cross aimed directly at Kirsten. 'I like to think I work well using my own initiative.'

'You don't need that cross, Dave. I'm not a monster.'

'I think you'll find that's exactly what you are,' Dave replied.

'We're just like you,' Kirsten said. 'We work hard. We pay our taxes. My one vice is that I enjoy feasting on the blood of innocent office temps, but who doesn't have their little quirks and foibles?'

'Foibles?' said Dave with incredulity. 'How many people are dead because of you?'

'There are some productivity statistics that are best not dwelled on.'

Dave was getting closer and closer to Kirsten. It would be time to act soon, but he had some questions he needed answering first. 'How did you do it? How did you keep Death from the building?'

Kirsten eyed him quizzically. 'How did you know about that? Who are you?'

'Let's just say I'm an employee with some concerns about his work environment.'

He was around ten feet away from her now. Kirsten looked terribly ancient and monstrous under the harsh glare of the fluorescent light. The proximity of Dave's cross was causing her to sweat and shake as if a terrible sickness had infected her.

'It was like that when we got here. It came with the building along with the furniture and computers. We simply took advantage of the situation. We have a benefactor, shall we say?'

'Benefactor?' Dave repeated. The truth dawned on him. 'Are you talking about Conrad West? He knows about this?'

'My poor Dave. It was his idea. It's just business. We needed jobs and he needed people to work the night shift. An entirely practical arrangement and Conrad West is nothing if not a practical man.'

'So, if it's not for you, what's it for?'

Kirsten shook her head. 'Mr West has bigger plans, apparently.'

As Dave processed the information, Jason stepped out from the shadows to his right. Dave swore under his breath. He thought he was being so clever extracting information from Kirsten, but she was in fact stalling him so she could trap him.

'Clever girl,' Dave muttered.

'You can't hold both of us off with that relic,' Kirsten said with a satisfied smile.

Dave shook his head with a resigned sigh. 'No. You're probably right.'

He scratched the back of his head. Then he reached behind him and grabbed the plastic bottle of holy water he'd taped to his back. He squirted a jet of liquid into Jason's eyes. He hit the ground like he'd been shot, writhing around in agony.

With Dave's attention elsewhere, Kirsten covered the distance between them quickly. She slapped the bottle from his hand and grabbed him by the throat. He felt his feet kicking the air as she lifted him up off the ground.

'I really don't know what to do with you,' she said. 'I could happily tear your head from your spine, but I can't deny that you've got potential.'

'That's a popular misconception,' Dave squeaked. He could see stars and his vision began to darken as Kirsten squeezed the breath out of him.

She drew his face close to hers, admiring his features like a gourmand examining a piece of well-prepared meat. 'How about it, Dave? We can escape the dawn. I'll need a new team and a new team leader. Would you like the position?'

Kirsten bared her razor sharp teeth. Dave thrust his hand in his pocket and rummaged around. He wrapped his fingers around the gossamer thin chain and pulled Melanie's necklace out. As Kirsten opened her mouth wider, he rammed the silver cross and chain down her throat.

'You can take your job and shove it,' he spat.

Gagging, she released Dave and staggered back. She coughed and choked. Thick plumes of smoke billowed from her mouth as if her internal organs were on fire. She looked at Dave with incredulous eyes one last time before every cursed atom in her body violently escaped in all directions.

When the dust - and Kirsten - had settled, Dave picked his wrecked and battered body up from where he'd been dropped. He surveyed the blood-splattered office and let out a low groan.

He was going to have to find that sodding necklace.

TWENTY-FIVE

Melanie was curled up with her eyes closed in the chair where Dave had left her. She was bathed in the warm golden sunlight of the new morning. Dave checked that she was breathing and wasn't smouldering around the edges. Satisfied that she was alive and unlikely to burst into flames, he gently shook her awake. She fluttered and then opened her eyes. She stretched her limbs and saw the sun climbing behind the skyscrapers of London. She laughed and sobbed simultaneously in a sudden burst of overwhelming and conflicting emotions.

'Good morning,' Dave said softly.

'We made it?' she asked in barely a whisper.

Dave nodded. She stroked his bruised and bloody face. 'Are you okay?'

His heart swelled to bursting at her touch. 'Tough shift at work,' he said. 'I'm knocking off early. Do you want to do something?'

She smiled. 'I'd like that.'

'I've got something of yours.' He pulled the necklace from his pocket and placed it in Melanie's hand.

'Thanks for looking after it.'

'No problem,' said Dave. 'You might want to give it a rinse under a tap.'

Melanie and Dave were hurried away in an ambulance as soon as they'd staggered out of the building. Dave refused treatment until the paramedics had seen to Melanie and confirmed that she would be fine. Now, as she slept in a hospital bed, it was his turn to keep a vigil at her bedside as she had for him.

Death casually wandered through the wall. 'Hello. I was just down the corridor. I thought I'd pop in.'

Dave looked up from the rack of machines monitoring Melanie's life signs. 'Oh, hi.'

'Is she going to be okay?'

'Yeah,' Dave replied. 'She's lost a lot of blood, but she'll be alright. Her parents are on their way down. It looks like I'll get to meet them after all.'

Death placed a hand on Dave's shoulder. 'And how are you?'

'I don't know yet. Numb.'

Death cleared his throat. 'I'm sorry for... Well, I'm just sorry.'

'You know something has gone terribly wrong in your life when Death is apologising to you.'

'Are there any biscuits?' Death asked.

Dave waved in the direction of the bedside table. 'The nurse left a snack box. I think there might be some in there.'

Death rummaged through the small cardboard box. 'Urgh. Rich Tea. Has there ever been a more disappointing snack food? It must've been like when Dylan went electric when they introduced the chocolate Hob Nob.'

'I know who's responsible for keeping you out of the UberSystems building,' said Dave.

Death sat at the end of the bed and flicked through a celebrity magazine. 'Who?'

'Conrad West.'

Death looked up from the magazine and shrugged his shoulders. 'Should I know who he is?'

'My old boss.' Dave held his hand out. 'Give me your phone. Mine's still drying out.'

Death gave his phone to Dave who pulled up a picture of West on its browser. He passed it back. Death looked at the screen and then back at Dave.

'This is Conrad West?' Death asked.

'Yes.'

Death sighed. 'I know him.'

TWENTY-SIX

Conrad West watched the rolling news from his Parisian hotel suite while he waited for his car to take him to the airport. Footage of Dave Marwood with his arms around a young woman wrapped in blankets being led out of the UberSystems International building looped every fifteen minutes.

He turned the television off. It looked like Kirsten's little project had failed. The UberSystems International PR machine had already rumbled into motion. How would he spin this unwanted publicity? A terrorist atrocity? An unbalanced, disgruntled employee? Where could the money be thrown to make the problem go away?

He sat down on the sofa and picked up his iPad. He clicked on a link tucked away at the bottom of the news website's landing page. He steeled himself and read about the life of Julia MacDonald. A life from which he had been wiped clean. When he finished, he wiped a tear from his eye. He knew that this day would come, as it would for everybody he had known, but still it crushed him. For humans it was relatively simple. They would meet someone and think 'Yep, you'll do. I want to spend the rest of my life with you. I don't need to look around anymore.' It was not that easy for him. Their time together had been as brief as the flap of a butterfly's wing, but the consequences had rippled and grown until they were a storm in his heart.

Conrad took a scratched and beaten pocket watch from his waistcoat; a gift from three old friends, crafted by Patek Philippe & Company in 1933. Back when he was somebody else. He had been known by many identities over the years, but he had only one true name.

He had seen the best that humanity could do, but he had also witnessed them at their worst and now he despised them for it. Their hatred. Their cowardice. Their stupidity. The Billy Joel album, "An Innocent Man".

Especially the Billy Joel album, "An Innocent Man".

When he had left Death behind on that hill, he'd returned home. He understood who he really was. He had realised his true purpose. He knew what had to be done. He'd unpicked his financial affairs and then stitched them back together so that there was no trace of his previous lives. He took a new name, Conrad Q. West (a poor joke), and became the darling of the finance industry. Corporations became the new superpowers.

He built an empire on which the sun never set. Not with swords or gunfire, but with ones and zeros, secrets and guile. You couldn't change the world with grand gestures. It had to be in tiny increments.

But his plan had not been without fault. He had realised too late the usefulness of the Marwood boy. He'd slipped through his fingers and had taken his place at Death's side. He would not make that mistake again. He would have to watch them all carefully. You never succeeded in business by underestimating the competition.

Now that Julia was gone, nothing remained of his old lives. He would return to his tower where Death could not touch him. He would give humanity what they craved. The Dark was coming. Soon, it would be time for his glorious rule.

He was waiting. He was good at that.

He muttered three little words.

'I. Am. Conquest.'

OLD HAUNTS

ONE

11 April 1986

It was a sign. A messenger from the Gods.

Halley's Comet was a smudge against the infinite black that stretched above Nathan Christou. It was closer to Earth now than it would be for almost a century and he felt he could pluck it from the sky with one hand and hide it in his pocket.

Like his great-uncle Archibald before him, Nathan had learned to interpret the messages passed down to all of humanity but heard by only a special few. This comet was the final dispatch. Goodbye from the universe.

Ten years earlier, he'd been a different man. He'd worshipped only money and craved only the wanton pleasures of the flesh. His excesses had taken their toll and one day his bloated, sin-filled heart failed him as he himself had failed so many. The doctors told him he had died for several minutes and the news left him distraught. There had been no light, no peace, no ever-loving God. He'd been alone in a single moment that could have easily turned into forever.

In the months that followed Nathan retreated to the family home; one of the few assets that hadn't been stripped bare and that remained in the Christou name. There he found Archibald's journals.

Archibald had been the black sheep of the family, dabbling in the occult before he'd had some kind of epiphany and dedicated the rest of his life to charitable works. His diaries had documented his attempts to bring about the end of the world and his reasons for doing so. He even claimed to have summoned the Four Horsemen of the Apocalypse who were, by his account, jolly nice fellows. In those pages, Nathan had found a persuasive argument.

He, too, saw the omens all around. The Earth was due a reaping. He would be the herald of its destruction and his belief would be rewarded. He would not succumb to the cowardice and mediocrity that had stopped Archibald.

Bringing about the end of the world took longer and more effort than he'd thought. His rituals didn't work and his sermons fell on deaf ears. If people needed to hear about the Apocalypse, they wanted the words to come from someone with more charisma.

Nathan's life changed when his Master entered his life.

Nathan didn't know where he came from, but he knew where they were going together. The Master performed miracles and spoke the truth and, in time, people listened. Soon they followed. They gave up their material possessions. There would soon be no need for them. They would be the pioneers; brave travellers setting off to an undiscovered country. The New Righteous Order of Armageddon moved into a disused warehouse in the docklands of London; a derelict land left behind by the march of progress. It was a fitting location for their ascension.

Now, Nathan looked for the last time upon the river and the city that had grown unchallenged along its banks like a virus. He smoothed his black trousers and white shirt. He was ready to leave. He would not miss this world. He turned his back on it and went into the warehouse.

The nineteen other Chosen were waiting for him in contemplative silence. They were all dressed in the same style as Nathan. Uniform and devoid of individuality as was humanity's proper station. Their Master stepped forward and took Nathan's hands in his. 'Brother Nathan. He who took the first steps along this seldom-travelled road. I trust you have said your goodbyes to this mortal realm?'

Nathan nodded, unable to speak. The Master turned to face the others. 'Then it is time.'

Twenty mats had been laid out in four equal rows on the vast empty floor. Next to each stood a small beaker containing a clear liquid. Everybody took their designated place in front of a mat and picked up their drinks. They stood with their heads bowed solemnly.

'Humanity is dead,' the Master told them. 'Like a cockroach with its head ripped off it crawls along on its belly, driven by instinct, too foolish to know it is doomed. It is no surprise. You have been sick for aeons. That sickness is freedom. You have no idea how to deal with it; like a baby with a gun. Take Jesus, your lord and saviour, for example. The first time someone comes along and suggests that maybe you shouldn't hurt each other and what do you do? You nail him to a big plank of wood. This is why you can't have nice things.

'You, to me, are prophets. I have made you no promises, but I make you this promise now. I will protect you from Death. He will not enter our home. You shall live forever. Now you will sleep and dream. When you wake, you will be the first to feel the joy of the new day's sunlight warm your soul, but the dream will not end. Let us drink.'

And, with that, twenty believers swallowed a cocktail of poisons and lay down. They crossed their arms over their chests. They were at peace with themselves and soon they would be at peace with the world. It had all been so easy.

Conquest, their master, pitied their foolishness.

TWO

Dave Marwood stood at the window of UberSystems International's empty boardroom. He placed his hands on the glass and basked in the warmth of the sun beating down from a sky painted pure blue by the steady hand of nature. Far beneath him, bodies and metal moved through the streets performing a precisely choreographed dance, oblivious to the audience of one gazing down. A shadow passed overhead and settled above the building. It flowed down the glass and steel, slick like liquid, and spread when it reached the ground. It flooded London with darkness, spilling over the tallest skyscrapers and outwards across the green parks, until it consumed the city in an unnatural night. Dave looked to the sky to find the sun was a flat black disc: a hole punched through the fabric of stars.

He felt a hand on his shoulder. He turned his head to find Death, hooded and silent, at his side. A creature so ancient and powerful his name was feared before humanity could even speak. A creature Dave called a friend.

'And the sun became black as sackcloth,' Death said, 'and the moon became as blood and the stars of heaven fell unto the earth and-- Shit! The bins!' Death slapped his forehead. 'I knew there was something I had to do.'

'What's happening?' Dave asked, nodding towards the black horizon. 'Why are we here?'

Death shrugged and took a bite of a chocolate-covered biscuit. 'I dunno. It's your dream.'

'Where'd you get the biscuit?'

'Again. Your. Dream.' Death repeated slowly.

Dave looked in his hand to find a biscuit already there and took a bite. 'Awesome,' he said, spraying crumbs over the thick carpet. 'What are you doing here, then?'

Death had a cup of tea now. 'I'm not here. I'm simply a representation of me produced by your own subconscious. I generally try not to poke around in the heads of twenty-six year old men. One time I did that I had to take a very, very long shower.'

'Some people say that dreams are visions. That some can predict the future or see into the past.'

'Yeah, well, some people say that a Rich Tea is a good biscuit. People are stupid.'

Dave was about to say something when he heard a noise in the distance; a low rumble felt as much as heard. It gradually increased in volume, a bass note from the soundtrack of Hell. The horizon had vanished, obscured by thick dust, and Dave realised that buildings were tumbling in waves. A chasm stretching as far as he could see was growing, rushing towards him. Offices, shops, houses, lives were sucked down into the black abyss as the city ate itself.

As the ground hundreds of feet below buckled and groaned, the window in front of Dave shattered under the stress, forming spiderwebs as sharp as knives. He turned to Death, who lowered his hood to reveal the face of Melanie, Dave's girlfriend.

'The Dark is coming,' she said with a voice that was not her own.

The wall of dirt and rock smashed into the windows, throwing razor sharp shards of glass into the board-room, slashing and stabbing at Dave and--

Dave woke with a moan; a pale imitation of the scream he left behind, rattling around his subconscious. He untangled himself from the duvet and sat on the edge of the empty bed, head in his hands. The night-mares of his childhood had returned, made worse with the knowledge that monsters were no longer found only in dreams.

It had been a week since two-dozen people lost their lives in UberSystems Tower. Seven days since Dave had found out that his ex-employer, Conrad West, was an ex-Horseman of the Apocalypse. Melanie was still in the hospital recovering from the injuries she'd sustained on that tragic night and Dave was wracked with guilt that he'd escaped the bloody madness relatively unscathed.

The story had already slipped from the front pages. UberSystems International's lawyers had descended on the publishers with the fury of particularly litigious Gods. All the footage from the building's security cameras from that night had mysteriously, and conveniently, been lost. When the police interviewed Dave and Melanie they both described how they'd locked themselves in a corner office the moment the carnage had begun. They couldn't explain how several of the victims' bodies had exploded, nor why at least five of the dead had been living under false identities. Dave choked back a sob as he remembered how many had died by his hand.

He did what he always did now when he began to think too much. He scrabbled around on his bedroom floor and located his tee shirt, shorts and trainers. He pulled them on and let himself out of the flat.

The early morning air was already heavy with heat. Unseasonable warmth had settled on London, baffling the Met Office and creating a topic for millions of idle conversations. The city was still half asleep and irritable after another stifling night during which sleep came only in fractured moments.

Since fighting for his life in UberSystems Tower, Dave had been drawn to the dawn streets to run mile after mile, trying to put as much distance between himself and his nightmares. He'd always been of the opinion that if humans were meant to run nature wouldn't have made all the hurty bits jiggle so much, but he found peace on the empty streets. The crisp early morning light helped him momentarily forget that there was a darkness growing in the heart of UberSystems International; a darkness that he would soon have to head back into. At best, there were some unethical business practices carried out in the building; at worst, something evil was waiting for its time to emerge.

Anne had told Dave to take as much time as he needed to recover and recuperate but he'd decided that tomorrow he would head back to Crow Road. A ghost of his earlier dream floated up and he wondered what Death had planned for his old friend Conquest.

He ran on, letting the twisted London roads guide him until he staggered to a halt. Breathing hard, his hands on his knees, he sucked air into his burning lungs. He looked around and found himself in an affluent residential street he didn't recognise. A young couple, walking home from the night before, argued on a corner. A middle-aged man cursed his dog for not relieving himself on a neighbour's lawn fast enough.

Dave could sense the same festering anger he'd felt a week before in the reception of UberSystems Tower. The same directionless rage the dead had told him was approaching was now right here among the Audis and shrubbery.

He turned and ran home as fast as he could.

Dave bravely took on the Quantum Shower of Doom and, to gather himself afterwards, decided to make a cup of coffee. The kitchen resembled the aftermath of a particularly brutal snack-based military campaign. He gingerly picked his way through the dirty crockery until he found a mug he could rinse under the tap and drink from with minimal risk of contracting a serious illness.

'I say we nuke the site from orbit. It's the only way to be sure,' Gary said from the doorway.

They had barely seen each other since Dave had returned from the hospital a week earlier. There had only been awkward inquiries and offers of support before Gary would disappear into his bedroom for the rest of the evening.

'Hi,' Dave replied stiffly.

Gary scuffed the carpet with his feet in an overly casual manner and avoided Dave's gaze. 'So, I was thinking about replacing the shower.'

'The Quantum Shower of Doom?' Dave replied. 'That's a pretty big undertaking. There'll have to be some kind of ceremony to cleanse the evil spirits.'

Gary failed to hide a small smile. 'You're probably right.'

Dave sipped his coffee in the uncomfortable silence. 'Everything alright?'

'Yeah. Fine. Why?'

'I get the feeling you've been avoiding me.'

'Well, I didn't know if you needed space after, y'know,' Gary said. 'You seemed pretty freaked out the first couple of days. Then there were all the news reports about what went on in there. And I was worried you might want to talk about your feelings or something, like when you wrote all that poetry when Melanie and you went through that rough patch. What was that one you wrote?

"Roses are red,

Foxgloves are purple,

I appear to have trapped myself,

In a linguistic corner".'

Dave burst out laughing. 'I'm really alright. Melanie's coming out of hospital today, I'm going back to work tomorrow. It's all good.'

Gary thought for a moment. They both knew there was only one way for him to make amends for his behaviour. 'Do you want to go out for a pint tomorrow night?'

'A pint would be fantastic.' Dave looked at his watch. 'I better get to the hospital.'

He headed out of the kitchen, but Gary put a hand on his shoulder. 'What really happened that night?'

Dave looked his friend square in the eyes. 'Vampires, Gary. Shitloads of vampires.'

Gary roared with laughter. 'Very funny. Now get out of here.'

THREE

As usual, Dave arrived at the hospital too early so sat in a quiet corner of the coffee shop waiting for visiting hours. Around him, tired members of staff in scrubs were making small talk as they took a break from their good work. Worried patients wrapped up in dressing gowns stared into their drinks as if they could divine the future from the formations of chocolate sprinkles.

Unseen by all of them, the dead drifted silently; those that had made the journey to this place but had never left. They cast no shadow in the low morning sun and Dave spotted them easily. An old man in a frayed dressing gown peered unnoticed over the shoulder of a doctor reading the football scores on the back page of a newspaper. When the doctor turned the paper over, the ghost gave an annoyed grunt and waddled off to see if he could find the rest of the results elsewhere. Football wasn't a matter of life or death; it was more important than that, and here was the evidence. Other figures stood on the periphery of conversations, eavesdropping on life. They smiled at jokes they couldn't reply to and heard problems to which they could offer no solution. The sadness hung thick in the air with the smell of ground coffee; a pain that wasn't caused by physical injuries.

Beneath the heartache, Dave could feel a familiar quiet rage tugging at him like an insistent and unruly child. He settled into the hard plastic chair. He exhaled slowly and the secret part of his mind opened like a flower in bloom. The darkness was all around him. It both clung to the coffee shop's customers like grime and rose like black steam. It swirled around table legs and drifted over Dave's body. It was cold and smothering, like suffocating in winter fog. Unbidden thoughts of his parents, and how they'd died in a place like this, filled his head. He resented them for dying and for not giving him a brother or sister with whom he could share the burden of grief. His eyes stung as the tears he never shed all those years ago formed. He was slipping under the surface of a calm black sea. If he didn't do something, he knew he'd be drowning in the Dark forever.

He wrapped his fingers limply around the handle of a fork that had been left by the table's previous occupant. With effort, he dragged it from the tabletop. It slipped in his sweaty palm. Tightening his grip, he stabbed the prongs into the meat of his thigh. The pain was a lifeline that guided him out of the darkness. He gasped as the fork fell from his grasp and he broke through into the light.

He slumped in the chair, his head spinning. A quarrelling middle-aged couple sat down at the table next to him. As a shadowless figure passed them by, the woman stopped mid-sentence, shivered and said, 'Ooh. It's like someone just walked over my grave.' Her hand flew to her mouth. 'Oh, bloody hell. I shouldn't say stuff like that here.'

Dave explored the hospital. He drifted down wide white corridors and through busy waiting areas. He sometimes wondered whether delaying patients' appointments was a recognised medical technique. Whatever diagnosis the doctor gave you couldn't be as bad as at least seven possible terrible scenarios you'd come up with yourself if left alone long enough with only old copies of "Take a Break" to read. Morbid curiosity made him peer into every room he passed. He saw consultations, worried faces and caring hands placed on heaving shoulders.

While he wandered the building, he tried to process what had happened to him in the coffee shop. The Dark crushed the heart like unrequited love but was as insubstantial as morning mist. It whispered to you, reminding you of every dirty little secret. It played back every terrible memory. A Netflix for every embarrassing moment you'd lived through and every angry thought you'd regretted. It was spreading across the city, afflicting both the living and the dead. Dave could see it on the streets and in the shadows with every petty squabble and each cross word between strangers. He was sure West was responsible, but where did it come from and what purpose did it serve?

Soon he found he'd arrived at Melanie's door. Dressed in jeans and tee shirt, she sat cross-legged on the large bed. An overnight bag was on the single chair in the room. She was ready to leave. She didn't notice him as her attention was focussed on the phone in her hand. Her thumb expertly flicked the screen as she scrolled the page she was reading.

Dave took the moment to drink her in. They'd experienced the usual problems of any new relationship. Misunderstandings. Doubts. Exorcisms. Vampire attacks. They'd made it through the other side and he knew they couldn't lose each other again. They'd come too close too many times and the scars they both carried would be a reminder of that.

He knocked on the door and Melanie looked up from the phone's screen. She smiled when she saw him. 'I've been stuck in here for a week with only social network sites for company and do you know what I think?'

Dave crossed the room and kissed her gently on the top of her head. He moved the bag from the chair and sat down. 'No, what do you think?'

'Very little social networking goes on. The majority of people just complain about things. Or complain about people complaining about things. Or complain about people complaining about the complainer and how the complainer is oppressing the original complainer's right to complain about things. And share pictures of cats in people clothes.'

Dave was content to say nothing and simply listen to her. It was a relief that so much life and energy coursed through her body when she'd come close to losing it. It was easy to forget the monsters and the fear when it was just the two of them like this.

'I've had an idea for the perfect site,' she said. 'Everyone's doing start-ups now, aren't they? I'm going to call it Howls of Impotent Rage dot com. You don't tweet or update or anything. You "scream into the ether" from your Procrastination Station. All the text is in Comic Sans just to get the bile rising the second you load up your account.'

'You'll make millions,' Dave said as, despite himself, he watched the spirit of an old lady float down the corridor.

Melanie noticed his distraction, his gaze towards a seemingly empty space. 'Is there one here now?'

Dave's attention snapped back to her. 'Yeah.'

Melanie leaned forward, inquisitive. 'What does it look like?'

Dave shrugged. 'Like a standard issue old lady.'

'So how can you tell who's alive and who's dead?'

'You pick it up as you go along. Little things. They don't cast shadows for one thing. And you can walk right through them. But that one is a last resort as, if you get it wrong, the living aren't keen on you bumping into them.'

Melanie shook her head. Her hand moved instinctively to the cross around her neck. 'I just don't get how this is even possible.'

Dave felt a mixture of awkwardness and relief when he talked to Melanie about his talents; confiding a long, bottled-up, dark secret to an understanding lover. 'Anne has a theory. She went for an MRI scan a couple of years ago. Do you know what the thalamus is?'

Melanie shrugged. 'It goes well with taramasalata?'

'It's part of the brain. Information about the world around us is collected by our senses, right? But all that abstract sound and light needs to be turned into understandable and useful information so you can deal with your surroundings. So it's all sent to specialised parts of the brain for processing. Visual information travels to the visual cortex, what you hear goes to the auditory cortex and so on. The thalamus acts like a gatekeeper. It decides what data will be filtered through, prioritises that information and weeds out irrelevant stuff so that your brain isn't overloaded and doesn't dribble out of your ears.'

Melanie nodded, beginning to understand. 'And yours is different?'

'It appears to be working much more efficiently. My perception of the world is different to others.'

'So you see things other people don't?'

'Exactly.'

Melanie thought for a moment. 'If it's something biological, is there anything they could give you? Drugs or something? If your brain is like a radio receiver that's stuck between stations you just might need the right medication to change the frequency so you tune out the random signals from other worlds and only pick up Radio This Plane of Existence? If you wanted to, of course.'

'Maybe,' Dave said. 'It's all about the dopamine and serotonin levels or something.'

'Is it hereditary?'

'I don't know. My parents never mentioned anything and you'd think it would be something they'd bring up. I'd be worried that any kids I'd have might have it.'

The implications of that statement hung awkwardly in the air between Dave and Melanie when the doctor arrived. He looked tired, with heavy bags under his eyes and grey greasy skin. He fell into a chair as if it was the first time he'd sat down all day.

'Ready to go home?' he asked Melanie.

Melanie was discharged soon after. Dave offered to book an Uber, but she insisted on taking public transport.

'I've been stuck in that place for a week,' she said. 'I want to stretch my legs. And maybe get some Chinese food.'

They walked to the Underground station, taking baby steps so as to not upset Melanie's patchwork of medical treatments. At the entrance, Dave watched a man trip over a suitcase being wheeled behind another. Instead of both of them awkwardly apologising, which would be the usual course of action, they both squared up to each other with accusations about their respective mothers and threats of violence.

Once they were on the train, the atmosphere didn't improve. The air was heavy with sweat and menace, crackling with the same tension Dave had felt in the hospital a few hours earlier. A man standing next to him was quietly sobbing to himself. Further down the carriage, an expensively dressed elderly man was discussing the relative merits of music with a teenager and what he would do with the iPod if the younger man didn't turn the volume down.

Dave leaned into Melanie. 'Do you fancy getting a coffee?'

Melanie smiled, feigning casualness. 'Yeah, it's a lovely day. Let's get off at the next stop.'

Melanie had already started crunching away on the bag of prawn crackers when they arrived at her flat, a trail of crumbs left on the laminate flooring of her bedroom. They curled up on the bed together eating takeaway and watching bad television. Whenever Dave stayed over at Melanie's, he was reminded that furniture wasn't supposed to crunch or snap when you sat on it.

'Do you want a cup of tea?' Melanie asked, getting up.

Dave placed a hand gently on her shoulder. 'I'll do it.'

He left Melanie on the bed, crossed the flat's hallway and went to the kitchen. Nobody who lived here was trying to play Bin Jenga and balance the rubbish as high as they could before it collapsed on the floor. He switched the kettle on and opened and closed the cupboard doors looking for mugs.

'It's the one on your right,' said a woman's voice behind him. He turned around. It was Emma, Melanie's friend and housemate, wearing a dressing gown in the kitchen doorway.

'Thanks,' he said, taking two mugs from the cupboard. The kettle clicked off. 'Do you want one?'

'No,' she replied. 'So you're back then?'

Dave poured hot water onto the teabags in the cups. 'We've worked things out. She asked me to stay over tonight. She's still in some pain.'

'Her knight in shining armour. Touching.' She didn't even try to hide the disdain.

Dave looked around for somewhere to put the dirty teaspoon, like it was a grenade about to go off in his hand.

Emma sighed loudly. Dave had learned that she had two hundred and seventy-six sighs covering the entire emotional range. 'Just put it in the sink.'

He did as he was told and grabbed the mugs. As he was passing Emma, she placed a hand on his arm and squeezed with just the right amount of pressure. 'You hurt her and I will kill you.'

'I'll keep that in mind,' Dave said. Pulling his arm free from her grip, he scurried back to Melanie's room.

'Has Emma always been that intense?' he asked.

'She's always been pretty highly-strung, yeah,' Melanie replied as she took one of the cups from him.

Dave sat back down on bed. He thought about telling her about the dark forces he'd been feeling around him, but decided there would be plenty of time for that. Right now, he was happy to just be with her. There was nobody he'd rather lie next to in bed while they both stared at their phones.

FOUR

Conquest had not been this close to Julia McDonald in over eight decades. She lay six feet beneath him, her coffin covered with sun-warmed soil and marked with a simple cross. The funeral had ended several hours earlier, the mourners had left for the wake and he stood alone by the old oak tree under which she had been buried. Once he had read of her death the week before, he'd anonymously made some phone calls and pulled some strings at the council to secure the most fitting location in the cemetery. She would've appreciated that she would feed the tree as her body broke down and returned to the soil. She so hated waste.

He placed the flowers he'd brought with him on the mound of earth. He rubbed his eyes beneath the sunglasses. He was so very tired. Part of him wished he could crawl beneath the grass and sleep alongside her forever.

A breeze sprang up, stroking the oak leaves above his head with a sound like waves rolling onto the shore. He closed his eyes and thought back to a time he and Julia had stood on the beach letting the sea wash over their feet almost a century ago.

A century. More than a lifetime for most people, but a blink of an eye for Conquest. He could barely comprehend how anybody could get anything worthwhile done in the infinitesimally short time they had on this planet. He regarded humans now as he would mayflies: they were dragged into this world kicking and screaming and had just enough time to make more of themselves before they died impossibly quickly. Sometimes kicking and screaming. Sometimes they never stopped the entire time they were alive.

In spite of their limitations, he felt humans could be great. His attempts to help them before had fallen on deaf ears, but there were other methods. They just needed to be led by a firm guiding hand; one that was careful to reward and punish in simple ways they understood.

He suddenly felt self-conscious. He could feel someone prying on his grief. He looked over his shoulder to see a familiar shadow standing in the distance. The moment he saw it, it slipped through a puncture in the universe and was gone.

Death was following him.

FIVE

Seventeen Years Earlier

Dave sat cross-legged, playing with his Star Wars figures on the carpet of his empty bedroom. Now that the room had been cleared of furniture, it seemed much larger. Large enough for Emily to skip around him in a circle, the hem of her summer dress bouncing around her knees. She always wore that same dress, even during the coldest winters. She span around. Dave didn't know why. She was a girl. They did stuff like that. He didn't understand girls. He was pretty sure he never would. They were weird. Anyway, he wished she wouldn't do any of that twirly stuff as it was distracting him from his attempts to educate her.

'This is Boba Fett.' His voice bounced off the blank walls. He's a bounty hunter."

Emily stopped mid-pirouette and her dress floated down to rest. 'What's a bounty hunter?'

'I don't know.' Dave shrugged. 'It sounds cool, though. It probably involves chocolate.'

'I'm bored. Let's play a game. And not with your stupid figures.'

'They're not stupid. Anyway, mum and dad have put away all the other toys in the lorry.'

Today was moving day. They were going to a new home. A better home, his parents had told him. He hadn't really talked to Emily about it. Every time he tried, he felt nervous and sick. He knew that she couldn't come with them. He wasn't bothered about his classmates, but the thought of not seeing her again made his belly feel like it stretched down to his toes. She was his best friend, though he'd never tell a girl that. She'd always been in Dave's life, for as long as he could remember. She was part of the fabric of his home. She came and went as she pleased, but she was always there when the bad dreams woke him. Now he was abandoning her.

'Let's play hide-and-seek,' Emily suggested.

'You always win and there's nowhere to hide.'

Emily span around again. Though the sun was shining brightly that morning, no shadow span around with her.

'I can always find places.' She balanced on her toes. 'You're not coming back, are you?'

Dave hung his head. 'Dad's got a new job. We have to go where the work is, he says.'

'Work sounds rubbish.'

Dave agreed, but he tried to sound enthusiastic. 'There'll be a new family. There'll be other kids to play with.'

'I don't want to play with them. I want to play with you.'

Dave hoped that she wouldn't start crying. 'I'll come and visit.'

'No you won't.'

'I'll run away if I have to.'

She looked cross. 'Don't do that. You'll get in trouble.'

'Dabbie!' his mother voice called from the bottom of the stairs. He hated it when she called him that. When he was a toddler, he'd had trouble saying his own name and the mispronunciation had stuck. He was nine years old now, not a babbling infant. Why couldn't she see that?

Emily looked sad now. It was a constant wonder to Dave how quickly girls' moods could swing from one extreme to another. He was amazed they didn't get dizzy. It was probably all the twirling they did. It was practice. He wanted to take her hand, but he knew that he couldn't. He remembered the time last year when he'd tried to hold Lucinda Maxwell's hand in assembly and she'd screamed so loudly he almost wet himself right there in the school hall. Girls needed some kind of warning if you were going to try something like that.

Instead, he uncrossed his legs and felt the pins and needles dance agonisingly along their length. He stood up and stretched to his full height, which wasn't that great. He fumbled in his jeans pocket and pulled out a small, battered stuffed rabbit. He'd won it out of a grabber machine on holiday a couple of summers ago. He'd kept it hidden; boys his age didn't admit to owning cuddly toys, but it had been a reminder of one of the few small victories in his young life. He didn't know what to say so he placed it on the floor between him and Emily. He knew that girls liked gestures.

'I've got to go.'

'Go then. I don't care.' Her bottom lip jutted out in a display of petulance. Dave turned and left the room. He hadn't wanted it to end like this. He closed the door behind him for the last time and headed down the stairs.

His mother was waiting for him in the hallway. She watched him descend with her kind eyes.

'The neighbours won't miss you thudding down the stairs. It's like a herd of elephants.' She ruffled his hair playfully. As he smoothed it back down, he noticed the dark square patches on the barren wall where the photos had hung; a comic strip depicting his childhood. It was then that he was struck by the finality of it all. Their lives as a family had been sealed up and transplanted elsewhere, away from everything he knew.

Through the front door, Dave watched as his father struggled to put the last boxes into the boot of the car. His face was screwed up in thought as he dealt with the logistics of the task. Dave was pretty sure he mouthed a rude word. Realising he was being watched, dad looked up and waved. Mum went out to help him. Working together, they pulled boxes out and squeezed them back in. They slammed the boot lid down with a triumphant thunk.

His parents were all right, he guessed. They were still together, at least. They still hugged and kissed (bleurgh!). It was different for a lot of kids at school. Mark Davies hadn't even met his dad. He claimed that his mum had told him it was that bloke off the telly, but Finn Hodges reckoned that was bollocks.

His parents came back in to do a final check of the rooms. Dave told his parents that he'd cleared his bedroom of his possessions and that there was no need to go back in there. The front door was closed and the keys dropped through the letterbox.

'Goodbye, house.' His mum patted the brickwork. The three of them stood on the porch as if unsure of what the next step should be.

Mrs Van Dresch was waiting for them at the end of the drive. She was a small woman of indeterminate age and nationality. Dave was still at the age where time could be divided into two categories: everything that happened before he was born and everything that happened afterwards. Whether it was dinosaurs walking the Earth, the Second World War, or his fifth birthday, all events were neatly partitioned. Mrs Van Dresch had moved to this country very firmly at some point in the first period.

'You go without goodbye?' she asked, her arms folded in mock annoyance.

'Of course not, Elena,' his father replied. They walked to where she stood. His father shook her hand gently, as if worried it would snap off at the wrist.

'Thanks for everything. Look after yourself. Don't scare off the new people,' he said.

'Me? Never. I am sweetness and light.' She smiled as his mother wrapped her in one of her enveloping hugs that Dave was all too familiar with.

'Goodbye Elena. Stay in touch. You've got our new address.'

Finally, Mrs Van Dresch turned to Dave. The difference in height between the two was slight and she didn't have to bend over too much to bring her face level with his.

'And you, Dabbie. Do great things.' She put her arms around him and he felt like he was bound in wire. She smelt of old person. He squirmed out of her surprisingly strong grip.

'I'll try.'

'You ready, kiddo?' his dad asked, ruffling Dave's hair. He really wished they'd stop doing that. Mrs Van Dresch returned to her front lawn and the Marwoods climbed into the car. With his parents in the front seats, Dave squeezed between boxes marked 'KITCHEN' and 'BATHROOM' in the back. He looked up to his bedroom. Emily was staring back from the window with the saddest expression that Dave had ever seen. He waved half-heartedly with a limp hand. He father saw this in the rear-view mirror and turned awkwardly to his son.

'Who are you waving to?' he asked.

'Emily.'

He saw his parents share a concerned glance. 'Isn't she coming with us?' his mum asked with a soft voice.

Dave looked down. 'No. She's stuck here.'

He kept his eyes fixed on the floor of the car until they reached the end of the road and were out of sight of the house, and Emily.

SIX

As Dave and Melanie slept and the city slipped into darkness, the world continued to spin. While the Western hemisphere rested, billions awoke and continued where they left off. Friendships were forged, lovers parted and life staggered onwards towards its unknown destination.

London reset itself, switching off and back on again in the hope that maybe it'd get things right this time. The sun dragged itself back up over the horizon like it was a bad idea and lazily spilled its photons, which spread over the concrete and steel and tumbled into Anne Mitchell's bedroom. She shifted beneath the duvet and felt the reassuring weight of Schrodinger, her cat, at the foot of the bed.

She rose, showered and dressed. With her long skirts, home-made jewellery and black cat, the kids who lived at the end of the hallway were convinced she was a witch with a broomstick hidden in her cupboard. To be fair, a broomstick would've been a convenient mode of transport when London's infrastructure imploded on a seemingly weekly basis.

She left the bedroom and crossed the living room to the kitchen. Her flat was immaculate. Everything was at right angles; sharp points and corners aligned, uncluttered and precise. She found the clean lines soothed her and cleared her mind of the noise of the dead. Reminders and recipes were pinned to the kitchen wall, including Death's instructions on how to recreate the Big Bang:

- 1 Bottle of Diet Coke
- 1 Packet of Mentos
- 1 Rubber Band
- 1 Particle Accelerator
- 1 Excitable Puppy

After feeding Schrodinger, she left for work. That morning, she decided to take the Underground. Lives brushed against each other, intersecting and spinning off in their own orbits, travelling down to the concrete and steel of the Square Mile, across to the ragged charm of Camden and over to the capitalist shrine of Oxford Street. The Underground's pre-programmed public address system announced every stop with such automated joy you'd believe that each one was a gateway to Narnia.

When she moved with the flow of the crowds, she felt that she was part of something bigger than herself. She had lived in London her whole life and thought of the city as some living, breathing creature in a symbiotic relationship with its inhabitants. It offered them a home and protection and it was their job to keep it alive with ideas and creativity. As they all travelled through the arteries of the beast, they were spreading the oxygen of humanity, making it glow and shine from within. She wondered from time to time whether she over-romanticised her relationship with the city, but then told herself that she deserved a bit of bloody romance in her life even if it was with a 1,200,000,000,000,000,000 tonne conurbation with halitosis, a bad attitude and serious commitment issues.

She arrived at the office on Crow Road to find Dave sat at his desk reading the newspaper. He was pushing a chocolate bar through the middle of a ring doughnut so the result looked like an artery-hardening spinning top. He took a bite and moaned with pleasure.

Anne wrinkled her nose in disgust. 'That is horrible.'

'Don't knock it. I've only been back ten minutes and I've already doubled my productivity,' Dave replied. 'Besides, I've been running this morning and need the calories.'

'How are you doing?'

Dave smiled. 'All the better for you asking.'

'How's Melanie?'

Dave's smile grew tighter. 'As well as can be expected.'

Melanie shared the burden of Dave's guilt. If she'd believed what he'd said, how many deaths could've been avoided? But Anne had learned from an early age that you couldn't second-guess your way through life. She nodded towards Death's office door. 'Is he in?'

Dave shrugged. 'I've not heard anything.'

A crash came from behind the door; the sound of paperwork filed to within an inch of its life being destroyed.

'What's going on in there?' Dave asked.

Anne winced. 'I rearranged his office yesterday, but forgot to tell him. He's probably just teleported into a desk or something.'

The office door swung open and clattered against the wall, the frosted glass rattling in its frame. Death staggered into the room clutching a crumpled ball of paper.

Anne smiled sweetly. 'Good morning. How are we today?'

Death walked over to Anne's desk and balanced the ball of paper at its edge. His voice was calm and measured. 'There I was minding my own business, drifting through the ether, when all of a sudden A STATIONARY BLOODY FILING CABINET JUMPED OUT AND HIT ME.'

Anne unfolded the paper and smoothed the creases out. 'Well, if somebody stuck to the clear desk policy like I asked them to, I wouldn't have to do everything myself.'

Over the years, Anne had become the type of person who could give Death himself a withering look. They held each other's gaze until Death broke it off and turned towards Dave.

'Dave! Good to have you back. How are you feeling?'

'Good, thanks. Keen to know what you've got planned for Conrad West.'

Death shifted uncomfortably. 'How do you mean?'

Dave looked as if he'd been asked to explain quadratic equations to a Victoria sponge. 'You have a Horseman of the Apocalypse at the heart of one of the largest multinational corporations on Earth.'

'Watch what you say about Horsemen of the Apocalypse,' Death said. 'I was one and I turned out alright. Anyway, he hasn't got a horse and I certainly don't see any apocalypse. He's just a man. That's all he ever wanted, anyway.'

Dave gave Anne an exasperated look. 'But the vampires and the dark and all the weird stuff that's happening. He's behind it all. He's up to something.'

'And it's exactly that kind of attitude that stifles enterprise in this country,' Death said, irritated. 'Now, we've all got plenty of work to be getting on with. Anne, do we have any of those biscuits? You know, the ones that are the opposite of custard creams?'

Anne thought for a second. 'Do you mean bourbons?'

Death snapped his fingers. 'Yes! Those bad boys!'

Anne shook her head. 'I'm afraid not.'

'Bugger,' he said and vanished into the fabric of the universe.

Anne could see the hurt and confusion in Dave's eyes. 'I'll put the kettle on,' she said.

She filled the kettle and waited for Dave to finish his emotional filing. When the last mental drawer was slammed shut behind his eyes, he spoke. 'What the fuck was that about?'

The kettle clicked off and Anne filled two cups with boiling water. She sploshed tea bags around with a spoon, watching the liquid swirl and darken. 'Look at it from his point of view. You don't see your friend for a few decades and then you find out he's been employing the undead. How do you bring that up when you first meet each other?'

Dave gave a hollow laugh. 'So the world might be destroyed because of social awkwardness?'

Ann dropped the tea bags into the waste bin. 'I don't think anybody is talking about the end of the world.'

Dave sat back in his seat and took a bite of his chocolate bar/doughnut hybrid. He chewed thoughtfully and then nodded his head. Anne was glad he'd seen sense.

'I felt the Dark again,' he said once he'd swallowed the mouthful of food. 'It's getting stronger. Whether

West is behind it or not, I don't think any good can come of it.'

Anne passed a steaming cup to Dave and patted him on the arm. 'Just give Death a few days. He's probably got some things to work through.'

Dave sipped his tea. 'I'll do that, but if nothing happens I'm doing something about it.'

Anne knew that was the best she could hope for. There was a knock at the office door. A deliveryman stood there with a box piled high with bananas.

'Got a delivery for Eamon Key?' he said, squinting at the invoice in his hand.

'Oh, they don't work here anymore,' Anne replied. The Infinite Monkeys had decided to move to Hollywood to continue their screenwriting careers.

'What am I meant to do with fifteen boxes of bananas?'

Anne shrugged. 'Massive banoffee pie?'

The deliveryman sighed and, heaving the box onto his shoulder, stormed out of the office.

'What's the plan for today?' Dave asked. 'Whose supernatural arse are we going to kick?'

'Are you sure you're alright? You don't want to take it easy? Do some paperwork?'

'I just want to get back to it.'

There had been something that Anne had needed to do that would require both of them. Dave seemed back to his old self. What could possibly go wrong?

'We're going to Eastgate,' she said.

'The shopping centre? Hasn't that just opened? How can that be haunted already?'

'It's what it was built over. A plague pit. When this was countryside, outside of the city walls, they buried the dead there. Some were less dead than others.'

'Buried alive in a mass grave? Lovely.'

'The seventeenth century was a busy time, I'm sure you can understand. I think it was about the time Death was fighting with Famine.'

'Of course he was.'

Anne pulled maps and blueprints from one of the filing cabinets. She smiled at Dave.

'Let's go shopping.'

SEVEN

Once Anne had parked the car and finished complaining bitterly about the price, they took the lift up to the mezzanine level of Eastgate shopping centre. The shoppers below swayed and rocked like a football crowd. They moved in and out of the shops in a ballet choreographed by marketing departments. The looks in their eyes ranged from consumerist joy through to murderous rage.

Dave stared up at a large chandelier hung from the ceiling above them. Thick with lights at the top, it tapered down like an inverted Christmas tree.

'Ostentatious,' he muttered to himself.

Anne took out a schematic of the shopping centre and flattened it against the balcony. 'There's two million square feet of retail space here,' she said.

'What's that in football pitches? Statistics mean nothing to me unless they tell me how many football pitches it would cover. Or its relation to the size of Wales.'

Anne shook her head. 'I've overlaid the blueprints over original maps of the area.' She tapped the schematic with her finger. 'The main burial ground is under a pound shop.'

'How undignified,' Dave muttered.

Anne folded the map away. 'I've wanted to deal with this for a while, but there's too many for one person. It's like herding cats. Are you ready?'

'As I'll ever be.'

They took the escalator down to the ground floor. It was like entering a medieval melee, but instead of swords and maces the combatants were armed with bags of shopping and boiling hot cups of coffee.

Dave spotted an ethereal female figure floating outside a shoe shop and the butterflies in his stomach took flight. She moved with a serene grace in contrast to the belligerent and frustrated shoppers.

'There's one,' he said, pointing over the crowds.

Anne gave him a gentle shove in the ghost's direction. 'Go get her, then. One word of warning. Don't let them gather in numbers. When you get a lot of them together, they generate some weird electro-magnetic fields that can be a nightmare.'

'Aren't you coming with me?'

'We need to split up if we're going to get this done. You'll be fine, but give me a call if you have any problems.'

'Hang on. What do you mean electro-magnetic fields?'

Dave looked around but Anne had already disappeared into the throng.

Shopping centres operate within a unique spatial field. Somehow, no matter what direction you head in, you will always go against the flow of the crowds. There are entire branches of physics dedicated to researching this phenomenon. Dave tried to keep the apparition in his sight, but it was harder than he imagined. He finally caught up and trailed behind her until the crowds had thinned out.

Dave coughed, but there was no reaction.

'Excuse me?' he said.

The ghost stopped and turned. There was a beauty in the fluid motion balancing on the edge of being and nothingness.

'What the bleedin' 'ell joo want?' she asked in a thick cockney accent.

'Oh. Hello. It's just that I... Well... Me and my boss... Well... We can sort of, y'know, help you out. Get you to the other side. Or something. Find eternal peace and all that. If you want,' Dave gabbled, wishing he'd rehearsed this introduction.

The ghost seemed to consider this. She turned away from Dave and yelled, 'Beryl! BERYL!'

Another ghost poked her head out of a wall between W.H. Smith and Pret a Manger. She had died middle-aged and toothless. 'What are you shoutin' about, Edith?' she asked impatiently, as if she had been dragged away from something important.

'This lad 'ere says he can give us eternal rest,' replied Edith.

'I never got any when I was alive, so I can't see me ever gettin' it in death.' Beryl sighed. She looked Dave up and down. 'He don't look old enough to shave.'

'Honestly, I can help you,' Dave said, trying to ignore the stares of passers-by.

'Joshua!' Beryl screamed at the wall she was leaning out of. 'Get your lazy arse out 'ere!'

Another spirit appeared, red-faced, overweight and yawning. 'Bloody 'ell, woman. You're loud enough to wake the dead.'

'Good thing'n'all or you'd never do anything. This boy 'ere,' Beryl turned to Dave. 'What's your name, son?'

'Dave.'

'Dave 'ere says he can help us.'

Dave noticed that more ghosts were gathering around as word spread on the ethereal grapevine. There must've been a dozen or so now, bobbing and floating around the living. The lights above them fizzled and flickered. Dave backed away.

'You shouldn't... swarm... like this. It's not good.'

The ghosts followed him, arms outstretched. 'Help us,' said Joshua, yearning in his voice. 'Help us stay away from the Dark.'

Dave stopped, tripping over his own feet. 'What's in the Dark?'

'Fear,' replied Joshua.

'Anger,' said Beryl. 'Hate.'

Dave had moved out into the main concourse. More of the dead drifted in his direction. They passed through shoppers like sleepwalkers through mist.

Trembling, Dave slipped his mobile phone from his pocket and dialled Anne's number. She answered on the fourth ring.

'Get back here now,' Dave hissed into the mouthpiece before she could say anything.

'What's wrong?' she asked and, then, to somebody stood with her, 'Paying by credit card.'

'I've found them.' He'd made it back to the escalators. 'Hang on. Are you shopping?'

'I thought I'd grab a few bits and pieces while I was here. I don't get much free time,' Anne said huffily.

'I'm being stalked by a Shakespearean rent-a-mob and you're shopping?' he spat into the phone.

'I'll be right there.' Anne hung up the phone.

Dave was directly underneath the giant chandelier. There were at least a hundred restless spirits surrounding him, all begging for Dave's help. People instinctively walked around them until a clearing had formed where Dave stood. His breath caught in his throat as their voices became an intense low hum that buried itself between his skull and brain. He clutched at his chest, feeling his heart race. His vision swam and danced. He saw sharp shining teeth dripping with dark red blood. He remembered warm breath on his exposed neck. The lights on the chandelier grew brighter and hotter as the ghosts closed in; tiny suns that burned Dave's scalp.

'Get back!' Dave yelled. The living had formed a second circle around the dead. Anne shoved her way through the crowd, some of whom were suspecting that this was some intellectually demanding new street theatre. When Anne reached the front, that's when Dave felt the first light above him explode. He jumped aside as the others followed, making a sound like God's own bubble wrap. Glass fell around him like boiling rain.

The silence that followed was punctured only by Dave's panting breath. Then, with a creak and snap, the light's steel frame tore itself from the ceiling and crashed onto the floor, throwing plumes of dust into the air. Wire and twisted metal thrashed and rolled on the smashed tiles casting monstrous shapes in the brown half-light.

Dave sighed with relief. 'That was close.'

It was at that moment every other light in the shopping centre exploded.

Anne pulled Dave to his feet and, sharing a single thought, they ran.

EIGHT

Back at the office, Dave sat at his desk and watched the news report through the gaps in his fingers.

'London's newest shopping centre was evacuated today due to what has been described as a catastrophic electrical fault,' the news anchor said to the camera.

The report cut to shaky camera-phone footage of Dave diving out of the way of the falling debris. It then cut to an eyewitness talking directly to the reporter. 'I thought it was a terrorist attack. All hell broke loose. There was this guy yelling stuff. I think he was trying to warn us. He probably saved a few lives today.'

The report ended and the news anchor told the viewers, 'Police have not been able to identify the man in the footage, who immediately left the scene, and are appealing for any witnesses to come forward.'

The broadcast returned to the news anchor. 'In other news, reports of violent crime including assaults and robberies had increased by almost twenty per cent according to Metropolitan Police sources...'

Anne switched the television off. Dave closed the gaps in his fingers and buried his head in his hands. She gave him a reassuring pat on the back. 'You do understand that we're meant to keep a low profile?'

'I thought it'd be like riding a bike, that I could get back to work easily.'

She opened her desk drawer and pulled out a beaten tin. She offered it to Dave and said, 'Would a biscuit help?'

Dave took the tin and pulled the tight lid off. He peered inside and rummaged around. 'Bleurgh. Malted Milks. That's worse than no biscuits at all. '

He put the lid back on and slid the tin across the desk

Anne pulled the chair over from her side of the office and sat opposite him. 'What happened out there?'

'I tried to tell them to not get so close, but they didn't listen. They were talking about the Dark. They were frightened by it. They wanted to get away from it.' Dave looked at Anne. 'They weren't the only ones who were frightened. I panicked. I don't appear to be as brave as I thought I was.'

'Life isn't about being brave. It's about getting through it even though you're scared,' Anne said. 'Why don't you go home? Let's try again tomorrow.'

When five o'clock came around, Anne locked the office door and went to see her mother. The care home smelt of bleach and hopelessness. Her mother was asleep when Anne arrived, but the care assistant told her that it had been one of her better days. She'd been lucid; chatting and making jokes with the staff and other residents. Anne was disappointed she'd missed an opportunity to catch one of the last remnants of her mother. The care assistant smiled sympathetically. Everybody who worked there wore the same painted-on grin, like it was the charity's logo.

Anne sat at her mother's bedside and brushed her thin grey hair, the strokes in time with her mother's slow breathing. The dementia had taken her away from Anne in tiny increments, a war of attrition that the armies of her mind weren't equipped to defend against. On the bad days, Anne wondered if she should just take a pillow and gently push down on her mother's mouth and nose until her breath stopped. Then she'd have her back for a brief moment. The soul was fine; it was just surrounded by a damaged shell. But she didn't get to choose when someone else died. Nobody did. Death was adamant about that.

Schrodinger was quietly shedding hair on the sofa when Anne came home. He rolled lazily onto the floor and plodded over to her to demand to know where she'd been. His claws clicked and scraped on the flat's wooden floor as he fought against Anne scooping him up into her arms. His annoyance had once again been mistaken for affection and Anne buried her face into his fur. Schrodinger's training of his owner was not going as well as he'd hoped, but he conceded that the hugs were quite pleasant. Despite himself, he let out a quiet purr of satisfaction. Anne told him about her day. She told him about the Dark and how much it concerned her that she didn't know what it was or where it came from. He didn't have any idea what she was talking about but, as she was preparing dinner for them both at the time, he thought it in his own interests to feign attentiveness. He found the meal acceptable, and then he curled up on her lap while she read a book.

At ten o'clock, Anne went to her bedroom. She undressed and took her bangles and bracelets off. She rubbed the ragged pale scars cut into each wrist. Sometimes they itched and irritated her; a reminder of another life. She changed into her pyjamas and climbed into bed. After waiting a suitable amount of time to demonstrate that he didn't have to be with her, Schrodinger pushed the bedroom door open and jumped up onto the duvet. He snuggled up to her cheek and they were both drifting off to sleep when a beeping noise jerked them both awake. Anne picked her mobile phone up off the bedside table. A text message from Death.

I'VE JUST HAD A KIT KAT THAT WAS ALL CHOCOLATE NO WAFER. WHERE'S YOUR PRECIOUS SCIENCE NOW?

Anne smiled to herself. When they had met all those years ago, they were both alone. Now, when he had these moments of wonder, Anne was the one person he would share them with. If they hadn't found each other, she couldn't say what would have happened to either of them.

NINE

After he left the office, Dave wandered around the city. The heat oozed from the sun and he pushed his shirtsleeves up past his elbows. He was already regretting ordering a hot cup of coffee. When he thought back to the shopping centre, it occurred to him that he'd never truly failed at anything before this job. Maybe, he reasoned, because he'd never really tried at anything. Still, at this moment, he missed the old apathy and mediocrity that had previously dominated his life.

Usually, he'd drift through the streets in the sonic cocoon of his headphones, but this time he let London's mood wash over and fill his senses. A low-level hum of annoyance reverberated all around him. It was every unsolicited sales call, every missed bus and every petty disagreement manifested as an energy building up and looking for a release.

'THE DARK IS COMING' was spray painted in thick letters against a wall. He took a photograph of the warning on his phone and hurried along until he came across a pub. Unable to resist the illicit lure of a beer on a weekday afternoon, he threw the coffee into a bin and ducked into the shade of the dimly lit building.

Sat by the window, he supped the cool pint of lager he'd bought and considered what he knew about the situation. The poltergeist that possessed Letitia had told him that the Dark was like a choking wind blowing around the streets. The ghosts in the shopping centre had told him it was full of fear and anger; exactly what he had felt while in the hospital. It was the same rage he'd felt in the foyer of UberSystems Tower; a building that was cursed in such a way that Death himself could not enter it.

It always led back to UberSystems International. Like a black hole, its gravity sucked him back towards the dark, mysterious singularity at the heart of the company. Black holes were the most destructive things in the universe. Arseholes were a close second and Conrad West was the biggest arsehole Dave had ever met.

Dave's phone buzzed. It was a text message from Melanie. She'd agreed to have a girls' night with Emma, if that was all right, but would see him tomorrow at the restaurant for Laura's birthday dinner. Dave couldn't remember agreeing to attend a birthday dinner, wasn't entirely sure who Laura was or which restaurant Melanie was referring to, but was happy to have the evening to himself to do a little research. He finished his drink and headed for the door.

When Dave returned to the flat, he microwaved and ate a lasagne that had the same taste and texture as the plastic container that it came in. He collapsed into the living room's sofa and channel hopped for a while, building up the energy to surf the internet.

A key rattled in the front door, quickly followed by the sound of various explosive bodily functions. Gary was home. He blustered into the living room like a tornado dressed in a Motorhead tee shirt and threw himself into an armchair.

'You going to get ready?' he asked.

Dave turned the volume down on the television. 'Ready for what?'

'We're going out tonight, remember?'

'I've had a really bad day at work.'

Gary leant over and prodded him in the shoulder with a podgy finger. 'All the more reason to go out for a pint. You promised me.'

'It's a school night.'

'You know what they say. Wednesday night is the new Thursday night. And as Thursday night was the new Friday night that makes Wednesday night the new Friday night. Also, Tuesday is the new Monday and May is now April. August is still August but renamed 31 Days of Awesome!'

Dave narrowed his eyes. 'Have you started drinking already?'

'No. A little bit. Yes.'

'What have you got planned?'

'I thought we could go along to the Truther Symposium?'

Dave groaned. 'Not those conspiracy nut jobs?'

'Those are my friends you're talking about. They are not nut jobs. Mostly. And we've got a guest speaker tonight. He's talking about the government covering up evidence of the afterlife.'

This got Dave's attention, but he tried to play it cool. 'Oh, right. That sounds like it could be quite interesting. And if I get bored, I can just play my usual drinking game.'

'What's that?'

'Every time I die a little inside, I down a cup of my own tears.'

The Truther Symposium was a rather grand name for what was basically about a dozen men drinking in the back room of a small Shoreditch pub. Dave calculated that roughly seventy-five per cent of all the facial hair in London was in the room. Chairs were set up against three of the walls, facing the front of the room where a pale, thin man was concentrating on a laptop. A PowerPoint slide was projected behind him. It read 'GHOST OF A CHANCE - THE AFTERLIFE AND THE

GOVERNMENT COVER-UP'. A box of paperback books sat in a cardboard box by his feet.

'Gary,' Dave whispered, 'Can we not tell people I was at UberSystems International? I'm sure there's quite a few people here with their own theories about what went on there.'

Gary slapped him on the back. 'Of course, mate. Low profile. I understand.'

Across the room, a man with mutton chops was talking animatedly about The Bilderberg Group.

'What's the Build-a-Bear Group?' Dave asked Gary.

'Bilderberg. They're a cabal of the world's richest and most powerful men – and it's always men - who secretly control all the world's governments. Most people have a speciality here. Trevor's is the New World Order. Nigel, who he's talking to, his is the moon landings. Or the lack of them to be more precise.'

Dave nodded towards a man with a small goatee. 'What's his?'

'Barry? I don't know. To be honest, I think he just comes for the beer.'

Dave took a sip of his bitter. These conspiracy theorists might be confused about a lot of issues, but they did seem to know where to get a decent pint.

A middle-aged man in a Marillion tee shirt walked to the front of the room. Dave could tell that he was in charge because he had the biggest beard. He exchanged quiet words with the pale thin man and turned to address the room.

'Gentlemen, if you could all take a seat, please. We'll begin tonight's talk.' Everyone sat down and, when they were all settled, he continued, 'We're delighted to have Nick Broughton come along. He's going to talk about a conspiracy that goes right to the heart of both the world government and the Vatican. So, please put your hands together for Nick.'

The Marillion fan scuttled over to a vacant seat. The audience clapped as politely as they could without putting down their pint glasses. Some beer was spilt. Nick stood with a finger pressed against his pursed lips as he waited for the applause and mopping up to stop.

'Thank you, Norman, for that introduction. Tonight, I want to share with you what I've discovered. Ghosts exist and the afterlife is real. But that's not the shocking part. No, I've uncovered evidence that governments are colluding with the Church to cover up this knowledge. There's a top secret agency whose mission is to hunt down these paranormal entities, exterminate them and hide the truth from you.' Nick paused for effect. An excited murmur rippled through the audience. Beards wobbled with anticipation.

'But to what end? What purpose does this serve? Control. If it was known that life didn't end when your physical form died, all organised religion would collapse. Religion is built on belief and faith. They tell you their truth and you must blindly accept it. If there's empirical, measurable evidence, belief and faith are redundant. So would the Church and governments which rely on its support in controlling the minds of the masses. We would enter a new age of wisdom and truth, and those are the two things that both the Church and State fear more than anything.'

Nick spent the next hour showing the group blurred satellite pictures and making leaps of logic that made very little sense to Dave. His thoughts had drifted off until a grainy photograph of a familiar woman dressed in overalls and carrying a tool kit was projected onto the wall. It was Anne.

'This female is one of the organisation's top agents. She has been observed at several locations where paranormal activity has been reported. After she leaves, the activity stops. It's thought that she harvests supernatural beings, possibly in some kind of containment unit hidden inside her tool kit.'

It seemed like a perfectly normal tool kit to Dave. He hadn't realised that he'd laughed out loud until he noticed all the eyes in the room staring directly at him. 'What? Like in Ghostbusters?' Dave asked.

'Do you have something to contribute to this?' Nick asked.

'He bloody does,' said Gary. 'He's had a near death experience and everything.'

'Thanks very much,' Dave muttered.

'What?' Gary asked, genuinely confused. 'You didn't say I couldn't talk about that.'

'Well, I wouldn't call it an experience,' Dave said to Nick through gritted teeth.

'So, you've seen the world beyond this?' A sly grin formed on Nick's lips.

I have touched the ethereal plane, talked with ghosts and monsters, seen souls destroyed in front of my very eyes and at night I dream of teeth and blood, Dave thought to himself. He smiled politely. 'Not really.'

'I thought as much. Bloody amateurs.'

The room laughed into their pint glasses. Dave suddenly felt very sorry for the other audience members. Nick was right. It was all about control. They were all so sure that somebody else had it. The world was full of both terrible and wonderful things. When they couldn't understand something, they saw a conspiracy orchestrated by the powerful. The human mind was designed to recognise patterns and often saw them where none existed. Whether you looked to religion or conspiracies, humans just needed to make sure that somebody, somewhere, knew what they were doing. They needed that thought to explain away this feeling of impotence they all had. But sometimes shit just happened. Princesses met their end in car accidents in Parisian tunnels. Terrorists flew planes into buildings. Elvis was dead.

So he told them that, including the bit about Elvis, which seemed to visibly upset an impressively quiffed gentleman sat a few seats down from Dave.

TEN

Sixteen Years Earlier

Roger Mitchell would soon be dead. Running a small business, he was stacking the shelves of his small video rental store until that moment came. Outside the window, a man bellowed into a mobile phone the size of a small brick. Roger thought back to a time when private telephone conversations were just that. Private. His teenage daughter had started pestering him for a mobile phone. He knew that he would finally give in, but he just couldn't shake the old feeling that only three types of people used them: drug dealers, poseurs and poseurs who wanted to look like drug dealers.

Roger understood that the world was changing. He knew that humanity stood at the cusp of a new millennium and the future was now. The analogue was being replaced by the digital. His daughter had started listening to something called MP3 on the family computer. At first, he thought that it was a band. She soon corrected him, accompanying the explanation with the now traditional roll of her eyes. Roger told her that he couldn't give up his vinyl. You couldn't convey an emotion within a digitally encoded bit. He was too old and it was too late to change his ways, though he didn't know how late it actually was.

The poseur outside the window continued berating the person on the other end of the call. Roger's own irritation began to grow. He considered stepping outside and giving the guy a piece of his mind. Roger loved a good argument but, since what his wife euphemistically called 'The Incident' at his previous job, he tried to avoid conflict. He had taken his redundancy money and invested it in this shop. To be surrounded by film had always been a dream of his. Twentieth century myths flickering in the dark at twenty-four frames per second.

He thought about his daughter. Things were getting more complicated. In the last couple of years, she'd started seeing strange, morbid visions and hearing terrible voices. She was scanned with expensive machinery, spent hours being questioned by psychiatrists and had been quietly shunned by her school friends. Frightening words like 'schizophrenia' and 'mental healthcare' were mentioned by people with lots of letters after their names. She had grown insular and distant; the popular, loving girl she once was had become a faded memory. He felt guilty at times. What if it was hereditary and he was responsible for burdening her with this? What if it was the way they had raised her? Had they made some terrible mistake in their parenting? Either way, what broke his heart most was that he didn't know how to protect his only child from the monsters in her head. He took a deep breath and concentrated on sorting the display case in front of him. The rigid order of the rectangular cases, uniform in design, soothed him. A place for everything and everything in its place.

The poseur finished his call and marched through the shop door. He walked up to Roger and waved a video case under his nose. He could feel the man's fury radiating out like body heat.

'I'd like my money back,' the man barked in Roger's face. Roger told himself to concentrate on the rhythm of his own breathing and smiled.

'Was the video damaged in some way?'

'There's nothing wrong with the video. It's just that the film sucked.'

'I'm sorry, but I can't give you a refund based on the quality of the film.'

'You should've told me how bad it was!'

'I don't have time to watch every film we stock.'

'Just give me my money.'

Roger gently prised the video case from the customer's grip, wiped the sweat from the plastic film and looked at the title. He raised one eyebrow. 'It is not our policy to provide refunds on the grounds of quality or, indeed, taste.'

'What's that meant to mean?'

Roger could feel the red mist begin to descend but spoke in measured tones, as if explaining a difficult maths problem to a small child. 'You rented a film called "Kung Fu Bikini Killers Battle Zombie Elvis". That would be like going to a restaurant, ordering a shit sandwich and then demanding a free meal.'

'I demand to see the owner!' Roger watched the veins in the customer's neck and forehead throb. He honestly thought for a moment that the guy's head would explode like a character in that Cronenberg film.

'I am the owner!' Roger spat back. He was sure he could feel his heart beat against his shirt.

The customer's mobile phone began to ring.

'I'd get that if I were you.'

The customer looked at the small green display on the handset and returned his gaze to Roger. 'I am never renting here again.'

'Yeah, well, you're not allowed to rent here again.'

The customer answered the call.

'What do you want?' he shouted into the phone as he marched out of the door, letting it slam behind him.

Roger threw the cassette box onto the counter. His head span in the silence. He was disappointed that he had let his temper get the better of him again, but he made a mental note to ask Grant the weekend boy to delete the customer's record from the computer. Tightness grew in his chest, as if the anger was pressing down upon him. Stabbing pain travelled from his heart and down his left arm. It crept up his neck and along his jaw. Roger realised that this wasn't normal. He knew what this was. His doctor had given him a pamphlet the last time he had a check-up, forced there by his wife who was concerned about his stress levels. He drew short darting breaths as panic took hold. He grabbed hold of the counter, his knuckles white with tension. The telephone was in the back office. For the first time, Roger wished he had one of those mobile phone things. He took a step forward, but his legs gave way like dry twigs and he crashed to the floor. His back twisted in furious agony. His last thoughts were of his wife and daughter. He was angry that he would never hold Marion again and never see Anne grow up. That was the real pain. His heart rattled in his ribcage; a juddering engine winding down until there was nothing left of Roger Mitchell.

Roger didn't remember how he had got back on his feet. All the pain had gone, even the dull ache in the base of his spine that he'd lived with for years. Perhaps the fall had somehow sorted it out.

'Oh, wow. "Kung Fu Bikini Killers Battle Zombie Elvis". I love this film.' The voice was behind him. Roger turned around and realised then why he felt no pain. The bright midsummer sunshine fell around the dark figure standing at the counter, as if it was afraid to touch him. Roger had seen Bergman's "The Seventh Seal" enough times to know who it was. 'The bit where the last Kung Fu Bikini Killer kicks Zombie Elvis's head off is brilliant.'

'I'm afraid I haven't seen it.' It wasn't the only thing Roger was afraid of.

'You should. Well, you should have. I don't know if they have films where you're going. And I've just ruined the ending for you,' Death said.

Roger's fear grew. Not being able to watch films was his idea of... Oh dear. 'You don't mean...? But I've tried to live a good life. I go to church regularly. Well, Christmas and Easter. Twice a year is regular, isn't it?'

'Church? What's that go to do with anything?' Death sounded confused and annoyed.

'Isn't there a heaven and hell?'

Death shrugged. 'Nobody tells me anything. I just work here.'

It was Roger's turn to be confused and annoyed. 'But what about what it says in the bible?'

'The bible? Is that the one that starts off well, tails off in the middle, ends up with the bloke dying and then coming back to life?'

'Yes.'

'And then beats up Agent Smith?'

'That's The Matrix.'

'Oh yeah. Now that's a good film.'

Roger laughed. Death seemed like a nice guy. Perhaps he would do him a small favour. 'Is there any chance I could talk to my family one last time?'

Death gave a sigh full of regret and pity. 'I'm sorry. It's a Do-Not-Pass-Go-Do-Not-Collect-Two-Hundred-Pounds kind of a deal.'

The words made Roger feel like he had lost them all over again. The agony was almost too much to bear. He had been taught that men don't cry, but he was no longer sure what he was. A sob caught in his throat. 'Promise me they'll be alright.'

'Death does not make promises other than itself.'

Roger couldn't believe how unfair this all was. 'So that's it, is it? That's my lot? Fifty-two years and I achieved nothing. I had so much I wanted to do, but I told myself there'd always be more time.'

'Hey, I know what you're going through. I've learned first-hand what it is to lose those close to me. My friends. My brothers. You were loved and you will be remembered. From my experience, this is the greatest of achievements.'

Roger smiled and wiped his wet cheeks with the back of his hand. 'You're quite good at this.'

Death shrugged beneath his midnight-black cloak. 'Not as good as I used to be. There are too many of you to keep up with and I often find myself tired and confused these days. I lose track. You're one of the lucky ones. You get to move on. Shall we go?'

'Yes. Thank you. I'd always thought you'd be--' Roger struggled to find the word.

'Taller? I get that a lot.'

'I was going to say scarier.'

'Don't believe everything you read. Now, come on. I'm working in a time frame here.'

Death placed a reassuring hand on Roger's shoulder, and they were gone.

Anne Mitchell looked up at the clear summer sky. When she was a kid, she asked her father why the sky was blue. He told her that it was because the sky loved the ground, but the ground was so distant. She hadn't understood his reply at the time, but now she loved that his mind worked like that. Though, as she was seventeen, she was in no hurry to tell him that.

Her mum had sent her down to the video store with his lunch, which she carried in a Tupperware box wrapped in a carrier bag. A well-dressed man shouting into a mobile phone barged into her as he headed in the opposite direction. It was one of the new Nokia models. She'd looked it up on AOL. She wrapped the bag's handle tighter around her hand. Perhaps she could use this good deed as ammunition to finally persuade dad to buy one for her. Her behaviour had been less erratic recently and she'd been trying to keep the darkness from creeping around the edges of her mind.

She arrived at the parade of shops, waving to Mr Ustunsurmeli in the newsagents as she walked by. She glanced through the video shop's window covered with one-sheet posters advertising the newest releases. The carrier bag slipped from her grasp and the box clattered onto the concrete path. A prone body was lying on the floor inside, though the shadows prevented her from being able to identify who it was. Her father was talking to a figure in a black hood. No, not talking. Pleading. He was incredibly upset. She wondered whether she should go in and see if she could help, but she was rooted to the spot as if the hot thick summer air had condensed around her. Then the dark figure put a hand on her dad's shoulder and they were gone.

She ran into the shop, the door's bell tinkling pathetically behind her. She fell to her knees by the body. Her eyes were still adjusting to the relative darkness, but she knew it was her father staring blankly up at the ceiling. She felt for a pulse and then, realising she had no idea what she was doing, ran next door to Mr Ustunsurmeli who phoned for an ambulance.

She sat in numb shock as the doctors explained how her father had suffered a massive heart attack and there was nothing she could've done. When her mind had finally caught up with events, she couldn't work out how her father had been on the floor and talking to the figure in the black hood at the same time. She didn't mention this paradox to anybody because she knew what the replies would be. Privately, she couldn't forgive herself. If she had been quicker, or less afraid, perhaps she could've saved him. Instead, she stood on the street looking into the shop window. A stupid, scared teenager.

She made a promise to herself in the waiting room. She was beginning to understand what these visions and voices were and why they wouldn't leave her alone. No matter what it took, she would find that dark hooded figure and she would find out what was happening to her.

ELEVEN

'That was exciting,' Gary said the next morning as he and Dave ate breakfast. 'Nobody's been thrown out of a Truther Symposium before. Well, Barry drank too much Badger's Fancy one night and tried tugging on everyone's beards, but nobody's been kicked out for ideological reasons.'

'Sorry if I've got you into trouble.' Dave smiled sheepishly.

'Don't worry about it. I told them I suspected you were sent by the intelligence services to infiltrate the group. They quite liked that. I can't believe you stopped to buy one of the guy's books on the way out, though.'

Dave bought a copy of 'Ghost of a Chance' to try and make it up to Nick Broughton for ruining his talk, but only made the situation more awkward when it turned out Nick didn't have any change. The other members of the audience had put their pints down and rummaged through their pockets as Dave felt himself become more and more embarrassed, until he just threw a ten pound note at Nick and ran out of the door.

In the pub garden, Dave persuaded Gary that he just needed some time on his own and he should go back to his friends. He then went to a different pub; one filled with less controversial opinions, and thumbed through his newly acquired book. It was cheaply self-published, the film already peeling from the glossy cover featuring a stock photo of a cheesy horror movie ghost. All he had learned from what he had read was that Nick Broughton was, without a shadow of a doubt, completely off his rocker. The opening chapter asserted that UFOs weren't from outer space, but were piloted by demonic entities scouting for tasty souls to drag back to the underworld. Naturally, the world's governments allowed the lie to perpetuate in exchange for access to the demons' advanced technology. He thought about texting Melanie, but then felt guilty about wanting to heap his burdens onto her when she was out enjoying herself. He finished his drink and took himself home to bed.

'So, what's up with you?' Gary asked as he chomped his way through last night's re-heated kebab.

Dave scratched his finger at a dubious stain on the table. 'What do you mean?'

'What was last night all about? Adrian was really upset about what you said about Elvis. Is it work?'

'Actually, I had a meeting with some--' Dave looked around the kitchen as if searching for the right euphemism to pluck from the air, '--clients. It got a bit intense and I had a panic attack.'

Gary chewed thoughtfully on some jalapeño peppers. 'Got a bit of that social anxiety, have you? I used to think that I had that, but it worked out alright.'

'What did you do?'

'Nothing. It turns out I just don't like people.' Gary offered the polystyrene tray to Dave. 'Pepper?'

'No thanks.'

'How's Mel? I forgot to ask.'

'She's on the mend.'

'And are you two alright now?'

'Yeah. Yeah, we are.'

'You thought about the future? About moving in together or anything?'

'What are you talking about? I live with you. Are you trying to get rid of me?'

'Not at all. Let me ask you a question. Where are you staying tonight?' Gary asked.

'Hers.'

'And tomorrow night?'

'Hers.'

'And the night after that?'

'Ah, that's different,' Dave said. 'She'll be staying here.'

'You spend all the time together so really it's just about what postcode your PlayStation sits in,' Gary said, sitting back in his chair. 'I just want you to be happy.

And living together? Hot and cold running sex? How could I stand in the way of that?'

'Let's just see how it goes, shall we?' Dave got up from the table and placed his coffee mug in the sink. 'I've got to get to work.'

Dave walked out of the kitchen as Gary called after him. 'And what about kids, Dave? I want to be called Uncle Gary by someone's kids at some point. I don't want your legacy to the world to just be a cautionary tale for others.'

Dave made a cup of coffee for the commute to work and left the flat. As he prepared to cross the road, a black Jaguar floated up to the kerb and blocked his path as if the driver owned the road. Gripped with white-hot, uncontrollable rage at the driver's dangerous inconsideration, Dave reacted like any true Englishman: he rolled his eyes and made a tutting noise.

As he considered what an over-dramatic sigh could add to the situation, the blacked-out rear door window silently glided down on expensive motors. A sly grin appeared from the car's dark interior. It belonged to Bowen, Conrad West's right hand man. He was the human equivalent of a clammy handshake. 'Can I offer you a lift, Mr Marwood?'

Dave felt his stomach knot. He smiled, feigning calm. 'On a day like this?' he said, looking up at the pure blue sky. 'I think I'd prefer to walk.'

'You look hot,' Bowen said. 'This model of car has a quite exceptional air conditioning system.'

'I wouldn't want to spill coffee on your seats.'

'There are many cup holders in here.'

Dave looked up and down the road, trying to gauge the situation and whether there was anybody who could come to his aid should he need them. 'I have to get to work.'

Bowen's smile grew wider. 'I'm aware that your current employer has a surprisingly flexible attitude to time-management. I'm sure he won't mind you being a few minutes late.' Dave hoped the shock he felt over Bowen knowing this secret hadn't travelled to his face. 'Mr West has a proposition for both you and Miss Watkins that he'd like to discuss.'

'Well, you can tell Mr West that I'm extremely flattered, but--'

'Of course, I could always approach Miss Watkins directly.' There was a chill to Bowen's tone. 'Get in, Mr Marwood. I can assure you that no harm will come to your person, or the upholstery.'

Dave could feel butterflies in his stomach as he grabbed the door handle. And the butterflies were puking.

He placed his coffee into one of the many cup holders and relaxed into the car's soft leather seats. Bowen's sole task had been to get Dave into the car and now that was complete, he turned his attention back to the paperwork on his lap. The black-suited driver didn't acknowledge Dave and simply stared directly ahead as he eased the car back into the slow-flowing traffic. Dave was in no mood to try and engage either of them in conversation so he simply sat back and watched the city glide past the tinted windows.

Soon, the familiar glass and steel of UberSystems Tower rose up in front of him, growing until it dominated the skyline like a metaphor for Dave's anxiety. The car rounded the side of the building and they reached the car park entrance. The security guard nodded a greeting and lifted the barrier. The saloon slipped under and headed down the slope until they were under the building itself. They pulled up into a reserved parking bay and the driver killed the engine.

Bowen tidied the papers away into an expensive brown leather suitcase and fastened its combination lock. He flashed a tight smile in Dave's direction as he opened the car's door. 'Shall we, Mr Marwood? I'm sure you're aware of how little Mr West likes to be kept waiting.'

Dave looked over at the driver who had already started to read a newspaper he'd pulled out from underneath the seat. Dave stepped out of the car and let Bowen lead the way across the car park. Bowen swiped his security card and held the door open into the building. 'After you.'

Dave hesitated. This was the first time he'd be entering the building since he'd stumbled out covered in blood and flesh.

'Life isn't about being brave. It's about getting through it even though you're scared,' he muttered to himself. With a slow, calming exhalation of breath, he stepped over the threshold and walked down the utilitarian corridor. When they reached the metal doors at the end, Bowen pressed the button to summon the lift. He fired another round from his arsenal of humourless smiles.

'You'll be pleased to know that we've fixed the lifts. I must commend you on the number of imaginative ways you managed to destroy the company's property. The water damage in some areas will take months to sort out, unfortunately.'

The lift whisked its two occupants up to the top floor, thirty storeys up. It was just as Dave had left it after the vampires' surprise attack. Desks were still covered with photographs of employees' loved ones, certificates for completed training courses and cuddly toys. All had been abandoned until the UberSystems International board members decided what should be done.

Some were happy to let the staff back in immediately, while others were in favour of torching the department and never speaking of it again.

Dave trailed behind Bowen as they headed towards the closed door of the boardroom. Then, with a startled cry, he stopped in front of a dark stain on the carpet that used to be Christopher Love. The realisation hit him like a punch to the gut, stars dancing in his vision. He felt the bile burn his throat as he choked it back down. His breath jammed in his windpipe and he had to let it slip out in tiny gasps.

Sensing Dave's sudden halt, Bowen turned on his heel. His eyes darted down to Dave's feet. 'As I said, you'll have to excuse the mess. We've lost quite a few staff.'

He rapped his knuckles on the boardroom door and let himself in, leaving the door open. After he had let the nausea pass, Dave stepped around the dried blood and, with a final glance back, followed him through.

Conrad West sat at the head of a vast conference table; Bowen at his right hand. He adjusted his cufflinks and waved a greeting. 'Dave! Take a seat, please. How are you?'

Dave pulled a chair out at the opposite end of the table and slouched down. 'Sick of people asking me how I am.'

West laughed off the rudeness. 'Of course. My apologies. Can we get you a drink? Tea? Coffee?'

In his many hours spent looking at job websites during his employment by UberSystems International, Dave had learned to always accept a drink when offered one in a high-pressure interview situation. This, apparently, projected a relaxed attitude. 'Coffee, please. White. No sugar.'

'Bowen,' West said. 'Can you get Mr Marwood a coffee?'

Bowen's body language said that he thought this menial task to be below his pay grade, but he walked the length of the room to the ludicrously expensive coffee machine located behind Dave.

'I know who you are,' Dave said over the sound of grinding coffee. 'Conrad Q. West. Conquest. Very cute.'

Dave tried to gauge West's reaction to the revelation that Dave knew the truth, but there was none. His was a poker face trained by years of negotiation.

'Ah, yes. I'm sure our mutual friend has filled you in. How is he? He never writes. He never calls.'

'Vampires, Conrad. How could you hire vampires?'

Conrad sat back in his chair. 'Kirsten and I met in Andalucía during the Spanish Civil War. Our paths crossed again a little while back. She was in the job market and I was looking to hire,' he said, as if it was the most obvious thing in the world.

'People died.'

Conrad nodded. 'And that's a pity, but there'll always be staff attrition in a company of this size.'

Dave was lost for words at this callousness. In the silence, Bowen placed the coffee on the table and returned to his seat.

'But that's not the big plan, is it? What are you doing here?' Dave asked once his senses had regrouped.

West tilted his head to the side. 'What do you think we're doing here?'

'You're manipulating people somehow. This dark energy, it's making people sad or miserable or angry. I don't know why.'

'And I'm not going to tell you. This isn't a movie where I reveal the details of my nefarious plan.'

'Death said you were one of the good guys.'

West laughed, a sharp bark that made Bowen and Dave jump in their seats. 'There's no such thing as good or evil. There's only corporations.'

'The Dark. Was it working on me? Is that why I was always so miserable working here?' Dave asked.

'No, you were miserable here because you did a terrible job for very little money. Everyone thinks like that,' West said dismissively. 'Bowen, could you show Dave the papers, please?'

Bowen rolled his eyes and gave an almost imperceptible sigh. He pulled his briefcase from under the table and lifted a sheaf of papers from it.

He retraced his steps back to Dave and placed the papers next to the steaming coffee.

'What's this?' Dave asked, confused.

'A contract,' West explained. 'It's obvious you have certain talents. I want to help you fulfil the potential I see.'

Dave pushed the contract away. 'I'm not going to work for you now, not after what you've done.'

'I thought you might say that. Bowen, show him the other paperwork.'

Bowen took a small piece of paper from his jacket's inside pocket and laid it on the table.

Dave's eyes widened at the sight of the cheque. It was more money than he'd ever hoped to earn in his life.

'Think of that as a golden handshake,' West said. 'Come and work for me and I will show you everything.'

Dave picked the cheque up with trembling fingers. He traced his name and the looping zeroes, rolling the idea of incredible riches around his mind.

He threw it back at West with a flick of the wrist. It skimmed and skidded across the varnished tabletop and spun to a slow stop. Dave savoured the confusion in West's eyes.

'I can't,' he said.

'Please don't say it's because of some misguided belief that you're doing the right thing.' West spat the last part of the sentence out as if the words were toxic.

'No. It's simple. You're my nemesis.'

'Your-what-now?'

'My nemesis. Don't worry. It's alright. It's healthy. A boy needs a nemesis,' Dave said.

'I don't think you understand the implications of your actions,' Bowen said at his shoulder.

Dave stood up and smiled. 'Now, I've got a job to get to. Be lucky.'

As Dave rested his hand on the door to let himself out, West spoke. 'Are you a betting man, Mr Marwood?'

Dave turned back. 'No, the look on the winning horse's face is reward enough for me.'

'Well, I am,' said West, 'and I bet you'll be back in this room within a week.'

'I seriously doubt that,' replied Dave and he marched out of the room, slamming the door behind him.

West tore the cheque into tiny pieces and scattered them over the table like confetti. Bowen immediately began to sweep the mess up into a cupped palm.

'I think we'll need to keep an eye on Mr Marwood,' West said.

Bowen dropped the remnants of the cheque into the nearest waste paper basket. 'Indeed, sir. I shall make some phone calls.'

'Thank you. Are all our investments in place?'

'I checked with the trading floor earlier on. The deals are ready to be executed when you ask.'

West steepled his fingers together. 'Very good. Perhaps we should move to the next phase of our plan?'

Bowen smiled. 'I think that would be an excellent idea, sir.'

TWELVE

Dave's body still shook with the adrenaline pumping through his veins as he reached Crow Road. He bounded up the stairs two at a time and burst into the office. Ignoring Anne sat at her desk, he headed straight for the smaller room opposite the entrance.

'He's not in,' Anne said.

Dave stood at Death's door. "Where is he?'

Anne shrugged. 'Doing his job, I hope.'

'I need to talk to him.'

Anne registered Dave's agitation. 'What's happened?'

'I've just talked to West. I know what he's up to.'

'And what is he up to?'

Dave hesitated. 'Something.'

'He told you his plan?'

'Well, no,' Dave said after a moment. 'But he definitely implied there was a plan. This is some next level Scooby Doo shit.'

Anne closed the lid of her laptop. 'So, what did he imply?'

'That energy I've been feeling? The poltergeist that possessed Letitia said it was spreading out over the city? It makes people angry or miserable. He's creating it.'

'Making Londoners miserable or angry? That's like shooting fish in a barrel. What's the point?'

Dave had to admit that he was having trouble figuring out how it would be a meaningful exercise. Angry and miserable was the average Londoner's default setting. 'Whatever the reason is, he's doing it. We need to figure out what we do next.'

Anne walked around to the front of her desk. 'Whatever we do next can wait. After yesterday, it's obvious you're not one hundred per cent yet.' Dave tried to say something but she waved him away.

'I'm sorry, Dave, but it's true. And we went in without knowing what was going on last time and look what happened. We almost got you killed. I don't know if Death will ever forgive himself. He can barely bring himself to look you in the eye.'

Dave thought this over. 'Is Death avoiding me?'

Dave realised that most people would be happy to have the Grim Reaper make an effort to keep out of their way, but most people didn't count him as a friend. He was lost in this world without him.

Dave sighed. 'So what do we do now?'

'After the shopping centre, I think we need to lie low for a bit.'

Dave groaned inwardly. He knew what that meant: filing.

THIRTEEN

Please, Master.

'No.'

We want to sleep.

'You want to rest now? When we are so close to our goal?'

You lied to us. You promised us eternal life.

'I promised to keep Death away. Is that not what I have done?'

This is not living.

'You must stop thinking of life and death in such simple terms. Your suffering does not go unnoticed. Soon you will be rewarded.'

Thank you, Master. We wish only to serve you. We have faith, but it is so cold and dark where we are.

'That is because you are the Dark. You are pure. You are perfect. You are humanity reduced to its very essence. This is a great honour.'

We thank you for the privilege of being chosen to be the first, Master.

'It is nothing less than your belief in me deserves. I'm going to have to hurt you now.'

We know.

FOURTEEN

When he'd filed all that he felt he could, Dave said goodbye to Anne and made his way to the City: the Square Mile of real estate where grand old financial institutions stumbled over each other, churning billions of dollars, pounds and yen before spitting them out and sucking in even more. Modern glass skyscrapers tiptoed around the older squat stone buildings that refused to yield to them. UberSystems Tower lurked in the background, looming like an ugly threat.

Mel was waiting for him with a kiss and a hug when he emerged from the Underground exit. With her high heels and glamorous dress and his jeans and tee shirt, Dave felt he was the very definition of "punching above your weight".

'You look amazing,' he told her.

'Thank you,' she said as she grabbed his hand and pulled him along the pavement. 'Come on, we're late.'

The streets thronged with crowds of drinkers. Office workers spilled out of pub doorways to take advantage of the premature summer warmth before the sun disappeared behind the walls of glass already turning orange in dusk's glow. The air was filled with chatter and laughter, but Dave could already feel an edge to the humour; as if the wrong word could cause the delicately balanced mood to come toppling down and smash into violence.

'How was work?' Melanie asked.

'Dull. Paperwork. It's not all ghosts and ghouls.'

'Oh. Fair enough.' Melanie couldn't disguise the disappointment in her voice.

'Today I saw--' Dave stopped before he finished the sentence. Melanie had enough to deal with concentrating on her recovery. He'd figure out what was going on before he told her about his meeting with West. More selfishly, here was an opportunity to spend just one evening pretending his was a normal life. A chance to eat, drink and talk about everyday topics rather than what was the most efficient exorcism method.

'You saw what?' Melanie asked.

'Nothing. It's not important. What did you get up to last night?' Dave asked.

'Just went for drinks in a bar round the corner from where Emma works,' Mel replied as she slipped her arm into Dave's.

'She's over at Canary Wharf, isn't she?'

'Yeah. It was nice to do something normal for once, but there was a weird atmosphere.'

'Define weird,' Dave asked, his interest piqued.

'People were really aggressive I mean, the traders are normally swinging their dicks around thinking they're the alpha males, but fights were breaking out in bars and in the streets. It was scary.'

'Anyone hurt you?'

'No, I can take care of myself, thank you very much.'

'Didn't say you couldn't.'

They walked along in an uncomfortable silence for a while until Dave spoke. 'So, whose birthday is it again?'

'Laura's.'

'And who's Laura?'

Melanie sighed. 'She's a friend from university. You met her at Gavin and Sally's house-warming party.'

'Right.' Dave nodded his head. 'And who are Gavin and Sally?'

Melanie stamped her foot in frustration. 'For fuck's sake, Dave. Can't you show any interest in anything that isn't about you?'

Dave looked down at his feet. 'I was only joking,' he said sheepishly.

Melanie placed a hand on his arm. 'I'm sorry,' she said. 'I don't know what came over me. My head's been all over the place today.'

'It's okay,' Dave reassured her, though her words hurt. 'Let's just get to the restaurant, shall we?'

The restaurant seemed a pleasant enough venue. There was candlelight and interesting works of modern art that Dave didn't understand hanging on the white walls. The waiter showing them to the table seemed a bit surly, but that was probably due to having to serve arrogant bankers all day.

Melanie's friends had already been seated and were studying the menus with furious concentration, all trying to avoid each other's gaze. Harsh words had obviously been exchanged recently. Dave was reintroduced to Laura, Gavin and Sally along with three others whose names he immediately forgot. While he was bad with names, he was also terrible with faces. There were awkward kisses on cheeks and handshakes, then he sat opposite Melanie at the end of the long table.

'We've already ordered drinks,' Gavin said before focusing his attention on the list of the specials in front of him.

'Do you want to share a bottle of wine?' Dave asked Melanie. She nodded and took the menu the waiter shoved into her hands. Dave quickly scanned the drinks list before ordering the second cheapest bottle of wine.

While Melanie made small talk with the others, he watched the other diners and, as he did so, he started to feel that something wasn't quite right. It was the couple sat at the table next to him that he noticed first. They were obviously having some kind of argument, their whispered accusations flickering the candle's flame. An office party near the back of the room traded snide comments. A well-dressed elderly couple both sobbed silently into their menus, each lost in their own personal tragedies. The atmosphere was toxic; thick with poisonous words.

'I must say, I'm surprised to see you two back together again,' Laura said as Dave watched darkness leak from her mouth like steam in negative. 'I've always thought you lacked the drive that Melanie normally likes in her men.'

Embarrassed, Dave studied his cutlery. Melanie held his hand across the table and smiled at him. 'Oh, he's doing very important work. Trust me.'

'Well, if you say so,' Laura said dismissively.

The waiter returned with a bottle of wine in an ice bucket and grudgingly filled their glasses. 'Are you ready to order yet?' he asked.

Dave smiled politely. 'Could we have a couple more minutes? Oh, and could I get another fork, please? This one has something on it.' The waiter rolled his eyes, snatched it from Dave's hand and stormed off in one flowing motion. 'Thank you,' Dave called after him.

'So what's with the jeans and tee shirt, Dave? Dress down Friday in your office?' Gavin asked.

'My boss Anne allows a casual dress code. She's pretty cool,' Dave replied.

Melanie's expression changed. Her eyes dulled and her smile was replaced with a scowl. 'Are you sleeping with her?'

The question caught Dave off guard. 'You what?'

'Are you sleeping with her?' Melanie gulped down her wine and refilled her glass to the brim, dropping the bottle back into the ice bucket.

'Of course not,' Dave hissed over the top of his menu, ignoring the gaze of the others. 'She's not even my type.'

'And what is your type?' She spat the words like a challenge.

'You. You are my type.' He blushed.

Her mood swung again. Dave's head was spinning just watching her. The smile returned as if she had come out of a deep trance. She held his hand across the table. 'Really? Aw, that's so sweet. I'm sorry. My head's...'

'All over the place. I know.' Dave waited until the others at the table continued their conversations and then leaned over to Melanie. 'Look, maybe we should get out of here. This place has a weird vibe.'

'But I'm starving,' Melanie whined, 'and Emma says the food is amazing.' She turned her attention to the menu. 'Everything looks so good. I don't know what to have. They've got lobster. They boil them alive, you know? It must be horrible. I can't think of a worse way to die.' Her eyes were wet with tears. She dabbed them with the corner of her napkin. 'Jesus. What is wrong with me today? You must think I'm a nightmare.'

'Don't worry. It's not really you.'

'Oh, so you think you know me now, do you?' she said through the tears.

Oh, come on! Dave thought, and he was grateful for the arrival of the waiter.

'What d'you want to eat?' he grumbled. They gave their orders – Melanie decided against the lobster – and he left them in silence.

'No, I don't think I know you,' Dave said finally, 'but there's something going on. It's not just you acting like this.'

'It's probably this heat.'

'Maybe,' Dave said, staring out of the restaurant's window. The street was a mime show of badly suppressed aggression; glowering faces and pointed, accusatory gestures. He thought about excusing himself and phoning Anne, but he could imagine the argument if Melanie caught him. He delicately made small talk with everyone, tiptoeing around subjects like a cartoon mouse approaching a trap laden with cheese.

Though there was a worrying moment when Sally brought up the subject of Melanie's dead dog, the next few minutes went relatively well until the first course arrived. The waiter placed Melanie's salad in front of her with a resigned sigh. He carelessly dropped a soup bowl from a great height, which clattered on the table and spilled its contents into Dave's lap. With a gasp, Dave wiped the hot liquid away with a napkin.

'Are you alright?' Melanie asked.

'Yeah,' he replied through gritted teeth.

'Hey! Come back here!' Melanie yelled to the waiter who was half the way back to the kitchen. The waiter turned and trudged back to the table like a petulant teenager.

'Really, it's fine,' Dave said. 'I've got most of it out. I don't want to cause a scene.'

'What now?' asked the waiter.

'You've spilled soup all over my boyfriend. What are you going to do about it?'

The waiter shrugged. 'Not my problem.'

Melanie jumped to her feet and grabbed him by the collar. She felt around the table until she found a knife and held it up to his throat.

'Jesus, Melanie! What are you doing?' Dave said as the others pushed themselves away from the table.

She ignored him. She was a stranger to him now. There was a cruel aspect to her gaze. 'You are going to apologise.'

'I'm sorry. I'm really, really sorry,' the waiter blurted out.

'It's not a problem,' Dave replied.

Melanie returned to her senses and, shocked by her actions, she dropped the knife as if it was red hot. She looked at Dave with horror and ran from the restaurant. With an embarrassed smile to the table and the waiter, Dave chased after her.

The streets were crowded and Dave shoved his way through in pursuit of Melanie. When he caught up, he grabbed her by the arm, pulling her back. She was wild, kicking and screaming, but he took the blows. He was solid and sure as he knew he had to be. Now, he wanted nothing more than to keep her safe.

Soon, she calmed down and fell into him, letting herself be wrapped up in his arms. 'What's happening to me?' Her wet eyes were wide with fear and confusion as she looked around her. 'What's happening to us?'

Around them, the thin veil of civilisation was tearing at the seams and all the tiny horrors that people kept hidden away from each other were revealing themselves. Couples argued and strangers barged into each other. Motorists hurled abuse through open windows. On the other side of the road, a charity worker chased a man who wouldn't give him his direct debit details.

'I don't know,' Dave said. 'But we need to get you home.'

He tried hailing a taxi and lost count of how many sped by until one finally pulled over and they got in. They sat on the back seat and Melanie put her head on his shoulder. He put his arm around her and could feel her shivering even though the evening was warm. He reached into his reserves of politeness once more as he nodded and muttered 'I know' while the taxi driver explained to him what was wrong with the world and who exactly was to blame.

When they got back to Melanie's flat, he helped her into her pyjamas. She climbed into her bed and Dave piled on layers of blankets, but that didn't stop her shaking so he kicked off his shoes and climbed in with her.

They held onto each other in the darkness, their breathing falling in time. Soon, she fell asleep. Dave continued to stare at the ceiling as he allowed the pieces to fall into place in his mind.

FIFTEEN

Fourteen Years Earlier

The classroom looked pretty much like it always did to Dave. Mrs McKenzie, who was slightly younger than the universe itself, sat behind her desk reading from a textbook in her nasal monotone voice. The walls were lined with posters of seventies French fashion and crude pictures drawn by the pupils. The institutional smell of disinfectant stung his nostrils. The desk he leaned on was covered in filthy limericks, carved into the wood with the point of a compass and written over in biro to preserve them for the ages. Though he didn't really understand some of the words and wasn't completely sure where Nantucket was, he'd memorised and repeated them in the playground to scandalised giggles.

There were two fundamental differences to a normal school day: Dave was the only pupil there and the room extended on behind him into infinity. If he looked over his shoulder at the endless rows of desks stretching back into forever, Mrs McKenzie shouted at him to turn back around and face the front. He wanted to get up from his seat and run the impossible distance, but he did as he was told. Mrs McKenzie's voice flattened out into a drone which he let wash over him until he felt his heavy eyelids begin to droop. At the moment they finally closed completely, the school bell rang.

Dave sat back in his seat, more awake than he'd ever been before. Mrs McKenzie was gone. He stood up, the chair's scrape putting his teeth on edge, and walked over to the teacher's desk. It was bare apart from two bloody palm prints. He wanted to call for help, but the icy fingers of terror had wrapped around his throat.

The room had shrunk so it was just large enough for the desk and chair. The walls pressed down around Dave. He made for the classroom door and tried to open it, his sweaty fingers slipping over the handle. He finally managed to get some purchase, pulled and it smashed against the wall.

In the corridor beyond the classroom's threshold stood Dave's classmates. They stared back at him with dead eyes in pale, lifeless faces. Stretching to his full height, balancing on tiptoes, he saw that the crowd stretched off in both directions, packed in tightly against the walls like a never-ending game of Sardines. He shoved past the blank gazes. The zombified children yielded easily to his nudges and elbows and he slipped and squeezed through the hordes. Still, it was an exhausting exercise. He continued for what seemed like hours, the throng never thinning or reducing in numbers, until his heart was ready to explode in his chest and the sweat drenched his uniform. He stopped to catch his breath when an open door caught his attention. He was back at the entrance to his classroom. He was sure the corridor led off in a straight line in both directions, but somehow he had gone around in circles. He felt defeated. He would've dropped to his knees, but the pressure of the surrounding bodies supported him and kept him on his feet.

Ahead of him, in the distance, something was approaching. Something big. Something dark. He could feel a ripple through the crowd as bodies were hurled aside. Soon, he could see the throng parting like a sea of flesh. Whatever was coming was invisible, but threw up shadows and left bloody palm prints on the shoulders and faces of his classmates as it pulled them apart and tossed them to the floor.

Then it was on top of him. Shadows moved within shadows. Dave could feel the heat of its excitement and smell the stench of its breath. Dave didn't know who was screaming, the invisible creature or him.

Dave woke up, his limbs twisted up in the duvet from wrestling the monsters in his nightmares. He lay panting in the half-light, his pyjamas sticking to his warm tacky skin. He heard the soft pad of his parents' feet on the carpet outside his bedroom door and a sliver of light fell over him as they came in. The bed creaked as his mother perched herself on its edge. She ran a hand through his matted hair and his father stood over them both, a look somewhere between concern and exhaustion on his face.

'Another bad dream?' his mother asked. He nodded. 'You okay?' He wanted to tell them he wasn't and that it would be best if he came and slept in their bed, because the monsters might not think to come and look for him in there. He simply nodded. Both his parents kissed him on the forehead and returned to their bedroom.

Dave didn't sleep for the rest of the night. He stared at the ceiling waiting until the sun rose. When morning arrived, he heard his parents' bedroom door open again and they trod down the stairs to the kitchen. He waited a while and then rolled out from under the Star Wars duvet. He dressed in his school uniform, the knees of his trousers still grubby from the battle in the woods the day before, and headed downstairs. Before he had reached the bottom step, he could hear his dad's voice complaining again about the job he would have to leave for after breakfast.

'The guy is an idiot wrapped in a moron inside another idiot. Sometimes I just want to punch him flat out. And I loathe violence, so he actually makes me hate myself.' Dave slipped into the kitchen. He chose the most sugary cereal available and filled his bowl.

'Dave,' his dad continued. 'What they never tell you at school is that, as an adult, you will be surrounded by arseholes. The key to life is working out who they are.'

'Bob, don't talk like that,' Mum said, then to Dave, 'How are you feeling this morning, tiger?'

'Good, thanks.' Dave worried about his father. While his new job had bought the house that they lived in and provided Dave with the breath-taking array of cereals laid out in front of him, it made him angry more often than he used to be. Dave didn't see what the point was of doing a job you didn't like. You had to do it for a really long time, so you might as well do something that you enjoyed. He made a promise to himself that he'd get a job that made him happy. He understood that he'd never be an intergalactic smuggler, but he'd made his peace with that. He had no idea what he would be, but he had plenty of time to figure that out.

Dave was sat as his school desk. Every now and again, he would chance a look over his shoulder to make sure that the back wall of the classroom was where it should be.

'David Marwood, I fail to see what it is behind you that could be more interesting than the Great Fire of London,' Mrs McKenzie shouted. Dave's gaze fell back down to his desk and he read a poem about a young man from Devizes. 'I don't know what to do with you,

Mr Marwood. There always seems to be something more important going on.'

Sat at the desk next to him, Penny Richards giggled. Dave felt his hot cheeks redden. When she looked at him with her big blue eyes, Penny made him feel both excited and confused for reasons he didn't fully understand.

'Sorry, Mrs McKenzie,' he mumbled.

Mrs McKenzie returned to reading Samuel Pepys's diary and Dave tried to think what kind of grand gesture he could make to impress Penny. Soon, the lunchtime bell rang and the children poured out into the playground. Jumpers became goalposts, skipping ropes appeared from coat pockets and a very brief bundle on the playing field was quickly broken up by the teachers on duty.

Dave hung on the periphery of the action with his friends Craig and Darren. He'd latched onto them soon after starting William Furling Junior School. They weren't sporty enough to join in the football games and not cool enough to hang out on the benches by the school garden. That suited Dave just fine, but he was feeling restless that afternoon.

'How about a piggyback fight?' asked Darren, tugging at his shirt poking out from beneath his school jumper. There hadn't been a good piggyback fight for several weeks, not since Matt Spiceley had fallen off Hamzah

Chaudhry's shoulders and needed stitches. Dave was tempted, but was sure that Penny Richards was too sophisticated to be impressed by acts of juvenile violence, no matter how much fun it was.

'We should go exploring. Somewhere nobody's been before,' Dave said. What girl could resist an adventurer?

'Like where?' asked Craig.

'Dunno.' They returned to kicking pebbles with their scuffed shoes. Darren broke into a smile. 'I know. The boiler room.'

Craig's eyes widened with fear. 'We can't go there. That's where...' his voice trailed off.

'What?' asked Dave, intrigued.

'You don't know?' Darren said, incredulous. 'You've, like, been here forever now.'

'No. What? Tell me.'

'Ages ago, there was a janitor who went mental and hung himself in there. Reggie Carter's dad came here then. He saw his dead body and everything. Now they say his ghost is in the boiler room and takes the souls of kids that wander in there. That's what happened to Marek Rakowski.'

'Yeah,' said Craig, doubtfully. 'But he also said his dad smashed up the Blue Peter garden.'

'I'll do it. I'll go in there,' Dave said. 'If you dare me.'

'You can't!' said Craig.

The logic of a twelve-year-old boy is bewildering, even to a twelve-year-old boy. You can't back out of a dare. It was a verbal contract. Penny would be impressed by both his bravery and commitment to the laws of the playground. First, though, there were the age-old formalities to perform.

'Alright,' said Darren. 'I dare you to go into the boiler room for two minutes.'

'Double dare,' Dave replied immediately.

'Triple dog dare you,' Darren said. There was no way to challenge or back down from a triple dog dare. The ceremony was complete.

'Let's do it now.' Dave wanted to act before he lost his resolve.

'Now?' Darren and Craig replied in unison.

'Yeah, the teachers are out here or in the staff room. Stinky Johnson doesn't ever lock it. We could do it and be back before the end of break.'

When the teachers were occupied by a fight breaking out between two of the footballers, the three friends snuck back into the school and crept through the quiet, eerie corridors.

They stood outside the boiler room door. Class 3G's crayon self-portraits stared down at them disapprovingly. Dave told himself that they'd never directly been warned that the boiler room was off limits. He was more worried about that might be waiting on the other side of the door. He reminded himself that Reggie Carter was lying. Probably. There had never been a suicidal janitor, there were no such things as ghosts and he'd stand in the dark for two minutes before being hailed a hero.

'Marek and his family moved to Lincoln, didn't they?' Dave asked. With Craig and Darren keeping a look out in either direction, Dave placed his hand on the door handle. He turned it and felt the lock give. He pulled the door ajar and the smell of dust and oil slipped into the corridor. Darren set the digital wristwatch he'd got for his birthday.

'Two minutes, alright?' Dave nodded and cracked the door wide enough to slip through. Once inside, the handle jabbed in his back as he felt Darren and Craig throw their weight against the door behind him. The only light came from a window high up on the opposite wall. He waited for his vision to adjust to the darkness and soon the dark latticework of pipes and levers solidified in front of him. There was a chill in the air, even though he could hear the rumble of the hot boiler in the corner of the room. He shuffled forward and his heart skipped a beat when his foot came into contact with something heavy, yet soft, lying on the floor. He bent down and fumbled around blindly. It was just a couple of paint pots and oily rags. He smiled at how silly he was being.

When he looked back up, he stared into the tired eyes of a middle-aged man. He wore a flat cap, blue overalls and had a surprised expression on his deeply-lined face. Dave screamed in shock and terror. The dead janitor's eyes widened in surprise and he echoed Dave's shriek. They both staggered away from each other. Dave tripped over a pipe sticking out from the floor and fell backwards. The wind knocked out of him, he shuffled on his bum, back towards the door.

'What are you doing here?' yelled the man, exposing his tobacco-stained, crooked teeth.

'Nothing.' Dave gasped.

'How'd you know I'm here? How can you see me?'

'You re not real. You're just a filament of my imagination.' Dave flipped over and pulled himself up off of the ground. He was filthy with the dust and grime. He began to hammer the door with his fists. 'Let me out!'

Darren and Craig laughed from the other side. 'You've still got a minute left!'

The janitor walked towards Dave, who pushed and shoved at the door but was unable to shift the weight of his two friends leaning against it.

'Don't you go anywhere! the janitor yelled. Dave felt his skin crawl as if it wanted to be somewhere else and wasn't bothered if the rest of Dave wasn't coming with it.

The door crashed open and Dave felt a hand grip his arm tightly. His relief was short-lived when he saw that the hand was attached to Mrs McKenzie.

'David Marwood! What do you think you're doing in here unsupervised?'

He was tugged out into the blinding sunlight.

'Get him away from me!' Dave cried.

Mrs McKenzie looked into the boiler room and saw nothing. 'Get who away from you, you silly boy?'

The door slammed in the janitor's face. He sighed heavily in the gloomy, solitary blackness.

'I just wanted somebody to talk to.'

SIXTEEN

Dave woke with a cry, tearing himself away from another bad dream. Next to him, Melanie was twisting and turning, caught up in the covers and her own private nightmare. He knew that it would all end today, whether for good or for ill. It was ridiculous and patronising keeping the truth hidden from her in some foolish attempt to protect her. She hadn't run from him when she found out what she already knew. She was a part of this. She'd fought alongside him. She had been as damaged as he had been. Together they could try and fix each other. He didn't have to do this alone.

Dave decided to go in search of coffee. He slid gently out of the bed. He was still wearing the clothes from the night before, having fallen asleep before he could get undressed. He crossed the flat's hallway and went to the kitchen. He could hear Emma in her room as he tiptoed past. The sharp staccato sound of items shattering provided a backing track to her monotone moaning and muttering. He didn't know whether she was usually this terrifying or if she was affected by whatever paranormal force was taking hold of the city. That was the problem with flat sharing. He wasn't going to take any chances, though, so turned on his heels and went straight back to Melanie's bedroom.

Melanie had woken up, but was fighting a losing battle with the duvet. She looked pale and tired, her smile a painted-on mask. 'Good morning,' she said with a sleepy drawl. She yawned and blinked away the tiredness. He wished he could just stay here, with nothing more important to do than look into those eyes and count each of the lashes that framed them. 'We need to get out of here,' he told her.

'What are you talking about?' she asked, confused.

Dave searched for a way to break the news gently. He settled on, 'I don't think Emma is feeling herself.'

This woke Melanie fast. 'You mean she's feeling like everyone was last night?'

Dave nodded as he looked around for his shoes. 'Get dressed.'

'Where are we going?' Melanie asked as she fell out of the bed and started to pull clothes on.

Dave stopped tying his shoelaces and looked up at her. 'I think it's time you met my boss.'

Melanie hesitated before asking, 'You mean Anne?'

'The other one. We're going to need his help if we're going to stop this.'

'Why do we have to stop this? Surely we need to leave this up to the authorities?' she asked, her questions coated in fear.

'When it comes to this sort of thing I am the authority,' he tried to say in his most heroic voice. Then he ruined it all by struggling to put his man bag over his shoulder and getting caught up in the strap. Melanie shook her head as she freed him.

'Are you ready?'

'One second,' she said and began searching the drawers of her dressing table.

Dave checked his watch. 'What are you looking for?'

'My make-up bag.'

'What do you need that for?' Dave asked, incredulous.

'If I'm going to face a supernatural catastrophe I'm not going to do it without my lip gloss. There it is!'

Dave shook his head, but held his bag open for her to put the make-up case inside. 'Getting ready to go out with you is always a nightmare.'

Dave slowly opened the bedroom door and gingerly poked his head out into the hallway. The noise from Emma's room had stopped. He took a calming breath, waited for his heartbeat to slow and signalled for Melanie to follow him. They crept along the corridor until they reached the front door. Melanie released the deadbolts on the locks, taking care to make as little noise as possible.

The vase smashed against Dave's head, detonating in a soggy explosion. He wheeled around, his hand clutching at his wet, matted hair. The blood pounded in his ears and the water stung his eyes, but he couldn't fail to notice a naked Emma stood at the entrance to the kitchen; hair wild, eyes dulled, a feral sneer on her lips.

'You're not taking her away from me,' she snarled.

'Oh, hi Emma,' Dave said through gritted teeth. 'Didn't realise you were in.'

Her teeth bared, Emma charged down the hallway towards Dave. Melanie stepped between the two of them, taking the full force of the impact. The two women wrestled to the ground, Emma biting at the air and slashing her fingernails indiscriminately. Dave came to his senses and pulled Emma up off of Melanie. They toppled backwards, Dave flipping her over and pinning her hands behind her back.

'Get the bloody door!' he yelled, but Melanie was already on her feet and fumbling with the locks.

The door sprang open. 'Come on!' Melanie urged.

'Go! Get the downstairs door open!' Dave said as he struggled to contain Emma as she kicked and screamed beneath him. Melanie nodded and sprinted out of the flat.

'I'm glad we've got this time alone,' Dave said. 'I really hope this doesn't make things awkward between us. I really would like us to be friends, if only for Melanie's sake. Anyway. Good talk. Nice to see you again.'

Dave counted to three in his head and then sprang to his feet. He turned and ran out the door without looking back. He could feel Emma bearing down on him as he reached the first flight of stairs. As he descended, fearful that he might trip over his own feet, he wistfully thought back to the last time he tried to exit a building without someone trying to rip his throat out.

As he reached the ground floor, he could see Melanie holding the street door open from him. The look in her eyes told him that Emma was nearly upon him and, with safety in sight, he pushed himself forward and into the sunlight. Inertia carried him forward and he hit the pavement as Melanie slammed the door in Emma's face. She beat the window, howling in frustration, fracturing the glass and slicing her hands.

Melanie pulled Dave to his feet. 'Let's get out of here,' she said and Dave dumbly nodded in agreement. They'd barely made it to the end of the street before they had to help separate two businessmen brawling against a parked car. Scuffles broke out as people tried to push in lines outside coffee shops and department stores. When the British started queue jumping, Dave knew that society was definitely crumbling. He took Melanie's hand, partly so they wouldn't be separated but also for comfort. The air crackled with animosity.

Dave and Melanie kept out of people's way as they headed to the Underground station, keen to avoid confrontation.

'What's going on?' Melanie asked.

'You know how I told you that your employer - my old boss - is, in fact, Conquest and one of the Four Horsemen of the Apocalypse?'

'Yes,' Melanie replied as casually as if Dave had told her the football scores.

'For centuries he and Death, my current boss, and the other Horsemen tried to stop the end of the world. Now it looks like he's reread the job description and, for whatever reason, decided to destroy it all.'

Melanie waved a hand at the crowds starting to mass together, spinning off into factions, weighing each other up like prize fighters. 'So, he's doing all this?'

'Yeah, he's created some kind of negative energy. It's centred on UberSystems Tower. I think the plan is for us to tear ourselves apart.'

'The whole of London? He couldn't do that, surely? It's a big city. There's a lot of love. I know it doesn't look like it, but it's there.'

'Well, he's doing a pretty good job so far.'

'How come it hasn't affected you?'

'I don't know. Maybe because I'm aware of it, or I haven't spent as much time where it's the strongest. Or maybe it's because I'm a stone cold super-cool badass.'

'Yeah, that's it,' Melanie said. Dave could practically hear her eyes rolling.

'You're taking this all rather well.'

'Trust me, beneath this calm exterior I am having a full scale, record-breaking freak out.'

Though social order was collapsing, with Melanie by his side Dave felt in control. He walked with purpose through the chaos until they reached the entrance to the Underground. A busker was making his way through the Radiohead back catalogue on an acoustic guitar. Dave and Melanie had to carefully step over the prone bodies of commuters lying on the floor sobbing.

Scanning their Oyster cards, they breezed through the gates and headed down to the platform. Jumping onto the next train, they collapsed into vacant seats. After a moment, Dave felt a wave of tweedy anger. Across the aisle sat his ghostly friend Fred Drayton.

Surrounded by the oblivious living, Dave gave a subtle nod of recognition.

'Oh, it's you, is it?' Fred spat. 'I wondered when you'd show up.'

Dave pulled a face that said, 'You what?'

'You've been too busy gallivanting around town with your skin and internal organs to come down here and see your friend?'

Dave didn't need to ask whether Fred was being affected by the Dark. He sighed, feeling as if he was dealing with a cantankerous old relative.

'I've been busy,' he said quite openly. Everybody else was dealing with their own private insanities, what was one more thrown in to the mix?

Melanie's eyes switched from Dave to the empty seat opposite. 'Dave, is someone else here?'

Dave sat back. 'Yes. Melanie, this is Fred Drayton.' He addressed the empty seat. 'Fred, this is Melanie.'

'She's a lot prettier than I imagined,' Fred said with a leer.

Dave turned to Melanie. 'He says he's pleased to meet you.'

Melanie squinted at where Fred was supposedly sat. 'I--I think I can see something. Just a faint outline.'

'Yeah, I think whatever divides their world from ours is becoming permeable. They're bleeding into our reality.'

'I am right here, you know?' Fred said huffily. 'I do not bleed anywhere.'

'I'm very sorry,' Dave said. 'How have you been?'

Fred leaned forward conspiratorially. 'I feel fantastic. I'm learning new things. Watch this.' He turned to the man sat next to him, who was engrossed in a paperback novel.

'The killer is the school teacher's ex-wife.' Fred's face was screwed up in concentration as if he was trying to physically push the words into the reader's ear.

The reader looked up from the page and glanced around the carriage, a befuddled expression on his face. He flicked to the back of the book, scanned the text and muttered an incredibly rude word under his breath. The train pulled into a station. He threw the book down onto his seat and shuffled off onto the platform.

'Excuse me.' Melanie called after him. 'You've left your book behind.' The man didn't acknowledge her.

Dave shook his head when he saw Fred's self-satisfied grin. 'That's not cool,' he told him sternly.

Fred shrugged off Dave's disapproval. 'Do you know how long it took me to read that book by glancing over people's shoulders? I'm sick of it.'

'Yeah, but still--' Dave trailed off.

'I'm glad you two have sorted things out,' Fred said.

Dave took Melanie's hand in his. 'Thanks.'

'What's he saying?' Melanie asked.

'He's happy we're back together,' Dave explained.

Melanie slid her fingers out from under Dave's. 'You talk to dead people about us?'

'Who's he going to tell?' Dave asked.

Melanie thought for a moment. 'Other dead people?'

'Can we not do this now?'

'Fine,' she said and crossed her arms.

'I'm sorry if I've made things awkward,' Fred said, the trace of a malicious grin on his lips.

Dave turned back to him. 'Have you noticed anything unusual?'

'I'm dead, Mr Marwood. My threshold for "unusual" is set pretty high these days.'

'Y'know. Anything apocalypse-y. Things that seem like humanity's heading towards the End Times.'

Fred considered the question. 'I did see a dog wearing a little top hat the other day.'

SEVENTEEN

Crow Road was still and calm as always, yet Dave could feel the darkness circling like a noose, pulling tighter and constricting the city.

He put his hand on the door handle, paused and turned to Melanie. He wondered if he was making the right decision. He was reminded of the first time he brought a girlfriend home to meet his mum and dad. The hope that everybody liked each other and the fear that his parents would say something embarrassing.

'I know I've told you this before, but I think I should warn you that the creature you're about to come face to face with is...' Dave said.

'Frightening?' Melanie interrupted. 'Terrifying? Horrifying? I understand. I'm prepared for it.'

'Actually, I was going to go with irritating,' Dave said as he opened the door.

He led her to the door at the top of the stairs, took a deep breath and marched into the office.

Death and Anne were stood talking by the water cooler. At the creak of the opening door they looked over to see Dave stood on the threshold.

'You look unusually focused for this time of the morning,' said Death.

'I've had an idea,' Dave replied.

'Good for you. Does it involve the kettle?' Death asked, waving an empty tea cup. Then he saw Melanie over Dave's shoulder and his mood darkened. 'What's she doing here?'

Melanie was already staggering backwards down the hallway. The embodiment of humanity's greatest fear stood in front of her and nothing could prepare her for the implications of that. Dave reached out and took her by the arm to steady her. With quiet words of encouragement, he coaxed her into the office. She lurched forward, her legs as unsteady and delicate as a newborn foal's.

'She deserves to know what's going on,' Dave said. 'She's part of this now.'

Anne walked over, her hand extended. 'It's good that we finally get to meet, Melanie. I've heard a lot about you.'

Melanie took Anne's hand, but her eyes were still locked like lasers on the dark figure on the other side of the room. Her mouth flapped up and down, but her voice had been scared away.

Anne gestured towards Death. 'Don't mind him, he's always moody until he's had his second cup of tea.' She turned to him. 'Did they teach you any manners at any point in the millennia you've existed?'

Death lazily waved a hand at Melanie. 'Hello Melanie. It s good to see you again.'

Melanie found her voice. 'Again? What do you mean?'

Dave turned to Melanie. 'There have been times when he's been around you, but you weren't aware of it.'

Melanie looked from Dave to Death and back again. 'That's handy, because I actually didn't want to sleep ever again.'

'Can we all focus on the matter in hand?' Dave said, disappointed that he'd lost his momentum. 'Have you seen what's going on out there? The place is tearing itself apart and you're sat around here drinking tea and eating biscuits.'

'It was a pain au chocolat, actually,' Death mumbled.

'Melanie threatened a waiter with a butter knife last night!'

'A good thing too. Too few people are willing to take a stand against the poor service you receive in restaurants in this country.'

'I'm just going to ignore you now.' Dave turned to Anne. 'Have you got that folder of newspaper cuttings?'

'It's on my desk. Why?'

'Letitia. Or George. Whoever. I'm not really sure how it works. They said that the Dark was coming in from the river. I'm pretty sure that it's coming from UberSystems International. If we can plot all the disturbance on a map...'

'...We can see if there's any kind of pattern,' said Anne.

Death folded his arms. 'Excuse me, but can I ask one question?'

'What?' Anne barked.

'Am I going to have to make my own cup of tea?'

'Yes!' Anne, Melanie and Dave shouted at him in unison.

'Unbelievable,' Death muttered as he walked over to the kettle. 'I'm not making anyone else one.'

Dave grabbed a map of London from a drawer and stuck it to the wall while Anne rifled through the folder full of cuttings. They each grabbed a handful of drawing pins and pushed them into the locations mentioned in the newspaper articles. Death busied himself with the ritual of making tea. Melanie fell into a chair and stared dumbly as they worked. After a while, she attempted to make conversation.

'You-- er-- You're not as--'

'Tall as you expected? I know. '

'I was going to say scary. Once you spend a bit of time in your company.'

'Thank you Melanie. You're not the first person to say that. What can I say? I've had a lot of bad press.

Would you like a cuppa?' Death said as he squeezed the teabag and dropped it into the bin.

'No. I'm fine, thank you.'

'Then, if you'll excuse me I've got some work to do. It really is good to meet you. I'm very sorry about before.' Death took his mug and disappeared into his office.

After a few minutes, Anne and Dave stood back and looked at the collection of coloured dots. They were definitely centred round where UberSystems Tower stood.

Death stuck his head from around his office door. 'I'm just popping out. Does anybody want anything?'

Melanie shook her head, but Anne and Dave ignored him as they tried to find patterns in the seemingly random position of the pins. 'Is there something going on here?' Dave asked, circling three closely placed pins with a marker pen.

'I can't see it,' Anne replied.

'Right. You lot seem to be doing fine without me. I've got to meet someone, anyway.' Death slammed the door for dramatic effect. Melanie flinched in her chair, but neither Anne nor Dave noticed.

'There's nothing there,' Anne said, turning her back to the map. 'It was a nice idea, though.'

'No,' Dave shook his head. He knew there was something they were missing.

Death opened the office door and stood motionless. He seemed confused. After a moment, he coughed to get everyone's attention. They all looked over their shoulders.

'I can't go out there,' he said in a stunned, flat voice.

'Look, I understand that you're finding things hard to deal with at the moment,' Dave said in a calm tone. 'It must be difficult to learn this is all being caused by your old friend, but you've got to deal with this.'

Death shook his head as if trying to dislodge terrible thoughts. 'No, you don't understand. I can't physically leave this place. Whatever it is that stops me from getting into Conquest's building has spread. It's all over London. I'm trapped here. You've got to figure out what he's up to and stop him.'

Dave looked around the room. He didn't know what to do next. Whatever it took to defeat Conrad West, he'd hoped he would have Death at his side.

Melanie got up from her seat and looked intently at the map. 'Maybe there's something in the history of the area,' she said. 'All that part of London was docks and wharfs for hundreds of years before it was redeveloped.'

Dave smiled at Melanie and took his mobile phone from his trouser pocket. 'I think I know someone who might be able to help us.' He dialled a number in his contacts. 'Hi, Gary. It's Dave,' he said as soon as the call was answered. 'Dave... Your flatmate...? About five foot eleven, medium build, dark hair...? We talked yesterday...? Yeah, now you've got it. I need to ask a favour. Can you get me in touch with Nick Broughton?'

EIGHTEEN

After several phone calls and promises to buy beer, Dave, Melanie and Anne made their way to Nick Broughton's last known residence.

The high-rise block dominated the skyline, a brutal monolith that loomed over the surrounding estates and cast them in shadow. The lift wouldn't work, so they climbed the five flights to the floor where Broughton lived. They headed along an open air walkway, counting the door numbers until they arrived at the flat. Anne gave a business-like knock and they patiently waited as they listened to a dozen locks being released. The door cracked open and two narrow eyes peered out from the gloom.

'Nick Broughton?' Anne asked with a smile. The eyes widened with recognition and, before it could be slammed shut, Dave jammed his foot in the door.

'How'd you find me?' Nick asked, panic-stricken.

'You'd be surprised what people will do for a pint of Badger's Fancy,' Dave replied.

'I don't want to die,' Nick whispered as he smashed the door repeatedly against Dave's shoe.

'What are you talking about?' Anne asked.

'You're here to kill me, aren't you? A government hit squad. I know you.'

'Don't be so stupid. Do we look like a government hit squad?' replied Anne.

Nick looked at Anne's beads and bangles and Dave and Melanie's tee shirt and jeans. She had a point. Melanie decided to appeal to Nick's ego. 'There's an emergency and we need your expertise. You're our only hope.'

The door opened wide. Anne looked impressed. Dave was just grateful that the slamming against his throbbing toes had stopped.

'Well, you'd better come in then.' Nick stood aside to let them in. After he checked the walkway was clear, he closed the door.

'Perhaps we can start this again?' Anne said, holding her hand out. 'Anne Mitchell. These are my associates Dave Marwood and Melanie Watkins.'

Nick grabbed Anne's hand as if he was handling a wet fish. Anne assumed he wasn't used to normal social interactions.

'You were at the Truther Symposium the other night, Nick said to Dave. 'You caused a scene. They told me you were a mole.' Before Dave could reply, Nick had already turned his attention to Melanie and taken her hand.

'I'm afraid I haven't made your acquaintance,' he said in a rough approximation of a seductive purr.

Melanie gently took her hand back and wiped it on her jeans. 'I'm just a fan,' she said.

Nick ushered his three guests along the dim hallway. 'What can I do for you?'

'You must've noticed what's happening out there?' Anne said.

'Who's at the door?' A woman's voice yelled from the living room.

'Just some work stuff, mum,' Nick shouted back.

'Tell your weird friends not to touch my things.'

Nick shook his head and pointed to a door. 'Go in there. I'll be with you in a second. The kettle's just boiled if you're interested.'

They went where they were directed. It was Nick's bedroom. It didn't look like the interior design had changed much since his adolescence. The walls were decorated with fantasy posters, old books and photos he had taken. Some of them were of Anne.

'Why does he have photographs of me?' she asked, backing away towards the door.

'I've told you, he thinks you're a government agent involved in an international conspiracy,' Dave said.

'A creepy, paranoid Dungeons and Dragons fan who stalks women and still lives with his mother? This is your plan?' Melanie asked.

'Melanie's right, Dave. This is a terrible idea. I'm not letting you reveal everything to him. What if he tells people? Anne said.

Dave took Nick's book from out of his bag and waved it at her. 'Have you read this? Nobody is going to believe him.'

Nick came into the room carrying a tray laden with tea and biscuits. 'Oh, you brought my book with you? Would you like me to autograph it?'

Dave looked at it in his hand and shrugged. 'Yeah. Sure.'

Nick put the tray down and looked for a pen. Dave handed one to him from his bag.

'And who shall I say it's for?' Nick asked, looking directly at Melanie.

'Dave,' Dave said, aware that Nick had already forgotten he was in the room.

Nick wrote a short message in the inside cover, pocketed the pen and handed the book back to Dave with a smile.

'Thanks,' Dave mumbled and put the book in his bag. 'Can I have my pen back?'

Nick's smile disappeared as he gave back the chewed biro. 'Sugar?' he asked as he picked up a cup from the tray.

'No, thanks,' Anne said. 'If we can get back to the reason for our visit, please? I'm sure you're aware of what's been going on out there?'

'Society falling apart? Groups of people moving around like packs of wild animals? Attacking each other randomly? Unstoppable and insatiable? Some people on the forums are saying this is the Apocalypse,' Nick said with a sense of foreboding.

Anne mulled that over before saying, 'A medium sized apocalypse, maybe.'

'More like a bijou apocalyse-ette,' Dave said.

'Very London,' added Melanie.

Nick passed a second cup to Melanie, leaving Dave to get his own.

'Zombies,' Nick said.

'It's not zombies,' Dave replied tersely. 'Zombies don't run. This is the situation. We work for an individual who would prefer to remain anonymous. Our job is to deal with people who... well... aren't as dead as they should be. There's something going on. Someone, or something, powerful is manipulating both the living and the dead.'

'I knew it!' Nick shouted, punching the air. He reached over to a cluttered desk and picked up a Dictaphone. Anne grabbed him gently by the wrist.

'This is strictly off the record.'

Disappointed, Nick dropped the Dictaphone back onto the desk.

'I reckon it's being controlled from one central location.' Dave put his cup of tea to one side and pulled the map out of the bag. He spread it over the bed and tapped it with his finger. 'Riverside Wharf.'

'But you don't know why or how?'

'Yeah.'

'And what's in it for me?' Nick asked.

'All that apocalypse stuff we just talked about? I think we'd all like to avoid that, wouldn't we?' Anne said.

Dave could tell that wouldn't be enough. 'I'm sure we could come to some sort of financial arrangement.'

'That's more like it.' Nick sighed. 'I'll admit that paranormal research isn't the growth industry I'd hoped it would be.'

Nick picked up a heavy book from the shelf above his head and flicked the through the dog-eared pages. 'Riverside Wharf rings a bell. Here we are.' He passed the book to Anne. 'It was the home of a cult in the mid-eighties. The New Righteous Order of Armageddon.'

'Armageddon?' Dave said.

'Well, it sounds like you're in the Armageddon business. It was run by a guy called Nathan Christou. His great-uncle was Archibald Christou. You might have heard of him?'

Dave shook his head.

'He was a Victorian occultist,' Anne said. 'He used to hold rituals to try and bring about the Apocalypse.'

'End of the world cults run in the family, then?' Dave asked.

'Then he had some kind of change of heart and dedicated his life to setting up hospices in memory of his fiancée Sarah Montague.'

'Oh yeah. My mum was in one when she had her cancer,' Dave said. Melanie placed a comforting hand on his knee.

'The New Righteous Order of Armageddon started off all new age, hippy-dippy, peace and love,' Nick continued. 'Then it went very dark very quickly. They fell under the influence of someone who called himself the Master, who preached a belief that the world was too sick to survive. They were convinced that Halley's Comet was a sign that the world was going to end and that a chosen few would be saved. They decided to get there first and committed mass suicide.'

'How many?' asked Dave, horrified.

'Twenty. Everybody except the Master. He disappeared without a trace. It was all hushed up.'

'What if they're still there?' Anne asked.

Dave shivered. 'Death's mistakes.'

'Something that psychically violent must cause an incredible amount of negative energy,' Nick said.

'Can you explain to me what you're talking about?' Melanie asked. 'Use small words. For the sake of argument, pretend I'm very drunk.'

'There are energies all around us,' Nick said. 'Many are negative. You might pass through one and feel inexplicably angry, or weepy. They're sometimes caused by violent death. This is on a scale that's never been seen before.'

Melanie shook her head. 'Just a few days ago I would've said that this talk of negative energies and auras was a load of holistic, tantric arse...'

'It doesn't matter what you believe in, Miss Watkins,' Nick said. 'Things are what they are, even if they are beyond the realms of your understanding.'

'Now UberSystems Tower sits on top of it,' Dave said, his voice wavering. 'The building's height and structure must be acting like a giant transmitter beaming the energy across the city.'

'Which is ironic because I could never get a phone signal in there,' Melanie said.

'UberSystems Tower? Where those people were killed last week?' Nick said. 'That's interesting. I had a few cool theories about that.'

'Theories?' Dave exploded. 'Theories? People died in there. Good people. They're not some intellectual exercise for you and your friends on the internet to stroke your neck beards over.'

Nick held his hand out in an attempt to placate Dave. 'Woah! I'm sorry, man. I didn't realise you'd be so sensitive about it.'

'Dave and Melanie worked there,' Anne explained.

'We were there that night,' Melanie said, stroking Dave's neck. She could feel him shivering and shaking as if trying to dislodge the pain that rattled around inside. 'Dave tried to save them all, but--' She ran out of words, unable to articulate the enormity of Dave's task that night. 'He saved my life.'

'Wow. Really? I'm sorry,' Nick said with feeling.

'Can you keep the noise down in there?' Nick's mother shouted from the living room.

Nick rolled his eyes and stood up. 'Excuse me,' he said before leaving the room.

'What now?' asked Dave, calm now. He already knew what the reply would be and that he would agree to it.

'Fancy a trip to your old workplace?'

'Yeah, I didn't steal nearly enough stationery when I left. Can I drive?'

'No.'

Nick poked his head around the door. He said, 'You might want to watch the news,' and then returned to the living room.

Using an old tennis racquet, Anne managed to excavate an ancient portable television from under a pile of dirty socks and underwear.

'...Appears to have started in the more affluent areas of the capital,' the newsreader said to the camera. 'We can go live to Jason Booth, who's on Oxford Street.'

The broadcast switched to an image of a nervous looking reporter. Over his shoulder, Oxford Street burned. There were dark gaping mouths where shop windows used to be. Black cabs, gutted by flames, were abandoned in the middle of the street. Around them, summer bunting was strewn like the entrails of some vanquished yet fabulous monster. Mobs prowled like hungry wolves; some clutched shopping bags while others had looted weapons, baseball bats and golf clubs. A Molotov cocktail made using a fine premium vodka bottle and monogrammed handkerchief flew through the air and exploded against a bus that had been parked halfway inside a Starbucks.

'Trouble flared soon after the shops opened for business,' Jason shouted into a microphone clutched in his shaking hand. 'Nobody knows what the catalyst was, but hundreds now roam one of London's most prestigious shopping districts. The violence is random and indiscriminate. We don't have any numbers when it comes to casualties, but it's safe to say that the emergency services are overwhelmed.'

A policeman in full riot gear ran into shot. 'What the bloody hell are you doing here?' he shouted at the reporter.

Jason shoved his microphone under the policeman's nose. 'Officer, what do you think caused all this?'

The policeman lifted his helmet's visor. 'How should I sodding know? Maybe they ran out of ra-ra skirts, or whatever's in this bloody season.'

The picture juddered, pixelated and finally broke up and went black. The newsreader in the studio reappeared. 'We seem to have lost the feed there. We apologise if the language used has caused any offence.'

Anne had located the remote control and, glad she didn't have to go near the television and mound of underwear again, turned the sound down.

Nick returned. Anne stood up. 'I'm sorry, but we're going to have to leave now,' she said.

'Really?' said Nick excitedly. 'Let me grab my coat.'

'I don't think that's a good idea.'

'Are you kidding me?' Nick replied. 'I've been waiting for this my whole life. I'm not going to sit here twiddling my thumbs. If it wasn't for me, you wouldn't even know what you were up against.'

'Alright. Fine.' Anne gave an exasperated sigh. 'Let's go.'

Nick opened a wardrobe and pulled out a shovel, its blade polished to a bright shine. He spoke to it lovingly. 'It's finally time.'

'What the hell is that?' Anne asked.

Nick shifted the shovel in hands, feeling the weight and balance. 'I call her Grace. She's my zombie killer.'

'Aren't zombies already dead? How could you kill them?' Melanie asked.

'They're not zombies!' Dave said. 'Why won't anyone listen to me?'

They bundled into the hallway. When they reached the front door, Nick called out, 'Mum! I'm just popping out.'

'What for?'

'Society's crumbling. I've got to go and sort it out.'

'You always say that.'

'No, it really is this time. If I'm not back in a bit, avenge my death.'

'Only if there's nothing good on the telly.'

Nick shrugged his shoulders. 'Parents, eh?'

NINETEEN

Nick and Melanie folded themselves into the back of the Morris Minor while Anne and Dave took the front seats. Anne wheel spun the car out of the car park and headed towards the financial hub of the country and UberSystems Tower. Soon, though, they were forced to slow down and join the gridlock that had ground the city to a halt. They sat in silence as they watched the violent scenes play out around them, soundtracked by the sirens of unseen ambulances and police cars. Anne switched the radio on.

'...This is being caused by the ennui that has gripped the country for a generation. We are a people defined by how large our widescreen televisions are and how thin our waists should be. This is a manifestation of the frustration felt in our daily lives. We are finally saying, as a society, "we have had enough"...'

Anne switched the radio off. 'I think we're done listening to Radio 4.'

She drummed her fingers on the steering wheel impatiently and then seemed to come to a decision. She put the car in gear, revved the engine and steered up onto the pavement. Dave grabbed the door handle and Nick and Melanie slid along the back seat as she sped past the stationary traffic. People put the objects that they were planning to throw through shop windows down and dived out of the way. A bin bounced off the windscreen and fell underneath the car's wheels.

'Shit!' Dave shouted.

'What's wrong?' asked Melanie as she extricated herself from underneath Nick.

'The bins. It's bin day.'

'Try and think of the bigger picture,' Anne told him.

Dave agreed and concentrated on their destination. UberSystems Tower stood in the distance, a beacon calling them in. At this very moment, he wished he'd never made that visit to Crow Road. He wanted to be anywhere than here, racing towards a force that was capable of destroying a city. Then he reasoned that, if he wasn't here, he'd probably be working at that same desk he was six months ago. He and Melanie would be sat right on top of it with no knowledge of what was beneath him. The traffic cleared and Anne twisted the steering wheel so the car jumped down onto the road. She looked at Nick in the rear-view mirror. 'You can open your eyes now.'

Nick sat up from the crash position he'd adopted. 'Are we off the pavement? Did we kill anyone?'

'Yes and no,' Anne confirmed. 'For someone who claims to live outside of society's rules, you're pretty conformist when it comes to the Road Traffic Act.'

Nick was putting together a witty retort when a car jumping a red light stole his thunder and smashed into the side of the Morris Minor. The cars span across the road, their tyres and brakes squealing and screeching in grotesque harmony.

The vehicles came to rest by the kerb. The driver of the other car fled the accident scene without looking back. The Deathmobile's passenger door fought and rattled against the pulverised bodywork before popping open. Dave tumbled out onto the pavement, quickly followed by Melanie, Nick and Grace the Shovel clanging on the concrete.

'Is everyone alright?' Dave asked.

Melanie checked all her limbs were intact and nodded dumbly. Nick gently picked up the shovel as if it was a precious family heirloom and dusted it down.

Anne stumbled out from the driver's side. She surveyed the damage, grief creeping into the corners of her eyes. The windscreen was cracked into fractals, the bonnet's curves transformed into blunt lines. The mathematics of disaster.

Dave scooted around the front of the car and steered Anne away. The accident had attracted the attention of a group of teenagers destroying an expensive 4x4 and he felt it would be better they returned to their work.

One of the teenage gang threw his head back, opened his mouth and let out a scream that Dave thought might rip the fabric of the air in two. Everybody else in the street turned in their direction.

'I think we should get out of here,' Dave said, slowly backing away from the car. He reached out behind him until he found Melanie's hand. Anne followed and Nick stepped in front of them protectively, shovel held out to repel any attackers.

The crowds slowly lumbered towards them. With their bloodied limbs, blank expressions and thoughtless working towards a common goal, Dave could see how they could be mistaken for zombies.

The howling teenager was the first to break into a run, leaping over the car's wrecked bonnet in a single bound. The others took this as the signal to follow and a seething tide of angry humanity surged forward.

'Run!' Dave screamed unnecessarily and all four of them spun around and sprinted down the road.

Dave hopped up onto the pavement and ducked down a passageway tucked between two buildings. It was narrow enough that he could touch both walls at once if he stretched his arms out. He allowed himself a glance backwards to check the others were with him.

Anne and Melanie were hard on his heels with Nick bringing up the rear. The feral teenager was trying to get a grip on Nick's shirttails. He turned around midstride and lashed out with the shovel in an upward swing. It connected solidly with the teenager's jaw with a sickening crunch. His head was thrown back, blood sketching a dark parabola in the air as he crashed to the ground at the alley's entrance.

Those behind, desperate to get through, tripped over him. More and more piled up, wedging themselves tight, until a dam of flesh blocked the advancing hordes. The air was filled with frustrated screams, raw and naked, stripped of civilisation's thin disguise. Their prey had stopped at the other end of the passageway and watched with morbid fascination.

'I think we need to find somewhere to lie low and work out what to do,' Melanie said, bent double and gulping lungfuls of air.

'Good idea,' Anne wheezed. 'Preferably somewhere with a kettle.'

TWENTY

Eleven Years Earlier

The dead were at Anne's door again. She could hear the urgent whispers, the plotting and the despair. She fumbled with the vodka bottle's lid and sloshed the contents into a glass. Knocking the drink back, she shivering as the burn travelled from her mouth to her stomach. The warmth radiated out and, as it did, the voices in the hallway grew fainter.

She crossed the grubby living room, five unsteady steps from one side to the other, and collapsed into the sofa. She pulled a throw over her shoulders. It would be all be fine, she told herself, if they just left her alone. But they followed her around like lost children, so she locked herself away in her flat.

With trembling fingers, she lit a cigarette. She hungrily drew the harsh smoke into her lungs, the crackle of the burning tobacco above the soft murmur of the muffled voices. She refilled the glass. Twenty-two years old and already broken. Everything changed when her father died. In a fit of grief, her mother had got rid of all his possessions and the video store was sold off to an entertainment chain. Every day she walked past it on the way to school wishing the store front still bore his name, for some reminder that he had been part of her world. She constantly played that final day over and over in her mind. The guilt clung to her; because that was the price she thought she had to pay to remember him. The ghosts still came to her and in greater numbers and she resented them. Why couldn't her father have stayed here, like them? What was special about them? Why was he taken away? Shouldn't the dead be with the people they left behind, rather than haunting her?

Her teenage years finished in a blur. University had been a disaster. It was there that she discovered that if she drank enough, the ghosts would fade away into the background noise and disappear. That kind of self-medication came with side effects; the failed courses, regrets and strangers in her bed the next morning.

Then there was her mother. She could deal with the arguments, the pair of them screaming. At least it showed that they both still had some fight left in them. It was the days spent in silence, dead to each other, which were the hardest.

She stubbed the cigarette out in the overflowing ashtray. She knew what she had to do. It was obvious, hiding from her in plain sight. She knew who was responsible. For the dead. For her father. For her situation.

She made a telephone call. It was short and finished with the familiar raised voice at the other end of the line. When she hung up the phone, she walked calmly into the bathroom. The cabinet in there was empty. Any painkillers that might have been there once had long been consumed. She ran the bath, the steam from the hot water fogging up the reflective surfaces. This was fine. She didn't want to look herself in the eye. She went to the kitchen, searching through the drawers until she found the one sharp knife she owned. She carefully cleaned it under a running tap and delicately touched the blade with her fingers. It would do.

She went back into the bathroom and closed the door.

Anne was looking at the bathroom door. The first thing she noticed was that her feet didn't stick to the faded linoleum. She felt her own weightlessness. She was clear headed, her thoughts sharper than they had been in a long while. She remembered what she had done. The phone call to her mother, a goodbye or a cry for help? She wasn't sure. Closing the bathroom door. Climbing into the warm water. A bright white light, a supernova of pain. She didn't turn around, didn't want to see the bath. She knew what was in there. Panic engulfed her, washing away her reason. He wasn't here. Why wasn't he here? She didn't want to die. What had she been thinking? This was wrong. She had screwed up her life and it looked like she'd screwed up her death too.

Voices started calling her name from behind her front door, fists beating on the wood, and she recognised them as the sounds of the living.

'Help me!' she screamed, knowing nobody could hear her.

Then he was there, standing right in front of her. The dark flaw that ran through her memory. She'd been right. She knew it. She'd always known it.

'Sorry I'm late. There was this thing and --' Death stopped and looked over her shoulder. 'Oh, bloody hell. What'd you go and do that for?' he asked, disappointed. 'You don't get to choose. Did you think about everyone you're leaving behind? It's not just your life your decisions affect. Wasn't there anyone you could talk to?' Then he waved a hand. 'Never mind. None of my business.'

'I don't know.' Anne's voice came in panicked gasps. 'It seemed like a good idea at the time. I thought I wanted to do this. I wanted to meet you. You were the one I wanted to talk to. I wanted to prove to them, to prove to myself, that you were real and this seemed to be the only way of doing it but now I don't want to do it and I'm scared and I need you to help me and I want to go back and pretend this never happened.'

'Shh,' Death hushed in a calming tone.

There was a sharp crack from the living room as the front door gave way. A second later, the bathroom door smashed open and two paramedics ran in. Carrying heavy pieces of medical equipment and cases, they barely squeezed into the room. They passed through Anne and she felt a cold shiver all down the memory of where her body used to be.

One of the paramedics looked in the bath behind her and simply muttered, 'Shit.'

Anne heard the urgent splash and splatter of water gushing over the side of the bath and onto the floor. Death took her by the arm and led her out into the living room. 'Perhaps we should do this out here.'

A nervous looking policeman was talking into his crackling and hissing radio, oblivious to the ghosts peering around the shattered remains of the front door. There were old ladies and young men. Sharp business suits, overalls, jeans and tee shirts.

'You might as well come in,' Anne said to them. They shuffled in and everyone stood around awkwardly, like the worst house party ever. 'You can sort this lot out while you're here,' she said to Death.

'You know these people?' Death asked, confused.

'They come over here every day. They think I can help them. I can barely help myself,' Anne explained.

'You don't have to be so rude about it,' replied a little old lady.

'I'm rude?' answered Anne. 'You've ruined my life!'

'There didn't seem to be much to ruin, if you ask me,' the little old lady sneered.

'What did you say?'

Everybody began shouting, talking over each other and refusing to listen. Death rubbed his temples. He didn't need this.

'Can you all BE QUIET?' he barked.

The ghosts fell silent, sullenly staring at their feet like scalded children. Thinking he was alone, the policeman picked his nose.

Death pointed a finger at Anne. 'Right. You. What's your name?'

'Anne.'

'Anne. So you could see this lot while you were alive?'

'Yes.'

'That's weird. I've never come across that before.'

'And we could see what she gets up to,' the old lady muttered.

Death rounded on her. His patience was wearing thin. 'I will get to you in a minute.'

There was something unusual about Anne. An energy radiated from her in a way that he'd never encountered. Though her blonde hair was matted and greasy, and her clothes crumpled and stained, there was an intelligence and sharpness behind those bloodshot eyes. If she was telling the truth, perhaps she could help him. And, maybe, he could help her. It looked like she could do with it.

'Clear!' shouted one of the paramedics from the bathroom. There was a dull thud and Anne doubled over in pain, like somebody had kicked her in the chest with a heavy boot. They were trying the defibrillator. Anne felt the charge explode in her body and ripple out in bioelectrical waves.

'I think I've got a pulse,' a voice called out from the bathroom. The policeman ran in to join them.

Death turned back to Anne. 'If you get out of this, I want to talk to you. There's something odd going on here.'

'Oh, really?' Anne replied.

'Don't be cheeky, young lady.'

'How are you going to find me?'

'I am familiar with the local hospitals. I'm sure I can figure it out.'

'But what about --'

Anne was gone, dragged back to the world of the living. The policeman, shouting into his radio, ran through the living room and out of the door.

'That s not fair. How come she gets to live?' asked a middle-aged man in a kipper tie and flares.

'Do you lot ever stop moaning? I don't make the rules.' Death took a deep breath and counted to ten. He sensed his world had just changed. Until two minutes ago, he thought he would be alone in the world. It was a simpler time. He already missed it. 'Right. Who wants to go first?'

TWENTY-ONE

Like many before them, Dave and his friends found shelter and peace in a bookshop.

It had obviously been abandoned in a hurry, the front door left ajar and books scattered across the floor. They locked the door and barricaded it with a display case filled with the latest ghost written celebrity autobiography. Anne located a kettle in the back room and made a pot of tea for everyone. When you're British, tea is a cure for all ills, a one-stop healing potion. Bad day at work? Put the kettle on. Wife left you for your best friend? Put the kettle on. End of the world? Put the kettle on and throw an extra teabag into the pot. Treat yourself.

She phoned Death and briefed him with what they'd learned about the suicide cult. He complained that there was nothing to do so she directed him to a stack of magazines in her desk drawer.

They were slouched against the bookshelves, hidden away from the window and the gangs of the Dark-infected that roamed the streets. Melanie rested her head on Dave's shoulder, both lost in their own thoughts. Anne flicked through a copy of the celebrity's autobiography, wrinkling her nose when she reached another sordid revelation.

Nick methodically cleaned the blood from his shovel with a cloth he'd found behind the sales counter. 'I'll be okay in the zombie apocalypse,' he said in between breathing onto the shovel's blade and polishing it to a shine.

'They're not...' Dave began to say before he realised that Nick was paying no attention.

'The zombies themselves wouldn't be much of a problem. They spend most of their time bumping into things and, quite frankly, they're a bit of an embarrassment. If you get caught and eaten by a zombie you deserve it.' He held the shovel up into the light and admired his handiwork. 'No, it's the nights you have to worry about. The dark nights that stretch out like a dark stretchy thing.'

He glanced up at the shop's entrance. 'You've barricaded yourself in. The zombies are bumping into the window of the artisan bakery down the road. You've got food and your shovel.' He looked at Dave. 'We need to get you a shovel. You should give it a name. How about Shovelly?'

Nick turned his blank gaze to Melanie. 'But what to do for entertainment? There's no "Cash in the Attic" during the zombie apocalypse, although watching daytime TV sometimes makes me think that the zombie apocalypse has already started. You're burning the contents of the bookshop for warmth. Apart from the Harry Styles biography.' Nick stroked a book lying at his side. 'Harry understands. Harry takes the pain away. Sweet Harry.'

Dave and Melanie exchanged a concerned glance.

'Are you alright, Nick?' Melanie asked.

Nick blinked as if coming out of a trance. He turned to Melanie. 'Pardon?'

Melanie placed a hand on his knee. 'Are you alright?'

He brushed her hand away and stood up. 'Yeah, I'm fine. I'm going for a slash.'

Nick placed the shovel carefully against a shelf and went in search of a toilet.

Melanie returned her head to Dave's shoulder and said, 'Well, that was weird.'

'I'm starting to think that Nick Broughton is not playing with a full deck,' Dave replied. He rested his cheek against the top of Melanie's scalp and let himself enjoy the weight and warmth of her body against his.

He tried to think of something to say, but the gravity of the situation rendered every conversational topic tiny and meaningless. So he asked the question asked in every relationship when there was nothing to say. 'What are you thinking about?'

Melanie sighed, but didn't look up. 'I'm thinking about how I'll probably have to find somewhere else to live.'

'We could live together?' Dave's mouth said before his body and brain could catch up with it.

Melanie sat up straight. 'What did you say?'

'We could live together,' Dave repeated with more confidence. 'If we get out of this alive, obviously.'

'Do you think we're ready for it?'

'We love each other, we spend most of our time at each other's flats and we both know we're capable in dangerous and hostile environments so Christmas with your parents should be a doddle.'

Melanie hit him on the shoulder. 'What about Gary?'

'I could ask him, but I think he'll want to spend Christmas with his own family.'

'I mean what will Gary think about it?'

'We've talked about it. He's cool. In fact, it was his idea.'

Melanie thought it over, a serious expression on her face, which flipped itself into a smile. 'Let's do it,' she said.

Though she had been pretending not to listen, Anne allowed herself a small smile. Not looking up from her book she said, 'You should probably kiss her now, or something.'

Dave shot Anne a look over his shoulder, then turned back to Melanie and kissed her gently.

'Oh, shit,' he said into her mouth and pulled away.

'What's wrong?' Melanie asked.

'Gary.'

'You were thinking about Gary?' Melanie asked.

'No. Yes. We should check he's okay,' Dave said as he pulled his phone out of his pocket. He dialled a number and waited impatiently as it rang. Gary finally answered.

'Gary! It's Dave. Are you alright?'

'Yeah,' replied Gary. 'Why shouldn't I be?'

'Haven't you seen the news? There's a city-wide riot.'

'Yeah. I heard.'

'Are you safe?' Dave asked.

'Dude, I've got a bucket of chicken, the new season of "My Big Fat Geek Wedding" and a shovel. I'm sitting pretty.'

The flat screen television hanging on Conrad West's office wall showed rolling news of the violence spreading through London. Conrad, though, preferred to watch the live show playing out on the streets below him. The crowds beneath him shifted and switched between the buildings like iron filings following a magnet controlled by an excitable child. Orange and red bloomed against the black and grey.

Conrad was satisfied with how the project was running. Sure, events might have been unfolding quicker than he would've liked, but he wasn't one to micromanage. A mobile phone on the desk rang. Bowen got up from the couch in the corner away from the window and answered it. Conrad had been so taken with the view he'd forgotten he was in the room with him.

'Yes?' Bowen asked the caller brusquely. He listened to the reply, rolled his eyes and held the phone out to Conrad. 'It's that writer.' Conrad could hear the speech marks around the last word. 'He says he wants to tell you something personally.'

Conrad took the phone and smiled into the mouthpiece. 'Nick. How wonderful to hear from you. How's it all going?'

'There's been a bit of a problem,' Nick whispered down the line from the bookshop toilet.

Conrad's smiled didn't falter. 'I've told you before, Nick, there are no such things as problems. There are merely opportunities to shine.'

'I was bringing them to you, but we hit a snag,' Nick said. 'Well, several hundred snags, actually.'

'Don't you worry about it,' Conrad said. 'I'll send someone to get you. Where are you?'

Conrad signalled for Bowen to pass him a pen and paper. He scribbled down the address Nick gave him.

'Stay right there,' Conrad ordered. 'I'll have this sorted for you.'

'I'll still get my payment?' Nick asked.

'Don't worry, Mr Broughton, you'll get exactly what you deserve,' Conrad said before terminating the call.

'Difficulties?' asked Bowen.

Conrad gave him the reassuring smile that had landed multi-billion dollar deals. 'A bit of scope creep, but that's to be expected on a project of this size and scale.'

'Marwood?'

'Yes. I think it's time that we deal with him once and for all.' Conrad turned away from Bowen. 'Where is my flock?'

We are here, Master.

Bowen shivered. The building around him seemed to breathe and sigh.

'I need you to ask our friends downstairs to do us a favour,' Conrad said to the walls.

Of course, Master.

Police Constable Andrew Tomlinson had originally joined the Metropolitan Police Force for the excitement. Unfortunately, there was a bit too much excitement barrelling its way towards him down Baker Street.

The sweat ran down his forehead. The gas mask he wore prevented him from wiping it away and it ran into his eyes, stinging and burning. He tightened his grip on the riot shield handle and adjusted his stance, throwing his weight onto his back leg. He was one link in a chain of reinforced polycarbonate that stretched across the road.

When he'd been called into the briefing room that morning and informed of the situation, he couldn't believe what was happening in his city. Yes, he'd seen some terrible things in his time on the force - he was one of the first officers on the scene at UberSystems Tower just a week before. Yes, he'd seen struggle and inequality on a daily basis. But he wasn't one of those coppers who'd become cynical and jaded. This was his city and he loved it. There had been no flashpoint or catalyst for the violence. It seemed that London had woken up and decided to burn itself to the ground. If what the duty sergeant was telling him was true, the city hadn't just jumped the shark. It was jumping up and down on the shark and screaming that its name was Jumpy McSharkface.

The mob filled Andrew's field of vision. He could see a couple of deerstalker hats that had been liberated from the Sherlock Holmes Museum gift shop. As the crowd pushed on, the windows of the Italian chain restaurants and money exchange outlets imploded one by one. The tear gas twisted and curled in the sunlight, the breeze washing it over the throng like an early morning mist, but did nothing to slow their progress.

When the pack was almost upon them, Andrew and his fellow officers drew their batons and rested them on the backs of their shields. His body tensed. Every muscle and nerve was preparing itself, running through a genetic checklist. He was ready.

Then, without warning, the rioters stopped in their tracks mere feet away from Andrew. Each one had the same calm, contemplative look on their face as if they were all having an identical thought. They turned and marched in an orderly fashion back the way they came.

TWENTY-TWO

'So, what are we going to do?' Dave asked the room.

Anne had found an A-Z in the Travel section of the shop and was furiously flicking the pages back and forth. 'If we stick to the back streets, I think we can make it to UberSystems Tower without being seen.'

Nick shifted uncomfortably on the table he was sat on. 'We should stay here until nightfall.'

'If we wait any longer, it will get even worse out there,' Melanie said.

'You've been in this game ten minutes and you're an expert already?' Nick asked with disdain.

'Don't talk to me like that,' Melanie snapped back.

Dave knew he had to put his foot down. 'Melanie's right, Nick. We can't stay here.' He pulled himself up onto his feet. 'Let's see if there's anything useful we can take with us and get moving as soon as we can.'

Anne saw her first. A young girl, no older than thirteen, stood in front of the shop window. She pressed her face up to the glass, her eyes trying to penetrate the dim light of the shop's interior. One by one, others stood by her shoulder in an intimidating silence: window shoppers of the soul.

'They know we're here,' Anne whispered.

'D'ya think?' Nick asked.

They moved back into the shadows, each step careful and deliberate, to avoid exciting those on the other side of the glass.

The girl tipped her head back, paused for a moment, and then smashed her forehead against the window. Dave jumped at the dull sound. She repeated the action again and again.

The glass cracked on the fourth blow, the fine spiderweb fractures smeared with her blood. All throughout, her steely gaze did not waiver, telling Dave of her solid sense of purpose. She would get to them even if she were torn to shreds in the process.

'Is there a back way out of here?' Melanie asked.

'I really hope so,' Anne replied.

They ran through the maze of bookshelves. Dave pulled some over, flooding the aisles behind them with wood and paper in an attempt to put some obstacles between them and their pursuers. He heard the savage melody of the window giving way swiftly followed by the crunch of feet on the shards.

He followed the others as they ducked through a small storeroom, scattering boxes as they went, and smashed their way out of the emergency exit.

The shock of the sun hit them like a fist of light as they ran down the alley behind the row of shops. Nick knocked bins over with the shovel, the contents vomiting over the concrete. The alley quickly joined the main road and exposed them. Random pedestrians looking for an outlet for their rage joined the chase until it seemed like the population of London was trailing them.

Dave's lungs burned in his chest and it was as if his trainers' rubber soles were sticking to the hot tarmac. The others around him were fading fast too and, though they'd had a head start, the distance between them and the mob was being eaten away. He was about to give up, ready to surrender to his fate, when a miracle appeared from around the corner.

A London black cab for hire when he actually wanted one.

'Taxi!' Dave shouted as he waved frantically at the driver.

'That'll cost a fortune!' Anne yelled after him. 'Maybe we can book an Uber?'

'Yeah, well, now would be an ideal time to treat ourselves,' Dave shouted back as the cab pulled up to the kerb. He almost ripped the door off its hinges and the four jumped into the back, scattered across the seats and floor.

'UberSystems Tower,' Dave gasped. 'And step on it!' he added, because he'd always wanted to say it after leaping into a taxi and he didn't know if he'd ever get the opportunity again.

The cab driver looked over his shoulder, trying to find a face amongst the mass of arms and legs. 'You wanna go south of the river? When there's a full-scale city-wide riot going on? You're havin' a giraffe.'

Dave pointed through the windscreen at the approaching hordes. 'You could always give them a lift instead?'

The driver's gaze followed Dave's finger and his face drained of all colour. 'Bloody hell lad. What have you been up to?'

'Making new friends. Now can we get out of here?'

The driver - his identity badge claimed his name was Keith - switched off the 'For Hire' sign and put the cab into reverse. When he reached the end of the road he snatched at the handbrake. The engine complained bitterly as the front of the car swung round in a shriek of smoking rubber. Keith threw the gear stick forward and stamped on the accelerator pedal, throwing his passengers around the back seats.

Keith casually guided the cab around abandoned and burnt-out cars. 'You know who I blame for this?' he asked Dave in the rear-view mirror, an arm rested on the passenger seat.

Nick, Melanie and Anne were already pretending to look at their phones, leaving Dave to make small talk. 'No. Who?'

'Them bankers. It all started around Canary and Riverside Wharves. The radio called it a manifestation of the middle-class malaise, but I told my Rita that's why I don't listen to Thought for the Day. I read on the internet that they'd put something in the water to send the workers mental and wreck the economy. They then swoop in and make a mint.'

'Where'd you read that?' Dave asked.

'Some website. New World Recorder or some such.'

Nick looked up from his phone. 'Those bunch of hacks? They don't know anything.'

'It was very persuasive stuff,' Keith said. 'Talked about an apocalypse brought about by a worldwide financial collapse. All currencies would be worthless and we'd be reduced to bartering for goods and services.'

Dave and Anne exchanged a look. 'I don't think it's the Apocalypse,' Dave said.

'Some kind of apocalypse expert, are we?' Keith asked.

'I have some professional interest,' Dave replied.

'So what makes you say it isn't the end?'

'Because we're going to stop it,' Dave said. 'Anyway, if you think the world's going to end what are you doing out here?'

'I'm self-employed mate. No days off for me even if society collapses.'

TWENTY-THREE

Death was bored. Mind-numbingly-fist-chewingly-punch-yourself-in-your-own-face bored. He'd filled in all the crosswords he could find and completed all the surveys in Anne's magazines (mostly C's: he was a woman who loved too much). He'd drunk more tea than was advisable and the biscuit supply was dangerously low. He'd been denied his powers for only a short while but it already felt like he'd lost one of his senses.

How did humans cope with this? How did they deal with the prison of their own humanity? How could they get up every morning knowing that the whole world in all its form and splendour was just over the horizon, yet they would only glimpse a tiny fraction of it in their maddeningly fleeting lifespan?

He switched on the television. The advertised programming had been suspended to bring rolling news of events happening just outside his door. The Shard was on fire, flame and smoke distorting the structure until it resembled architecture Saruman would've been proud of. Canada Square's windows had been smashed out, leaving random black puncture wounds among the glass squares so it looked like a diabolic crossword puzzle with no solution. The whole skyline was blasted and broken. Only UberSystems Tower stood pristine and untouched, like a gleaming needle in a burning haystack.

What would his old friend be thinking, sat there at the top of his kingdom? Death knew he'd become disillusioned with humanity in the 80s, but who wasn't disillusioned in that decade? The threat of nuclear war, the depletion of the ozone layer, Bon Jovi. The list of humanity's crimes against nature was long and hideous. But to want to destroy them all? That seemed like a bit of an overreaction. He should've talked to him at the cemetery the other day, but he looked so tired and lost. So human. He was a stranger to him now.

But the time to talk had passed. Death opened the door to what used to be the Infinite Monkeys' office. The stench hit him like a slap to the face. No matter how many times they tried to clean it, they could never completely remove the smell of monkey.

Inside was a cupboard. He searched through the contents, throwing aside screenwriting guide books and broken keyboards, until he found what he was looking for. It was heavier than he remembered, but the steel shone with the same brilliance as the day it was forged and was as sharp as the time it sliced the Devil's own head from his shoulders.

War's sword.

Ooh. And a Van Morrison CD. He'd been looking for that for ages.

TWENTY-FOUR

The taxi pulled up around the corner from UberSystems Tower and let Nick, Anne, Dave and Melanie out. Dave passed a twenty pound note to Keith through the driver's window.

'Keep the change,' he said. 'Oh, can I have a receipt?'

Keith scribbled the fare onto a scrap of paper and handed it to Dave. 'Whatever you've got planned, good luck,' he said. Before Dave could thank him, he revved the engine and pulled off in a cloud of tyre smoke.

Lightning carved through dark, boiling clouds that had gathered above the city. Underneath a lacerated sky, UberSystems Tower shone like never before. Each window was lit up with a dazzling glow. It was a star-bright arrow pointing up to the heavens. When he closed his eyes, Dave could see a negative after-image burned into his retinas.

There were running battles in the streets around the skyscraper. Restaurants and bars that should've been full of Friday evening crowds had become refuges for the terrified victims of the savagery outside. Paul, an accountant that Dave recognised from the UberSystems International Finance Division, ran down the middle of the road snarling like a wild animal. His shirtless torso was smeared with grease and soot and he threw punches at anyone who went near him. He suddenly switched direction and, before Dave could react, rugby tackled him to the ground. Paul's fists flew, battering Dave's body wherever he could land blows. Dave pushed his attacker's face away with both hands as Anne and Melanie jumped on his back, trying to peel him off. They succeeded and Paul stumbled backwards, knocking the two women onto the pavement. He continued to stagger into the path of Nick, who swung his shovel at the side of his head. Paul immediately crumpled into a heap.

Melanie helped Dave to his feet. 'Maybe you're right. I should get one of those,' he said, nodding to the shovel in Nick's hands.

A woman wandered around in a slow, sad circle. She lifted her head and Dave could see that it was Sophie from the club last week. 'Are you okay?' he asked, immediately realising the stupidity of the question.

She simply howled in reply. She clutched at Dave, her cheeks streaked with tears. He tried to gently push her away, but she grabbed and scratched and it took Anne and Nick's help to drag her off of him.

'Who's that?' Melanie asked, her eyes narrowing.

Dave brushed over the question as a photocopier crashed through a tenth floor window and exploded on the street below. 'We'd better get out of here,' he said after they'd propped Sophie up against a lamppost.

Nick looked up the sheer face of the tower in front of them. 'I'm guessing we can't just walk in through the front door,' he said.

'There's a car park underneath,' said Dave. 'Perhaps we can find a way in there.'

They walked around the side of the building until they reached the car park entrance. The security guard had long since left his post at the barriers. They slipped under and headed down the slope until they were under the building itself. A handful of cars had been abandoned for the night. A fluorescent light blinked and flickered, making the shadows jump and dance around. Sheltered from the noise above, the four trespassers walked slowly across the empty bays.

Anne said, ''Twas the night before Christmas and all through the house not a creature was stirring...'

'Apart from the creature of unspeakable horror,' finished Dave.

'We should use the service lifts,' Melanie said, leading them across the car park. 'They won't be expecting us to come that way.'

Dave was impressed by his girlfriend's newfound skill at subterfuge. 'How are we going to get in? They need a security card.'

Melanie took her purse out of Dave's bag and pulled a security pass from a pocket. 'Let's see if this still works.'

She tapped it against the security panel and gave a tiny surprised laugh as the control panel blinked awake. A motor far above them kicked into life, sending the lift downwards.

'What do we do when we get up there?' Melanie asked.

'West's a businessman. We have a meeting. Find out what he wants,' Dave said. Nobody argued with the idea. The silence was broken by a strange creaking sound. Curious, Dave looked around but couldn't find the source of the noise. Unknown to him, it was the suspension of three of the cars as they were slowly raised into the air. The tyres dropped with a soft thud as the vehicles they supported defied gravity and hovered several feet above the ground, bobbing gently in the air.

The lift door slid open, revealing a functional square steel box lacking the style of the passenger lifts elsewhere in the building. 'After you,' Dave said to Melanie as he stepped aside.

When she stepped into the lift, the cars were hurled across the car park as if they were toys thrown by an angry toddler. Anne, Dave and Nick dived out of the way as Melanie flung herself into the far corner of the lift.

The cars smashed into the walls, glass and rubber flying in all directions. The lift door slammed shut, trapping Melanie on the other side. Dave was up on his feet before the hubcaps had finished spinning across the tarmac and beat the steel doors with his fists. He tried to pull them open with his fingers, shouting Melanie's name.

Anne and Nick dragged him away. His ears were ringing from the impact and it took him a few moments to realise they were talking to him. Anne pointed to where the fire escape door used to be. A tyre had pulverized it to matchwood on its final journey.

'We can get in that way!' Anne yelled too loudly.

TWENTY-FIVE

Two Years Earlier

Anne badly parked her Morris Minor outside the William Furling Junior School. She'd collected the car from a second-hand dealership that morning and was still trying to get used to the absence of power steering. It needed some work doing to it; a new paint job to start with. And the clutch would need replacing. The brake pads seem to be made from slices of wafer thin ham. And there was a strange knocking from the boot that she had to stop and check wasn't a kidnap victim. Oh, and the chassis was held onto the bodywork by rust and good thoughts. Apart from that, she was rather pleased with her purchase.

After their first meeting, Death kept his promise and visited Anne in hospital as he 'was in the area'. They got on well and Death continued dropping in to her at home after she had been discharged. They talked to each other about their losses and worked through their grief together. As they grew closer, Anne cleaned up both the flat and herself. Soon, she found herself looking for something to occupy her time. Anne suggested to Death that perhaps he needed some help in organising the day-to-day aspects of his life. She was sorting out bank accounts, paperwork and generally helping him adapt to the modern world. Through trial and error, they discovered what powers she had and her job description and responsibilities grew. She decided that something had to be done about the mistakes Death had made through the ages and started gathering information about hauntings and possessions. Newspaper clippings, rumours and blog posts filled folders and drawers. Though Anne was very vague about her new life, her mum was just happy that she'd found a job and a nice young man to help her through her problems.

She grabbed the tool kit that sat on the passenger seat, got out and adjusted her overalls. She locked the car door. This was an optimistic gesture as a) nobody in their right mind would try and steal the car and b) the lock didn't actually work. Out of the corner of her eye, she saw something flash in the bushes on the other side of the car park, like sunlight reflecting off glass. She looked closer. It looked like a telephoto lens poking out from between the leaves. She started walking across the asphalt when a thin pale man leapt up from the hedgerow in a panic. Shoving his camera in a kitbag as he went, he ran off down the road until he disappeared around the corner. Anne shook her head, wondering what that was all about.

She walked into the school's reception with purpose. She'd learned early on that confidence was key in this job. If she gave the impression that she knew what she was doing, people were happy to leave her to get on with whatever it was. There was little chance that it would become their problem.

'Morning,' she shouted to Gloria the receptionist through the window of the school office. 'I've come to look at your boiler.'

If you looked up jobsworth in one of the dictionaries in the school library, there would be a picture of Gloria Kendrick. But before you could go to the library, she'd want to see a permission slip signed by the class teacher and authorised by the librarian. She pursed her lips and scanned her eyes down the diary open on her desk. 'I don't have that written down here.'

Anne sighed theatrically. 'Look, all I know is that I've got paperwork that says to come down here because you've got a possible issue with the boiler.'

'You've got paperwork?' A little thrill of pleasure ran through Gloria. She fondled the rubber stamp that she always kept close at hand. 'Well, I'll have a quick chat with the Head.'

Gloria disappeared into the Head's office at the back of the reception area.

She returned with Mrs McKenzie. She was older and more successful since her days of teaching the likes of

Dave Marwood, but she was no happier. The years spent raising other people's children had convinced her that kids were great until they developed an opinion. Sometimes, she thought the same about her staff.

'How can I help you?' she asked.

'Anne Mitchell. Council Maintenance. I've come to look at your boiler.'

'We weren't aware that anybody was coming.'

'Emergency call out. We're inspecting all properties that have the model you've got installed. You don't want to end up like that school in Lincolnshire, do you?'

'What school?'

'Didn't you read about it in the papers? Cut-off valve gave out. The boiler went off like a rocket.'

Mrs McKenzie's cool indifference vanished to be replaced with concern and visions of potential lawsuits. 'Like a rocket? They can do that?'

'Took the roof clean off. Boom. Whoosh.'

'Boom?' Mrs McKenzie asked.

'Whoosh,' Anne confirmed. She pointed off down the corridor. 'This way is it?'

'Yes. I'll show you.'

Anne and Mrs McKenzie went to the boiler room at the back of the school. Mrs McKenzie unlocked the blue doors that had been locked vigilantly since Dave had snuck in there all those years before.

'Thanks,' said Anne. 'I'll let you know when I'm done.'

'Oh, don't you want me to stay?'

'Boom. Whoosh. Remember? It's for your own protection.'

'Of course.' Mrs McKenzie retreated to the safety of her office. When she was out of sight, Anne opened the door and stepped into the hot, dark and noisy boiler room. She fumbled along the wall until she found a light switch. A single naked bulb barely illuminated the pipework with its pathetic glow.

'Joe?' Anne called out. 'Joe Walker? Are you here?' The light bulb flickered and swung. Shadows danced around the walls. She felt the familiar chill wrap around and saw her misted breath that told her she was not alone. A lanky middle-aged man stepped out from behind the boiler. 'What do you want?'

'I'm here to help you.'

'Have you got any tabs? I'd kill for a ciggie. A roll up. Anything. I quit, but I can't see it doing any harm to my health now.'

'Sorry, I don't.'

'How comes you can see me?'

'I don't know. I just can.'

'I can hear the kids playing outside sometimes. It's good to hear them, so full of life. Not like me, dead in the dark. It's good to talk to someone though, good to be noticed. It's been a while, not since that boy.'

Usually, Anne would let the dead talk for as long as they'd like. People got rather attached to being alive and were often very angry they weren't anymore. Nothing and nobody finished neatly. Life and death was just a tangled mess of loose ends. Thoughts and regrets gathered over the years with nobody to listen or confess to. This comment, though, made Anne curious. 'What boy?'

'A pupil. He could see and hear me just like you can now.'

'He could do what I can? Did he tell you his name?'

'The teacher said it. That scary one. She used to terrify me when I worked here. Dave Marwood, that was his name. Always hoped he'd come back some day for a chat.'

TWENTY-SIX

Melanie could feel the lift's ascent begin to slow until it came to a stop around halfway up the building. She braced herself, ready to spring out when the doors opened, but she remained trapped.

The light above her head grew in luminosity until she had to shield her eyes or risk damaging her sight. The electrical buzzing filled her head and pushed up against the front of her skull until the noise subsided and the glare dimmed.

Shadows cast by the bulbs shifted and moved around. Impossibly, more appeared from the cracks in the door and gaps in the metalwork. They flowed along the floor like thick oil and crawled along the walls and ceiling. Melanie crouched down in a corner trying to keep as far away from them as possible.

The movement stopped as suddenly as it has started, forming a perfect circle of light around her.

Melanie.

She felt a chill pass over her. Her breath and heartbeat quickened as if she had been dropped in ice water. 'Who's there? How do you know my name?'

We are the Dark. We have watched you work here. We did not mean to frighten you. We merely wished for us to have some time alone.

Melanie relaxed slightly, sliding down the wall to sit on the cold metal floor. 'Nathan? Nathan Christou?'

We were Nathan once. We were many. No longer.

'What do you want from me?'

You are the lover of Mr Marwood.

A small smile appeared at the corner of her lips. 'They aren't exactly the words I'd use, but that's right.'

Mr Marwood has certain gifts.

Melanie's smile grew wider. 'He certainly does.'

Events have spiralled out of control. We cannot stop what we have started. We cannot stop what we have become. We want to. We will need his help. And yours.

Melanie got to her feet. 'What do you need me to do?'

TWENTY-SEVEN

None of the lifts would work so Dave, Nick and Anne climbed the thirty floors to where Conrad West would be. Through the doors leading from the stairwells they could see the building was deserted, desks abandoned when the staff had taken to the streets.

As they passed the fifth floor, Nick left Grace the Shovel behind.

Around the twelfth floor, Dave thought how his actions had once again led directly to Melanie's life being threatened by supernatural forces. He was beginning to wonder whether he was not quality boyfriend material.

At floor seventeen, Dave considered throwing up over the railings.

On the twentieth floor, Nick beat him to the punch and did actually throw up over the railings.

When they finally reached the top floor, Nick and Dave slumped against the wall in a sticky heap. Anne, still looking fresh and alert, grabbed the handle of the door leading out of the stairwell.

'Ready, boys?'

'Just-- Just give us a minute,' Nick gasped. 'Nobody ever tells you how physically demanding stopping the Apocalypse would be.'

Anne rolled her eyes and stood waiting, arms folded, foot tapping impatiently. With a flick of her wrist, she checked her watch. 'Right. Come on.' She opened the door and marched through. Nick and Dave staggered behind her, mopping their faces dry with their tops.

The still, silent office had been completely devastated since Dave had been here last. The furniture had been thrown around and broken into pieces by a tornado of rage. Fluorescent lighting tubes hung from the ceiling, fizzing and popping like electric stalactites.

Dave pointed to the far end of the room. 'He'll be in the boardroom,' he said.

He was right. Conrad West sat at the head of the conference table, casually sipping from a glass of water. He smiled as Anne led Dave and Nick into the boardroom. 'It seems I've won my bet.'

'Where's Melanie?' Dave asked immediately. 'What have you done with her?'

West ran his finger up and down the glass, drawing lines in the condensation. 'I'm sure I don't know what you mean.'

'You took her. The Dark attacked us and snatched her away.'

For the first time he could remember, Dave saw West's assured demeanour falter for a fraction of a second. 'I really can't help you.' West switched his attention to the window. 'Do you like my little project? I admit it's got a bit out of hand but I didn't appreciate just how bloody angry you English are. You really need to learn not to suppress it all. It's not healthy. I'm also a little disappointed that you're still alive. You really can't do anything right can you, Broughton?'

'What do you mean?' Anne asked. 'How does he know you?' she asked Nick. He shrank away from her gaze.

'Oh, Mr Broughton has worked for me for years,' West said.

Nick stammered for a moment before his mouth could find the right gear. 'He pays me for information about you. I was researching you anyway, so I thought what was the harm? I thought if I told him where you were, he'd make sure I was safe. I didn't know he'd send his zombie army after us. I didn't know he was going to try and destroy humanity.'

'They're not zombies!' Dave said, exasperated.

Anne lashed out at Nick, punching and kicking him all over. He hunched over, trying to protect his head with his arms. 'We trusted you!' she shouted. Dave grabbed her around the waist and hauled her off of him, her legs bicycling in the air.

'Calm down!' Dave said. 'This isn't helping anyone.'

She did, but didn't take her eyes off Nick. If looks could kill, then Anne would keep Death very busy.

'Have you all finished? What are you talking about?' West asked. 'Destroy humanity? Why would I want to do that?'

'You're a Horseman of the Apocalypse. It's what you do,' Anne said.

'Oh dear me, no. I'm just trying to make a bit of money. London is the financial hub of the world. Emotion, not logic, runs the stock markets. Feed the fear, feed the irrationality, and you can control it. Have you seen the markets? I've made the single biggest profit ever in one day. If this continues, other markets will collapse and I'll sweep up there. Businesses will be driven to the wall, entire economies will fail, and governments will topple. I'll be the one to pick up the pieces.'

'So those guys on the internet were right?' Anne asked.

Nick shrugged. 'A stopped clock is right twice a day.'

'I'm not talking to you,' Anne replied.

They heard footsteps.

A figure approached the boardroom, thrown into silhouette by the damaged lighting. Shadows followed in its wake, swirling and shifting around its feet like a dark cloak. They watched in awe as it stepped through the doorway.

Melanie was staring back at them.

'Melanie? What's going on?' Dave walked towards her. 'Are you alright?'

'She is safe,' said a voice that came from Melanie but was not her.

'And who am I talking to?' he asked.

Dave looked for an escape route, but he, Anne and Nick were surrounded and the Dark started to consume them.

'We are the Dark,' said Melanie. 'We are the shadows. We are anger, suffering and pain.'

Dave heard sobbing. At first, he thought that it was his own, but turned his head to see Nick lying on the floor. He was curled up in the foetal position, wrapped in an overwhelming grief that threatened to tear his heart in two.

Dave took some deep breaths. He could feel his control slipping. He had to fight the urge to throw it away completely. He turned to Anne. 'It looks like it's just the two of us. Got any ideas?'

There was an inhuman rage in Anne's eyes. 'Oh yeah. As usual it's up to me to sort everything out, but do I ever get any recognition for what I do? No. I don't know what we should do. It's your bloody girlfriend. You deal with it. Why don't you do what they did in that film my dad liked? What was it now? Cross the streams?' She began to giggle. 'Yeah. Do that. Cross the streams.'

Tears mixed with her laughter, creating an awful sound somewhere between pain and hysteria. She slumped to the floor, helpless with the laughter and misery.

West stood up from his chair. 'That's it. Finish them,' he said to Melanie.

'No!' Melanie screamed. She waved a hand at West and he flew through the air and slammed into the wall behind him. Dave was just glad it wasn't him for once.

'What do you want?' Dave asked Melanie, unable to disguise the fear in his voice.

Melanie looked at him with pleading eyes. 'Help us. Our master has lied to us. He has used us for his own ends.'

Dave took a step forward into the Dark. All his energy was being used just trying to keep himself teetering on the edge of sanity. 'How?'

'Your touch can release us. Melanie has allowed us to possess her. We hope your feelings for her will stop the anger from taking control of you.'

He understood. They'd possessed Melanie the same way the poltergeist had Letitia. They'd taken a form that allowed Dave to touch them. If he could get to her, he could release them from this world.

Dave suddenly realised how much he hated Melanie. How many years had she ignored him for? She had probably been laughing at him behind his back the whole time. She only noticed him once he'd saved her life. Then he'd save her again. How many more times would he need to do this? He wanted to break something. He wanted to join the mobs on the streets and watch the world burn. Better yet, he wanted to start the fire.

'You can keep her,' he snarled.

Just as he turned away, he briefly saw the soul behind her eyes. He remembered the feeling when he first met her and clung to it. He remembered that it was her strength that had saved his life more than once too. He felt a warm glow inside and knew where it came from. The shadows receded around him and he stood in a small pool of light. The Dark would not be able to touch him now. He knew what he had to do.

Dave took another step. He remembered what he'd felt in the foyer the week before. 'Your master promised you something didn't he? But he broke that promise. He did this to you, instead.'

'Yes,' Melanie whispered. 'All are lies. There is nothing to believe.'

Dave walked towards her. He was a tiny chink of light in the dark tower of glass and steel. 'Well, that's a load of wank. I believe many things. I believe that

"Wouldn't It Be Nice?" by The Beach Boys is the greatest piece of music ever recorded. I believe cats are better than dogs. I believe most problems can be solved by cake. I believe in a thing called love.'

'We can feel only the hate.'

Dave was face to face with Melanie now. 'Oh, trust me. It's a big city. There's a lot of love.'

'No!' screamed West.

Recognition flickered in Melanie's eyes as he kissed her. The light around them intensified and then, for a fraction of a second, they were the light. They radiated out, burning away the darkness.

When the light had faded, Melanie opened her eyes and Dave knew that the Dark was gone. Her legs gave way and she collapsed into his arms. Dazed, she looked around the room. 'Did it work?'

He smiled. 'Yes.'

Melanie patted him gently on the cheek. 'Good kiss.'

'Thank you.'

Anne and Nick got to their feet, dusted themselves down and exchanged embarrassed glances. Nick saw something over her shoulder. 'Well, that's the single most terrifying thing I've ever seen,' he muttered.

Death. And he was carrying a flaming sword.

TWENTY-EIGHT

'Hello Conquest,' Death said.

'Hello Death. How have you been?' Conquest replied.

'I can't complain. Nobody listens. You look terrible.'

Conquest gave Death an exhausted smile. 'I'm tired, old friend. I've had a very hard century.'

Death turned to Nick, who had been edging towards him with his mobile phone out. 'I'm trying to have a private conversation. This isn't the time to try and take selfies with me.'

Nick put the phone back in his pocket and scurried to the other side of the room. Death turned back to Conquest.

'What's all this about, then?' he asked, waving the sword around.

'It's just business.'

'Just business? What about the bloody vampires? After I told Dave they didn't exist. You made me look like a right tit.'

Dave was first to notice the ripples on the surface of the water in Conquest's glass. He nudged Melanie and pointed to it. That was when they heard the creaking in the roof.

'It was means to an end,' Conquest said.

Death shook his head angrily. 'How many have you killed? They were innocent.'

'You shouldn't have been sleeping on the job.'

Everybody felt the floor shift beneath them. Something metallic clanged above their heads. It was quickly followed by a terrible scraping noise that put Dave's teeth on edge. Then objects whistled past the window. Dave was no architect but he knew that couldn't be good. The building was tearing itself apart.

'How did you do it?' Death asked.

'It was relatively easy. They're all so malleable as a species.' Conquest looked at the small group of humans cowering together. 'They're lost, searching for something; some meaning to their short pointless lives. You just have to tell them you can help them find it. And yet, they think so much of themselves. Ideas above their station.'

'Kicked *your* arse,' Dave muttered.

'All of these preening, vain individuals squander what they possess but we don't: a soul,' Conquest continued, looking at Dave out of the corner of his eye, 'Did you know you could torture a soul? I didn't. Get enough of them together and hurt them and you can infect an entire city with their pain and suffering. They've been doing it for centuries apparently. Civilizations throughout the ages have fallen to it.' Conquest shot a glance at Dave. 'It was going quite well until I had a little boardroom takeover.'

'Oh God, Conquest--' Death began.

'Don't you bring God into it. Where is he? One time it seemed that you couldn't shut him up. Fire and brimstone. Burning bushes. Then nothing. He's abandoned them. That's if he was ever interested in them in the first place. Somebody needs to take charge down here.'

'You know who you sound like?'

'Beezelbub? No, I assure you we're quite different. I don't want to destroy. I want to help. Strong leadership. That's what they need.'

A constant low rumbling was rising up from the foundations, a bass growl that Dave could feel in his chest. The glass slipped from the table and smashed on the floor. Dave tapped Death on the shoulder. 'Look, we're going to head off now. You seem to have this under control. It's getting late and it feels like the whole building is going to collapse.'

'Oh, that?' Conquest said wearily. He was looking his age. 'The Dark were integral to the construction of the building. They were in every brick and every girder. It was part of them. Now you've banished them to the great beyond, you've also doomed the building. It will follow them into the netherworld. So thanks for that.'

'You what?' Dave said, astonished. 'It's going to be sucked into the afterlife? I didn't think--'

'That's the problem with you humans. You never bloody do.'

Nick was already out the door. Bowen, worry etched into his face, cleared his throat. 'I should probably escort them off the premises,' he said to nobody in particular before following him. Anne was next. Melanie grabbed Dave by the hand and pulled him towards the doorway, leaving Conquest and Death alone.

Conquest pointed to the sword. 'Are you going to do anything with that?'

'Probably not.' Death threw it onto the table with a clatter.

'Would you like a drink?'

'I thought you'd never ask.'

Death and Conquest sat opposite each other. Their heavy crystal glasses filled with whisky hummed and vibrated on the wood of the table. 'How do you cope with it?' Conquest asked.

'Cope with what?'

'Immortality. Nobody ever tells you how incredibly tedious eternity will be.'

Death sipped the rich brown liquid. 'I suppose you need keep busy. To have a purpose.'

Conquest looked out across the city. 'I had a purpose once, but she rejected me when she discovered the monster that I am.'

'She never thought you were a monster.'

'You spoke to her?'

'Yes. She had a good life. I think she missed you.'

They drank quietly, the silence broken by the groans and cracks of metal and glass. 'Do you think she's there? On the other side? Waiting?' Conquest asked after a while.

'I honestly don't know. They didn't give me a manual when I started this gig.'

'I suppose I'll find out soon enough.'

'What are you talking about?'

'I've failed.'

Death looked around the opulent room. 'Yeah, you seem a complete loser.'

The lights rattled loose from their fittings and crashed onto the boardroom table. Conquest waited for the dust to settle before speaking.

'I will travel with the building when it slips from this world. I built this tower, this ridiculous tribute to my vanity. It's only fit that I am consumed by it at its end.' He waved a hand at the skyline. 'Like them, I have tried to fill my life with ambition and meaningless toil. I just have too much life to fill. Time stretches out before me like an endless ocean. I am drowning in time.'

'That doesn't sound like the Conquest I know talking.'

'I am not Conquest anymore. I am Conrad West. That is the name people will use when they remember me.'

'Is there any point in me trying to talk you out of this?'

Conrad shook his head.

'You're sure?'

Conrad nodded. 'I need to find Julia. I need to ask for her forgiveness. On the other side, perhaps she will see we are the same. This is the only way I can make the journey.'

Death held his glass up. 'To Conrad West.'

They clinked their glasses together.

'To Conrad West.'

TWENTY-NINE

By the time Dave and Melanie reached the street, Nick had disappeared into the crowds. Anne was on tiptoes, searching the blank faces, but he was gone. The shattered streets were eerily quiet in the aftermath of the destruction. People stared dead-eyed into the distance, or wandered aimlessly. The crunching of glass beneath their feet was the only sound. Melanie looked around at the burned-out shops and offices. 'Now, this looks like the zombie apocalypse.'

A deep, resonant rumbling from UberSystems Tower grew louder. It was growling like a wounded animal. Anne, Dave and Melanie pushed their way through the crowds trying to put as much distance between themselves and the building as they could. They yelled at people, telling them to get away - and out of their way.

When they were far enough, they turned to watch the death throes of Conrad West's empire. An intense light burned from the centre of the tower and spilled out of the windows. It grew until the edges of the building softened in the glare. Then the light intensified and completely devoured the structure until it was a white star glowing in the middle of the city. Then it was gone. And so was UberSystems Tower, ripped from its foundations, leaving a hole in the skyline. A thunderclap echoed through the streets as the air rushed to fill the newly-created gap in the world.

The roar's echo died away, replaced by a confused silence. A giant question mark seemed to hang in the air, nobody able to believe what they'd just seen.

'Death,' whispered Anne.

'I'm fine,' he said, standing next to her.

Unable to control herself, she threw her arms around him. Unsure of what to do, Death embraced her.

'Don't you dare do that again,' she sobbed. 'I was so worried.'

'Where's West?' Dave asked.

'The captain went down with his ship,' Death said through a mouthful of Anne's hair as he tried to untangle himself from her. 'It's over. No Dark. No Horsemen of the Apocalypse. Everything's back to normal.'

Dave looked around. 'I'm not sure that's possible.'

They made their way back to where the Deathmobile had met its end. As they walked between abandoned vehicles, Dave noticed that groups of people were once again roaming the streets. This time, though, rather than wielding baseball bats they carried brooms. Pavements were swept clean of the debris. Neighbours helped each other repair the damage to their properties. Cups of tea were passed around along with handshakes, fist bumps and hugs. It would take time, but London was starting to repair itself piece by piece. It was a big city. There was a lot of love.

Dave knew then that he was home. It wasn't perfect, but he was among the people he loved and who loved him back. Wasn't that all that really mattered? Anne, Gary and Melanie were his family. And there was Death. He was alone now, the last of his kind, and he would need Dave's help.

'What you said back in the boardroom. Do you really prefer cats to dogs? Because that's something we need to talk about if we're going to live together,' Melanie said.

He took Melanie's hand in his. Everything was going to be all right.

Anne wasn't thinking the same thing at that moment, though. The car was, unsurprisingly, where they had abandoned it. A parking ticket had been attached to the window.

'I don't believe it,' Anne wailed as she ripped the plastic envelope from the glass. 'The place was being torn apart, but they still find time to go around persecuting innocent drivers?'

'It's good to see the infrastructure didn't completely collapse,' Dave said. Anne gave him a look that made him think that he should stop talking.

'What's everybody doing now?' she asked.

'If it's all the same, I think I'll start that holiday,' Dave said. 'Does anybody fancy a pint?'

'That sounds like a plan,' Melanie said. 'Then I need to go to bed. Possession by restless spirits takes it out of a girl.'

'Arne?'

'Yeah, I think we could all do with a drink.'

'Death? We could hide you in the pub garden and bring you out a can of Coke and a bag of crisps.'

Death shook his head. 'No, I'm alright. I think I need some time alone.'

'What are you going to do?'

Death looked at the road ahead of him. 'I think I'll go for a walk.'

ABOUT THE AUTHOR

Dave Turner is an award-winning writer of science-fiction, fantasy and comedy.

His first joke was published in a national newspaper when he was nine years old. Since then, he has won the Best Screenplay Award at the London Screenwriters' Festival and published three best-selling novellas.

He lives in the south of England with his wife, three children and a crippling biscuit addiction.

Printed in Great Britain
by Amazon

44595981R00302